Defining Moments
of a Free Man
from a Black Stream

To: My brother Shil whose love and discipline made me who I am today. Thanks.

Kenneth.

Defining Moments
of a Free Man
from a Black Stream

DR. FRANK L. DOUGLAS

Printed in the United States of America
ISBN 978-1-948828-70-3 (sc)
ISBN 978-1-948828-71-0 (e)

Autobiography

2019 | 07 | 02

Access Media Group
Frank L. Douglas Books

REVIEWS

EDITORIAL REVIEW

I liked that the book reveals the trend of racial discrimination in educational institutions and in business organizations....I also liked that the memoir instills a spirit of hope despite the presence of daunting obstacles.

EmunahAn
(OnlineBookClub.org) 4 out of 4 Stars.

AMAZON CUSTOMERS

A Must Read for the Aspiring Professional
Defining Moments could easily have been 3 books in 1. The first section (Book 1) describes the struggles of a young man dealing with childhood trauma....and finally coming to the realization that despite all obstacles, he alone was responsible for his own destiny. The second section (Book 11) takes the reader through the author's migration from his country of birth to the culture shock of and adjustment to life in his new country.....the writer paints a picture of his love of science, wonderment and the parlaying of newfound knowledge into a storied career. The third section (Book 111) deals with the author's coming of age professionally and is essentially a treatise on science, drug discovery and development. It is also a how-to on navigating the minefields of the professional world.

schmd711

To The 'Underrepresented'.....
This memoir is an empowering testimonial that one can have a successful career without the betrayal of self and intrinsic values.

Reginald

The Definition of a Free Man
....the events that truly defined the life of Frank Douglas, were forged not in corporate boardrooms or high level meetings, but instead in how he chose to act when faced with beatings, homelessness, outright racism, and political intimidation...

Robert Goldberg

Inspiring Story of a Wise Man
....Few have overcome so many challenges, and fewer yet have done so with both strength of character and principles intact....

Robinswood

A Great Inspirational Gift to Society
....Given the current climate around the world, this book is a must read if you are a university/college professor or administrator......working in corporate America...a parent or grandparent....

Dr. Henry Odi

A Compelling Read
Dr. Douglas' book is an excellent testament to the theory that hard work conquers all. It is a compelling story of a young man from a poor country and from low economic status whose determination to succeed in life and with some spiritual push manages to succeed.

Aubrey Bonnett

An Inspirational and Compelling Memoir
....It's a clearly written chronicle of his journey from very humble beginnings, taking 'the path less travelled', working hard, doing what was 'noble and fair', significantly adding value to the lives of others....

Talk about Inspirational
If you ever feel like you need to evaluate your life, you should read this book! Talk about hardships and making things work! ... honest, down to earth and humbling in some respects, this book will be worth every second and penny! Buy it!

What a Journey!
Dr. Douglas' journey is truly inspiring. His defining moments he shares throughout the book are detailed and powerful. His mental toughness is his cornerstone.

Paulie

A Compelling Immigrant Story of Success
A courageous telling of how grit, integrity, remarkable intellect and most of all, to thine own self be true resolve, enabled him to reach the zenith of the global pharma industry.

Judith Lee

From Humble Beginnings
...In a life filled with accomplishments, he explained how he endured and overcame the challenges he faced in a racist society and how he fought for equality and justice in higher education. I highly recommend this book.

Dr. Trevin London

Humble Beginnings to Insightful Righteous Man of our Times
...I believe this book could and would help our future educators and corporations bring about changes in attitudes towards perceived racial inequities.

Wanda1313

An Inspirational Book for Everyone
A memorable representation by Dr. Douglas of an absolutely extraordinary life. This inspirational memoir validates how success is achieved through hard work, honesty, and above all, ethics...It is a moving personal story that also provides important lessons about leadership, stimulating innovation, and staying true to one's beliefs.

Peter L.

Important to Read
As a German Citizen it was interesting to read of the experiences of Dr. Douglas as he worked at one of the largest companies in Germany. Although I felt sad, at times, that he experienced problems both in the US and in Germany, I was delighted that he found helpful colleagues in both countries. This book is a must read for everyone interested in how to deal with cultural differences.

Tina D.

An Inspirational Book for Everyone
Dr. Douglas' book is a great testament that determination to succeed and hard work conquers all. A young Black man from very humble beginnings who took the road less travelled by many-his study and work ethics propelled him to become a world renowned scientist while remaining humble.

Mignon Murray

A "How To" in Effectively Changing the World We Live In
The life story of a brilliant scientist, who lived by the principle of "do the right thing."….Dr. Douglas has an uncanny gift of being able to objectively look at an issue and determine if change is needed because it is unjust/unfair or if change is needed in himself-and influencing that change.

Bonnie K. Griffith

This Autobiography is dedicated to my daughters
Katrina, Nataki and Diah

And to my grandchildren
Abisayo, Ayodeji, Theodore, Adelayo and Otis

Contents

Prologue

When I was sixteen, I was already on a path less well travelled with several questions preoccupying my somewhat troubled soul.

"Why does God relegate people of color to poverty and being the colonized?" I asked Brother McInnis, my minister. "Why do I behave differently from my brothers and sisters and cousins?" Before Brother McInnis had a chance to reply, I continued. "Why does God have favorites?"

He furrowed his brow, thought for a moment and in his deep Scottish accent replied, "Shall the thing formed say to him that formed it: Why hast thou made me thus?"

Out of respect, I remained silent. But inside, a loud voice shouted, "If the thing was made with the powers of reasoning, would not he who formed it, expect it to ask questions?"

In my early twenties, I stopped asking this question, primarily because what I was observing in America, from the time I arrived in 1963 at age 20, was that many Christian ministers and leaders, regardless of denomination, did not practice the teachings of Christ, as they had taught it to us in British Guiana (Guyana). My observation of these hypocritical and even inhumane behaviors only intensified my anguished attempts to reconcile what was being practiced with what was being preached. Ultimately, after suffering a bleeding ulcer, I recognized that this was not just a religious dilemma but had become an existential question. Thus, the only sensible solution was to cease asking this question because the answer did not lie in any rational explanation.

This autobiography therefore deals with the second question and describes Defining Moments in my life. This is not an answer as to why I behaved differently from my siblings and cousins, but rather recounts those things that kept defining who I was and who I was becoming. It traces the impact childhood events had on me and perhaps gives some insight into why, frequently, I tended to take 'the Road Less Travelled'. In fact, the process of writing this book has given me a greater recognition of this 'Less Travelled Road' tendency.

Finally, why have I decided to share these recollections publicly?

The first reason is as a tribute to my mother, and her two inseparable friends, Uncle Willie (Mr. William Nurse) and Auntie Chrisie (Mrs. Christabel Paris) who gave us food, shelter and courage whenever we needed it, and without whom, I would not have had this blessed journey.

The second reason is for my children: Katrina, Nataki and Diah; and my wife Lynnet, so that they will finally learn some of the challenges that I faced, the knowledge of which I often concealed from them.

The third reason is for my grandchildren: Abisayo, Ayodeji, Theodore, Adelayo, and Otis. My hope is that they will learn earlier than I did, when to keep their "swords in the scabbard", and when to "stiffen the sinews" and "imitate the action of the tiger", and learn never to allow anyone to limit their aspirations.

The final reason is that this is the 50th year since the murder of Martin Luther King, assassinated about 5 years after I arrived in America. In those brief years, I had gone from being the questioning, innocent, poor kid from a colonial country fighting for its independence, to a young adult confused by the racism, hatred, and evangelical hypocrisy aimed against Black Americans who were free but had not achieved independence. Independence—the right to live, to fail, to achieve, and to experience all that is associated with the dignity of being human -was still being contested in the streets and in institutions. Today we go from Dr. Martin Luther King's "I have a dream that my four little children will one day live in a nation where they will not be judged by the color of their skin, but by the content of their character", to DACA (Deferred Action for Childhood Arrivals) Dreamers fearful of being deported, to children of asylum seekers being housed in cages.

What a distortion of all that for which Dr. King had a dream.

Thus, this autobiography contains life episodes in which I was judged by the color of my skin, as well as, thankfully, moments in which I was judged by the content of my character. At a time when Truth and Values change with the whims of the wealthy and powerful, I found that taking the less well-travelled road and having True Grit do more to determine one's future and ultimately how one will be judged.

Frank Douglas FMBS
(Free Man from a Black Stream)

Cecil Miller Is Your Father

The Pan Am airlines plane took off smoothly and within a few minutes we were above the clouds. Fortunately, I had a window seat and could marvel at the clouds that looked like so many bales of cotton and wonder whether all of this condensed water could actually support the weight of the plane. Everything appeared so still in the bright clouds outside of the plane. I wondered: Am I in the Sky? Where does the Sky actually begin? My thoughts turned to the events of the previous few days. In some ways everything felt unreal. Were these events preordained? Were they a harbinger of the next phase of my Life's journey?

On August 3rd, 1963, two weeks prior to this flight, I was engaged to Lynnet Grant. The engagement was held in her parent's home a small family affair with my mother, brothers and sisters; her father, aunt, brother and sisters, and Lynnet's best friend, Ruthann Cannings. Brother Webster, the minister of Brethren Church, which Lynnet attended, blessed the event, after which we had tea and cake. A few of my close friends expressed surprise that I would take such a major step before embarking on an unknown future in the U.S.A. It never occurred to me at the time that this was especially brave or particularly noteworthy it just felt right. I drifted slowly and further into a reflective state.

I relived the first moment that I fell in love with her. I had arrived at the Cambridge Academy where we were teachers and went directly to her classroom. There she stood in this peach colored dress that seemed to epitomize all of the gentleness and loveliness of her personality that I had observed and had come to appreciate. Unknown to me, she had periodically given my mother loaves of bread from those she had baked on the respective day. My mother revealed this to me when I told her that I had asked Lynnet to become my fiancée prior to my leaving for the USA. This quiet thoughtfulness was not unlike one of the characteristics of my mother that I deeply admired.

We had attended different churches but at least one Saturday each month, away from our place of employ, I could enjoy watching her as she sang in the choir at our Youth for Christ Rallies, for which I had become the director and leader at the tender age of 19. Youth for Christ Rallies were previously directed by Pat Huntley, who had returned to British Guiana to fulfill his missionary obligations. In 1962, when Pat Huntley unexpectedly decided to return to England, I became the natural successor to lead Youth for Christ, British Guiana, because I had distinguished myself during the Bible quiz team competitions. I had led Cambridge Academy, a small private high school, to the Bible Quiz Championship victory over Queens College, the prestigious Number One Boys' High School. Later, when I became a teacher at Cambridge Academy, I coached its team to a similar victory. The Bible quiz competition was the highlight of the Youth for Christ Rallies. This main event was accompanied by beautiful choral renditions from the choir and occasional solos and duets. In fact, Lynnet and I did sing a duet together on my last and farewell Youth for Christ Rally.

My attending high school had almost not occurred. I was 12 years of age and in what was called School Leaving Class in Christ Church Elementary School. Unfortunately, I did not perform well enough at the common entrance examination, taken between the ages of 9 and twelve, to get a free ride to Queens College. A few days before what was to be my final opportunity, in which all my teachers felt that I would be among the top performers, it was discovered that my birthdate had put me just over the eligible age.

Since my mother could not afford the tuition at any of the small private high schools, I had no choice but to spend 3 years in the final grade, until I became 15 and age eligible to take the 'School Leaving Examination'. This examination qualified one for jobs such as at the Post Office, in factories, and the possibility to attend the Teachers' Training college. One day, Uncle Willie said to my mother, "Stella, Lennie is a bright little boy. It makes no sense to keep him in primary (elementary school). I shall pay the fees for him to go to high school." My mother demurred, but he insisted. Fortunately, my cousin Joan was attending Cambridge Academy and when my mother approached the Principal and owner of the school, he offered to give me a partial Scholarship, which I could retain provided that I maintained good grades. Thus, suddenly the summer of 1955 became the point that shaped my future life. Since neither colleges nor universities existed in British Guiana, attending high school was the sine qua non for any potential to gain entry to a university overseas.

Prior to this development, I had already decided that I would learn my grandfather's trade. My mother's father was a shoemaker and always refused to teach me how to make shoes, even though I would sit for hours and admire how he shaved and pounded the leather on his shoe anvil, until it was smooth and ready for the shape of the sole to be cut. And I would watch closely as he carefully made the holes with his awl and fasten the metal eyelets to hold the shoelace. Finally, he would stitch, by hand, the upper part to the sole and the major shape of the shoe would be evident. However, my grandfather, on hearing that Uncle Willie had offered to pay the tuition for me to go to high school, promised to buy me a second-hand bike. He had bought a new bike for Joan when she started high school at Cambridge Academy. Cambridge Academy was located about two miles from my home. Without a bicycle, I would have had to walk about 8 miles each day going between home and school at the beginning and end of each day and during the lunch recess. Unexpectedly, the possession of this bicycle precipitated a chain of events that further influenced the course of my life.

My grandfather bought the bike that had belonged to Ian McInnis, the eldest son of the minister of Elim Evangelical Church, which I attended. I was so proud of it. I bought two small cans of enamel paint and over painted the frame black and the corners of joints and ends of the frame to which the wheels connected, blue. A few days later, Saturday morning arrived. I hated Saturday mornings because it was my task to go to Bourda Market and Su Quan Grocery store to purchase the groceries for the week. I hated it because it was always my task. My older cousin Joan, 3-4 years older than I, was the Queen Bee. She was required to do nothing. She was "brown skinned' and therefore it was understood that she was privileged. Joan's brother was about one year younger than I, and he was considered too young for any of these chores.

But this Saturday morning was different. I awoke early. I got my basket and looked forward to the half-mile trip to Bourda Market, because I would not have to walk back home with a heavy basket of goods. I had a bicycle!

It was indeed a glorious day.

The sun was still rising and the dew had not yet fully disappeared from the red petals of the hibiscus and bougainvillea flowers in the trees that lined the avenue, which ran for four blocks down the middle of Camp Street. There were few bicycles and pedestrians, and even fewer cars disturbing nature's awakening. As a result, I could ride leisurely and enjoy the perpetual refrain of the kiskadee that seemed to resonate with the excited but quiet beat of my heart. When I reached the market, I placed the bicycle against one of the walls of the Chasberth Bookstore. The Bookstore was diagonally across from the Northwest entrance of the market and directly across the street from Bedford Elementary School. I headed for Auntie Gertrude's stall. Auntie Gertrude, as she was called by all, owned a fish stall in the market and was a known stalwart and ardent supporter of Mr. Burnham, the vice chair of the People's Progressive Party. As I approached her stall, which was crowded as usual, she spied me.

"Dat's Stella's boy." She pointed me out to her waiting shoppers. "Ya know Stella. She sews. He bright boy, ya know." With a wave of her hand in my direction she directed the gaze of her shoppers towards me.

"Wha ya wan today, boy?" she asked me.

"Six Banga Mary, auntie Gertrude." I replied with respect. I knew from experience always to be polite to Auntie Gertrude.

She gave me the six fishes wrapped in newspaper. "And dis one is fa you." She handed me a separate fish wrapped in newspaper.

"Thanks, Auntie," I shouted with glee, and then made my way to my favorite spot at the end of the fish stalls.

There were always three to four barrels with crabs tied on a string. I used to love to watch the crabs climb over each other to the top of the open barrel and then get pulled back by other crabs below, which were climbing on top of the crabs ahead, in their attempt to get out of the barrel. But none of them ever succeeded. I would stand and wonder why did the crabs not figure out how to get out of the barrel? I was sure that ants would have solved this problem.

From there I went to the Ground Provisions section to buy eddoes, cassava, tania and plantains. It was nice to leave the rank smell of fish and crabs and breathe in the subtler earthy and fruity smell of this section. Usually I would buy one or two of each of these provisions. That accomplished, I fetched my bike, positioned the basket on the handle bar and stabilized it with my right hand as I pushed the bike into Robb street and mounted it from the left side. I pedaled without incident to Su Quan's grocery store and bought rice, flour, oil, sugar and salted fish. I say bought but, actually, I was 'trusting' everything. That is everything was being bought on credit and my grandfather would sometime later go to all of these vendors and 'settle up' what was owed, or at least some portion of it, depending on how much money he had.

By now the basket of goods was quite heavy but I could balance it well on the handle bar for the rest of the ride North on Camp street and left turn into Murray Street for the final 200 yards to arrive home. As I approached the yard where we lived, in a flash, but too late, it occurred to me that the entrance not only sloped downwards but was sandy.

No sooner did the front wheel of the bike hit the sand it skidded and down went the basket, I and the bicycle on top of me. The packages of rice, flour, oil and sugar all exploded and the spilled contents quickly became soaked with oil and mixed with the sandy soil. My heart sank into the puddle of rice, flour, sugar, sand, and oil. I knew that this would mean little to eat for the next one to two weeks, as we basically lived from a week to week budget.

I picked up the basket, ground provisions, fish and bicycle and went to the house. As soon as I stepped into the room my mother started lashing me with a belt while telling me that my aunt Edith had told her that she saw me purposefully push the basket off the handle of the bicycle because I hated this Saturday chore. I ran out of the house engulfed in anger as I headed for the street. I could not understand why this aunt, sister Edith, as we called her, repeatedly and purposefully misrepresented things that were associated with me, when she knew that my mother would punish me after each of her complaints. I had resigned myself to this fate as I recognized that this was the path of least resistance for my mother. But today's lie was an order of magnitude greater than others. It was vicious and I was convinced that the source of her own anger had to do with the fact that my grandfather had bought a bike for me. I also found it difficult to forgive my mother because she had flogged me with a violence that I had never experienced in her before.

I decided impulsively to go to the seawall and drown myself in the Atlantic Ocean. I headed to Waterloo street and to the Promenade or Small Gardens. I entered the Garden and stopped awhile by the mami tree. I observed it for what I thought would be the last time. It was a tall stately tree and many a morning I would hurl stones to dislodge its luscious fruit. However, today I had no interest in hurling stones and certainly not at the mami fruit. Then I continued diagonally to the exit on the Carmichael street side.

Across the Carmichael street exit was the Governor's mansion and fenced compound. A guard with bayonet affixed to his rifle stood at attention in front of the gate. This was the backside of the compound. The front side and official entrance was on Main street, which was parallel to Carmichael Street. The tops of hibiscus and rose bushes rose above the fenced wall and above these, one could see the top floor and roof of the main residence of the compound. Governor Sir Alfred Savage, who had arrived in Georgetown in 1953, was derisively referred to as 'My wife and I' because, whereas many officials often used the royal 'We', he used 'My wife and I' instead, as a way to avoid using the responsible 'I'. And once more, in my wounded rage, I wondered why this Englishman, this symbol and executor of colonialism, was allowed to live in such luxury while we, the citizens, struggled every day. My own home, a short distance away, consisted of a single room in which one adult and three children lived, without an attached kitchen or bathroom.

I continued past the train station and into the Kingston area, by which time I was now walking more slowly but resolutely. My emotions had solidified and nothing could assuage the pain in my soul.

As I passed the Eve Leary Ground, I thought of the many parades to celebrate various British holidays, such as May Day, the coronation of Queen Elizabeth and the visit of princess Margaret to Guiana. I used to enjoy watching the soldiers in their dark blue uniforms and rifles march in various formations as the band played. It was always festive, even though at times I felt that I really was not a part of that scene and something always felt a little incongruous with my daily life. Now, this day, they had even less meaning. I had heard Mr. Burnham rail against these symbols of imperialism as added barriers against British Guiana's struggle to get the right to govern itself. What hope does that offer a boy of twelve when in his own home he cannot even defend himself or be defended against injustice? There was really only one way out of this unbearable existence and that was to exit.

Finally, I got onto the seawall and went to the end jetty. I walked to the end of it and watched the barnacles on the large boulders below and observed them as the water slapped powerfully against the boulders. With each slap of water against the boulders the barnacles remained still firmly attached to the boulders as the water receded. I asked myself, 'Should I climb off the wall and onto these boulders to get to the deep water?' I shuddered at the thought of losing my footing and banging my head on one of these large, slimy rocks.

'What if I slipped and got caught between two boulders and died there without ever making it to the sea? Would I be attacked by the crows and experience a painful, slow death?'

I began to feel an increasing sense of panic and sought a different approach. 'What if I waded into the water from a different part of the wall and walked towards the jetty?' I asked myself.

Parents often warned us to stay away from this jetty because the strong currents and undertow resulted in several drownings.

I walked back towards the adjoining part of the jetty that was parallel to the shore. I wondered how far out into the ocean I would have to walk before I would arrive at a level where I would drown.

That should not be far, I thought, particularly since I cannot swim. 'How long does it take to drown?' I asked myself.

I remembered hearing someone describe drowning as having a lot of water in one's lungs and being strangled slowly. I thought of my lungs filling up with salty, fishy smelling water. I thought of the fact that the water close to the shore was muddy because of the silt and refuse that were released into the ocean from the farms further up the coast. And suddenly I became incredibly frightened as I pictured being suffocated from the inhalation of muddy, refuse filled water. I started walking away from the shore, climbed back onto the seawall and lowered myself onto the street. I concluded that there had to be a different solution to my dilemma and my desire not to return to my insufferable life and home.

I thought of going to Auntie Chrisie. Auntie Chrisie was a very good friend of my mother. In fact, when my mother decided that she could no longer tolerate the beatings from my father and left the apartment with my sister and me, she took us to Auntie Chrisie and asked her to keep us. Unfortunately, Auntie Chrisie said that she could not keep us during the day as her husband, Uncle Oscar, would not allow it. But she said that my mother could bring us at night and we could all sleep on the floor in the kitchen. Of course, my mother accepted and was able to convince my grandfather and grandmother to allow us to stay at their dwelling during the day.

My grandmother Bea Bea and grandfather, whom we called 'daddy', lived in one half of the first floor of a duplex. A kitchen and a shower were both attached on the side where they lived.

However, it was crowded, because in addition to Bea Bea and Daddy, my aunt Edith and her three kids as well as my aunt Ina, lived in those two rooms. The front room served as a living room, dining room, a makeshift bedroom at night, and a space where daddy repaired and made shoes.

Mommy would go to her sewing job at Ms. Melville, while Myrtle and I sat on the steps all day. I had learned to read at a very early age and so I read the one book that I had over and over again. I never tired reading the stories, such as The Dog and its Shadow, The Tortoise and the Hare in this book of some of Aesop's Fables. When it got dark, Mommy would pick up our bundle of 'beddings' which were made up of old clothes and one to two old sheets and walk us the 6-8 blocks to go to shower and sleep at Auntie Chrisie. I could not recall how long this lasted, but one day, the tenant in one of the two rooms in the other half of the duplex, where my grandparents lived, vacated and we were able to occupy that room. I was very happy that we had our own room, particularly since I was always fearful when I took my quick shower, in the semi dark, in the yard where auntie Chrisie lived.

My mother got a double bed and a table on which she placed a table top kerosene oil stove on which she could cook our meals. In the remaining corner she set up a sewing machine and chair and began to supplement her income from Ms. Melville by making dresses for her own customers. Given my mother's attempts to avoid all conflict, her fallback position was to punish us whenever my aunt Edith made a complaint against us. Actually, the complaint was always against me as my sister Myrtle had some sort of brain damage and could not speak. As a result, she was quite withdrawn and mostly sat swaying gently from side to side as though trying to comfort herself. So, I could not simply return to the house and I knew that going to auntie Chrisie was not an option. By this time, we had lived in that room for about 6 years and it was home. We used an outdoor shower and three latrines that were shared by several families. Most important was that this room had its own landing on which I could sit and do my homework. Now I was homeless again.

As I began to retrace my steps through Kingston, past Eve Leary grounds, the train station and approached the Promenade Gardens, it hit me. I will go to Moms! I immediately felt as if my problems had been solved. I would not ever have to return to my home in Murray street. In fact, I would probably be able to sleep in a bed, instead of on beddings on the floor.

Moms was Ms. Gravesande. From about age 11, my mother would have me visit Ms. Gravesande after Sunday School. I was told to call her Moms. The visits were always strange. She was clearly 'well-off'. She lived in an 'upstairs' apartment that seemed quite large for one person and the living room was well furnished. I never saw the rest of the apartment, but I guessed that it had at least two bedrooms and a kitchen. The ritual was the same at each visit. I would come in and say, 'Good afternoon, Moms. How are you?' She would reply, 'Fine, son. Sit here.' She would point to an armchair that sat close to the window in a hallway that led from the door to the living room. A photo of a man in some type of uniform was mounted on the wall across from the window. She would bring me some 'sweeties' (candies) in a little bowl and we would then sit in silence for about half an hour as she alternated between looking at me and then at the framed photo on the wall.

Occasionally, she would ask, "How is your mother, Stella? "

Fortunately, this time she asked the question shortly after I had sat in the chair and it gave me the opportunity to recount what had happened.

I told her, "As I was riding into the yard the basket with all the goods fell off the bicycle handle and everything was spoiled. I could only save the fish and the ground provisions."

"And what did Stella do?" She asked. "I guess that was all the money that she had." She continued.

"She beat me very badly because sister Edith told her that she had seen me intentionally push the basket off the bike." I showed her the welts on my arms and legs.

She was silent for a while, then said, "Stella must have been really angry with you to have whipped you so badly. Did your mother not know it was an accident?"

"I think she did, but she always punishes me when sister Edith tells stories against me." I explained. "That is why I want to stay with you." I said tearfully. I refrained from telling her that I had contemplated ending my life by drowning.

Moms then said, "I cannot do that because Stella would be very angry with me. She depends on you to take care of your sister, Myrtle, when she is at work."

I immediately tuned out as I began frantically to think of an alternative to returning home. Suddenly, I was jolted out of my frenzied search for a new solution by a question from Moms. It was, "Do you know who is your father?"

I said, "Yes. Mr. Douglas."

She continued, "Do you know who gave you the name Lennox?" I said, "Mommy?"

Then she said, "Do you know whose Photo that is?" I said, "No."

Then she said, "He is my son, Cecil Miller. He gave you the name Lennox. Cecil Miller is your father! He is now a lawyer in Lagos, Nigeria, but he intends to return home to Guiana soon."

Suddenly, a number of things became clear.

Moms continued, "Do you know a boy named Lennox Miller? He is about one year older than you."

I replied, "Yes."

She said, "My son has always told me that he had nothing to do with that boy's mother. But that he liked your mother and you are his son."

Now it was clear why I had to call her Moms. Why she always spent time alternatively looking at the photo and at me. It also suddenly made me understand why, whenever Mr. Douglas came to the gate of the yard where we lived in Murray street, and my mother sent Myrtle and me to talk to him, he would ignore me and just cuddle Myrtle. The frenzy in me seemed to have disappeared and a sudden calm came over me. It was almost like it was an acceptance that things were beyond my control. And yet, in some ways, I felt empowered by this information. Ending my life as a solution disappeared and I began to repeat slowly as I returned home, 'Cecil Miller is your father!' When I arrived home I found my mother lying in the bed. I said derisively, with this strange sense of power, "So what's wrong with you now?"

She said, "Boy, I don't feel good and there is something I wan you to know in case I die." "Do you know why I send you to see Moms? Well Mr. Miller, her son, is your father."

I said very matter of fact, "I know. I went to see Moms and she told me." We were both silent and after a while, I got up and went next door to my aunt Edith and, in as threatening a voice as I could muster, I told her, "This is the last time that you will tell a lie on me. If you ever do that again I shall hit you."

I then left, got on my bike and went for a long ride.

That Sunday, I decided that I needed to give my heart to The Lord, because I was becoming fearful of the dark thoughts within me against my aunt. I had seen her do something wrong and I thought of exposing her. I also began to think of ways to hurt her physically.

After giving my heart to the Lord, Brother Mc. Innis began giving me more responsibilities in church. At that time. we actually had a Phenomenon, that had captured everyone's imagination and soul. It was a nine-year old boy preacher who began to attend our church, the Elim Evangelical Church. I decided not to go the route of boy preacher, but to study the bible and be a teacher rather than a preacher.

"Sir, lunch is ready," the stewardess said, yanking me from my reveries.

I looked around and found that others were having lunch, so I accepted to be served.

I looked out the window again and marveled at the fact that the airplane was still flying above the clouds and that these clouds still looked like many bales of cotton. Lunch was a typical curry and rice dish with a soda. I ate without giving much thought to the meal, instead I listened to the steady chatter of other passengers. I knew no one else in the plane and as was my usual preference, avoided eye contact with others so that they would not be tempted to engage me in conversation. I was also lucky in that I did not have a passenger in the seat next to me.

After lunch, I returned to my memories.

In September, 1955, at age 12, I entered Cambridge Academy and began to soak up everything like a sponge. Because we were now five of us in the one room (Myrtle, who was one year younger than I, Cheddie, my first brother, a second sister Faye, my mother and I), I could not study at home. I would go directly to the Promenade Gardens after end of the school day and do my homework until the six o'clock bees (the Circada Bees) loudly signaled 'closing time'. I would then go home, have tea and biscuits, pull the curtain that separated the part with the bed from the table with the kerosene oil stove and the sewing machine, spread my beddings on the floor next to the bed and go to sleep. I would then awake at about 3 am and start to study with the aid of the kerosene oil lamp. This usually consisted of reading future chapters and working on problems. I got A's in every subject and was first in the form at the end of the year. Towards the end of the first year Ms. Bacchus, one of the teachers called me to her desk. She was a kind looking woman and reminded me of my mother. She was direct and asked, "Would you like to take lessons from me?"

"Yes, Miss Bacchus," I replied, "But my mother cannot pay for it." "That will be no problem. I tutor your friend Winston Vierra. You could come and listen as I teach him."

I was excited by the prospect of working with her in the summer. I told my mother and she agreed. Since we did not have money to buy books, Ms. Bacchus loaned me the Latin Step 2 and Ora Maritima Latin books and the Geometry book by Comacho. I raced through Step 2 Latin and completed most of the Geometry section of Comacho, including many of the problem sets at the end of each chapter. Miss Bacchus was quite impressed and would correct my self-imposed home work.

During the first week of my second year in Cambridge Academy, Ms. Bacchus convinced Mr. Pinkerton, the Principal and owner of Cambridge Academy, to have me skip the third form, enter the fourth form and take the College of Preceptors Examination at the end of that school year. Mr. Pinkerton agreed, somewhat reluctantly, but the other teachers, such as Esther and Doris Ledoux, who had taught me a number of subjects in my first year, agreed with the recommendation. The LeDoux sisters were cousins of Mr. Pinkerton, so their opinion carried weight with him.

Fourth Form was exactly what I needed at that time, because there was where I learned the difference between regurgitating what I had memorized and studying for understanding, and synthesizing answers to questions. I took the College of Preceptors examination at the end of that year and justified Ms. Bacchus' confidence in me. I had the best performance of all students in British Guiana, that year, having earned a distinction in every subject.

This recollection evoked a smile as it caused me to recall an incident that was associated with this event. After the results were published, I visited some acquaintances where I periodically went to play ping pong. They really did not know me, as I had never talked about myself. One of the boys, who had attended Central High School, had taken the College of Preceptors Examination and had done quite well, having received a distinction in all but one subject. There were four of us together. Kamal said, "Harry really show dem all. He got 9 distinctions and 1 credit in de exam."

"Da must be de best in de country," the other boy said.

Harry, who was playing with the other boy, halted playing and said, "I don't know. They say some boy got 10 distinctions. He must be first in the country."

"No matta," said Kamal. "You gwan beat him next year at Senior Cambridge exam."

"Guys, I have to go home," I said, before they could ask about my performance, and quickly left.

Mr. Pinkerton was delighted and told me that since I would be under 16 at the end of the following year when I would sit for the Senior Cambridge Examination, I had an excellent chance of winning a scholarship to go to Queens College, if I placed among the top five students in the country. On average, students who sat for the Senior Cambridge examination were between the ages of 17 and 19.

In 1958, I sat for the Senior Cambridge Examination and the three-month wait for the results was unbearable. Finally, one day, Mr. Pinkerton, whose desk, along with that shared by the other teachers, was positioned on a raised platform of the open classroom school, beckoned for me to leave my seat and join him and the other teachers on the platform. The entire school went silent as I walked to the platform.

He shook my hand warmly and said, "The results of the examination came this morning. I think that you probably have come first in the country again. In your eight subjects you earned four Distinctions and four high Credits."

He continued with a smile. I had never seen him smile before. "This means that you have the equivalent of having scored, on average, a Distinction on each of your six best subjects, because you scored a '1' in Latin and Geometry." Distinctions were graded 1 and 2; Credits, 3 and 4; and Pass were awarded scores 5 and 6.

It was indeed the best performance that had been achieved in Guiana in several years. He was correct. I had placed First in Guiana and had won a scholarship to Queens College. I experienced a strange mixture of emotions. I felt a sense of pride and thanked the Lord for blessing me with this wonderful result. I also refrained from initiating conversation about my performance and humbly thanked those who congratulated me. Some students and adults observed me from a distance with a mixture of respect and curiosity. My very good friend and 'sister' Leila Adams, with whom I used to study, had also passed the examination, so there was great jubilation at Elim Evangelical Church. Elim's Boy and Elim's Girl had both passed the examination and many prayers of Thanks to the Lord were offered in Church that Sunday. Equally important for me was the gratitude that I felt and expressed to Uncle Willie, Auntie Chrisie, Miss Bacchus and of course, Mommy (my mother). It struck me that my mother did not appear to be at all surprised by my performance.

As was often the practice in these small high schools, the best performers at the Senior Cambridge Examination would be offered a job as a teacher at their high school. So, at age 15, I became a teacher at Cambridge Academy. I taught Latin and Geometry to students in the second form, while waiting to be admitted to Queens College in September of 1959.

Queens College Days

I motioned to the stewardess and asked if I could use the toilet. She pointed to the rear of the airplane. Three other passengers were ahead of me waiting to use the toilet. As I stood in line, I mused about whether there would be communal toilets at Lehigh University. I had grown up using toilets that were shared by several families. 'Will my personality change in the next few years?' I asked myself. I was told that I would be studying Engineering at the University and I wondered whether that would conflict with my evangelical religious upbringing. I had no idea what things would influence my life in the future. When I returned to my seat, after voiding my full bladder, I continued to reflect on the last 4-5 years of my life in Guiana.

September 1958 to September 1959 were incredible months of growth. I was teaching students, some of whom were anywhere from 3 years to 1 year younger than me. I taught Latin and Geometry which were among my best subjects. I also began to emulate Mr. Pinkerton's teaching methods that had had an impact on me. Mr. Pinkerton taught the Senior Cambridge class Literature and Geometry. Many students, particularly, the girls, were quite fearful of incurring his wrath when they could not solve the geometry problems. And I could still hear him repeating his words of encouragement, 'I don't care if you make 100 errors as long as you do not repeat the same error twice.' I also remember him bringing The Merchant of Venice alive as he read aloud Portia's words as she begged Shylock not to insist on receiving his pound of flesh,

"The Quality of Mercy is not strain'd
It droppeth as the gentle rain from heaven
Upon the place beneath. It is twice blest:
It blesseth him that gives and him that takes.
'Tis mightiest in the mightiest. It becomes
The throned monarch better than his
crown….."

Portia's focus on Justice, tempered by mercy and wisdom made an indelible impression on me.

No less of an impression was that of the speech of Gratiano on being genuine and true to one's self as he declared to Antonio,

Let me play the fool.
With mirth and laughter let old wrinkles
come….. There is a sort of men whose visages
Do cream and mantle like a standing pond,
And do a wilful stillness entertain,
With purpose to be dress'd in an opinion Of
wisdom, gravity, profound conceit, As who
should say 'I am Sir Oracle,
And when I ope my lips, let no dog bark.'

Wisdom and Justice tempered with Mercy as Portia told Shylock that he was to cut exactly one pound of flesh from Antonio, no more no less, and Gratiano's declaration that authenticity was more important than feigned seriousness, became key traits to which I aspired.

Another characteristic that I came to admire was self-control coupled with inner and outward physical strength. As with Shakespeare's Henry V and The Merchant of Venice, I had memorized many stanzas of Sir Walter Scott's poem, The Lady of the Lake. I had also studied this book for the Senior Cambridge examination. I reflected on one of my favorite stanzas from The Combat Scene,

"Now, clear the ring! For, hand to hand, the
manly wrestlers take their stand, Two o'er the
rest superior rose,
And proud demanded mightier foes,
Nor called in vain, for Douglas came. For Life
is Hugh of Lambert lame; Scarce better John of
Alloa's fare,
Whom senseless home his comrades bare.
Prize of the wrestling match, the King
To Douglas gave a golden ring, While coldly
glanced his eye of blue, As frozen drop of
wintry dew.
Douglas would speak, but in his breast
His struggling soul his words suppressed;
Indignant then he turned him where, Their
arms the brawny yeomen bare,
To hurl the massive bar in air.
When each his utmost strength had shown,
The Douglas rent an earth-fast stone
From its deep bed, then heaved it high, And
sent the fragment through the sky A rood
beyond the farthest mark;
And still in Stirling's royal park,
The gray-haired sires, who knew the past, To
strangers point the Douglas cast,
And moralize on the decay
Of Scottish strength in modern day.

Not only was I delighted by the octosyllabic iambic metre
of the poem but was impressed by the emotional and physical
strength of the banished Douglas in his struggle against King
James V. And, of course, I was secretly proud that I bore the
Douglas name.

As I began to prepare to enter Queens College, Mr. Pinkerton
called me to discuss my course of study. He knew that I wanted
to study the sciences which to this point I had not had an
opportunity to do. I had two options. I could enter the Lower
6th form and take the Advanced (A) Level exams after two years
of study; or I could enter the 5th Form Removed and spend one

year learning Chemistry, Physics, Applied Mathematics and Biology, at the end of which I would take the O Level exams. Successful performance at this exam would be followed by progression on to the Lower 6th Science form and the start of the preparation for the Advanced (A) Level examinations in those four subjects. Mr. Pinkerton advised me to choose to go directly to the lower 6th Science form and work on three subjects: Pure Math, Applied Math and Latin. He told me that Mr. Sangar Davis, the principal, would probably object because Queens College had a Science Track and a Classical Track and he would resist a mixed program. Mr. Pinkerton told me that this had been done before and I should insist. Mr. Pinkerton had two reasons for this suggestion. The first was that Math and Latin were my strongest subjects and more importantly was that I would have two chances at getting a Guyana Scholarship which was given to the top 2 performers under 19 years of age at the time of taking the Advanced Level examination. A Guyana Scholarship provided full scholarship to universities in England and The University of the West Indies.

I elected to enter the 5th Form Removed and I performed well at the O Level in all four subjects, chemistry, physics, math and Biology at the end of the school year. I entered lower 6th in the Science stream and things began to unravel. Events that could not have been predicted seemed to have justified Mr. Pinkerton's advice that I should have taken Latin, Pure Math and Applied Math. We lost our Physics teacher in the final year. At the end of the year in lower 6th, the talented and highly respected Botany and Zoology teacher, Mr. Ramsammy left for England and we had to study the remaining part of the curriculum by ourselves. Thus, for one year we had to study Botany, Zoology and Physics on our own, as the replacement for Mr. Ramsammy, who had received his B.S. from Howard University, was unfamiliar with the Flora of Guiana and the A Level Examination curriculum. In spite of these setbacks I did well on the A level examination, but not well enough to win a scholarship. The Guyana scholarship was won by Roopnarine and D'Anjou, both of whom were taking the A Level examination for a second time.

Fortunately, I had had the job as a Teacher at Cambridge Academy, so I had money to buy the white shirts and khaki pants which were the required uniform for Queens College. I received the yellow tie and bughouse (cork helmet) on my first day of school.

Nonetheless, I was anxious. Only a few of the students who went to Queens were on scholarship. That means that the rest came from either middle class or wealthy families. I began to worry about how uncomfortable it would be for me when I could not participate in any activities that required additional expenditures. I also wondered whether the fact that I lived with my mother and three siblings in one room would be personally embarrassing. Suddenly, Uncle Willie came to the rescue again.

Uncle Willie's wife had taken his two daughters to England and after a year had not returned. Uncle Willie invited us to move to his place in Thomas Street. His was also a small place but larger than our room. His flat had two small bedrooms each of which was large enough to hold a single bed. There was a small living/dining room, that was large enough to accommodate the sewing machine and still have room for a small dining table and two chairs. There was a small attached kitchen. Like our place in Murray Street the shower and toilet were unattached and we shared them with one other family, who lived in a similar and adjoining unit. This was a marked improvement over having to share the single shower and three toilets with six other families when we lived in Murray Street. I assumed that the house in Murray Street, in which we had a room, was probably owned in previous times, by one of the slave owners; and the row of six two-room apartments was probably the quarters for the slaves and later servants. So, we moved to Thomas street when I then discovered that my second brother, Gary, was in the womb.

This move, although practical, created some silent tension between me, and my mother and Uncle Willie. I was fully involved with Elim and often was asked to deliver sermons. I had become a boy preacher. According to the teachings of the Evangelical church, my mother was living 'in sin' with Uncle Willie. This meant that I was teaching and preaching against such life choices, while simultaneously living in the situation. Since I was highly respected as a Boy Preacher in my church, I felt significant inner conflict. I worked hard to justify my family situation and finally decided to simply accept it without comment.

Of interest, Ruby Holder lived in the house at the back of the yard in Thomas Street. Ruby and I had attended Christ Church Elementary School and at age 12 she had entered Bishops, the Girls equivalent of Queens College. Bishops High School was located at the corner of Murray and Carmichael Streets, which was a little more than one block from where I lived. That meant that every morning, I would encounter former classmates who were in Elementary school with me and who were now attending Bishops. They all would ride pass without acknowledging me, except Ruby. She would wave or smile. When we moved into Thomas street, Ruby stopped by and introduced herself to my mom. Ruby and I became fast friends and on occasion I would visit her. Ruby and her family lived in a large house at the back of the yard and her family was comfortably in the middle class. Ruby's acceptance and friendship made me feel less self-conscious about being poor. I felt accepted by someone attending one of the two top High Schools in spite of the economic conditions of my family. Queens College provided my first experiences with discrimination. Mr. Sangar Davis, the Principal, who was an Englishman, differentiated between boys who had entered Queens in the first form and those of us who had entered in the 5th Form Removed or lower 6th Form. To him we were not really Queens College Boys. For example, one day a stop watch was missing at the end of an experiment in the Physics Lab. Mr. Trotz, our physics teacher reported the event to Mr. Sangar Davis. The 5th Form Removed had three other boys who like myself had come to Queens College via performance on the Senior Cambridge Examination, and boys who had been in the classical stream and were switching to the science stream. Mr. Sangar Davis arrived unannounced during a physics session. He appeared angry. He was about 5' 10" tall with a pleasant face that could assume a stern visage whenever he was annoyed. His pate had a small central balding portion that was often red from the Guiana sun. Today the red color was in his face and not on his pate. He asked immediately, "Which one of you boys took the stop watch?"

Silence. No one spoke. No one moved. He asked again, but this time with anger in his flushed face. Mr. Trotz, a Guianese who had received his B.S. in Physics from a British University, in deference to the Principal, had moved away from the front of the class and was standing on the side of the room, next to the windows.

"Which of you boys stole the stop watch?"

Silence.

He waited a little longer for an answer. I thought to myself, 'why would he assume that someone had stolen the stop watch? Perhaps it was simply misplaced.' However, I too remained silent. I was afraid to offer my thoughts.

Finally, he said, "This is what we get for letting you boys into Queens. No true Queens College boy, who had grown up in this School, would ever steal.

You are simply ingrates! We have given you an opportunity and this is how you repay the school.

I expect this stop watch will be returned to the laboratory within the next 24 hours."

He pulled the door firmly behind him as he left the room.

I felt my anger rising as we all exhaled. He had clearly stated that one of the four of us, who had recently been admitted to Queens College, was guilty. Two weeks later we learned that one of the long-term Queens College Boys had taken it to practice for the upcoming Sports Day. He had neglected to inform the Physics teacher that he had borrowed it.

At the end of each term the names of the best three performers in each Form were read out during a special general assembly.

Mr. Sangar Davis read three names from my form, but my name was not among them. I was quite sure I had performed in the top three.

I went to see the house master, brandishing my report – proof.

He shook his head, denying the facts. "You placed fourth," he said. "There's nothing more to be discussed. Dismissed."

I wasn't recognized as being among the top three performers until the final performances for the year were announced at General Assembly.

Then came lower 6th and my being voted as President of the Bible Club. The Bible Club had been led by Bobo Young for several years. Bobo had insisted on offering Scripture as one of his A Level subjects. This had displeased Mr. Sangar Davis as Scripture was not one of the subjects being taught at Queens. At the last meeting of the Bible Club, before Bobo left, I was elected to succeed Bobo. During the first week of the new school year, Mr. Sangar Davis summoned the new officers of the Bible Club to his office to discuss the plan for the Bible Club.

Three of us, the President, the Vice President and Secretary of the Bible Club, appeared at his office at 3:15 pm, the end of the school day. He directed my two classmates to sit together on one side of his rectangular conference table and me to sit on the end directly opposite him.

"What is your study plan for the semester?" he asked without any preamble or unnecessary pleasantries and looking directly at me.

I responded, "Sir, we have decided to study the Prophets of the Old Testament. We have selected Jeremiah, one of the major Prophets."

"What is the goal of this Plan?" he asked

"Sir, our plan is to track the prosperity of the Children of Israel as they either accepted or rejected Jeremiah's prophesies." I explained.

Abruptly, he said, "I will be taking over the Bible Club. I studied Old Testament in the University and I will develop a Plan." He continued to talk, now addressing the other two officers of the bible club. I did what I tended to do in such situations. I tuned out. Finally, he looked at me and said, "Now, Douglas, what do you have to say for yourself?"

I replied, "Sir, may I ask a question?" "Go ahead, Douglas."

As he was talking to my two classmates, I had thought, 'Why was he so resistant to BoBo's studying Scripture as one of his A Level subjects, when he had studied Old Testament at the University?'

23

I looked directly at him and said, "Sir, I am trying to understand why you have chosen to run the Bible Club?"

He sputtered in anger, "As Principal, I run every club in this school."

I immediately shot back, "Sir, I am the vice president of both the Debating Society and the Bee Keeping Society, and you do not run those clubs."

Now, his face flushed, he exploded, "This is dogmatic pigheadedness. That is what I call this. Dogmatic pigheadedness, and furthermore, I will hear nothing more from you Douglas. Dismissed!"

My classmates exited the room trembling with fear.

They wanted to know what I planned to do. They said I would probably be expelled. They were sure that I would never become a Prefect. Prefects were usually selected from students in the lower 6th Form and served two years.

They were selected by Mr. Sangar Davis. I told them that I planned to attend the club meeting as scheduled. The meetings were held after School, on Wednesdays. Wednesday came and a few brave souls, primarily the officers and a few others appeared. We waited the entire hour and Mr. Sangar Davis never came. In fact, he never showed up and I ran the Bible Club for the next two years, without interference from him. Thereafter, everyone noticed that Mr. Sangar Davis totally ignored me. If I were in a group with two or three other students and he happened to walk by us, he would stop and address the others by name, while ignoring me.

The final signal was that when Walter Rodney and Ewart Thomas, who both won the Guyana Scholarship in 1961, and who were the leaders in Cunningham House, graduated, I was not named as Leader of Cunningham House. However, to everyone's surprise, Mr. Sangar Davis did appoint me a Prefect when I entered upper 6th Form. On my last Day as a student at Queens College, I learned why he had appointed me a Prefect.

Other aspects of being at Queens College were both challenging socially as well as enjoyable. I stayed away from joining teams or activities that required uniforms, such as cricket, or the cadets, as I knew it would be difficult for Uncle Willie to support that. However, I did participate in a number of other activities such as the debating competition, the Verse recital and Baritone competitions at the National Guiana Cultural Festival. The music teacher, Ms. Dolphin had insisted that I participate in these latter two and I placed second in both. Perhaps, however, the most notable event was being selected to play the Major General part in the Pirates of Penzance. I was in the lower 6th and it was assumed that Spencer, an upper 6th student would play the part. I was quite surprised when Ms. Dolphin insisted that I play the part, particularly, since, unlike many of the other boys, I had not had any musical training.

The first night's performance of the Pirates of Penzance was almost a disaster for me.

Each year Mr. Sangar Davis and his wife produced and directed one of Gilbert and Sullivan's operettas. Mr. Sangar Davis also conducted the orchestra whose members were professional musicians. One of my classmates, Clement Marshall, was given the task to tell me whenever it was my turn to make my entrance on stage. The performance started and as I peeked out I could see that the hall was full. I was quite nervous. My outfit had been borrowed from the Police Department and had been modified by Mrs. Sangar Davis, with the appropriate ribbons and chords that befitted a proper major General. I kept adjusting and readjusting my Major General's hat.

I became aware that Clement was waving to me and pointing to the stage which was the agreed signal when it was time for me to make my entrance. I was confused because I did not hear the daughters of the Major General sing, "Yes, Yes, our father is a Major General." The stage was empty and I walked out somewhat timidly, saw the puzzled looks from the members of the orchestra. They stopped playing momentarily and I noticed that Mr. Sangar Davis was making a somewhat circular motion to the orchestra. Then there was a down wave with his wand and I heard the introduction to my piece.

I sang somewhat tentatively, 'I am the very model of a modern Major General.'

My voice strengthened on the next lines, 'I've information vegetable, animal and mineral

I know the kings of England, and I quote the fights historical
From Marathon to Waterloo, in order categorical.'

As I sang the daughters and pirates flooded back onto the
stage and we continued the scene. The rest of the performance
went without a hitch. On the second night, I was a hit. It turns
out that Clement had given me the incorrect cue on the first
night.

The other activity I loved was track. I would get up at 5
am and run a mile to the seawall, then to the school grounds.
Queens College school was close to the seawall. I would do my
wind sprints and run back home. I thought I should do well
in track because my aunt Ina was actually for many years the
best woman 100-yard sprinter in Guiana. My best events were
the 220, 440 and 880 yards. I usually ran second place to either
Ivor Fields or Clement Marshall. I was also athletic co-captain
for Cunningham House in my last year at Queens. However, I
was never as dedicated to winning as were my peers.

The final surprise to my classmates came in our final
days at Queens. At the end of our years at Queens we would
each receive a typed recommendation letter from Mr. Sangar
Davis, copies of which were used to support applications to
University and for jobs. Naturally, we eagerly read each other's
Recommendation Letter. All had assumed that I would get at
best a tepid letter of recommendation from Mr. Sangar Davis.
To everyone's surprise not only did the Principal praise my
academic achievements but also my leadership and courage.
His last sentence read, 'And I wish we had more boys such as
him.' As I read his words, my bitterness and my feelings of
having been treated unfairly by him were replaced by a sense
that determination and being true to my values ultimately had
led to success. His last sentence in my recommendation letter
altered my perception of my world.

Waiting for a Scholarship

Since there was no University in Guiana, students often would work 2-3 years to earn enough money, and with help from parents and close friends, travel mostly to England or Jamaica to attend University. I had started that process with my teaching assignment at Cambridge Academy. But political unrest would thwart this path.

The previous ten years had been quite politically charged. As a ten year old boy I could sense the excitement as the country prepared for the first general elections under adult suffrage. Aunt Ina and Daddy were very active foot soldiers of the People's Progressive Party (PPP). The corner of Waterloo and Murray streets, close to where we lived, was a popular spot for political rallies, thus our small home became an informal meeting place for many of the speakers at the rallies. I remember how often they talked about Cheddie (Jagan) being fiery, but that Burnham was an orator. The Peoples' Progressive Party (PPP) won the election but the constitution was suspended one month thereafter because England was opposed to the PPP's association with and orientation towards the communist bloc countries. In addition, it was reported that Ms. Janet Jagan's aunt and uncle, the Rosenbergs, had been recently executed in the US for spying for the Soviet Union.

British soldiers with rifles and in trucks could be seen everywhere in Georgetown. I could sense danger, particularly when my grandfather had me help him gather all the political pamphlets in the house. He put the small coal pot in the shower and burned all the pamphlets. It seemed to take an eternity to burn them all, and I feared that at any time the smell of burning paper and smoke would attract informants of the British soldiers and my grandfather would be hauled off to jail.

As I started high school at Cambridge Academy, I recalled the reappearance of political excitement. Burnham, the then Chairman of the PPP had split from and formed the People's National Congress (PNC). Aunt Ina and daddy were excited and they would take me to Bourda Green, an open grassy area next to the market, to hear Comrade Burnham speak. I remember thinking that I would like to be able to speak as fluently and confidently as he.

In 1957 a limited constitution was reinstituted and the PPP, Jagan's party, won the majority of seats. Four years later the PPP again won the majority in the General election. However, the PPP won by 1.6% of the vote but received twice as many seats as the PNC.

Riots against the PPP's austere budget and continued move towards the communist bloc broke out in 1962, a few months before the A Level examination. This was followed by an 80-day general strike in 1963. This was quite difficult because it now seemed to have had a racial overtone. During the 1961 election, the Indian population that unanimously supported Cheddie Jagan, who was Indian, had run through the streets, shouting "Apan Jaat", meaning 'Our Kind'. And although one could find prominent African politicians, such as Sydney King, who supported the PPP, there were very few Indians, except Lachmansingh, who supported the PNC.

Teachers were also on strike, although we held classes for students studying for examinations. The Trade Unions Council (TUC) had arranged for supplies from abroad and we would stand in long lines to get rice and seafood. The seafood was mostly squids which was the first time I would eat squid. This racial tension made a reconciliation between Jagan and Burnham impossible and it led to the British government changing the constitution to provide for more proportional representation. New elections were arranged in 1964. The PPP won 46% of the vote and the PNC 40%, and the United Force won 11 % of the vote. Burnham and the United Force formed a coalition government and Burnham became Prime Minister, and The PPP became the opposition party.

I steadfastly refused to join either Party, particularly the PPP Youth movement, of which my cousin Aubrey Bonnet was a member. Members of the PPP Youth movement were being offered scholarships from declared Communist countries such as Cuba and East Germany, and it was clear that had I joined the Youth Movement I would have received such a scholarship. Aubrey received a scholarship to University of Puerto Rico.

I am not sure why, but I also began to receive offers of scholarships to attend universities in East Germany, Rumania and Israel. I was quite keen on going to Israel as it would have been an unusual opportunity to study in the land where Jesus, our Savior, and his disciples had lived, preached, and performed miracles. I began to prepare to respond to the offer of a scholarship to Tel A Viv University when I received a message to attend a meeting at the USIS office.

I was puzzled but went anyway. The meeting was very brief.

They handed me a letter and explained that I was being offered a Fulbright Scholarship to study at a University of my choosing in the USA. The only requirement was that I study Engineering and return to work in Guiana after I completed the Bachelor's Degree. They needed an answer as soon as possible. I recalled how with a rapid heartbeat I pedaled home as fast as I could to tell Mommy and Uncle Willie. Then I pedaled over to Church street to tell Lynnet and to propose to her. As I told her I wanted to be sure that I did not return to Guiana with a foreign wife. I asked a couple of individuals which University I should select and the only guidance that I got was that the best colleges and universities were on the East Coast of America. I communicated to the USIS that I wanted to be on the East Coast. A few days later they summoned me to another meeting where they handed me a large packet of documents and told me that I would be attending Lehigh University. I immediately said that I had already completed High School. The man smiled and said, Lehigh is one of the best Engineering Colleges on the East Coast.

I took the large package and went directly to inform Mr. Sangar Davis of my good fortune. When I entered his office, he invited me to sit in a chair close to his desk.

I said, "Sir, I would like to thank you for the very positive recommendation that you gave me and for the opportunities I had at Queens College." He smiled and remained silent.

I continued, "I have just come from the U.S.I.S. office and they have offered me a scholarship to attend a University in America." He nodded and I got the impression that he was already aware of the scholarship.

I waited for him to speak.

Finally, he said, "Douglas, I always thought that you would go to Oxford or Cambridge."

I said, "Sir, that was my desire. But, unfortunately, I do not have the necessary money. This Fulbright Scholarship from America pays for everything." He leaned forward and said with emphasis, "Oh Douglas, you can do better than that!"

He rose. Extended his hand, and said, "In any case, I know that you will do well."

I thanked him and left.

Uncle Willie sent me to a special tailor who made a robe for me. He explained that it is cold in America and I will need a robe. The robe was purple and looked elegant. This robe, clothes and toiletry were placed in a blue grip that Uncle Willie had purchased for me.

I went to say goodbye to Moms. I had continued to visit her periodically and to keep her abreast of what I was doing.

I was quite excited when I visited her as I thought that she would have been very proud of me.

I started the conversation by saying, "Moms, today, I have great news. I have received a Fulbright Fellowship to attend a University in America. The Fellowship pays for everything."

She smiled and said, "That is great news. Your father would be very proud of you."

I said, Moms, I doubt whether he sees me as his son."

She expressed surprise and asked, "Why would you say something like that?" I took a breadth and debated with myself, whether I should say more. Finally, I explained. "When he was here in Guyana, I would go to his office every afternoon to try to get to see him. I would sit and wait for nearly an hour and at the end of that time, the receptionist would tell me that unfortunately, he had left for the day. One afternoon, I was ushered into his office. He apologized that he was very busy and had been unable to see me on the previous occasions. He asked to see one of the text books that I had with me. He looked at the inside front cover of the book and returned it to me. He then gave me a shilling and told me to study hard. That was the only contact that I have ever had with him."

She remained silent and returned to her alternative looking at me and at the photo of her son on the wall.

I could see that she was embarrassed by this, so I decided to change the subject.

"Moms," I continued, "The good news is that America is paying my tuition and I get a monthly stipend to cover my living expenses and books." I paused to make sure that she had heard this.

I continued. "I have used all of the money I had and wondered whether you could lend me 50 Guianese dollars. I will be able to repay you in a month, after I receive my first stipend."

Moms looked away for a moment. Then she said, "You know that I would really like to help you, but two of the houses I own need repairs, and I don't have any free cash."

I immediately tuned out and did not hear the rest of her excuse. When she was done, I thanked her and told her that I was sure that I would find a solution. I bade her farewell. I resolved not to ever contact her again.

The last Sunday before my departure as I was closing the worship service at Elim, I saw two guys that I knew slip into the back of the Church. They kept signaling to me that they wanted to talk to me. I ignored them and completed the service.

At the end of the service they rushed up to me and said, "Comrade Leader has been waiting for you. He is pretty mad. Did you not get the notice that he wanted to see you, urgently?"

We got on our bicycles and rode to Mr. Burnham's (Comrade Leader's) office. We entered his large office where there was one other person present. He addressed me angrily, "How dare you keep me, the most important Leader in this country, waiting?

I responded, "Mr. Burnham, I meant no disrespect but I was in the service of someone who is greater than you." He glared at me incredulously, then invited me to sit down.

Mr. Burnham then said, "Soon you will be heading to America on a scholarship. You need to know how this occurred. I spent several weeks in America talking to officials of the American government. I told them that many of our brightest young people were being offered scholarships by the communist bloc countries and they will return to Guiana committed to communism. They finally agreed to give a limited number of scholarships. Last year they offered one and this year they have offered two scholarships." He paused for effect. He looked directly at me and continued.

"You will be asked frequently to explain my political philosophy. Your answer will be that I am a democratic socialist. That means that we are committed to Democracy and will involve the workers and population in building the economy."

I thought to myself, "Sounds good. I wonder what it means in practice."

He continued to expound on Democratic Socialism for about another 15 minutes. At the end he asked whether I had any questions.

I said, "I do not have any questions and thank you for explaining Democratic Socialism."

He got up from his desk and approached me. As he shook my hand, he said, "I am happy that you have gotten this scholarship. I know your mother and aunts and I know that they are strong supporters of the PNC."

So here I was on my way to America, to study Engineering at Lehigh University and explain Democratic Socialism, when asked. And it was clear that without the help and care from Uncle Willie and Auntie Chrisie, who were always there for my mother and her five children, and particularly for me, who knows what my life would have been.

Perhaps, I would have been a Postman.

I drifted off to sleep, letting the vibrations of the plane's engines soothe me for the remainder of my flight to the U.S.A.

First Impressions—
Lehigh University

The stewardess tapped me on the shoulder. "The airplane is landing, Sir," the stewardess said. I blinked the sleep from my eyes. The landing was as uneventful as the take off, but I had my first culture shock as I started down the stairs of the Pan Am airlines airplane to enter into the customs area of a building that was about 50 yards distant from where the airplane had stopped.

There were many buildings and planes at the Idlewild Airport compared to the small building and at most two planes that were at the Guiana Atkinson Airfield. I went through customs and it dawned on me, that although I had seen white people in Guiana, mostly British, I had never seen so many white people in any one place. I asked myself, 'Where are the Black people and East Indians? Why do they not smile more frequently? Why do they seem in a hurry? Why are there so many official looking people?' They did not appear to know each other.

As soon as I exited the customs area with my blue suitcase, a man and woman approached me. They both wore smiles. The woman seemed friendlier than the man.

"Hello Frank. Welcome to America. We are from the Institute of International Education and will be responsible for you during your study time in America." The woman greeted me. The man was silent.

"Hello. I am fine, thank you," I responded.

"How was your trip?"

"It was fine, thank you."

"We have a letter for you." The man gave me the letter. "In it you will find our names and the address and telephone numbers of our offices at the Institute of International Education. We refer to the Institute as IIE." The woman explained.

"Thank you." And I accepted the letter.

"We shall take you to your hotel and tomorrow morning, at 9:00 am, we will come to take you to the bus for your trip to Yale University."

"Thank you. Is Yale University a part of Lehigh University?" This time the man smiled broadly and the woman continued.

"Yale is a separate University. Yale University is one of the places where we hold an orientation program for new Fulbright scholars. There will be about 100 Fulbright scholars from all over the world."

"Thank you." I said, a little bewildered.

"Let us get a taxi and take you to your hotel."

We climbed into a yellow taxi. The woman sat in the front seat and the man and I sat in the back seat. There were many of these yellow cars intermixed with mostly black and blue cars on the road. The density of cars increased as we entered the city. There were many buildings and they were all taller than buildings in Guiana. At the hotel, the man helped me with checking in. I was given my room key. The man was thoughtful and took me to the elevator and up to my room. This was the first time that I had ridden in an elevator. I opened the door to the room and saw that there was a bed, a dresser, a table and a chair. My own bed for the night! I was on one of the upper floors. I looked out of the window and the people walking around below looked very small.

It was dusk and the buildings were brightly lit with many neon lights. I decided to go for a walk. I noted my room number, went to the elevator and out into the streets. The hotel was not far from what I learned was called Times Square. It was Sunday and the stores were open! There were colored lights on all of the buildings. There were many traffic lights. Guiana had gotten its first and only set of traffic lights in 1961. Suddenly, I understood why Brother McInnis during his final prayer for me, had asked God to protect me from being tempted by 'the

Bright Lights'. However, I was still puzzled as to why I would be tempted by these lights.

After walking about 4 blocks I retraced my steps to the hotel and my room. I undressed, took a shower and went to bed. I slept until awakened by light streaming into the room. The clock on the dresser said 8:00. I did my morning ablutions, packed and took the elevator to the lobby to await the officials from the IIE.

The IIE officials arrived promptly and we walked a few blocks to the Greyhound Bus Station. There they took me to a bus, gave a ticket to the bus driver and asked him to be sure that I got off in New Haven. They told me that someone would meet me at the New Haven Station and take me to Yale University. I took a window seat in the bus and waved good bye to them. A quiet excitement descended on me as the half-full bus pulled out of its station. The bus ride to New Haven was a blur as we drove by so many cities. The following morning, however, I entered yet another different world. I was in a large hall at Yale with graduate students from many countries. All spoke English, but accents were clear and they were obviously quite accomplished and educated. We learned that among the 100 or so Fulbright Scholars that year seven were undergraduates. We were then divided into small groups based on our area of concentration. Since I was going to study engineering I was placed in a group of Chemists and Physicists. In each session, 2-3 members described their research. I was told to go to the Library and look up the work of one of the professors in the Chemistry Department at Lehigh and prepare to give a report a week later.

I also began to look at the evening news on TV and became quite moved by the planned March on Washington organized by Dr. Martin Luther King. I went to Chaplain William Coffin to ask him how I could get to Washington to witness this March. He invited me to sit. He was silent for a while and then asked, "When did you arrive in the US?"

"About 3 days ago," I replied.

"Why is it important for you to go to this March in Washington?" he asked. I reflected for a moment and answered slowly, "I am not sure, but something within me is drawing me to it."

"You have only been in America for three days." I interrupted and said, "I listened to the news last night and learned that Black people are being treated very badly in America. I could not believe it, because my minister at home always taught us that Christians love each other and America is of course a Christian country."

The chaplain responded, "Regrettably, that is true. Do you know where you will stay when you get to Washington, DC?"

I replied simply, "No."

"How much money do you have?" "About ten American dollars."

He looked at me and I could sense his concern and compassion. Then he said, "They are expecting many thousand people on this March on Washington. The hotels will be full. It will be relatively easy to get lost and there would be no one to help you. Do you think that this is a good idea?"

I did not respond because I knew that he was correct. It was not a good idea. I stood up and thanked him for his advice. He raised himself slowly out of his chair, as though he was reluctant to end the conversation. Then he said, "Please come to me if ever you want to discuss these issues."

A couple of days later, I began to have severe pain in my groin that was aggravated by walking. At the beginning of the section meeting I asked the professor if I could speak with him privately. We stepped outside the room and I explained the problem to him. He immediately launched into a long diatribe about my being in America and that I would be expected to work very hard. He further told me that in America excuses to avoid hard work is not acceptable and I needed to determine whether I was really up to the task. I was really puzzled. He clearly believed that I was malingering. I sat through the session, wracked with pain. At lunch I went to one of the organizers of the orientation program. Unfortunately, she was female, so I could not tell her the precise problem. I told her that I was having a male problem. She clearly observed that I was in pain. She got one of her male colleagues to take me to the hospital. When I told the doctor my complaint, he briefly examined my scrotum which was exquisitely tender to touch.

"How long have you had this pain?" he asked "It started yesterday," I replied.

He turned to the organizer who had accompanied me and asked, "Why was this man not brought to the hospital sooner?"

The organizer explained that he had brought me to see him immediately on learning that I was suffering from scrotal pain.

The doctor shook his head slowly, and said, "It is obvious that this man is in a lot of pain. I shall admit him to the hospital immediately."

I had never been admitted to a hospital so I had no idea what to expect. I was asked many questions by the doctor and he told me that I was scheduled for a test to check my kidneys because my blood pressure was high. Then he asked me the big question, "When last have you had sex?"

I told him I was engaged two weeks before coming to America, but I had never had sex. He nodded.

Then the parade began. Every morning a Doctor, in tow with 3 – 4 young doctors, would come by, ask questions, do a brief examination of my lungs, abdomen and look at my scrotum, then leave. Later individual ones of the young doctors would come by to do their own examination and before leaving would ask the big question, when last did you have sex?

After 2-3 days of this, I decided to tell a fantastic tale. When the big question was posed, I responded, "Don't tell the doctor. But I had three girlfriends in Guiana and since I was leaving they each gave me a lot of sex so I would not forget them. At home we call it, 'Giving Farewell'."

They must have believed it because the Big Question was never asked again. I was discharged after about a week. The diagnosis was Epididymitis.

The Fulbright Orientation had already concluded when I was discharged from the hospital, so I was taken directly to the New Haven Bus Station for my trip to Lehigh University to start my studies in Engineering. I was registered as a Freshman in the class of 1967 and then taken to Price Hall. Price Hall was a small residence hall next to Grace Hall where the wrestling and basketball games were played. I immediately liked Price

Hall because it was small and the first floor had two suites with four rooms in each. I was in one of the suites which I felt offered a certain privacy. I was also quite excited because for the first time in my 20 years I would be sleeping in my own bed and not on a bunch of old clothes (beddings) as protection from the hard floor.

The next two weeks at Lehigh were quite enjoyable. I slept late, then walked to the cafeteria and had breakfast. This was followed by lunch and I could not believe that one had another main meal for dinner. At home in Guyana, meals consisted of breakfast, namely a cup of tea and two slices of bread with butter. Lunch, the main meal of the day, was usually a plate of rice with various beef or fish stews and dinner was a cup of tea and bread. Sunday lunch was often soup with ground provisions, such as cassava, plantain and eddoes. This was usually very filling, hence a real treat.

Since there was no TV in Guiana and I had never seen a movie, I spent most of the day watching TV. I looked forward to the Soap Operas, such as, As the World Turns and General Hospital and the roller Derby at 4 pm, followed by the early movie. This was interrupted by dinner. After dinner I watched the news, the sitcoms, which I thought were short movies and thereafter went to bed about 9 pm. In the evening many of the students played cards while I watched TV. At the end of the first week one of the students told me that there was a student from one of the African countries who, like me, watched TV all day and he had flunked out of Lehigh. I had no idea what flunked out meant but gathered that it was not a good thing.

At the end of the second week Geoffrey Stiles, the Gryphon or Dorm Counselor for Price Hall came to see me. In addition to the bed, there was a desk and a chair in the room. Geoff sat on the chair as I sat on the bed.

"I hear that you have not been attending classes."

I said, "I will. I have not yet decided which will be my main courses."

"Do you mean that you really do not have your course schedule? Geoff asked, somewhat surprised.

I replied, "I will probably take Chemistry, Math and Physics in the first year. I shall go to the Bookstore and select some books. Then I will have to determine how to find a professor to guide me."

Geoff looked somewhat alarmed. "We do things differently in American Universities. I will take you to see the Dean tomorrow."

The next day Geoff took me to see Dean Buchanan, who on hearing the story smiled and told Geoff that he knew what was happening and that he would handle it. Dean Buchanan had studied in England and knew the British University system. Dean Buchanan then arranged for me to take a number of tests, at the end of which I received credit for first Semester Chemistry, first Semester Calculus, Freshman Physics and Freshman English. He then enrolled me as a Chemistry Major in the Engineering College.

Following the placement tests, I had to take a number of psychological tests. The following day I was called to discuss the results of my tests. The psychologist explained that he did not think I would be successful in the engineering department. He felt that I should probably do sociology or perhaps business. I asked why and he explained to me that I did not have the profile to be an engineer. I asked him to explain that further and to tell me how he was able to ascertain that from the tests that I had taken. He explained that my answers did not reveal a sense of urgency and showed more sympathy for animals than they normally see in engineers.

He also told me that my reading rate was 283 words a minute, whereas most Lehigh students read at a rate close to a thousand words a minute. I told him that since I was planning to do science and engineering I only needed to read for comprehension and not to see how many books I could devour in a night.

When I returned to Price Hall I found that one of my fellow classmates was quite upset. He was one of the very talented wrestlers, was quite young, and had received unfavorable news and advice from the psychologist. I told him that I too had received discouraging advice from the psychologist and my plan was to ignore it because that psychologist did not know me from 'a nail in the wall.'

I was enrolled in Advanced Freshman English, World history, Metallurgy, Second semester calculus, and economics. I found all of the classes stimulating particularly the enlightened lectures by professor Dowling on world history. He brought it all to life. I could not wait to attend his lectures. On the other hand, I quickly got into trouble with the English professor. On one occasion he was extoling the virtues of America in that it had become a Melting Pot and had embraced all cultures in the USA. While at the orientation program at Yale, I had received a book entitled, Beyond the Melting Pot by Moynihan and Glazer. I told the professor I disagreed and in fact the recently published book by Moynihan and Glazer challenges that view. He promptly told me that I was new to America and therefore had no basis for making such a comment. A second incident involved an ancient Chinese Poem. I think that the author was Lao Tse. It said,

> At 60 years of age
> He is a man of promise, still
> Me thinks he'll need eternity
> That promise to fulfill.

The professor insisted on one interpretation and I challenged him that there could be another interpretation. I do not remember which interpretation I supported, but it could mean that since at 60 years of age he had not accomplished anything he's unlikely to do so during his lifetime. Or, it could mean that his potential is without limit because at the advanced age of 60 years he still showed great promise. The professor expressed his displeasure in no uncertain terms and in fact demonstrated this displeasure by giving me a B in the course although I had obtained A's on the examinations. I was quite angry at the arbitrariness of this decision, but at the same time I felt powerless because I did not believe that there was anything that I could do to change this result.

Metallurgy was a particularly disappointing experience. On the first hour exam, which occurred about two weeks after I joined the course, I earned a C grade. Prof. Pense called me to his office because my answers were quite unusual. Many of the questions that I had answered incorrectly had to do with selection of the correct manufacturing process for various items, for example, a TV tower, or camshaft. I had no idea what a camshaft was, having never seen what was underneath the bonnet of a car. A tower to me meant a very large building like the Eiffel Tower. Prof. Pense took me around the lab showed me examples of several of the items that were being studied in the course. He also told me that if I got an A grade on the research topic and an A on the final, he would forgive the C grade and give me an A overall. I had missed a field trip to Bethlehem Steel but I was able to arrange a visit during the Christmas holidays. I received an A for my paper on the basic oxygen method for making steel and received an A on the final examination.

Nonetheless I received a B in the course. I asked Prof. Pense why he had not fulfilled his promise and he simply said that it was not fair to the other students. What I found very disturbing was that he had told me that he was a 'Born-again' Christian. In fact, he had invited a number of us, who were members of the Intervarsity Christian Fellowship, to his home that semester and I had enjoyed the fellowship and singing some of my favorite Christian songs. In Guiana, a 'Born-Again' Christian was expected to be fair and just. The contradiction between statement of Faith and action both puzzled as well as annoyed me. Needless to say, I avoided any contact with him thereafter.

Economics was another lesson in the difference between the British versus American system. The First exam was multiple choice. I had never had a multiple-choice type exam and I was the last to leave the classroom and still had not completed all questions. Later Jim Stamoolis, one of the students in the class asked me why it had taken me so long to complete the test. I told him that I had never done a test like that and I was confused by the many choices. He also asked what grade I had received and I proudly told him that I had received a 78. He then told me that his grade was in the 90s and that most students would have scored above 80. I was stunned because in the British system final grades were often curved and thus 78 on one of the preliminary examinations probably would have been one of the highest grades. Nonetheless I enjoyed economics, but fortunately, it was the last multiple-choice exam that I had to suffer through. I was entered into the honors program and all my examinations thereafter were problem oriented.

Jim Stamoolis and I became very close friends and in fact he helped me understand and deal with many of the cultural conundrums that I faced that first year. A somewhat comical situation occurred one morning when Jim came to my room and I was still lying in bed under the blanket.

"Why do you sleep on both sheets with the blanket over you?" he asked. I looked at him somewhat puzzled and said, "Actually, I have been wondering why there are two sheets."

Jim said," You use the top sheet to cover you, and you add the blanket if you want to get warmer."

I mused aloud, "So one sleeps between the two sheets." Jim said, "Yes."

I began to laugh and said, "Now I understand what they mean when they say, at home, that someone was not born between the sheets."

"Between the sheets?" Jim asked.

"Oh, it is probably a British expression to describe someone born out of wedlock." I said and decided that it was not worth trying to explain further.

Another of these conundrums was actually quite scary. One night I saw a very large burning cross at the back of one of the Dorms that was uphill from Price Hall. I think it was Drucker Dorm. I do not know why, but I had the same inner dread as I had had a few months earlier, when I had witnessed the murder of a man by a mob in Guiana. No one in Price Hall commented. The next day when I saw Jim, I asked, "Did you see the large cross that was ablaze in the woods above the dorms?"

Jim said, "Yes," and fell silent.

"I don't know why, but somehow it felt scary."

Jim looked a little bit uncomfortable. Then he said, "It was not directed at you, because you are a foreign Black. It was against Harold who lives in that dorm."

Then it became clear and I shuddered as I recalled reading about the Klu Klux Klan burning crosses as a threat against Black people in the South.

This was another one of those occasions when I could not believe the degree of hatred for Blacks in America. There was a total of four Black students among the 3000 male undergraduates at Lehigh in 1963. Three of us were foreign students, a senior from Cameroon, a junior from South Africa, and I, a Freshman from British Guiana. There was only one Black American student, Harold, who was the other Black Freshman in 1963. I did not see much of Harold after Freshman year as the following year most of my courses were junior level and not sophomore level. Both Harold and I had run Freshman track and when I discovered that he had not been invited to the end of the season banquet, I refused to attend.

Many of the students professed that their families were of Republican persuasion. It was therefore a breakthrough when a debate between the right wing conservative William F Buckley Jr. and the socialist, Norman Thomas was organized at Lehigh in 1965.

I attended the debate and felt that Norman Thomas had made many compelling arguments. The Lehigh students all felt that William Buckley had 'demolished' Thomas. I actually found Buckley's speaking style stilted and arguments somewhat artificial, whereas Thomas was rational and fact laden. It became quite clear to me that it was best not to discuss the debate with any of my colleagues. This puzzled me because I thought that the University was the place where opposing ideas could be aired and debated. In fact, when I shared this general surprise with Jim, he advised that I should try to transfer to Yale because the environment there would be more open to such discussions.

I continued to thrive academically. Chemistry was the right home for me. I did two courses of organic chemistry during the first Summer and on each test scored 10 -20 points ahead of the next student. I simply loved organic chemistry and Professor Young, who taught the course, was quite encouraging. On one lab I noted that everyone had crystals for their final reaction product but my final product was a clear, colorless liquid. Prof. Young returned the graded paper to each student and gave me mine last.

He said, "Your product was a clear liquid. Did you find that strange?"

I said, "I saw that everyone had white crystals and felt that something was wrong with my product."

He continued, "Specific Gravity of your product is 1.0, Ph. 7.2, freezing point, 0 degrees. What do you think you produced?"

I said, somewhat embarrassed, "Water?"

He said, "And to think that you could just have gotten it from the faucet." I could have died. Everyone was looking at me. I thought, I am glad that I am not white, because my face would have been red from embarrassment.

Then he said, "Do you know what happened here?"

I said, "Yes. At the final separation step, I discarded the wrong fraction." He said, "Right!" and gave me my graded report. It was a C; the only C that I had received in any test or lab exercise in his courses that Summer. I received 'A' as final grade.

I never made that mistake again! What struck me, however, was that Prof. Young had made his point in a kind tone and one that was not demeaning!

Among my courses in the First Semester of my second year were Physical Chemistry (Thermodynamics), Advanced Organic Chemistry, A creative Concepts Seminar and Physical Chemistry Laboratory. I found writing up the Lab reports quite challenging, so I tried to work carefully. This created a problem for track practice because I often missed the bus that took us to the track in Saucon valley. On one occasion when I did make it to practice, the coach was conducting the run offs to determine who would represent Lehigh at the Penn Relays. A decision needed to be made as to whether Charlie Parker or I would represent Lehigh in the 400 meters. I won the run off, but the coach said we should run it a second time. Charlie won the second trial, so we had to run it a third time, which I won.

The coach exploded; more out of frustration, than anger, was my impression. "I would rather have someone who had no talent but who worked hard than someone with talent who did not take track seriously." He said in exasperation.

"Coach," I said, "I have Physical Chemistry labs which often run late."

"You need to decide whether you are going to run track or be a physical chemist." Was his rejoinder.

I thought about it very briefly. I Removed my running shoes, gave them to the coach and said, "Coach, you are right. I have decided for Physical Chemistry."

The rest of the team looked on in disbelief. On the bus back to the campus several explained that the coach did not mean it. He was just a bit angry. I responded with, "The coach is right. The reality is that I did not come to America to be a track star. I came to get a Bachelor's degree."

That was the end of my track career.

I particularly enjoyed Thermodynamics. All the problems were practical, based on the fundamental equations and the solutions always seemed straight forward if one selected the relevant equation and worked through it logically. I did very well in the midterm and I also thought that I had done well on the final because I went over the posted answers and I felt I could not have been more accurate compared to these posted answers. I received a C. I went to professor Lovejoy and told him that I was really puzzled. I asked to see my exam paper and he refused and said there was nothing to be discussed. I was really upset because although I had done extremely well in the organic chemistry courses, applying mathematics to solve chemistry problems really delighted me.

I had one other similar unpleasant experience and that was in the advanced level Biochemistry course. I was doing very well in this course. During the final, professor Merkel said that there would be an extra 5 points for answering one of the problems correctly. I was sick on the day that students went to pick up their final exam books and get their grades on the test. My friend Butz, who was a senior brought my examination booklet to me. As he gave it to me he told me that I should never ask professor Merkel for a recommendation. I asked why. He told me that he had looked at my booklet and had noticed that I had answered the special question correctly but had not received the extra 5 points. He told me that he had brought it to the professor's attention and the professor said that he did not care what Douglas scored on any tests, because he will never become a scientist.

On the positive side, however, I had won both the Freshman and Upperclassman Williams Extempore Speech Contests. I had had a wonderful summer on an NSF Undergraduate Research Project in Prof. Sturm's lab. I was inducted into AED premedical society, and at the end of the first Semester in my third year, I received the notification that I was to be inducted in Phi Beta Kappa and Tau Beta Pi.

I declined both.

Almost immediately thereafter I received a call from Dean Ross Yates. He wanted to know why I had declined these honors.

"Each honor requires twenty-five dollars," I told him with a shrug and a show of empty hands.

"You've spent all your stipend?" I could hear in his voice that he was perplexed by this.

"No, sir," I said, a bit uncomfortably. "I send most of it to my mother and step father. They need it more than I do."

"Ah," Dean Ross said. He was quiet for a moment. "Phi Beta Kappa is important. I'll pay the fee for you. You should also consider applying for the Rhodes Scholarship."

Lehigh had just received its second Rhodes scholarship and his idea was that I would apply as a student from the Caribbean. In that case I would be competing against students at, for example, the University of the West Indies and I would have an advantage because I could be a strong candidate from a US University.

I declined.

I told the Dean that I thought that that would be unfair, but I promised to think it over. I could not convince myself that it was fair.

The most rewarding experience was an unusual call from the Psychologist who had told me that I should study sociology because I did not have what it takes to succeed in science or engineering at Lehigh.

He called me into his office and said directly, "I want to apologize to you." "Why?" I asked, being a little unsure about the purpose of this conversation.

He continued, "I discouraged you from entering the Engineering school and here you are a top student and Phi Beta Kappa in your third year." He paused, stroked his chin and said, "Now I understand what is meant by culturally biased assessments."

He stretched out his hand towards me. I shook it and said, "Thank you."

Reconciling Religiosity and Developing Personal Philosophy

In my first week in the Bethlehem area, my reputation having preceded me, a member of the National Youth for Christ movement visited me.

"We've heard of your leadership and speaking ability," he praised, then invited me to speak at a church that Sunday.

I was excited by the invitation and agreed. I never quite knew where the church was located but it was less than an hour by car from Lehigh. It was a large church and the first thing I noticed was there was not a single black person present. I delivered a sermonette at the end of which I received many compliments, making me feel warm with a sense of belonging. On the way back to the campus I asked the Youth for Christ official why there were no Black people in the church. He then explained to me that this was one of the churches where Blacks were not allowed to attend. I immediately decided not to accept any more invitations to speak in white churches.

My Freshman year was one of continued discovery of the American, or at least of the upper class American culture. I leaned on my friend Jim Stamoolis for explanations of simple things. One weekend a couple of the students were bragging that on the previous night they had picked up some Pigs in town. I asked Jim what did that mean. When he told me, I said, if they consider those girls Pigs, why don't they also see themselves as Pigs?

Another time I asked Jim what was a Hay Ride? He laughed and asked why I wanted to know. I told him that one of the

48

girls in the church that I had been attending, who was a math major at the Moravian College, had invited me to attend a Hay Ride with her. Jim advised me to decline. I asked why. He said that often on a Hay Ride, on a nice moonlit night, the boys and girls would use it to be close and kiss each other. That would probably be awkward for the others with you and your date along for the hay ride.

I agreed to decline.

I also told him that I had gotten the impression that some of the members of our Intervarsity Christian Fellowship Club were doing more than just kissing their girlfriends. I thought that Christians did not have such activity before marriage. He told me yes that is true, but when they are going 'steady' they are almost married.

I spent my first Christmas alone on the campus. It was cold so I did not venture outside the dorm. The empty, cleaning agent smelling rooms in Price Hall heightened my longing for the sweet smell of Pepper Pot meat sauce and the black colored fruit cake that were cooked primarily during the Christmas season. I also missed the joyous laughter and gaiety that filled the homes and streets of Guiana during the Christmas season. One day my loneliness and homesickness were interrupted by the ringing of the phone in the hallway outside the suite. I answered it. The person said that he was one of the Assistant Deans and a Lady in the town was interested in inviting any students who were on campus to dinner. He said he had told her that all the students had left but one of his colleagues thought there was someone staying in Price Hall. I was actually quite hungry, as I had been living off of peanuts from the vending machine, so I eagerly accepted.

Miss Hadie seemed like a lady around sixty and I liked her immediately. She served a sumptuous meal consisting of baked turkey, turkey stuffing, candied carrots, and potatoes. There was cake for desert. I think she observed that I was quite hungry and she offered to give me a 'care package' of food. I declined, a decision that two days later I began to regret. She also noted that my jacket was more like a summer jacket. She offered to buy me a warmer jacket. She took me to Hess Department store and bought me two jackets and two pairs of slacks and a pair of gloves. Although somewhat embarrassed, I was very thankful. She took a happy and no longer hungry student, back †o Price Hall and said if I would like she would take me to church with her that Sunday. I accepted.

Two days later, as the vending machine yielded its last bag of salted peanuts, Geoff Stiles arrived. He said he knew that I was alone on campus and wanted to see how I was doing. He immediately surmised my predicament. It was quite a walk from the campus to the restaurants in the town and it was cold so I did not leave the warmth of Price Hall. He took me downtown in his car to buy some fruit, bread and peanut butter. I thanked him for his thoughtfulness and he drove back to his home in New Jersey. That Sunday Miss Hadie took me to her Church. It had a welcoming feeling. People seemed genuine and when they said hello, they actually looked at me directly and waited for a reply, before either continuing to speak or moving away. I decided to make that my place of worship, although no other members were Black. One of the members, Don Matz, introduced himself and said that he and his wife would invite me to dinner soon. Don and his wife had one daughter about 10 years of age and they began to invite me regularly to have lunch at their home after church. I liked the Matz.

Another family that I liked was a family (the H's) that sat in the front row every Sunday, Father, Mother and four daughters. I noticed, however, that although church members greeted Ms. H., the greeting seemed quite guarded and no one spoke to Mr. H., who always had a very large bible in tow.

Finally, one day Ms. H brought me a Cherry pie and invited me to have dinner with them. I asked Don Matz whether I should go because I had noted some awkwardness in the interactions of other church members with the family. He encouraged me to do so. I accepted the invitation and later discovered that the problem was that Mr. H was physically abusive to his wife and the girls. The girls looked forward to my occasional Saturday afternoon visits as they were not allowed to have friends. Two of the girls were already in High school and seemed quite able students. They had two older brothers who had both left home because of the behavior of their father. And although I had ceased to worship at this church, I continued to enjoy visits with them throughout my remaining time at Lehigh.

Two events occurred close to each other that led me to leave this church and stop communicating with both Ms. Hadie and The Matz. At the end of one church service a female member approached me, and said: "That must be the outfit Hadie bought for you. It looks so nice," she continued, smiling at me as she shook my hand.

I was embarrassed and inwardly furious. We left and went over to Don's home. He had invited several other people to lunch. It was a celebratory meal. I do not remember the reason for the celebration but I was happy to be a part of it. Conversation turned to me and one of the diners asked, "How large is your father's Kingdom?"

I replied, "My father does not have a Kingdom."

Another asked, "Then are you an African Prince, or something like that?" "No," I said, getting a little uncomfortable. "I am from British Guiana and that is in South America."

The first diner then offered, "Lehigh is a very expensive University and we figured that your father must be very wealthy."

I am not sure why, but I decided that the way to stop this was to shock them.

I said, "I come from a poor family and I am a bastard child."

Silence descended on the room. Desert was served and Don offered to take me back to the campus. We rode in silence and that was the last time that I saw either Ms. Hadie or Don Matz.

I was saddened by the loss of my relationship with both Miss Hadie and Don because I felt that they were kind to me and they themselves meant no harm. I had hoped that Don would have changed the conversation. I also recognized that Miss Hadie probably had no idea of how demeaning it is for a poor person when he feels that his poverty is the subject of discussion and pity. The two episodes occurring within about an hour of each other were more than I could bear.

Meanwhile back on campus I was having outwardly 'the best of times.' Inwardly I was experiencing fierce battles as my evangelical religiosity was clashing with a personal philosophy that was evolving in response to my experiences.

In my second year I became a member of one of the most prestigious organizations on campus. I had been appointed a Gryphon and assigned as Dorm Counselor to Taylor Hall. Gryphons were often among the best students and leaders in other areas. In Taylor Hall I became close friends with Harold (Hal) Ward, another Gryphon, and like Jim Stamoolis, Harold did quite a lot to help me understand conundrums in America. For example, Hal, who was a gifted French Horn player and artist, but struggled with the premed courses, received acceptance to Cornell Medical School. At the same time Sam S., who graduated Number 1 in our class was very disappointed. He was not accepted by Cornell Medical School which was his first choice. He was accepted by Harvard Medical School. When I asked Hal how was that possible, namely that he was accepted by Cornell but Sam was not, Hal explained, that although no one admits to it, many of the medical schools limit the number of Jewish students they accept. I found that inexplicable.

The Gryphons had a table in the student union where we ate together and had many enlightening discussions. We also sponsored several extracurricular events. Gryphons differentiated ourselves from the Fraternities some of which were infamous for their lechery and debauchery. So, when I was asked to find a chaperone for the Gryphon homecoming party I gladly did it. I asked one of the administrators in the Chemistry Department to chaperone the party. He was probably in his thirties. The party started quite well with lots of dancing. I spent most of the time outside the party area talking with the chaperone. After a while the music had changed more to slow mood songs. We stepped in and found that some couples were slow dancing, but there were a few that were in corners writhing on top of each other. I stopped the music and said that unfortunately our chaperone had to leave. This brought the party to an end.

Added to this confusion with respect to moral practices, hypocrisy by Mr. H., insensitivity to the feelings of others, rank racism and prejudicial behavior at Lehigh, I found the general culture and mores confusing and somewhat frightening for a foreign black man. Within 1-2 weeks of arriving in America there was the Dr. King's march on Washington in August, 1963. This had been preceded by those horrible scenes of cops attacking black men, women and children with dogs in Birmingham, Alabama. There was the murder of Medgar Evers in his driveway in June, 1963. There was the killing of four young black girls in the bombing of a church in Birmingham, Alabama, in September, 1963. In November, 1963, there was the assassination of President John F. Kennedy. Further, in 1965 there was 'Bloody Sunday' connected with the Selma March. This was the country whose missionaries went to Guyana and preached that we were equal before God and that confessing Christ as Savior guaranteed one a place in heaven. And here in America, some of the churches they attended denied Blacks the opportunity to worship with them.

Churches were fighting to uphold and reinforce segregation.

I found the deep seated systemic hatred for the Black race by presumed 'Born-Again' Christians unfathomable and incredible. How could Evangelical Christians say they love God whom they cannot see but do not love their brothers whom they can see. (1 John 4:20 King James Version).

In 1965, I began to have severe stomach pains and often felt hungry. On occasion, I noticed that my stools were darker than usual. I visited the student health center with these complaints but they felt that I was probably just tired from studying. They also suggested that I drink more milk. I explained that I could not drink a lot of milk because it gave me diarrhea. Finally, The Health Services referred me to a local Gastroenterologist. I underwent an upper GI series and I was diagnosed as having an ulcer.

The Gastroenterologist asked, "Do you have major problems?" I responded, "None that I am aware of."

"This is unusual. You are an excellent student; a campus leader and you do not smoke or drink. It is not often we see an ulcer in someone with your profile."

I returned to the campus with my instructions to eat a bland diet and to try to avoid stress. As I lay on my bed shortly after receiving the ulcer diagnosis, my classmate Butz had brought my Biochemistry examination results and had told me of the negative comment from the professor. When he left, it hit me like a bolt of lightning.

Of course I was experiencing significant stress.

Butz' report of what for me was another instance of discrimination against me had not evoked much anger in me. My stress had less to do with these outward issues and more to do with an internal struggle.

I was struggling to reconcile my religiosity with the hatred and other behaviors by professed Christians in America. I decided that there was only one thing to be done and that was to give up my religiosity.

I used to pray for guidance before making any decision and always accepted the outcome as 'God's Will' and Plan for my life.

I decided to stop going to church, to stop praying for Divine guidance.

I would accept the consequences of my decisions. If the results were negative I would accept them as learning experiences and if they were positive I would thank the universe for its kindness.

I decided that I would pattern my life after Uncle Willie, who never professed any faith, but was the kindest and most considerate human being I had ever known.

I repeated the decision to myself and as I lay on my bed I felt both as though a weight had been removed and that it had been replaced by a mild anxiety over the uncertainty of my future. Being a 'Born-Again' Christian gave one a feeling that one's life was preordained and under God's control. Now I would be traveling along a different spiritual path.

Hard Work and Perseverance
– Cornell University

It was Second Semester of my third year at Lehigh and I was struggling to determine my course of action for my final year of my Fulbright scholarship, when I was summoned to Prof. Daen's office. Prof. Daen was a Physical Chemist and I was taking one of his courses that Semester. He invited me to sit as I entered his office and said, "Tell me about yourself."

"I come from a poor family in British Guiana and was admitted to Lehigh University on a Fulbright scholarship." I said.

"And what was life outside of the classroom like for you in Guiana?" Prof. Daen probed further.

"I grew up in the Evangelical Church and was an ardent believer?" "Why do you say 'was'?"

"I have found it difficult to maintain my religiosity while adjusting and trying to understand the differences in America." I said.

Then Prof. Daen said, "I have been observing you. Do you know that you have enough credits to graduate?"

"No. I am not aware of this."

"My observation is that you are not feeling challenged and you are undergoing a personal struggle. We are considering placing you into an experimental six-year Ph.D. program. That means that you would get a Ph.D. in three years. However, I think that you would benefit all around by going to graduate school at another institution. It is now March, and a bit late, but if you would like, I can call around and see if I can get you interviews at some graduate schools. Are you interested in this?"

I said, "You are correct. I am a little unsure of my future life steps. I would really appreciate it, if you were to call the graduate schools."

Two days later, Prof. Daen gave me a list of interviews that he had arranged, complete with place, time and contact professor. The Universities included Columbia, Cornell, MIT, Harvard, Brandeis and Washington University. My interviews went well. When I returned from my road trip Prof. Lovejoy, who had obtained his Ph.D. from Washington University called me in to understand why I had gone to all of the interviews except the one at his University. I told him I did not have money for a plane trip to Seattle, Washington. I could get to all of the others by bus and they were all on the East coast. He became angry and told me that I was a typical Lehigh student. Lehigh University was their second choice and so they work hard at Lehigh with hope to get into an Ivy League graduate program. I thought that was rather strange. He had given me a 'C' in Thermodynamics and had refused to even discuss and justify it when I knew that my answers were almost identical to the posted answers. I chose to give no further explanation but knew that he would not be one of the professors that I would ask for a reference, if needed.

I returned to Prof. Daen to discuss each interview. "How were your visits? He asked.

"I felt that they went well. I felt most comfortable at Brandeis, MIT and Cornell."

"What did you like about them?" he asked.

"I felt that each of these three were not only interested in how I was doing academically at Lehigh, but they told me about the academic environment and how they support graduate students to achieve their goals."

"I have already heard from each of the departments and each is interested in your joining them. I would recommend that you focus on Cornell. I tell you this, not because I received my Ph.D. from Cornell, but because it would be the right environment for you. You will be challenged academically, while at the same time benefiting from the intellectual environment. This will help you in your personal journey."

"That sounds good to me", I said.

"I would like you to read the research areas in the department of Chemistry at Cornell and see which area interests you. This is one way to find a Ph.D. thesis Professor."

I decided for Cornell for two reasons. Prof. Daen had had me look at the type of research being done in the Chemistry department in each of the schools and the application of Physical Chemical methods to the study of RNA by Dr. Gordon Hammes at Cornell had attracted my attention. The second and more important reason was that Prof. Daen had observed me, had sought to understand who I was, and had gone the extra mile to help me navigate what was a critical point in my life.

I was convinced that he had chosen an environment that he thought would be best for my maturation. In a subsequent meeting he had told me that he was Jewish and was aware of the struggles that a person with a religious background could have as he developed intellectually. I felt his empathy and that he wanted to provide the best environment where I could develop fully.

Apart from Mr. Pinkerton, who had advised me on the best way to optimize my academic success at Queens College, no one had ever taken the time to discover my formative years, my present aspirations, and give me advice based on that knowledge.

On arriving at Cornell, I was immediately thrown into the life of a graduate student in the Chemistry department. I went to see Prof. Harold Scheraga, who was the Chairman of the department at that time. He pointed out that I needed to immediately take a series of tests that every incoming student had to take. These tests were important so the department could determine whether there were any weaknesses that would be improved by taking one of the undergraduate courses before taking the required graduate level course. I passed all four tests – organic chemistry, inorganic chemistry, physical chemistry and analytical chemistry. Prof. Roald Hoffmann reviewed my results with me and asked why I had decided to study physical chemistry since my performance in organic chemistry was extremely strong. I told him that I had read of the work of Prof. Hammes and was interested in that area. Thus, began this phase of my life at Cornell University.

I immediately liked Cornell. I could feel the energy and excitement in the atmosphere everywhere I went. Each day on my walk from Cascadilla Hall, where I lived, to Baker Lab I would take a left on College Avenue and cross Cascadilla Creek onto the campus. Leaving the earthy smell of the flora on the banks of this small creek, I would continue on College Avenue towards the arts quad where Sage Chapel stood like the Guardian of the quad supported by Uris and Olin libraries behind it. Before reaching Sage Chapel, I would stop in front of Willard Straight Hall, which is the student union, and watch as male and female students entered and emerged from Willard Straight. Lehigh's undergraduate college was all male so the presence of female students was one noticeable difference. Past the libraries I would take a diagonal direction towards and beyond Golden Smith Hall and finally cross East Avenue to Baker Lab, which would be my home away from home for the next five and one half years. When one entered Baker Hall one could smell the history. The walls had that scent that comes from the admixture of the multitude of chemicals, infinitesimal quantities of which were released over many years. It is the scent that tells every chemist that s/he is in a Chemistry building. Peter Debye, the Nobel Laureate was still active and one could feel that important science was being pursued in the labs and small discussion rooms.

At the end of the Day I would retrace my steps occasionally stopping in Sage chapel or Willard Straight Hall to see if there were any interesting activities or lectures. Other times I would return to Cascadilla by walking South on East Avenue past Rockefeller Hall, and Statler hotel on the left, Day Hall and Sage Hall, that house the administration and Business School, respectively on the right, then right past the north end of the Engineering Quad, and back on College Avenue to Cascadilla Hall. Later, in the early evening, I would visit one of the restaurants on College Avenue, outside of the campus, where the scents of food, car emissions and dwellings were a stark contrast from the quiet odors of the campus and its buildings.

Several events coincided with my starting graduate school at Cornell and served to add to that atmosphere that Prof. Daen predicted would contribute to my personal development. In June of 1966 Betty Friedan, Shirley Chisolm and several other women founded the National Organization of Women, whose purpose was to "take action to bring women into full participation in the mainstream of American Society now, exercising all the privileges and responsibilities thereof in truly equal partnership with men." This was a slightly foreign concept to me because women were not denied leadership positions in Guyana. I grew up with the knowledge of strong women leaders like Dr. Janet Jagan and Ms. Jesse Burnham, the sister to Mr. Forbes Burnham, Prime Minister of Guyana.

In October, this same year, Huey Newton and Bobby Seale founded the Black Panther Party for Self Defense. Their original purpose was "to patrol African American neighborhoods to protect residents from acts of police brutality and racism." The Nation of Islam (The Black Muslim) movement was at the height of its appeal to Blacks, particularly since the Heavyweight champion of the world had given up his slave name 'Cassius Clay' for a Muslim name, Muhammad Ali. In 1966, Muhammad Ali was stripped of his boxing titles and imprisoned for refusing to be drafted into the military and be sent to Vietnam. I had always admired Muhammad Ali for his artistry in the ring and for always achieving his promise to knock out his opponent in the predicted round. Now, I held him in greater esteem, because he had the courage of his convictions and did not let penalties deter him from his moral decisions.

In 1966, opposition to the Vietnam war was gaining significant traction on campuses such as at Columbia, Berkley and Cornell Universities. The leftwing Student for a Democratic Society (SDS) was very active on Cornell's campus and I still recall meetings when the leader would be brought in secretly to speak and would leave surrounded by a crowd of students to protect him from being apprehended by the police. These rallies, demonstrations and teach-ins reminded me of the politically charged and sometimes dangerous periods during my teen age years in British Guiana.

In fact, after one of these rallies I was visited by two men in suits. They immediately reminded me of the men who periodically visited Liu, a student from Mainland China, who lived in Price Hall, at Lehigh University, and with whom I had frequently played ping pong. They must have followed me after one of these SDS meetings. They stopped me as I was about to enter Baker Hall. One of them said, "We would like to talk to you."

I said, "OK."

"Are you a member of SDS?" "No. Why?" I asked.

"Do you agree with the war?" "I am not sure."

"You either do or you do not."

I remained silent, becoming quite uneasy.

"When last have you talked with the people at the Institute of International Education?"

"I don't know." I answered.

"As you know, you are a guest of this country and as a guest you are not permitted to demonstrate against our government."

I remained silent.

"You have a choice. You can join the army and go to Vietnam, after which you will become a citizen. Or you can stop all of your activities against the government."

I remained silent, now experiencing real fear. "We will check back in a couple of months."

They walked away and I went into the nearest lecture room in Baker Hall and replayed the conversation several times. I chose the latter option. I decided to cease my political activities.

I ceased attending SDS rallies and other events that expressed opposition to the Vietnam war.

In addition to anti-Vietnam war activities, civil rights activities, Black Power movement, women's rights, and activities against apartheid, the sexual revolution was alive and well at Cornell. The 'Pill' had been approved for prevention of Pregnancy in 1960 and now could be added to IUDs, diaphragms and other barrier methods such as condoms to the armamentarium of methods of contraception. I was amazed that students were able to pursue intellectual, academic, political and social advancement while dealing with nature's call to reproduction-free sexual experimentation.

In 1963, President James Perkins had created the Committee of Special Education Projects (COSEP) to increase the enrollment of African-American students at Cornell. Under COSEP Cornell began to enroll several African American students, many of whom came from the inner cities.

In 1968, I began to offer tutoring in Freshman Chemistry to Black students who were interested. These sessions were held in Wari House. I had been encouraged to do this by John Bloor, who was a very good friend of mine and also, like myself, a second-year graduate student in Chemistry. We were both teaching assistants in Freshman Chemistry and he was concerned because a couple of the Black students in his section were rarely in class and had performed poorly in the first examination. Few students, except on the night before a major examination, attended my sessions. I was unsuccessful in convincing them that one learned and retained more if one studied the material regularly and several times in a week. I was frustrated by this lack of appreciation of my attempt to help them do well in chemistry.

One night, before a major test, one student, Amos C., came to my lab to ask for help. He had not attended my review session earlier that evening.

I asked, "What happened? You did not attend the review."

He looked down at the floor and did not respond. I continued, "Mr. Bloor told me that you are frequently absent from his class."

Amos responded, "Mr. Bloor is a racist. He does not teach me anything. He only teaches the white students."

I asked, "Amos, how can he teach only the white students if you are also present in class?" There was no response from Amos.

"Amos, that is really weird. Let's go for a walk."

We walked in silence over to Uris Library. We walked around the stacks of one floor then I motioned for us to leave. We did the same in Olin Library and finally walked back to my lab in Baker Hall. However, before entering Baker, I suggested we walk around in Clark Library which lay between Baker Hall and Rockefeller Hall.

When we returned to my lab, I said: "OK, Amos, tell me what you saw?" Amos said, "Oh lots of books."

"And what else?"

"Oh, lots of white boys studying."

I said, "Bingo! Amos, that is the point. It is Sunday night. These white students probably partied Friday or Saturday night and on Sunday they are hitting the books again. What did you do this weekend? Probably you listened to your boom box all weekend."

Then to my surprise Amos responded. "I don't need to study. They owe us for making us slaves for years. They owe us!"

I responded angrily, "Amos, my fore parents were slaves but I am no damn slave. Never, ever, say that to me or anyone again!"

He grew pensive, then said, "let's do the chemistry."

I had my own 'Come to Jesus' moment a few months earlier and this made the conversation with Amos quite poignant.

I was very excited and enjoyed my first semester courses. I had done relatively well and was comfortable with the pace and level of the courses. One disappointment was Dr. Hammes' course on Physical Chemistry of RNA. I could not get excited about it and could not wait for it to be over. Potential of working for Dr. Hammes was one of the reasons that I had selected Cornell for graduate school, and unfortunately, I did not feel that I could discuss this with him. That probably had more to do with my usual reluctance to approach Professors than it had anything to do with Dr. Hammes.

The second semester, however, was a different matter. My own experiences with discrimination and the reports of acts of racism in the American society were impelling me to become involved. I was beginning to feel the weight of Elridge Cleaver's statement, 'You either have to be part of the solution, or you're going to be part of the problem.' I began teaching people in Ithaca how to apply for food stamps and going to anti-war rallies and lectures on philosophy and poetry. These activities began to take on a greater priority than studying.

Then came the finals for second semester Advanced Math. Although I had turned in all of the homework sets, I was rarely in class. I showed up for the final examination and found myself struggling to solve some of the problems.

Panic engulfed me and I began praying to God for help. Suddenly, I stopped and said, 'God, forgive me. I have decided to give up religion and be responsible for all my actions.' I calmed myself and refocused on answering the questions.

A few days later John Bloor and I went over to Professor Widom's office to get our final grade. I was inwardly in a panic and fearing the worse. Prof. Widom reached for his little notebook. He said Bloor, 'B'. Douglas, he paused, looked at me and said, 'C'. My trepidation and anxiety disappeared immediately. I had dodged the bullet and immediately thought that having appeared with John Bloor might have helped. Perhaps I was on the cusp and being in the company of a serious graduate student might have influenced Prof. Widom to give me the benefit of the doubt.

My attendance at Quantum Mechanics course that was taught by Professor Roald Hoffmann was similarly inconsistent. However, I turned in every homework set. I had noted that the Graduate Assistant often had added an 'S' to Douglas on my submitted homework. At the end of Semester, I explained to the Graduate Assistant that my name Douglas is spelled with one 'S'. He said he knew that and that the extra 'S' was to let Professor Hoffmann know that I had had access to the solutions because many of the homework problems were repeated from the previous year. He had basically accused me of cheating.

I was furious because I had done the homework on my own, with occasional help from one of my classmates. We had one week to complete the final at home. After 5-6 days of work, there was still one problem for which I felt that my solution was probably incorrect. However, I decided that I would find no solution better than the one that I had and so I turned in my examination effort. As I was entering Baker Lab, one of my classmates hailed me and came over and said,

"You did Number 4 wrong."

I said, "how do you know how I solved number 4?"

Then he looked at me and said, "Oh you have not been working in a team. We have been working in teams and we had split up the problems. I just found a book in the library in which Problem 4 has been solved."

Feeling righteously indignant, I took my examination papers, nonetheless, to Prof. Hoffmann's office. I gave it to him and said, I would like to say two things. This is my work and mine alone. Buchwald, the Graduate Assistant claims that I had access to the previous year's solutions of the homework problems. This is not so. I was unaware that they existed. Then I told him of my encounter with a classmate a few minutes ago, and I wanted him to know that I have not changed how I solved number 4. To my surprise Professor Hoffmann replied, "If your classmates were smart enough to work together, you should not blame them for that."

Confused, disappointed and angry, I marched off campus, oblivious to the grand old buildings, and sought refuge in my apartment.

At the end of the first year, I had passed all of my courses but did not have a Thesis adviser. I was feeling like a man without a place, or was it a man out of place?

Maybe the best solution was to return to Guyana, which had won its independence from Britain on May 26, 1966 and the University of Guyana was now 3 years old. Certainly, the Guyana University would need help in Chemistry. So, I went over to the registrar's office and applied for a leave of absence, filling out the paperwork with relief. I was going home. That done, I headed back to Baker Lab to inform Prof. Scheraga, the Chairman of the Chemistry Department, that I was taking a leave of absence. Doing this 'ass backwards' was intentional on my part. I feared that the Chemistry department might argue that I should stay at least one more year and complete a Master of Science before taking a leave of absence.

I entered Baker Lab and went to the restroom before going to see Prof. Scheraga. Prof. Albrecht came in after me and used the urinal beside me.

He said, "Frank, that was a good seminar you gave a couple of weeks ago." (Each graduate student was requested to give a seminar on her/his undergraduate research project.

Fortunately, I had done an NSF summer research project with Prof. Sturm during my second summer at Lehigh).

"Thank you", I responded, making sure that I kept my head down and focused on my urinal as I spoke. I was a little embarrassed to be having a conversation with a famous Professor while taking a 'whiz'.

"What are your plans?" He continued.

"I have just discussed taking a leave of absence with the registrar's office and I am on my way to get Prof. Scheraga's sign off on my request."

"Why do you want to do that?" he asked.

I tried to end the conversation by saying: "It is a bit complicated." I made an extra effort to empty my bladder quickly so that I could get to the sink to wash my hands and leave the restroom before him. As I was about to discard the paper towel, he came to the sink beside the one I had used and continued: "I would like to discuss this with you before you go to Harold (Scheraga).

Let us go to my office."

After we were seated in his office, somewhat uncomfortably, I said, "I am at the end of my fourth year on the Fulbright and I need to return home and give back to Guyana. After two years at home, I hope to return to continue my Ph.D. program."

He said directly, "I would like you to join my group. I will talk with Harold to look into Cornell taking over the sponsorship on the Fulbright Program."

"Would you be interested in doing this?" He asked.

I responded, "I would prefer to return to Guyana after I completed my Ph.D. Thank you, indeed."

I left his office feeling much more positive with the knowledge that as was the case with Professor Daen and Dean Ross Yates at Lehigh University, there were also people at Cornell University, who would take interest in the career and success of a Black student.

Professor Albrecht was a Physical Chemist, who combined theoretical analysis with laboratory experiments, and used low temperature organic solids to elucidate phenomena in Raman Spectroscopy and Photoconductivity. I told him that I was interested in using Physical Chemistry to study Biological molecules such as DNA, RNA, Chlorophyll. He told me that he studies simple molecules because it is a real challenge to make calculations on complex molecules. However, he said, that Herschel Pilof, who had received his Ph.D. a year earlier, was interested in applying his system to chlorophyll. He gave me Herschel's thesis and told me that I might be able to rebuild the equipment that he had used for his thesis. I was excited and immediately started delving into this. By the end of the summer, I had located the condenser, a major piece of equipment, and had engaged the machine shop to make the metal thermos to house the Photoconductivity cell from Herschel's excellent drawings.

I discussed my progress with Prof. Albrecht, who was very encouraging and then surprised me by suggesting that I schedule my Ph.D. candidacy examination. Normally, this examination is taken between the end of the second and third years. I was in a panic because I doubted that I was ready to take this examination.

I decided to consult some of the more advanced students. They had two comments: 1) I needed to change a couple of the members of my committee because they disliked each other and their students always suffered as a result; and, 2) I needed to go to each of them and ask if they thought that I was ready to take the candidacy examination. I did as they recommended and encountered no problems until I ran into a potential catastrophe, Prof. Roald Hoffmann.

Prof. Roald Hoffmann, was the Theoretical Chemist on my committee. I told him that Prof. Albrecht had recommended my scheduling my candidacy exam and I wanted to know his opinion.

Without a pause, a clearing of the throat, or any sign of what was to come, in a measured tone, Prof. Hoffmann said, "Mr. Douglas, you are not my impression of a graduate student. In my view a graduate student spends 9-12 hours studying every day and I think that you do not even spend four."

My head was spinning, but I realized that given his criteria, he was correct. I asked, somewhat pleadingly, "What do you suggest I do?"

He replied, "I don't know."

I thanked him and as I turned to leave he said, "I have a question for you." "Yes?" I said hesitantly, more as a question, afraid of what was to follow. "Three of your friends work for me. I know you live in the same house.

How would you rank them?"

I answered immediately, "That is easy. J. is the brightest student in our class. When it takes the rest of us 6-8 hours to complete a homework set, he completes it in 4 hours and we often go to him for help. "D. is the weakest student in the class. He has struggled with one or more of the courses. And R. is somewhere between the two."

Prof. Hoffmann said, "Here is how I rank them. D. is the best student in my group. He works very hard. Is here early in the morning and works till late at night. He is the best student of these three. R. is the worst student of the three. Like you he can't decide whether he wants to be a chemist or a revolutionary. I hear that you two guys spend your time teaching people in the town how to apply for food stamps. And J. is somewhere between the two."

I was stunned by his answer to the question, I was transfixed and did not know how to take my leave from this encounter.

Fortunately, he continued, "Of the 33 students in your class, one third will never get their Ph.D. at Cornell, not because they are not bright, but because they are not committed to work hard and persevere when things do not go well in their research." He waved his hand to signal that the meeting was over.

I went directly to Prof. Albrecht and reported what had happened. I asked his permission to postpone the exam until I felt more confident. He acquiesced.

The last two comments from Prof. Hoffmann reverberated in every part of my being: It *is* about hard work and perseverance.

About the same time of my encounter with Prof. Hoffmann, Black undergraduate students at Cornell were complaining loudly of perceived institutional and actual episodes of racism at Cornell. However, when Prof. Hoffmann indicated that 10-11 of my classmates would not get their Ph. D., this had NOTHING to do with racism because there was only ONE Black student in my class – I. He saw my lack of resolve **not** as a matter of the color of my skin, but as a matter of the limited extent and quality of my commitment.

Resolve steadied me. I knew that since I was the only Black student, they would see me as I sat in the front row of every class and attended Friday Journal Club. I also would periodically walk by Prof. Hoffmann's office with the hope that by accident he would see me. At the beginning of the following Semester, during one of those 'accidental' meetings in the hallway, Prof. Hoffmann stopped me and asked, "Have you scheduled your exam?"

I responded, "Do you think that I am ready?"

He said, "Well in a couple of months I will be leaving for a year's sabbatical, so you might want to schedule it."

I scheduled the examination for about six weeks later and started my preparation. A couple of weeks before the examination I gained experience with a different Institution of Learning in America. I was on the Pennsylvania Turnpike, close to Scranton, PA, driving back from Philadelphia to Cornell University, when I was pulled over by the sheriff. He claimed that I was going over the speed limit and I could either pay the fine or go with him to the Justice of the Peace. I told him I could not have been speeding because I was just overtaken by a large trailer truck, whose legal speed limit was 10 mph lower than that for a car. I elected to go with him to the Justice of the Peace. The office of the Justice of the peace was in a small building that seemed to also be his home. He sat on an elevated platform and had a friendly demeanor.

"Why did you not pay the fine?" He asked, "I only have about $5.00." I explained.

"Here is what I recommend. Leave your spare tire and you can redeem it when you return to pay the fine."

"Your honor," I said, "That is very considerate. However, if I were to get a flat, I would have a double problem. No money. No spare tire."

"Well, you will have to spend one week in the Lackawanna County Jail." "Your honor, then I guess I have no choice but to spend the week in jail," I said.

Then he detected an accent and asked, "Where are you from? Where do you go to college?"

I responded: "I am from Guyana and I am a graduate student in Chemistry at Cornell University in Ithaca."

On hearing my answer, he said, "Here is what I am going to do. I don't want you ever to say that you never met a nice American. So, you will sign this paper, continue on your way back to Cornell and return with the money within a week."

I thanked him and headed to Cornell.

I told a couple of my friends what had happened and told them that since my Ph.D. candidacy exam was still a couple of weeks away, this would be a great opportunity to study for a week without disturbance. About five days later, I asked a fellow graduate student, Marty Gazourian, to take me to the office of the Justice of the Peace. The Justice seemed pleased to see me, but then expressed confusion as to why I would choose to spend a week in prison, instead of paying the fine. What I did not tell him is that I was simply curious to see the inside of an American prison. He told the sheriff to take me to the county jail. Marty looked at me a little uncertain about all of this, having not succeeded in persuading me to simply pay the fine, he waved a weak goodbye.

On the intake at the prison, the sheriff told the officer that I was one of those radicals that had been causing trouble. They took all of my books and the small chess set that I had brought with me. My lab mate, Bob Ott, was teaching me to play chess. They also confiscated my pen and pencils. Then they placed a large book in front of me and told me to sign for my confiscated property. It was then I noticed, written in large letters, 'A.T.' I asked what did A.T. mean and I was told it meant Awaiting Trial. In short, I could be there a very short time or a very long time, depending on when my case was called. I protested that I was sentenced to one week in lieu of paying a fine, but to no avail. I was whisked away. I heard three sets of iron gates sequentially slammed and locked behind me, before I was taken to an area that had cells around the periphery of a rectangular area with a stairwell to a floor below. My cell was in the middle of the long side of the rectangle, and on one of the short sides were the gates giving access and egress to the block of cells. The door to my cell gave only a very limited view but, each morning, I could see the other prisoners, who, at a specified time got their daily exercise by walking around the perimeter of the cell block. My door had one opening through which my meals were delivered. I did not eat much as everything seemed to be swimming in some kind of white sauce. I spent my days playing a game of guessing the source and place of every sound that I heard. Then on the third day one of the other prisoners stopped by my meal 'slot' and asked, in barely audible tones, "Wha you in hey fa, bro?"

I told him, "for speeding on the Turnpike."

He broke into peals of laughter and then asked again, "Wha you in hey fa?" I repeated, "for a speeding ticket."

He said, "Look hey. This is where dey keep de bad cats. We ga people hey who waitin trial fa murder."

I said, "I need to speak to the warden immediately."

He laughed.

"This is serious. Somebody might get executed from an instrument in my Lab at Cornell."

That seemed to have impressed him.

A few hours later someone opened my cell and said that the warden wanted to talk to me. He took me to the gates of the cell block entrance and there two closed gates away stood the warden. "What do you want?" he asked. I told him, "I am a chemist at Cornell and I forgot to turn off my high voltage capacitor and if anyone accidentally touches it they could be executed."

He then said, "What do you want me to do?"

I said, "first you need to call Cornell University, then ask for the Chemistry Department. When you get the Chemistry Department, ask them to transfer you to Prof. Albrecht. When you get him, please tell him the following because he won't know how to turn off the capacitor."

At this point he said, "Ok, you do it yourself". He called for one of the guards to escort me out of the block and to a desk with a phone. I went through the procedure that I had given him. Even though I knew Professor Albrecht's office number, I called Cornell, asked to be transferred to the chemistry department, and to Prof. Albrecht's lab. I identified myself to be sure that they would put me through to him. I had good fortune. He was in his office.

I told him, "Please ask Bob Ott to check the 1500 Volt capacitor and disconnect it so no one could be accidentally hurt." Then I said very hurriedly, "Incidentally, if you don't see me on Friday, I am in the Lackawanna County Jail. Please come and get me!"

With that I was returned to my cell. The warden must have been impressed because the next morning I was allowed to go down stairs, take a shower and have breakfast with other prisoners. Shortly after returning to my cell, a guard came and took me through the iron gates, back to the intake area, where I signed that everything that was confiscated was returned to me and I was let out into the street without further explanation. I walked a few blocks away from the prison before I started trying to hitch a ride, first to the Turnpike and then to Ithaca.

In the remaining week I studied assiduously. The day before this 3-hour oral exam I kept thinking about the types of questions Prof. Hoffmann would ask me and how I would handle myself if I were to have difficulty answering one of his questions. I confided to one of the advanced students that I had prepared as well as I could but was still fearful that anxiety might prevent me from turning in a credible performance. He advised me to take a glass of red wine a few minutes before the exam and that would calm me down. I did not consider that I was still a teetotaler at that time when I decided to purchase a bottle of red wine. About 10 minutes before the beginning of the exam I drank a glass of red wine. Prof. Albrecht brought me into his office and said that the examination would begin immediately. Sitting facing the board were Profs. Albrecht, Clayton, Hoffmann, and Plane. Prof. Hoffmann asked the first question. It sounded like it had come from a far place. I don't know how long I stood like a deer caught in the headlights of a car, but from that distant place I heard Prof. Albrecht saying, "Frank, why don't you turn to the board and start working."

I asked, "Prof. Hoffmann, would you please repeat the question?" His question required me to develop a quantum mechanics equation. The intentional act of pressing the chalk against the board seemed to sober me and I began to work steadily. When I completed the equation, I felt relieved and wanted to shout Q.E D. as I used to delight in doing on solving a problem in geometry. This sense of victory, however, was short lived as Prof. Hoffmann asked a couple more questions about the meaning of the equation and then asked me to sketch the topography of the equation.

I asked, "What do you mean by topography." He responded, "Were you never a Boy Scout?"

"Unfortunately, no." I responded feeling somewhat uncomfortable. "It is a three-dimensional plot."

I sketched the three-dimensional representation of the equation at the end of which he scribbled something on a piece of paper, passed it to Prof. Albrecht and left the room.

My heart sank. I re-entered that fog place and vaguely heard a question from Prof. Clayton. Then I heard Prof. Albrecht again saying, "Frank why don't you begin by developing an equation?"

I turned to the board for a brief second, then turned back to face the examiners and I asked, "Prof. Clayton, would you mind repeating the question?" As he repeated the question, I recognized which equation would be applicable in answering his question. In fact, it was one that I had reviewed thoroughly. Working through the answer to this question rebuilt my confidence and I was able to answer the remaining questions with greater ease.

Prof. Hoffmann returned, at which point Prof. Albrecht said, "Frank, you may leave the room now." Their deliberation was brief as Prof. Albrecht opened the door and beckoned me to rejoin the panel of examiners. My heart sank again as I thought, they must have all said, 'Failed'. Now the discussion would be about scheduling a written examination. Depending on my performance on the written exam I would either get a terminal Master's degree or entry into the exciting and challenging phase of hypothesis generation and design and implementation of experiments for the Ph.D. Success in this phase led to thesis writing and defense, the final step for the Ph. D. When I reentered the room, Prof. Albrecht shook my hand and everyone said, "Congratulations!" Whew.

Prof. Albrecht took me to lunch and smiled often during lunch. I could not recall ever hearing him laugh nor witnessing a smile. He was clearly pleased with the outcome.

I said, "thank you for getting my engine in gear at the beginning of the exam. Can you tell me what was written on the paper that Prof. Hoffmann passed to you before he left the room?"

He smiled again, and said, "Roald had a conflict and was not sure that he would be back in time for the panel discussion at the end of your exam. So, it was agreed that he would ask the initial questions and his note said, 'Pass'."

I told Prof. Albrecht about drinking the wine before the examination as explanation as to why I was in a fog.

Then, I said, "I wish you had given me a small thumbs-up sign as Prof. Hoffmann was leaving the room. His departure made me wonder whether he was displeased with my answers."

Prof. Albrecht invited me to call him Andy! This was quite an honor, particularly for someone from my country, where one would never address an adult, and particularly a superior by his first name. After lunch with Andy Albrecht, I headed to the registrar's office to deliver the one page document, signed by my Ph.D. Thesis Advisory team. This stated that I had passed my candidacy examination and will be awarded the Masters of Science degree. I was ecstatic and bursting to share the news with all who would listen, but I restrained myself.

With my Ph.D. Candidacy exam behind me, I continued to work through the night as this was required to avoid electrical interference from instruments, such as mass spectrometers, in use in neighboring labs. This critical electrical signaling problem was further reduced when I enclosed the entire instrument in a large copper Faraday cage.

At about this time, in late 1969, Prof. Albrecht left for sabbatical at the University of California, Santa Cruz. I worked diligently on optimizing the system, concentration of chlorophyll a and b microcrystals, Voltage across the photoconduction cell, and selection of the nearinfrared wavelength range. Once these were optimized, I began to design experiments to capture these photoelectric effects. Once I had consistent results from each experiment, I would write up the results as though I was submitting it for publication. Of course, some sections, such as materials, methodology, etc. did not have to be repeated.

Fortunately, these new, structurally enclosed labs were specifically built to exclude extraneous light and thus infrared stimulating light could be focused and applied to the cell. Most mornings, I would emerge from my bunkerlike lab bleary-eyed and excited as a very nice relationship between concentration of Chlorophyll a microcrystals and shape and size of the current signal, as well as that between current signal and light intensity, were being consistently reproduced. I also evaluated a couple other porphyrin molecules and found similar activities. What was problematic, however, was that the slope of the plot between photocurrents and light intensity was consistently less than 1.0, suggesting that the charge separation was a monophotonic mechanism.

I became frustrated because I would periodically send these reports to Prof. Albrecht, but never got a response. Finally, Prof. Albrecht returned from his Year-plus Sabbatical, but announced that he would be continuing his sabbatical for another 6 months. I asked his view on the reports that I had sent him and he admitted that he had not really looked at them.

Why had I spent all these nights in a dark lab, if my Advisor had no interest in the work I was doing? I gathered together all of my reports and slammed them on Prof. Albrecht's desk.

"Here are all of the reports that I sent you. I have been offered a job by Xerox," I said, then continued before he could. "I will clean out my lab and head to Xerox. A Ph. D. is not that important."

I left him sitting behind his desk, looking stunned by my action. I still had a couple of experiments that needed to be completed, so I went into the lab as usual that evening, and worked through the night. About 6 am, as I was preparing to leave for my apartment, the lab phone rang. It was Prof. Albrecht.

"I'm glad I caught you," he said. "Don't quit until we talk."

About 7:30 am Prof. Albrecht arrived. I was sitting at my desk in the hallway outside of my lab, somewhat bleary-eyed and in a not-so-good humor.

I could sense that he was excited as he gestured me into his office. He did not sit behind his desk and began speaking immediately.

"I read your experiments last night and I want you to stop doing experiments and start writing your thesis," he said.

"Do you think that it is enough? I don't think it will be a very thick thesis," I replied, shaking my head.

"I want you to start writing your thesis." he repeated, emphasizing his words by handing me the stack of reports. "You have more than enough for a Ph.D. thesis."

I left exhilarated, walking on sunshine past other students and smiling at the grand old buildings as I went by them. I was not dying from sleep as was normal at this time of day. I called a friend of mine, Nancy Wyatt, who occasionally had come over at night to help me align the system to ensure optimal activation. She suggested meeting at Noyes Lodge for a celebratory breakfast, as she would be able to get away from her office in about an hour. Unfortunately, I was too tired to accept. I did need to sleep for several hours and hopefully awake to discover that this was not a Dream.

It was not a dream. It was my new reality.

Prof. Albrecht worked closely with me as I drafted the thesis. I was surprised as he often removed several paragraphs that I thought necessary to explain what I thought we had found. Finally, he scheduled my thesis defense after each member of my committee had signed off on my draft. Thesis defenses are open to the department so I was not surprised to see a few faculty members in addition to my thesis advisor team. I also had a sense that they were really interested in my presentation. The presentation went well and, of course, I gave the interpretation that Prof. Albrecht had advised, which I did not quite understand. At the end of my presentation and questions, a couple Faculty members asked why I was not staying on for at least one post-doctoral year to continue work on these intriguing results. Prof. Albrecht was clearly delighted with the outcome of the presentation. He took me to lunch and after all of the congratulatory handshakes from others who had learned of my major academic achievement, I asked

Andy the big question, "Why did you insist on this particular interpretation of the data?"

He explained, "I am a consultant at Kodak and their scientists are seeing a similar phenomena in a different system, which we could not explain. Your work explains it."

At that time, the dogma was that one needed to excite a molecule to its singlet state for an electron to be emitted. Alternatively, the molecule could relax back to ground state with emission of fluorescence, or could relax to the triplet state followed by emission of light as phosphorescence on transition from triplet to ground state. My work demonstrated that one could, in some systems, excite directly to the triplet state with the emission of an electron. This was a totally new discovery, hence the excitement.

The unrest among the Black students was increasing. Their requests for establishment of a Black Studies program and for Cornell to address their complaints of institutional racism were being ignored. Another Black graduate student and I had tried to convince a couple of the leaders, Tom Jones and Ed Whitfield that they were making progress. For example, James Turner had been identified to be the first Director of the Africana Studies Center. However, they told us that things were moving too slowly. In one meeting, one of the students challenged my credibility. He declared, "You are not Black. How many niggers do any of you know that are working on a Ph.D. in Chemistry or Physics at Cornell?"

I decided that it was probably best for me to refrain from attending these meetings. So, when the Willard Straight Hall was occupied on April 19, 1969, I was unaware that it had been a possible action by the students. On learning that this had occurred, I refrained from joining the students in Willard Straight Hall for two reasons. One was that they were suspicious of my motives, and the other was that I felt that I would probably get another visit from the 'men in suits' (the FBI?) and be immediately deported. However, I stood outside of the Willard Straight Hall and witnessed the emergence of the Black students from the Straight fully armed with guns, after it was rumored that white fraternity students planned to storm the building with guns.

In the aftermath of the occupation of the Straight, I was able to reengage with the Black students, many of whom were traumatized by the experience. A small number transferred to other colleges and several feared for their safety. The Constituent Assembly (CA) was created to address the many issues of the student body, and Dean Donald Cooke, who was asked to lead the Constituent Assembly, invited me to become a member of the CA. The Constituent Assembly was the beginning of Shared Governance at Cornell.

One of the tasks I assumed was visiting Historically Black Universities to recruit students for Graduate programs at Cornell. This was quite an experience. I travelled with another Black Graduate student and we visited six HBCUs. Joseph had served time in Vietnam and was from the South. We flew to Raleigh NC and rented a car for the rest of the trip. Joseph chose to drive because, as he said, he knew the South. Two things caught my attention. The first was that he never drove at night. As he told me, it was dangerous for two young Black men to be driving late at night. We ran the risk of being pulled over by the cops, and that could not end well for us. I could appreciate Joseph's concern given my own experience that resulted in my being incarcerated in the Lackawanna County Jail. Today the need for organizations, such as Black Lives Matter, shows, regrettably, that almost 50 years later, little has changed.

The second was that every time we entered a town where we planned to spend the night, he seemed to be in a significant hurry. He seemed to know exactly where to find the railroad tracks and hence find a wine store in the Black section of the town, before it closed for the night. Getting to a hotel was secondary. Joseph explained that we should never have alcohol in the car, because if the cops stopped us for any reason, that would be one of those issues that could land us in jail for the night. Hence, he left finding a wine shop as the last thing that we did just before going to the hotel.

The months following the Straight takeover were tense as this event collided with the many other political and women's right issues smoldering at Cornell. With respect to President

Perkins, this was truly a case of the Road to Hell being paved with Good Intentions. In my view, it was not appreciated then, and perhaps not even today, that there could be an enormous cultural chasm between young black students coming from the inner cities or rural areas and the predominant white students at Cornell, who come from homes or families where they were not the first college-bound generation. Nonetheless, the leadership and courage of President Perkins in creating the Committee on Special Education Projects charged with the administration of the recruitment and retention of Black and other minority students at Cornell, catalyzed increase in enrollment of minority students in many predominantly white universities and colleges.

My tutoring of minority students took on added significance when I was approached by a West Indian student for help in Chemistry. The Agricultural College at Cornell collaborated with the Agricultural College in the West Indies. The college in the West Indies, which was a two-year program, would send selected students to complete their B.S. at the Cornell Agricultural College. The West Indies Agricultural College gave priority to graduates who had worked for several years in agricultural departments of the Jamaican or Trinidadian government. The result was that these students invariably were much older, mostly in their forties, had families and had been away from the rigors of college courses for several years.

One of the courses at Cornell that a few of them found quite challenging was Freshman Chemistry. One of them, Bertie Saunders, approached me and asked if I would tutor four of them. I agreed and all four of them passed and graduated with their B.S. degree. I was elated that I had had this opportunity to positively impact their lives.

A Free Man from a
Black Stream

I arrived at the Xerox Webster Labs full of enthusiasm and anticipation. I wore my best Dashiki and Sandals, although I knew that I would have to change out of sandals to more secure shoes once I was in the Lab. Dr. Don Seanor, who would be my direct supervisor met me and escorted me to my office, which was two doors from his. It might have been because Don was a Brit and I was still more comfortable interacting with Brits than I was with Americans; or it could have been because Don understood the significance of my thesis, I liked him instantly. Don took me to meet Mr. Steve Strella, who was the Director of the area to which I was assigned. Steve explained that his section was responsible for all materials and specifications of the conducting surfaces and toners for the Xerox machines. He seemed pleasant enough. When I returned to Don's office, I asked him why I was in the materials section, since I was not a surface chemist. He then explained that the group who had recruited me had disbanded and I was assigned to the Materials group. I was quite disappointed because the group that had recruited me was exploring an imaging approach using electrophoresis. Given my work in photoconductivity, they thought that that might also bring an additional new approach.

I never heard about this approach at Xerox again.

Initially, no project could be found for me so I wandered around various labs learning about the electrophotography or xerography process. I also discovered that Xerox was developing several projects, including a color printer, the

ARDRI process which was intended to copy on both sides of the paper continuously, so that books could be fed into the machine and be copied, and the PONC process. The PONC was planned to use thermographic instead of electrostatic method to copy images. I was ultimately assigned to the PONC team and was responsible for specification of the toner consistency, the thermographic (heatmeltable) surface coat on the paper and release characteristics of the toner from the coated paper.

The project went very well and 9 months later the team was ready to present to the VP of Development, who would decide whether the project should get the green light for further development and commercialization. I was quite excited to witness my first Product Development presentation. The presentations seemed to have gone well. Then came three questions from the VP:

1.   How easy is it to copy this technology? STRIKE 1
2.   What will it cost to make the machine? STRIKE 2
3.   What is the ROI? STRIKE 3

At that time Xerox' business model was to lease copiers and make the returns on the number of copies made. It was estimated that cost to make the copier would be about $350 per unit, hence the lease model would not make sense. The units would be sold outright. The technology was easy to be copied, and finally, the ROI was estimated to be about 18%. At that time, Xerox would not market any product that would not bring at least 24% ROI. The project was terminated. The subsequent marketing and present common use of both black and white, and color low volume copiers demonstrate how shortsighted this decision was.

I went to Mr. Strella and asked him what my next assignment would be. "It is always difficult to find assignments for young scientists," he said, his upper lip twitching.

"Steve, Robert has just joined us. He has not completed his Ph.D. Nonetheless you have put him on the ARDRI project." I hesitated, should I tell him my opinion? I continued despite my doubts he'd listen. "Here is what I suggest. Don't think about me. Pretend that I am Robert. What assignment would you give me, if I were Robert?"

He admitted I was right in that it did not take him any time to decide to put Robert on the ARDRI team. I left Steve's office and went directly to Dr. Myron Tribus' office to describe yet another example of discrimination against me by Mr. Strella.

Dr. Tribus was the new SVP of Research and Development at Xerox. Dr. Tribus had three stated goals. These were to increase the number of PhDs at Xerox so that Xerox could move from phenomenological to mechanism-based product development; more rigorous decision making about the portfolio of projects; and greater diversity in the work force. Two other Black PhDs were hired at the same time as I was in 1972. This brought the number of Black PhDs to four.

Dr. Bill McCain had been at Xerox for about three years. Bill was a metallurgist and expert in Scanning Electron Microscopy. Bill was somewhat introverted but basically kept a low profile and avoided all conflict. I had gone to Dr. Tribus twice before to complain about episodes of discrimination. This time, I could give him a concrete example. Dr. Tribus offered a couple of options. I could transfer to the Xerox PARC in Palo Alto which had been established a couple of years prior (1970) to work on cutting edge research projects. For example, mammography would be developed at PARC. (And, very importantly, several years later, the work of PARC scientists on the mouse, on window-based interfaces and other technologies in their Alto computer inspired Steve Jobs to incorporate these in the Lisa and Macintosh, after his visit to PARC in 1979. PARC became a very creative and inventive Lab).

The second recommendation was for me to go to Stanford University and study Decision Analysis and return to work for him. I thanked Dr. Tribus and told him that I would think about it. I returned to Mr. Strella and told him that Dr. Tribus had offered the two possibilities and that I wanted to think about it. He angrily spoke as he told me that although he did not have a Ph.D. he had been at Xerox for many years and was promoted because he knew how to create products, something that PhDs do not know how to do. I returned to my office eager to complain to my office mate, Chuck Levine.

Chuck was about 55 years of age, had several important xerography patents, and as he described it, he was one of those non-PhDs who were kicked out of their labs by Tribus and forced to take early retirement. Chuck asked about the presentation to the VP of Development. I told him that the product was cancelled and recounted to him my meetings with Strella and Myron Tribus.

Chuck listened, allowing me to complete my report before he spoke. "I have been watching you and have been wondering why you stay here. You are an academic. You should return to Cornell and pursue an academic career."

I told him that Cornell was quite disappointed that I did not stay there and continue my work.

"Why don't you take some time off and explore returning to academia?" he advised, knowing I had received a letter from the Institute of International Education telling me that since I was on a J-1 visa, I had a few more months in the USA after which I must return to Guyana.

I had reached out to the Xerox lawyers and Xerox HR and was assured that they would be able to either get the visa converted to one where I could work fully or they would be able to get the practical work experience extended. Subsequently, a Xerox lawyer came to see me and informed me that Xerox was advised not to interfere with this process. He refused to explain further. I had appealed to the Institute of International Education for an extension on the basis that I had not received the requisite post graduate training in my field. Given these circumstances and Chuck Levine's advice, I decided to visit a few graduate programs to seek a post-doctoral position in Biophysics, which I thought would strengthen my argument in my appeal for an extension.

First, I visited University of Rochester and much to my surprise they raised the question as to whether I would be interested in entering medical school that Fall. I don't recall my answer, I just kept thinking that this was impractical for two reasons. The first was that it was already March and they were certainly close to completing their acceptances. I could not complete an application in time for the Fall semester and time was a critical factor. The second was that it was 1973, and soon I would be 30 years old. That seemed a little old to be starting medical school.

I got into my car and drove to New York City intending to visit Cornell and Columbia Universities. As I drove, I reflected on the question of medical school and could not convince myself that this was feasible due to application process requirements, nor that it would meet the exigency to justify an extension of my stay in the U.S. Then there was the practical issue of money.

As I drove, I thought of Dr. Rev. Walter V. L. Eversley, my close friend since childhood. During my last Summer at Lehigh, Walter had arrived in Bethlehem with Daphne, his wife and son, Colin. Walter, who had joined the Moravian Church, was on **vacation with an intent**. Walter did everything with intention and intensity. His plan, as he explained it to me, was to attend Moravian College. I was less than encouraging, having explained to him that it was already July and it would be unlikely that he would get a place in the incoming Freshman class. I told him that, nonetheless, we should try to meet with the Dean of Moravian College. We arrived at the Dean's office for what I thought would be, perhaps, a 15-minute meeting.

About one hour later, Walter came charging out of the Dean's office and said, "We have a lot to do! I have been accepted into this year's Freshman class. The Dean has also assured me that the College will help me find an apartment and a part time job!"

I congratulated Walter, but I must admit that I was amazed at this result. I expected that he would have been assured admission for the following year. It did however, remind me of the help that I had received from Prof. Daen, although the situations were quite different.

Four years later, when Walter was admitted to Harvard Divinity School but had neither scholarship nor personal funds, I asked him how he planned to manage this situation. He said simply: 'The Lord will provide.' He received his Ph.D. in Divinity from Harvard.

I had driven about three hours on this trip to explore a Post Doc position in Biophysics at either Cornell or Columbia Universities when I decided to stop, take a bio break and stretch a bit. I got back into the car and pulled back onto Interstate 81 towards New York City. I began to think about what my life would be like if I had to return to Guyana. This thought led me to reflect on events involving a potential return to Guyana that had occurred during my years at Cornell.

In 1968, five years after I had left my home, I had returned for a brief visit to Guyana. It was a good time to go because I had passed my Ph.D. candidacy examination and had received an M.S. The family had moved to a larger place in Kitty, a suburb of Georgetown, and I could see that my mother and Uncle Willie appeared less stressed. I took the opportunity to let Uncle Willie know how much I appreciated what he had done for my mom and me. I also discussed my desire to help him start any small business that he would like.

My mother informed me that Mr. Cecil Miller was visiting Guyana and was staying at the Pegasus hotel. She implored me to call him. I did with some reluctance and an immediate growing sense of anger within me. I identified myself and he responded with enthusiasm. "I have heard that you are doing very well at University."

I said, "In fact, I just received my M.S. in Physical Chemistry."

He responded, "Unfortunately, I leave in a couple of days, but I will give you my address in Lagos so we can stay in touch."

In as steady a voice as I could muster I said, "Mr. Miller, I called you because my mom insisted that I should do so. I have done my filial duty. Now here is what I have to say to you. I have achieved what I have with help from my step father and friends of my mother. I owe you nothing. Here is what I have to say to you, "Go screw yourself!" and I hung up. My mother who was standing nearby was mortified. She said nothing and never mentioned him again.

The PNC had won the 1964 elections and with support of the US government was able to achieve Independence for British Guiana, new name Guyana, in May 1966. Shortly thereafter I had received a call from Counsel General Saul in New York, who told me that the Comrade Leader wanted me to return to Guyana and become his minister of Education. I told him that although I was very interested in helping the Government, it made better sense to do this after I had completed my Ph.D.

I did not hear from The Comrade Leader again until I returned to Guyana three years later (1971) to bury Uncle Willie, who had died suddenly and unexpectedly. I felt robbed, because I had begun to help him start a small money lending business. That was important to his desire to help others. So, I travelled to Guyana with a very heavy heart.

However, about two months prior to this trip, I had gotten an unusual call from the Aluminum Company of Canada (Alcan) Ltd inviting me to a meeting at their Headquarters in Montreal, Quebec. I flew to Montreal and was overnighted in a top hotel. The next day I met with one of the Vice Presidents who came directly to the point. Alcan was offering me the Job as Manager of the Guyana Bauxite Company (Demba) which was a wholly owned subsidiary of Alcan. Demba was a prized resource in Guyana. Along with rice, sugar and forestry, Bauxite was always listed as one of the key resources of Guyana, particularly because at one time, Guyana had an effective monopoly in supplying higher grade calcined bauxite.

At the end of the day's visit, a firm offer was made. I would be General Manager of Demba. Prior to assuming this post in Guyana, I would be trained over 18 months, 6 months of which would be in Montreal and one year at the bauxite company in Jamaica. They wanted me to start immediately after completing my Ph.D. I told them that I would think about it. A few days later I received a call for my answer.

"Hello, thank you for the follow up. Could you tell me what the salary would be?" I asked immediately.

"You will be paid the same as the present Canadian General Manager." "Is he paid in Canadian or Guyanese dollars?" I asked

The woman on the other end of the phone said, "Naturally as a Canadian, he is paid in Canadian dollars. You will be paid in Guyanese dollars."

"The Guyana dollar is half the value of the Canadian dollar. Are you telling me that I will be paid half of the salary that the Canadian is paid for the same job and in my own country?"

No response.

I continued; "Will I get a car and housing allowance, as is provided for the present Canadian General Manager?"

"Unfortunately, you will have to provide your own car and accommodation." She said without emotion.

I said, "Madam, I consider this a personal affront. My answer is that I have no interest."

I then began to think in greater earnest about what I would do after completing the Ph.D. I decided to look into paper making and applying for Post Doc positions at Virginia Polytechnic Institute (VPI) and Oregon University. Both expressed interest and I actually visited VPI. The visit went very well. They said that they had been interested in the paper making properties of trees from Guyana and if I could arrange to get samples of Guyanese woods, they would teach me paper making. This seemed like a good deal and I was quite interested in doing this although I had one concern which was living in Blacksburg, Va., having driven past Blacks Run and Lynchburg on I-81.

I mused on the history of these names and what they signaled for Black people.

It reminded me of the trip that I had made to Historically Black Colleges and Universities with Joseph, a Black American fellow graduate student, and what I had learned from him about the dangers for young Black males in the South.

I constructed a proposal and sent it via Counsel General Saul to the Comrade Leader. The proposal would cost the Guyana government no money, since VPI would pay me the usual Post Doc stipend. All the government would have to do is to agree to send samples of specified Guyanese wood. I never got a response. My visit to Guyana to bury Uncle Willie occurred shortly after these discussions with Alcan and the beginning of the writing of my Ph.D. thesis.

During this visit I had a meeting with the Comrade Leader. I did not have a long wait. I was ushered into his office and after asking me to take a seat he got straight to the point. "I want you to come home immediately and become the General Manager of the Bauxite company."

"Comrade Leader, I have no management experience."
"You are a smart man. You will learn rapidly on the job," was his brief retort.

I tried to change the subject and asked, "Comrade Leader, did you receive the proposal on use of Guyana's woods to make paper?"

"Yes, I gave it to the Minister of Forestry and they are discussing it with Litton Industries. Now back to Demba."

"You will receive $540 Guyanese per month, but you will have to provide your own housing and car." He continued.

I took one of my usual silent deep breaths and said, "Comrade Leader, it is clear to me that you know that Alcan has made the exact offer to me, which offer I declined. I was incensed that Alcan would pay me far less than that which they were paying their Canadian General Manager. In your case, I have a different problem. I know at least two former classmates of mine who are undersecretaries in your government, and who do not earn enough to explain the several real estate properties and cars they possess. Either you will pay me enough so that I am not distracted or we might have a problem."

He abruptly said, "This meeting is over", and waved me out of the room. A few months later, Mr. Burnham (Comrade Leader), Prime Minister of Guyana, announced the nationalization of the Demerara Bauxite company (Demba).

My reflections on contacts with Comrade Leader ended as I pulled into a hotel in mid-town Manhattan and decided to have a good night's rest before my visits to Cornell Medical School and Columbia University on the following day. I puzzled over whether I should pivot from Post doc in Biophysics to Medical School if this opportunity were offered. I decided to make the decision on the spot if the opportunity arose. At 9 am on the following morning I went to the office of the Dean of Cornell Medical School and asked if I could speak with him for 5-10 minutes. Dr. Meikle was in his office and he invited me to take a seat. Midway through my Biophysics post doc pitch he interrupted me and told me that I might want to consider Cornell's MD program. Cornell had recently decided to admit 1-2 students, who already had a Ph.D. They expected these students to return to doing research after receiving the MD. I told him that I was definitely interested in this. Dr. Meikle told me to return the following day for some interviews.

On the following day I arrived at Dr. Meikle's office where he conducted a more formal interview. At the very end, he asked, what would be my goal after obtaining an MD. I said, I would probably train in general medicine and set up practice in Harlem, which is an underserved area. He looked at me directly and said, "When we take a man like you into the medical school we expect to hear that he plans to go back into the lab and work on medically relevant research problems. I cannot tell you what to say in your other interviews, but I will tell you that that is not the answer that would be expected." I appreciated his being direct because although I felt that providing medical care for in Harlem would be an important contribution, Research still ran through my veins.

I thanked him and headed for my next interview with Dr. Du Vigneaud. Dr. Du Vigneaud had received the Nobel Prize in Chemistry in 1955 for the first synthesis of a polypeptide hormone and had done his research at Cornell University in Ithaca. So, it made sense to me that I would be interviewed by him as he could get a rapid read on my capabilities from his colleagues in Baker Lab in Ithaca.

On my way up to his lab in New York Hospital, a nurse entered the elevator with a patient on a bed and IV lines and bottles hanging from poles and his arms. I braced myself against the wall of the elevator and willed myself not to pass out. I stepped carefully out of the elevator the next time the door opened and took some deep breaths. I reentered the elevator once the faint feeling passed and continued to Dr. Du Vigneaud's office. We discussed my thesis and I was careful to tell him that, as he knows, normally Professor Albrecht does spectroscopy on small organic molecules, but he had graciously agreed to accommodate my interest in bioactive molecules. The interview seemed to have gone well. I then went to an interview with Dr. Curtis, the associate Dean responsible for minority students. I left the interview a little discouraged because Dr. Curtis mentioned all the barriers: I was married. I had two young children. I had not had the prerequisite Biology courses. I felt a little puzzled because as a black Dean I expected him to have solutions and not just problems. I was careful to let him know that in spite of all of these challenges, I was prepared to work hard to get an MD and return to lab-based research.

The drive back to Rochester was a blur as I replayed all of the possibilities. Entering medical school in September, 1973 would probably solve the extension of my stay in America problems.

When I arrived home, I found a letter and phone message. The University of Rochester Medical School had sent me an acceptance for the September class and the phone message from Cornell was also to inform me that I had been accepted to the medical school and that an official letter would follow. I returned to my office the following day and as I entered Chuck said immediately, "Back already? I thought you would be gone for at least a week."

"Chuck, I only visited University of Rochester and Cornell. Both raised the possibility of medical school and I took your advice. I expressed interest."

"And?" asked Chuck, impatient to hear the outcome.

"I have been accepted to medical school at both Cornell and the University of Rochester. But I am not sure what to do."

Chuck said, "What is there to think about? Go!"

He continued after a brief pause and said in a somewhat fatherly tone, "Do you know how many people each year try to get into medical school?"

I said, "What about the offers from Dr. Tribus?"

He said, "Go and thank him. Tell him that you have been accepted into medical school and you have decided to go."

I did as Chuck suggested. Dr. Tribus was magnanimous in his support. However, Professor Albrecht expressed his disappointment, when I told him of my decision to go to medical school. As he said, he could not believe that I would give up research to become a medical Doctor. He nonetheless agreed to send a letter of recommendation to both University of Rochester and Cornell.

As I made the rounds to say my good byes, a couple colleagues said that they wished that they had had the courage to make the switch to medical school. Others wondered why, since I had been promoted to Associate scientist after only 15 months at Xerox, was I choosing to go to medical school.

My promotion, they thought, was a signal that management thought that I would be a very productive scientist at Xerox.

The most memorable comment, however, came from the senior technician in the Engineering Lab with which I had collaborated on the PONC project. He was middle-aged and a Brit. His boss was not in the lab, so I spoke directly to him, "I just came by to thank you and Alan (his boss) for your collaboration on the PONC program. Of course, you guys did the Lion's share of the work."

"What a shame," he said. "But the boys at the top make the decisions." "I also want you and Alan to know that I would be going to medical school in the Fall, so this is my last week at Xerox."

"Congratulations. I will tell him."

As I was leaving the Lab, he suddenly said, "May I ask you a question?" I said, "Sure. Of course."

He asked, "Do you know what your name means?" I said, "No."

He said, "Well, Frank is Celtic and it means Free Mason or Free Man and Douglas is Scottish and it means, From a Black Stream. And that is YOU: A FREE MAN FROM A BLACK STREAM!"

I smiled and thanked him. What he did not know is that he had lifted a small burden from my shoulders. In the mid to late sixties, many Black revolutionaries were changing their names to African names. Examples such as Amiri Baraka (LeRoi Jones, Poet, writer, activist); Malcolm X (Malcolm Little. Leader of Nation of Islam, activist); Kwame Ture (Stokely Carmichael, Leader of Student Nonviolent Coordinating Committee and member of Black Panther Party). I never succumbed to this pressure because I always felt that since I did not know from which country in Africa my fore parents were kidnapped and brought to British Guiana as slaves, I did not have a basis for selecting an African name. Now, I learned that my 'slave name' described me well, so I wear it proudly.

Cornell University
Medical School

Two questions my family raised almost stopped me from going to medical school. The first was that they doubted that I would tolerate medical school because it is all about memorization and it is very hierarchal. The second was that they were skeptical that I would have the patience to stay with it. Coupled with the loss in income they questioned whether this was a good move. Then came the killer. My petition brief was rejected by Institute of International Education and I was given one month to leave the USA. Given my last interaction with the comrade Leader, returning to Guyana did not seem like a feasible choice. So, I decided to travel to Canada and see whether I could get asylum there. Another possibility was going to Ghana, but I quickly dismissed that course of action as the distance and uncertainty would have increased the stress on my family.

I packed a suitcase and drove to Buffalo from my home in Rochester with the intent to cross into Canada at Niagara. As I approached Buffalo, it occurred to me that since there is a major office of Immigration and Naturalization in Buffalo, I could seek advice from one of the many immigration lawyers in that city, before crossing into Canada. So, I drove into the city and stopped at the first telephone booth. I found Lawyers in the yellow pages and one name jumped out at me: Runfola.

I went directly to his office. As I stepped into the spacious and well decorated suite of offices, the carpet under my feet was so plush, that I knew instinctively that I had picked a winner. The receptionist told me that Mr. Runfola would be back at 1 pm. I said that I would wait. Mr. Runfola arrived shortly before 1 pm and invited me into his office.

"How did you learn about me? Did someone refer you to me?" he asked.

"Sir, first, thank you for seeing me without an appointment. I walked into a nearby phone booth and selected your name from the Yellow Pages."

"How can I help you?"

"Sir, I would like to be very brief. Here is a copy of my petition brief that I sent to the Institute of International Education."

He took the three-page document and began to scan it as I spoke.

"I came to America as an undergraduate Fulbright Scholar, in 1963. I completed my B.S. at Lehigh University in three years and my Ph.D. from Cornell last year. I have just been admitted to do an MD at Cornell Medical School starting this Fall."

I paused to see if he was paying attention. He was.

"I have recently received this letter from IIE stating that I have to leave the U.S in a month. I need help from a lawyer."

He looked at me and said, "I am not an immigration lawyer. There is something about you that I like. I will help you." He made a copy and returned the brief to me.

He asked why I did not want to return to Guyana and I briefly described my last interaction with Comrade Leader and told him that I doubted that he would welcome my return.

He said, "I want you to enroll at Cornell Medical School. Send me $500 when you return to Rochester."

Since I was planning to stay in Canada, I had $500 cash with me. I gave it to him.

He then stressed, "You will hear from me in about three weeks. In the interim, do not leave the country, not even to Canada."

"Thank you, Sir." I left feeling a mixture of hope and skepticism. However, I said to myself, "That is the only game in town, young man."

On the selected date we walked over from his office to the Immigration and Naturalization building. As we walked into the lobby, he introduced me to a man by saying, "This is the young man than I mentioned to you." We met a second person on the way to the meeting with the judge and the greeting was repeated. Finally, we entered the room where a female judge was waiting. She invited us to take a seat and then said, "I have a copy of your brief, so we don't need to go over it."

She then asked a few questions which were somewhat incomprehensible to me. At one point, Mr. Runfola said, "As in the case of (name of a person) vs court," and said no more after that. Then as abruptly as it started it was over.

As we walked back to his office I asked Mr. Runfola about the individuals to whom he had introduced me. He said, "Oh, the first guy is responsible for deportations and the other is a longtime colleague of mine." Then I asked about the importance of his comment to the judge and he said that was to signal to the judge that should we get an unfavorable decision, he would appeal. When we reached his office, I asked him how much more money I owed him. He said, "None. Just sit tight. Enroll in medical school and wait for a call from me to get your green card."

In October 1973, several weeks later, that call came, and I travelled to the US Consulate in Toronto to receive my Green Card. The Visit to the consulate was remarkable in one instance and that is I had to sign a statement stating that I would not meddle in Guyana's politics. This was easy for me to sign because I had never had political aspirations nor interest in politics. I had a mixture of emotions. On the one hand I was relieved that now I could stay in the US. On the other hand, the requirement that I not meddle in Guyana's politics made me wonder whether Comrade Leader had been consulted before a decision was reached. And if so, what did this mean for my family in Guyana.

Orientation week at Cornell medical School was quite memorable. The tales and advice recounted by Dr. Ben Kean, the famous Parasitologist are legendary. More advanced students often attended his session during orientation week to hear more of his anecdotes. One example included the tale of a Saudi prince who had a tape worm.

As described by Dr. Kean, the Saudi Prince and his entire retinue, including bodyguards, had taken over the entire 16th floor of the New York hospital. The Saudi Prince had been treated once before for a tapeworm, but evidently, the entire worm had not been expelled. When Dr. Kean entered the room the anxious Prince said, "Doctor, I have expelled the worm, but I don't know if that is all of it."

Dr. Kean had the gloved nurse retrieve the worm from the stool can that the Prince had used for the occasion. The nurse placed it on a table in the room as Dr. Kean donned his gloves. He carefully uncoiled it to its full length of about 5 ft. and examined the ends. The Prince was looking anxiously over his shoulder.

With a triumphant "Aha", Dr. Kean announced to the Prince, "We have it all. Here is the Scolex (head) with its hooks and suckers."

The Prince was so delighted, he opened a suitcase and started stuffing its contents of $100 bills into the pockets of Dr. Kean's white coat.

The embarrassed Dr. Kean explained. "Your Highness, this is absolutely not necessary and it is not allowed. You can, however, make a donation to the New York Hospital."

The Prince thanked him once more as members of his retinue smiled and said, "Thank God."

Dr. Kean also gave us some personal advice. He said, "For heaven's sake, if you need a girlfriend or boyfriend, do not select somebody from your class. Find someone from any of the colleges and universities in New York City."

"Can you imagine," he continued' "having a romantic moment when both of you are smelling of formalin from the corpse on which you had worked, that day?" "Now, if your girlfriend or boyfriend from another university can tolerate the smell of formalin on you, he or she is a keeper."

Another memorable presentation during orientation was that by Dr. Michael Gershon who held up the enormous purple two volume Robbins Pathology text and said, "By the end of the second year we expect that you would have memorized everything in this text book." The image of young doctors walking around with purple brains appeared before me as my eyes glazed over at the thought of really having to do this.

The major reason for choosing Cornell over the University of Rochester was Cornell was in New York City where there are many colleges, so the opportunities to find a teaching position would be greater. My first stop was Hunter College where Aubrey Bonnet was a professor of Sociology.

Aubrey and I refer to each other as cousins although we are not actually related. His aunt and my mother and aunts were very close friends and when we moved to Thomas street we lived a few yards from each other. One year prior to my taking the Senior Cambridge examination, Aubrey was expected to be among the best performers at this examination, but inexplicably had performed below his potential and the expectation of his teachers. Nonetheless he remained a leader among his peers and his home was often a place where many young gifted Guyanese gathered. One day, while I was still in a fog from having placed First in the country at the Senior Cambridge I decided to visit Aubrey. It was just an impulse because usually I stayed alone except when it had to do with church activities. As I entered Aubrey's home where several of his friends were gathered, I heard Aubrey say, "Here comes one of Guyana's brightest sons." I have never forgotten his magnanimous gesture, even though a year prior he had had a personal disappointment with respect to this examination.

Aubrey introduced me to Ms. Ruth Jody who was responsible for the coaching of students and she immediately embarked on helping me. She introduced me to the chemistry department and I got a job to teach a section of the freshman chemistry course. This, however, meant that I could not attend some of my classes at Cornell. I made attending gross anatomy sessions, where we worked in teams on the cadaver, my number one priority in the first year. I found the lectures in the other courses quite uninspiring, but they raised many research questions. And that always captures my interest because posing the right questions starts every intellectual journey. I would ask many questions, which apparently was not appreciated by the Lecturers. This became clear when one of the biochemistry professors invited me to work in his lab, which frankly, I would have done eagerly, except it offered no stipend and I needed to earn money.

"What do you think of the lectures?" he asked me one day.

"I find them disappointing since most of the professors will only give 2-3 lectures all year. Three hours in the library and any student could give a better lecture." That was the last time he spoke to me.

Since I was working part time, I did not have much time to socialize and study with my classmates. I did become fairly good friends with Carl Ritchie, who lived in the same Livingston Ferrand building as I did. Carl was a slightly older student, who had spent time in the military, before returning to college and applying to medical school. It was during my chats with Carl that I began to realize that there was something amiss with the treatment of minority students. For the second year in a row, the same three minority students were being made to repeat the first year.

At about that time I had cause to visit Dr. Gershon's Lab where I found that he was grading the microbiology examination, which was essay based, with the class photos in front of him. I asked him why it was necessary to have the class photos in front of him and he replied simply that he likes to know whom he is grading.

I went to Dr. Curtis to understand his view on the minority students and I found that he seemed to hold the view that the targeted three students should consider themselves lucky to have gotten accepted to Cornell. I told him that since I had been a teaching assistant in graduate school, I had developed an ability to assess students' capabilities and it was my view from my interactions with some of my classmates in gross anatomy and microbiology that there were white students less capable than these three classmates. I also told him that I found his approach to the issue somewhat odd. Why did they have to repeat all the courses, rather than having them focus on the ones in which their performance was presumably judged unsatisfactory?

The more questions I asked of more advanced minority students, the more I became convinced that there was a bias against minority students. Working on a formalin drenched cadaver several days per week provided opportunities to hear natural candid comments from my team mates. On one of the early gross anatomy sessions, the conversation turned to our backgrounds and life experiences. I was surprised by the candor among the group. The youngest among us complained about having to wait until she was 25 years of age before she could access her Trust Fund. All three of my class mates working on the cadaver with me had Trust Funds. One of the others described being sent to Europe by her parents because she was pregnant. She returned to the US after a couple of years in Europe and was working for a small liberal newspaper, when her father, himself a Professor at a Medical School, convinced her to take premedical courses. Eighteen months later she was in medical school. The difference between their life experiences and expectations and that of many Black students was remarkable.

Generally, the students were all collegial and seemed to have a genuine concern for each other, regardless of ethnicity. I was so concerned by what I was hearing that I was able to get a couple other minority students to help me develop and make copies of a petition. I had learned that the Cornell Board of trustees would be meeting at Cornell. We slipped in before the meeting and left our petition and a position paper in front of each name tag on the table. The petition asked for the board of trustees to examine the unfair and unusual practices against minority students. I hoped that given the experiences at Cornell's Ithaca campus that this Board would request to learn the reason for this unusual action and that would make the Medical School review its practices. Disappointingly, this action turned the spotlight on me.

The following Monday I was summoned to see Dean Santos-Busch. The Dean, though serious in his visage, seemed sympathetic. He said, "We have some serious doubts and concerns about your commitment to medical school."

"Why do you have doubts?" I asked.

"A number of complaints have been brought to my attention. For example, I have been informed that you have stated that medical school is not challenging and as a result you do not attend classes but are teaching at one of the local colleges. Further, you have a poor opinion of the faculty in that you have said that students can prepare better lectures. In addition, whenever you attend lectures you bait the professors with difficult questions."

I responded, "Dean, believe me I am quite impressed with the enormous challenge that the medical curriculum presents. My situation is that with the loss of income that I had when I was working at Xerox and the additional burden of medical school expenses, I have no choice but to work. I also ask a lot of questions because I am intellectually stimulated by the many research opportunities presented by these lectures."

Dean Santos-Busch leaned forward. "Here is my advice to you. This is not graduate school. Medical school is a trade school. So, memorize the crap and forget it."

He continued, in a graver tone. "Further, there is something of which you need to be aware." He opened the catalog to the section on promotion and I read the indicated paragraph it stated clearly that students were advanced based on assessment of seriousness of purpose, overall attitude and numerical grades. "This means you could pass numerically and still not be advanced. This is how we prevent students, who prove behaviorally or mentally unfit, from entering the profession."

'Very interesting', I thought, 'if the school does not like me it can simply dismiss me regardless of the quality of my academic achievements. Interesting.' I thanked Dean Santos-Busch for his candor and reached out to Dean Don Cooke in Ithaca for advice. I had gotten to know Dean Cooke, who was also a Professor in the department of Chemistry, during the aftermath of the Willard Straight Takeover. He was responsible for the running of the Constitutional Assembly and had an open and sensitive ear to all students. He held many informal sessions with students and listened without prejudice. As a result, he was instrumental in returning the Ithaca campus to normalcy, a contribution that has been underappreciated. In fact, he served as a true Ombudsman for all sides. Dean Cooke got back to me and told me that he was told that the actions were not directed at me, but at a small number of students and I was getting in the way. It was therefore up to me whether I wanted to involve myself further. I felt that I had no choice but to be supportive of my black classmates that seemed to be the targets for unfair treatment.

A few days later, Dean Santos-Busch summoned me to his office and stated that they had looked into my financial situation. They had decided to give me a tuition free scholarship for the first two years and a tuition loan for the last two years, on the condition that I terminated my teaching job at Hunter College immediately. I explained that I could not quit immediately, but since it was close to the end of the semester I would let Hunter know that I was not available for the second semester. He allowed this approach. And thus, a major financial burden was lifted. However, we still had significant credit card debts so I did not let Cornell know that I had agreed to design and teach a chemistry of materials course at the New York Fashion Institute of Technology in the Spring Semester, because this was a night course.

I joined a study group with Walid Michelen and Ron Johnson and began to learn quite a lot from them. Jan Clarke was also a good source of help on how to do multiple choice examinations, which I had only experienced once while a Freshman at Lehigh University. I also suggested to my classmates that we needed to find a way of getting old exams which we could use to prepare for our upcoming examinations. Somehow, they managed, on occasion, to get a copy of an examination from a previous year which benefitted us significantly. The importance of studying in groups and getting previous examinations was a lesson I had learned in my quantum mechanics course with Prof. Hoffmann. The rest of the second semester of first year was relatively uneventful until at the very end when I was summoned by the Dean, who told me that I had to meet daily with one of the professors during the summer to review microbiology.

I went to see Dr. Meikle, who had taught Neuroscience and told him I could not believe what I was told.

He said, simply, "You did not do well in the Neuroscience final."

I was dumbfounded. I said, "that is not possible. I want to see my final, because you posted the answers to the final and there is no way that I did not do really well on that final."

"Unfortunately, it is not allowed for me to show you or any student his or her final examination."

The tears began to roll down my cheeks. What he could not know is that I had had a similar experience in one of my Physical Chemistry finals at Lehigh University. I also thought, 'If I did poorly in Neuroscience, why the hell do I have to study Microbiology in the Summer? That makes absolutely no sense.'

Instinctively and with emphasis, I said, "I would like to take another final right here and now!"

He then looked at me curiously and said, "It is amazing how rational you remain even though quite emotionally upset. Unfortunately, I can't give you another exam."

Feeling absolutely defeated. I left his office and went to see the professor with whom I was to do the Microbiology sessions in the summer. I had received a summer lab position with Dr. Anthony Cerami at Rockefeller University to develop an HPLC method, and I needed to know whether I could still accept this summer position. He told me that I needed to spend 2 hours a day reviewing microbiology materials, at the end of which he would quiz me on the material I had reviewed. I was relieved because developing the HPLC method was an important challenge which I thought I could solve.

After a few sessions the professor said, "Look, this is really about adjusting your attitude and it is wasting my time. If you agree to come here at the appointed time and study microbiology, without my being present, I will give you occasional quizzes and will sign off at the end of the summer that the objective was achieved."

We continued in this fashion until I received the sad and very disturbing news that my mother had suffered a massive stroke. I immediately feared that given the state of medicine in Guyana, she might not recover. I was devastated. Earlier that month, my cousin Joan had called me to tell me that Sister Edith, her mother, who had ovarian cancer, was not doing well and asked whether I could to go home to Guyana to check on her. As I could not go because of my Microbiology sessions, I asked Lynnet to go and take Nataki, who was two years old, with her. About six days after Lynnet arrived she called to tell me that she had found my mother standing under the shower, motionless. My mother was taken to PHG (Public Hospital in Georgetown). I told the professor what had happened and immediately flew to Guyana.

My mother was lying on a bed in an open ward with an IV in her arm. She was motionless and the nurse told me that she was comatose when she arrived at the hospital and had remained in that state. I sat beside her bed with the overpowering scent of the cleaning agents used to wash the floors and other areas in order to attain some level of aseptic conditions in the ward. The overpowering scent came from the liberal use of iodine and Lysol, two chemical agents with which I always associated PHG. After an hour of sitting in silence I feared that there was nothing that could be done, nor should be done, given that it was PHG and much could go wrong. I decided to go and check on my aunt, Sister Edith.

The ride to Norton Street where she lived in a comfortable house was filled with many unpleasant memories. Memories of the way she insisted on Joan having a special status among the rest of us primarily because she was 'brown skinned', that is, of lighter complexion than the rest of us. She was the 'Queen Bee' amongst us. Joan was two years ahead of me when I entered Cambridge Academy. One year later I would have been taking the College of Preceptors examination at the same time as she, so Sister Edith took her out of school and hired a private tutor to prepare her for the examination. I have no idea how she performed. It was a secret. The most amazing episode of this preferential attitude towards Joan occurred when I learned that I had gotten the Fulbright Scholarship. Sister Edith insisted that I should give the scholarship to Joan, since she was older than me. I explained to her that that could not be done. Nonetheless she persisted. Fortunately, I was independent enough and could just ignore her, although I was thinking that the unmitigated gall of this woman knew no bounds.

I arrived at the Norton Street home and went upstairs to her room. She was lying in bed and seemed to be in severe pain. I pulled up a chair and sat beside the bed. She reached and held my hand in her limp hands and tried to smile.

She squeezed my hand and said, "I am glad that you have come. I don't know how long I have but I want you to stay here with me."

I let out an audible sigh, a sigh more of sympathy than sorrow, as I said, "My medical school classes start in a few days, so I have to head back. I can't even stay with mommy."

In typical fashion she insisted, "You have to stay with me."

A long silence followed as I sat there with my hand in her feeble grasp. Then slowly she said, "I was not nice to you when you were growing up.

Forgive me."

"Sister Edith," I said, "I forgave you a long time ago."

After a couple more minutes of silence, I removed my hand and placed hers on the bed. "I will be back at Semester break."

I rose and stroked her cheek as she said, "Promise?"
"Promise."

On my return to Cornell I went to Assistant Dean Kline to let her know that I had returned. She then told me that she was told that I had concocted a story about my mother being sick and had gone to Guyana in order to escape completing my Summer assignment. I asked for a sheet of paper and wrote down the telephone number for PHG and the name of the Doctor in charge of the ward. I gave it to her and said, "Dean you are free to call the Public Hospital in Georgetown and I actually would appreciate any help you can give her doctor."

The second-year courses were quite exhilarating. Like Physiology and Neuroscience in the first year, the second-year courses required less brute force memorization and more understanding of principles. Interestingly, I had worked out a system to help me remember the pathology of various organs. I worked on the geography or physical location of the organ, its vasculature, the nerves associated with it, its functions and the parts of the body that are involved in those functions. It then became easier to know what gross pathology would look like and what areas and cells to look for under the microscope to identify the microscopic characteristics of the pathology of that organ.

Simultaneously, I began to observe white students who were having difficulties, but whose academic challenges did not hamper their advancement each year. I also learned that some of the best performing male students felt that some female students were getting better grades than they deserved. On learning this, I approached Vinnie, one of the top students in our class, and suggested that they push for anonymous grading. They did achieve this in the second semester, and the result was astounding. Not a single Black student failed. Carol Storey, a black student got three Honors and I got two Honors out of the four subjects!

I had joined the Student National Medical Association (SNMA) and discovered that Black students in other medical schools in NYC were experiencing similar problems with respect to their academic advancement. I decided to attend the SNMA convention and run for President of the Association. I felt that as President of SNMA I could bring minority students together to address common problems and effect changes that would improve the conditions for minority students in medical schools.

Walid was my campaign manager and we decided that our strategy would be for me to stay out of sight as my colleagues distributed my one-page Program and Rationale for seeking this leadership position. This plan was successful. I was voted president-elect of the SNMA in the Spring of 1975. On my return to Cornell from New Orleans, where the conference was held, I was summoned to see Dr. Ellis, the Chairman of Pathology.

As soon as I walked into his office, he arose from his desk and said angrily, "I hear that you went to the SNMA convention in New Orleans and besmirched Cornell's name all over the globe."

"Dr. Ellis", I said, quite surprised, "That is absolutely not true. In fact, I would be happy to give you a copy of the speech that I made prior to the voting for the position of President-Elect."

He made no response, so I continued, "I feel that some of my black class mates are being treated unfairly. I know of at least one white student who failed pathology and he is **not** being made to repeat the year."

He was surprised that I was aware of this and said; "As a matter of fact we are very concerned about this student."

"It would be nice if Black students received the same type of concern that you have for white students." I countered.

I also invited Dr. James Curtis, the Dean for Minority students, to an SNMA meeting to discuss how minority students were being treated. He made an apology for the administration and then made an assertion that I knew could not possibly be true. I then started asking him questions about his assertion and as he continued to defend it, I continued to attack his inconsistencies. Suddenly, he looked at his watch and said he had to leave. The meeting broke up and I noted that none of the other students looked at me as they hurried out of the room.

Finally, Sam Hunter came over to me, "You need to know that when you have an animal cornered, you need to step back and allow that animal to escape," he said. Sam was in the first year and like me had earned a Ph.D. before enrolling in medical school. I felt that my perception that he had been avoiding me was probably accurate. I thanked him for his advice and asked him directly whether he was avoiding me, since we lived in the same building. He told me that he was advised by the administration not to associate with me. I thanked him again for his advice and letting me know that my suspicions about his avoiding me were correct.

Although I had done extremely well in the second semester and had passed Step 1 of the National Medical Board Exam, I was told that I could not start my third-year clerkships and that I would have to repeat the first Semester of the second year.

I was devastated.

I decided to offer an alternative to repeating the first semester of the second year. I explored doing an elective at another medical school in the Washington, DC area, as this would allow me to work in the SNMA office before starting my presidency. I was lucky and got a spot in a medicine clinic connected with The Johns Hopkins Hospital. My assumption that they would not turn down my going to a Hopkins clinic was accurate. I had assumed that what was important to them was not permitting me to move forward with the rest of my class as that would be a visible punishment. There was nothing that I could do to prevent the delay in advancement to the third year Clerkships. I simply wanted to avoid the personal humiliation of having to repeat a semester that I had not failed. We agreed that I would be allowed to move on to third year Clerkships, after successful completion of the elective at Hopkins and repeating the Pharmacology exam when I returned.

The 3-month elective in the clinic run by Dr. Ira Morris at The Johns Hopkins was most exhilarating. Each morning Ira and the fellow would review the scheduled patients and identify the patients I would see. This often gave me time to review the charts and read about the respective medical problem before seeing the patients. I would review my examination of the patient and course of action with the fellow before implementing any treatments or instructions. I never made it to the SNMA office in DC during those three months. At the end of the elective Dr. Morris asked me where I was planning to apply to match for Residency. When I told him that I had not yet done my third-year clinical clerkships, he was shocked. He told me that completion of third-year clinical clerkships was a prerequisite for his elective. He then told me that I should apply for a sub-internship or other fourth year elective at Hopkins at the end of my third year.

I returned to Cornell with a real sense of achievement and confidence. I went to the Pharmacology department to take my exam. I was quite nervous because I was afraid that there would be another barrier at the end of this one. At the completion of the exam Dr. Riker told me that they would have the results in an hour. It was three hours of multiple choice. When I returned to his office, he asked, "What was going on with you during this exam?"

"Why do you ask?" I responded, beginning to fear the worse.

"You answered the first five multiple choice questions incorrectly. After that you did extremely well."

"I was really nervous", I confessed. "I was afraid that regardless of what I scored I would not be allowed to join the Third Year Class."

In a very kind tone, he said, "I don't think you need to worry about that." The next day I got the good news that I could join the group assigned to surgery and that I would spend the first six weeks at North Shore Hospital. Now I knew that I had probably faced the last hurdle to getting my Medical Degree. The amount learned during the six weeks of Surgery Clerkship at North Shore Hospital was enormous and demanded long days and nights. These long days and nights were a mixture of reading about the upcoming surgical procedures and the medical issues involved; post operation management of the patients assigned; practicing how to tie knots; holding retractors during surgery; and, finally, helping to 'close' the surgical wound at the conclusion of the operation. Probably because it was a satellite hospital to the New York Hospital, students got more opportunities to observe surgeries and manage patients pre- and post-op. We spent a lot of time holding retractors during operations, helping 'close' the incisions and worked closely with the residents in post-op care of the patients.

Two experiences are imprinted in my memory. One was having to stay up all night and call the resident at the first sign that the patient, who had received one of the early cardiac multiple bypasses, had begun to urinate. The resident told me to page him as soon as I saw 'that gold liquid' appear in the catheter bag. The 'gold liquid' appeared about midnight, several hours after he was brought to the unit and a happy resident busied himself checking other signs and drawing blood for laboratory tests.

The second memorable event occurred during a review of patients when the attending physician asked the resident, who had presented the patient, what was Courvoisier's sign. The tired resident could not remember and gave an incorrect answer. He then turned to one of my classmates, who did not know what it was. Then he called on me. I remember feeling uncomfortable because I knew what it was and it would embarrass the resident that a student knew the answer.

But I answered: "It is the ability, on palpation, to feel a large gallbladder jutting beyond the edge of the liver. It usually means that the swollen gallbladder is not due to the presence of gallstones." That was the correct answer.

There were also a few humorous moments during this intense rotation. The chief resident liked to have my help in the OR when he was in charge of the surgery. During one surgery, the nurse who passed a large needle to him jammed it into his outstretched palm. I was sure that he was going to explode in anger over what I thought was incompetence. But he said nothing. He stepped out of the OR, removed his gloves, washed his hands and had a nurse pull a new set of gloves over his hands, and returned to operating. Later I asked the chief resident why he had not reacted angrily. I had heard that he was very intolerant of careless errors in the OR. He smiled. "It is personal," he said with a shrug. "I am having an affair with her and she is mad at me."

Another somewhat light-hearted moment occurred as I was at the nursing station writing my notes in the charts of the patients that were assigned to me. Dr. Jean Paul P., a senior resident at that time and well respected by all, came to the nursing station and asked for one of the nurses who was taking care of one of his patients. She was not at the nursing station. Shortly thereafter, she returned to the nursing station and one of her colleagues told her that Jean Paul was looking for her.

"Do you know what he wanted?" she asked.

"I am not sure but he wanted something from you," the colleague replied. "Jean Paul can have anything he wants. All he has to do is ask," she said, somewhat wistfully. Several of the nurses grinned probably because Jean Paul was not only well respected as a surgical resident but was courteous and quite handsome.

The remaining six weeks of surgery and all other clerkships were done at the New York Hospital. By the end of six weeks of the Pediatrics rotation I knew that I could not be a pediatrician. The evidences of child abuse and neglect among so many of these children disturbed me greatly. I felt that I would be working more with the police and social workers than with the kids.

The Clerkship in Obstetrics and Gynecology was a fascinating mixture of the practice of surgery and medicine, focused on the female reproductive organs. My joy of having had the opportunity to deliver six babies was accompanied by the observation of how differently women reacted to the pain of child birth. The labor period of one of these deliveries stands out among them. A young black girl was admitted in labor. She was the most stoic patient in labor that I have ever seen. She lay in her bed, never asked a question, never complained, and only asked occasionally for a sip of water. At the same time her mother, who was well dressed, middle aged, with a rather strict demeanor, frequently berated her daughter for having gotten pregnant and for having loose morals. I got the distinct impression that the mother felt that the pregnancy was God's way of punishing her daughter.

Another notable episode occurred during examination of a patient, who thought that she might be pregnant. She was in her thirties, white and wore an expensive looking diamond bracelet and diamond ring. As I took the brief history, she told me that her husband was a pilot and traveled quite a lot, which made her feel very lonely. I reported my brief history to the attending and he then told me to do a full physical, including a gynecological examination, as this was her first visit. The physical examination was uneventful until I came to the gynecological examination. The nurse positioned and draped her with knees up and thighs apart as I donned a pair of latex gloves. I stood in front of her as she lay on her back draped, prepared for the examination. I explained that I was first going to examine her vagina after which I would do an internal examination to assess the size of her uterus and whether there were any areas of tenderness. She then asked if I could do it without gloves. I told her that although I had washed my hands thoroughly, as she had witnessed, before I had donned the gloves, the gloves were an additional precautionary measure. I enquired whether she had a sensitivity to latex and she said that she did not. I initiated the internal examination. It was quite brief and I told her that I would now withdraw my fingers as the exam was over. To my surprise she bore down on my fingers and started moving her hips. I kept a straight face placed a little more pressure on her abdomen and calmly said, "You can relax now. It is over."

After extricating my fingers, I removed my gloves, placed them carefully in the disposal bin, and washed the latex powder from my hands. I told her that I will report my findings to the attending physician, who would probably repeat parts of the examination to be sure that I had not overlooked anything. As I was leaving the room, she asked whether I would continue to be her assistant doctor. I told her that decision is made by the attending physician. I left the room, somewhat shaken, as I wondered whether this woman was trying to set me up and complain that I had done something inappropriate during the internal examination. My concern was immediately relieved when the white nurse, who was in the room, came to me and said, "You handled that really well." Fortunately, I never saw this patient again.

The other two rotations of note were psychiatry and medicine. Psychiatry was interesting but exhausting. In fact, although my days ended at about 6 pm I was always exhausted when I arrived at my apartment, which was only two blocks distant from the Payne Whitney Psychiatric Clinic. Dr. Stokes, the Director of Payne Whitney clinic welcomed me personally and offered the opportunity, if I so desired, to do lab work with one of his junior faculty. The Attending for the rotation, who had sat in on a few of my interviews of patients told me that I had an unusual ability to get patients to open up and I also had an obvious empathy with patients. One memorable event near the end of the rotation was with the psychologist with whom we met weekly for instruction on psychology theory. He asked about our post graduation plans. One of my classmates mentioned that he was taking a year off and he and his girlfriend were going to travel across Europe. Some of us expressed surprise that he had decided to delay Residency. "The trouble with you students is that you delay life. You work hard in undergraduate college to get into the best medical schools. Then you work hard in medical school to get the best Residency, and then the best Fellowship and finally the best position in academic medicine or with the best practice group," the psychologist said, unapprovingly. "And finally, when you are about 45 with 1-2 kids you and your wife decide to have that postponed honeymoon to Venice. And guess what happens. You get there. The Gondolas are the same, the moonlight is the same, the gondolier sings with the same romantic voice and you and your wife only notice the garbage and stench in the canals. Your classmate and his girlfriend will enjoy the romantic setting and never smell the stench of the canals."

This description made an impression on us because it rang true.

Medicine was exhilarating. It was what I loved: trying to ask the right questions, the answers to which, in the case of medicine, led immediately or in a short time frame, to the improvement of the health and well-being of another human. One thing I discovered was that whereas Vinnie D. and others could give about 8-10 conditions in the differential diagnosis, they often struggled with the question: the patient is in the Emergency Room, which diagnosis will you choose as your first choice? I, on the other hand, could only give 3-4 conditions in the differential diagnosis, and they were invariably the most relevant ones for the particular patient.

The final examination was very challenging. We reported to a room where we were given a 3x5 card with the location of a patient. We were given two hours to do a history and physical, make our notes, and return to the room to present the patient. At the end of the presentation of the history and physical, we were asked to specify the lab tests we would like and in what order.

During the history I found that the patient was a pleasant middle aged white woman with a positive history of severe rheumatic fever in her teens and 'heart problems'. During the physical examination, I paid keen attention to the border of the left ventricle and listened for mitral and aortic murmurs. And there were Rales in her lungs. I was fairly confident that she had rheumatic heart disease so in the oral examination I asked first for an x-ray (these days I would have asked for an ECHO). I identified global cardiomegaly, an increased left atrium and evidence of heart failure. I then asked for the EKG, which showed left axis deviation (LAD) and occasional PVCs. Finally, I asked for biochemistry labs to see BUN, serum creatinine and LFTs. At the end of which I told them that my diagnosis was Rheumatic Heart Disease. There were smiles from the three examiners and I was dismissed. Later that afternoon I happened to run into one of the examiners on the exam team and she briefly complimented me for a job well done.

Now I was ready for a fourth-year elective at Hopkins and I secured a spot on the endocrinology service. This was great because the two other students on the elective were Hopkins fourth year medical students and I could compare my performance and knowledge with theirs. They turned out to be very strong students, which was good for me.

As with my experience at Dr. Morris' clinic, I read deeply on every patient we saw and responded as precisely as I could, when I was asked to give a brief history, physical findings and discussion of diagnostic possibilities. Two days before the end of the elective the Residency Director called me into his office and asked very simply, "Where are you planning to match?"

I said, "I have not yet decided, but certainly Cornell and Hopkins would be high on my list."

"We are quite impressed with your work and we would like to have you at Hopkins. I can assure you that if you rank Hopkins No. 1 you will match at Hopkins."

"I have really enjoyed my experience here. I have learned a lot in this month and would be honored to be a Resident in Medicine at the Johns Hopkins." I told him.

He shook my hands and said, "We look forward to seeing you here."

On my return to Cornell, I was called to see Dean Kline. I was quite puzzled by the request to see her and began to wonder if another graduation inhibiting issue had raised its ugly head.

I entered her office somewhat hesitantly. Actually, I never had a reason to believe that Dean Kline was less than forthright.

"Come in Frank", she said. "What happened at Hopkins?"

My heart sank. I began to fear that perhaps something negative might have occurred after my meeting with the Residency Director. So, I asked simply, "Was there a problem?"

She said, "No. But they called us and it seems that they want you to do your Residency at Hopkins. We want you to do your Residency at the New York Hospital with us. So, if you rank New York Hospital No.1 you will match with us."

"Dean," I said. "That is really good news. I will do that."

She shook my hand and as I left, I felt terrible because I had purposely given an answer that was ambiguous, but was meant to sound as an affirmative response to her final statement.

I ranked Hopkins No. 1 and I matched at Hopkins. One interesting note about this match process was the Dean's letter. I was unsure who would write me a strong letter for the signature of the Dean. This was solved when I got a call from Dr. Walter Riker. I went to his office and he said, "I do not want you to worry about anything. I will draft your letter for the Dean's signature."

I thanked him and said, "Dr. Riker, this is very kind of you."

We were permitted to read our letter in the Dean's office. It was a very strong letter and of note was one contribution from the Psychiatry department which read, "Unfortunately, he has decided to go into internal medicine. We think that he is a loss to psychiatry." As I read that I recalled the advice that I had gotten from Dr. Myron Tribus, SVP at Xerox, when I told him that I had decided to go to medical school. After repeating that he had hoped that I would have stayed at Xerox and worked for him, he said, "I have one bit of advice for you. Never go into Psychiatry." I knew nothing about the discipline of psychiatry, so I asked simply, "Why?" "Well because the problem is not the rest of the world. You are the problem."

I found that statement odd and troubling. Did he just accuse me of something that made a lie of all the positive things that he had said before?

He continued. "You are the problem, because when others see the issue, you see the issue, the consequences and the unexpected complications. Psychiatry will ruin you emotionally."

As I reflected on this, I realized that what he had said contained the reason why I was exhausted at the end of every day during my Psychiatry rotation.

In March of 1976 I was inaugurated as national President of the SNMA. This was a notable event because Presidential Candidate Gov. Jimmy Carter presented his healthcare plan for the nation at my inauguration. This was an auspicious occasion and a significant honor. Gov. Carter had hoped for an endorsement from SNMA. I told his staff that I could give a personal endorsement but could not commit the entire association without approval of the executive committee. His staff did not push the issue. (Gov. Carter went on to become the 39th President of the United States of America).

During 1976-1977, Silas Norman, Chairman of the Board of SNMA, and I spent significant time trying to raise scholarships for minority students. Our first stop was to the Ford Foundation, where one of the Vice Presidents, Mr. Thomas, was Black. The Foundation had been very supportive of minority medical students. The meeting was cordial and brief. They said that they had supported many students who were now in practice. They would like to see the National Medical Association (NMA) step up and support students. They would renew their support if this occurred.

Thus, our next visit was to the executive committee of the National Medical Association (NMA). It was the day before the NMA Convention, so we were able to get a meeting with the NMA Executive Committee. Silas and I each introduced ourselves and our academic backgrounds. I took the lead after that and said, "Thank you again for seeing us during these busy few days. I would like to come directly to the reason for our visit."

"Go on", said one of the members.

"As you know, for several years the Ford Foundation has provided scholarships for minority medical students. They are threatening to terminate or reduce this support."

"Why is that?" asked another member of the NMA Exec. Committee.

Silas responded, "They said they would continue the scholarships when minority physicians, many of whom are doing quite well financially, begin to provide scholarships for these students."

Without discussion among themselves, without a pause, the Chairman of the meeting said, "that is not going to happen. We worked hard for what we got, and you guys will have to do the same."

I was so surprised that I said immediately, "This is about your sons and daughters."

They indicated that the meeting was over.

Needless to say, I immediately decided never to become a member of the NMA, which I dubbed the 'Not with My Assistance' organization. I have never joined the National Medical Association.

I also visited a few chapters on the East Coast and learned more about problems similar to those at Cornell. I began to research the performance of white students in medical school. This turned out to be quite easy because each year JAMA published an issue on medical schools. These issues included data on enrollment, graduation rates at 4 years, 5 years and 6 years. I looked at years prior to 1970, when there were rather few blacks in predominant white medical schools. I was amazed to find that there were students who did not graduate in four years and a small percentage actually took 6 years to graduate. I wrote a letter to JAMA with these findings and questioned whether there was a concerted effort to stigmatize minority students by having them repeat the first year, thus ensuring that they now comprised the students taking more than four years to complete the MD.

They totally ignored my letter. I did publish a more detailed report of this JAMA analysis in the Black Bag, the journal of the SNMA. However, I do think that my concern was recognized in the Report of the Association of American Medical Colleges Task Force on Minority Student Opportunities in Medicine, headed by Paul R. Elliott Ph.D. Chairman, June 1978. I was a member of the Task Force.

The Report carefully stated, "Retention rates for minority medical students in 1968– 72 are about what they were for white medical students a relative few years ago. As medical school becomes a more common and natural experience for carefully selected minority students it is probable that their retention rates will be even more similar to that of white students." For the years 1971-1974 the three-year retention rates for Black medical students was about 86% compared to 96% for all medical students. These numbers clearly suggest that with the enrollment of Black students, the failure rate of white students had decreased. This could only have occurred if advancement decisions were not made solely on numerical performance on the courses.

Prior to graduation I did a one-month sub internship at the Memorial Sloan Kettering Cancer Center. This was absolutely the experience I needed before starting my Internship and Residency at Hopkins. In a sub internship one acts as a full intern but has a lighter load of patients. Sloan Kettering is a research-based cancer center and many of the patients were referred by other physicians for advanced therapeutic interventions. Thus, these patients are often quite ill or have advanced disease. This was a tremendous experience of examining patients; following their physical and laboratory values closely; treating any infection aggressively because these patients are often immune compromised; paying attention to every detail and knowing when to request advice from the fellows or attending physician was paramount. It was again another very supportive teaching environment.

Finally, graduation time came and I was called to see the Dean. Dean Kline, who was quite supportive of students, told me that she was disappointed that I had elected to go to The Johns Hopkins Hospital instead of staying at The New York Hospital for Residency. However, she had good news for me. I had been selected to receive the Prize for the student who had showed the greatest improvement over four years. I thanked her but told her I could not and would not accept it because it would suggest to others that I was in agreement that my performance was poor in my first two years. She reflected for a moment and then said, "You are correct. In fact, we really should not give such an award to anyone." A couple of days after graduation I encountered Dr. Meikle. He stopped and congratulated me for having the fortitude to stick to my principles.

While dealing with the challenges of medical school, I had a final interaction with the Comrade Leader, the President of Guyana, in July, 1975. I had returned to Guyana to see my mother, who after lying in a coma for several weeks, had made an amazing recovery from what was apparently a significant hypertensive hemorrhagic stroke.

Her speech was still affected and she was weak on her right side, requiring the aid of a walking stick to ambulate. I also noted her ability to estimate measurements was markedly impaired. This was a major problem for her because she was a seamstress. Before making this trip, I was approached by Dr. George Reader, Head of the Department of Public Health, who wanted to establish a fourth-year elective in Guyana. I asked him whether he would also be willing to develop a training program for practical nurses to help relieve the nursing shortage in Guyana. He agreed and gave me a detailed proposal to submit to Guyana. As was my custom, I sent the proposal to Mr. Saul, the Guyana Counsel General in New York City, since I knew that he would forward it directly to the Comrade Leader.

I arrived in Guyana about 1 pm and visited my mother. Without unpacking I told her I wanted to go to the offices in Brickdam to see Walter Rodney before the end of the business day. Walter Rodney was one year ahead of me at Queens College, was a Guyana Scholar, and had returned to Guyana from his studies in England with the announced purpose of opposing the Comrade Leader. With this announcement his activities and movement within Guyana became very constrained and I and others would arrange for him to deliver lectures in the US in order, periodically, to get him out of Guyana. No sooner had I arrived at Walter's office than a messenger appeared at his office and told me that the Comrade Leader wanted to see me immediately. I told him I would like first to go back to my mother's place and change my clothes. He said that the Comrade Leader had instructed him to bring me by car to his office immediately. So, I bade Walter goodbye with a promise that I would return the following day. That was the last time I saw Walter.

We arrived at the office of the Comrade Leader. He was sitting behind his large imperial desk and he invited me to sit in the chair opposite him, on the other side of his desk. He went directly to his point. He said, "Comrade, I have a job for you. I want you to go into the interior and run a Leather factory for me."

I said, "Thank you, Comrade Leader. As you know I am now a second year medical student at Cornell and in fact, Dr. Reader sent a proposal that would help train practical nurses and have advanced medical students come to Guyana and work in PHG clinics."

He said, "Yes. I received that proposal and I have given it to a nurse to evaluate it."

I said, "Comrade Leader, Cornell is quite eager to do this and will cover all of the costs."

He leaned forward in a threatening manner and said, "Comrade, you have this uncanny habit of telling me how to run my country."

I countered with, "On the contrary, Comrade Leader, I am trying to find how best I can serve the country."

At which point he said, "Comrade, here is my advice. I want you to leave this country right now and not return before I die."

I thought of replying, 'Certainly Comrade Leader, but you will die before I do.' However, luckily, before I could make my response, I heard a click behind me. I turned around in the chair and saw a Guyana Defense Guard with drawn gun pointed at me. So, I replied, "As you know Comrade Leader, I need an Exit permit and the first plane back to New York leaves tomorrow morning."

He said, "All is arranged. You will fly to Trinidad this evening and back to the US in the morning."

I was taken back to my mother's home where I gave my puzzled mother a kiss and hasty goodbye. I was taken to Atkinson Field Airport and boarded a plane to Port of Spain, Trinidad, from which I departed for JFK Airport, New York, the following day.

Six months later Walter Rodney was assassinated via an explosive device that was placed under his car. About three months after I had returned home, I had a visit from a former Queens College classmate, named Armstrong. We were mere acquaintances during school, so I was surprised when he called and asked to visit me. I welcomed him and as we shook hands I saw the revolver in his belt.

I offered him a seat close to the door of the apartment, thinking that if it came to a struggle I might be able to push him out of the apartment. He came directly to the point.

"You know, comrade, some of us are very unhappy with the direction that Comrade Leader is taking the country and we are developing a resistance effort against him. We would like you to join us."

I refrained from asking, "and who is WE?" I said, "I have been away from Guyana over 12 years and have no basis to oppose anyone. In fact, my stay in America carries with it the condition that I not meddle in Guyana's politics."

He rose from the chair and said, "Too bad. We were hoping that you could help us." And without another word, he left.

I shared this strange visit with Aubrey, who had recently returned from Guyana. He told me to be careful because the Comrade Leader was very angry with me. Aubrey stated that he was at a meeting where the Comrade Leader angrily talked about this comrade who studied Chemistry of Chlorophyll and refused to return home to help him. A couple of weeks later, Aubrey called me to tell me that Armstrong was working for the Comrade Leader. For several months thereafter, I would write to Comrade Ackman, a very close friend of our family, who was very close to the Comrade Leader, and each time she advised me to stay away from Guyana as the Comrade Leader was still very angry with me. So, I stayed away from Guyana and its politics, even after the passing of the Comrade Leader in 1985.

The Johns Hopkins and NIH

I hired a moving company to pack and move us to Baltimore. I had vowed never to move myself again after the adventure of moving from Rochester to NYC for Medical school. I had rented a 24ft U-Haul truck, got a couple of friends to help me pack, hitched the car to the truck and decided to leave at midnight because I had never driven a truck before. Everything went well until we had driven a few miles on the Palisades Parkway when the car began to come loose from the tow dolly. I quickly pulled over to the side of the road, unhitched and parked the car and continued onto the new apartment in Manhattan. We entered Harlem River Drive and the FDR Drive and took the E. 96th St. exit to get to our apartment at 423 E.69th St. It was Monday morning and cars were parked on both sides of E. 69th street so there was no way we could unload.

I continued out onto New York Avenue and back onto FDR drive on my way to Brooklyn, accompanied by vigorously honking cars. Finally, I saw the sign. 'No Commercial traffic allowed.' Well too bad, I thought, I will probably be pulled over and get a ticket. I was lucky and got to President street, Lynnet's father's home in Brooklyn, and parked the truck without being pulled over by the cops.

The following Sunday, my brother, Cheddie, who I discovered lived in Brooklyn, and two of his friends came into Manhattan and helped us move into the apartment. This was also fortunate, because our apartment was on the fifth floor of a five-floor walkup and after the first three trips with boxes it occurred to me that there had to be a better way of moving into this building.

The Livingston Farrand buildings were three apartment buildings in a row, the third of which had the only elevator. This elevator was used to transport furniture and other items to the fifth floor, then up a short flight of stairs to the roof and across the roof to the other buildings. Once we discovered this the rest of the move into our apartment at Cornell was easier.

This time, for the move to The Johns Hopkins Hospital in Baltimore, we hired a moving company to pack and ship everything. And they did ship everything! We were having breakfast when the packers arrived, and interrupted our meal for us to answer some questions from a member of the packing crew who was in a different room. When we returned to the dining room the dining table was clear. We checked the kitchen to see whether our breakfast was placed on the table there. It was not there. However, as we unpacked boxes in the house in Baltimore we found our plates of eggs and toast neatly packed with other dishes.

The house was at the end of a set of two storied row houses and had two presumably attractive selling points. The most important was that the lower level apartment was occupied by a tenant whose rent covered all but $5.00 of the monthly mortgage. The second selling point was that because Wyanoke Avenue was adjacent to the wealthy Guilford section, there was the potential that this area would be developed and thus the prices of these houses would increase significantly.

What I did not know was that in the alley behind the row of houses there was an open area where drug dealers met. Several neighbors in the street, however, were quite friendly. We became good friends with the Dawsons, a black family who lived three houses over from ours and Mrs. Dawson often served as babysitter for Nataki and later also for Diah. Sharon Hargrove, the tenant on the first floor, retained her apartment for many years and became a close family friend.

Orientation for new interns (Year 1 Residents) was held the day after we arrived in Baltimore. Three things have remained with me and became part of my work habits.

First, it was explained that Hopkins had perhaps the most demanding 'on call' system. It was 'Long, short, off'. **Long** meant that you would be in the hospital 24 hours and were responsible for all patients on the service during the night. **Short**, meant that you remained in the hospital until all of your own patients were stabilized and could be easily managed by the Intern on Long call. This often meant that you were in the hospital until about 8 pm on Short days. **Off** meant that you left the hospital about 5-6 pm if all your patients were stable. They explained that the purpose for this rigorous program was that after one year, if you were called to the E.R. to see a severely ill patient, you would, almost in a reflex manner, rapidly assess that patient and start therapeutic interventions to stabilize that patient until the patient could be transferred to the floor or intensive care unit, as needed.

The second principle was that the Intern was the Doctor of Record. This means that the Intern was totally responsible for the outcome of the patient. The Intern had at her/his disposal all the experts at Hopkins and could call any one for a consult. However, the Intern was responsible for determining if and how to implement the recommendations of the consulting experts.

Finally, the Esprit de Corps at Hopkins was that your fellow interns expected you to stay and manage your critical patients, or to return to the hospital to do so if your patient unexpectedly decompensated after you had left the hospital for the evening. It was about hard work, performing thorough patient assessments, diligent follow up of labs and patient progress, and assuming full responsibility for the outcome of the patient.

It was quite sobering to hear what was expected, particularly learning that we were the physicians responsible for the outcome of the patients in our care. Non-private patients were assigned to one of the Osler services or Firms.

I was assigned to Osler 6 Firm. This meant that any patient who was admitted to Osler 6 when I was on call became my 'private' patient. I took care of that patient on the ward and followed that patient in my clinic. On my first month, fortunately, I was assigned to the private service. I say fortunately, because the private patients were often not as sick as the general patients and were often referred from other institutions, so that they came with fairly good histories and record of previous treatment and outcomes. On my first night On Call, I could not sleep. I read and reread all of the charts. I asked the night nurses which patients they felt should be monitored frequently during the night. I let them know that they should feel free to call me if they had any concerns.

The night was uneventful, except for one female patient who had great trouble sleeping because she could not keep her legs still. No sleep medication was prescribed for her by the previous team so I decided not to do so. I did, however, check on her periodically and described her on rounds the next morning as having a sort of 'restless leg syndrome', whose etiology I did not know. The rest of the month was noteworthy for three events.

The first was a patient who was referred to Dr. Tumulty because of a dime sized defect on his lung x-ray. No previous x-rays were available for comparison to the one which led to his being referred. Dr. Tumulty mentioned the importance of having this comparison before doing any bronchoscopy and or attempts of needle biopsy, or worse, opening his chest to remove the 'tumor'. I had learned the importance of follow up and so I called his referring Physician and other physicians whom he had seen and was finally able to get a copy of an X-ray that was taken three years prior to his admission to Hopkins. The same defect was present and had not changed in size over the three years. That day I carried a secret glow inside of me that in my first two weeks at Hopkins I had assisted in the diagnostic evaluation of one of Dr. Tumulty's patients.

The second instance occurred when my colleague on the service, Dr. Liu, who had admitted a patient for chest pain, signed his patient out to me so he could take a brief lunch break. Shortly thereafter the nurse called me and told me that the patient was complaining of return of chest pain. I rushed to his room and saw a slightly obese, elderly white male lying on his back with obvious signs of distress on his face. I attached the leads of the EKG machine which revealed ST segment elevation in the V leads. I asked the nurse to page the resident, Dr. Mark Levine, because we needed to get the patient to the CCU stat. As I began to explain to the patient that he was having severe angina and probably a heart attack, he looked at me and said,

"I don't want any nigger doctor touching me!" I immediately thought, 'Wow. He is going to have an even bigger heart attack when he realizes that he did not only have a Black intern, and an Asian Intern, but he was going to have a Jewish Resident!' Mark and Liu arrived promptly and took over getting him to the CCU, where he recovered from his heart attack.

The third episode that month was with another private patient who had Munchhausen syndrome and who insisted that she did not want any interns taking care of her. She was assigned to me. Her attending physician ordered a lumbar puncture. I told her that I would be doing the procedure. She insisted that I could 'prep' her for it but she only wanted her Physician to perform the LP. I called her physician and he decided to perform the LP. After 2-3 tries he motioned to me to take over. I was actually very good at procedures and got in on the first try. This was another confidence builder that made me less apprehensive about my first month on Osler 6, the Firm to which I was assigned, and where I would be the physician responsible for the total care of 'my' patients.

During that first month I discovered that there were three first year Black interns at Hopkins: two in medicine and one in surgery. David Bush (dec.) and I, were the Black interns in medicine and Ben Carson was the intern in surgery. I also discovered there was the first Black Chief Resident in Cardiac Surgery, Dr. Levi Watkins (who went on to become a distinguished member of the Department of Cardiac Surgery at Hopkins).

I was also amazed at the availability of the attending physicians who literally would come to the bedside to discuss a patient and give the interns their recommendations. Everyone, including the attending physicians, worked extremely diligently. And never once was a distinction made based on ethnicity by the Hopkins Physicians and staff.

A major highlight of being an Osler Resident at Hopkins was what was called: 'Tumulty Rounds'. Residents would present one of their patients to Dr. Tumulty and he would then engage us in the differential diagnosis and the treatment options of that patient, sometimes even taking the group to the bedside for this didactic discussion. We interacted with world leaders who treated us as equals. The learning curve at Hopkins was intense, steep, and exhilarating. I felt I was in my element.

On my second month, I was assigned to the Osler 6 floor, my firm. The patients on the Osler floors were usually sicker than those on the private floors.

These patients were poorer and often healthcare was of lower priority, which led to their delaying medical attention until symptoms were severe. The nurses were excellent on all the floors but seemed to have more empathy for the Osler patients than I had expected. I inherited a few patients from the Osler 6 Resident who had completed his residency and every new patient who was admitted to the floor when I was on call became my patient and was thereafter followed in my clinic.

One of these admissions from the ER was a mildly obese white woman in her mid-forties. She was diabetic and had complained of chest pain, but her EKG in the ER was unremarkable and unchanged from previous admissions. Shortly after I had completed my examination and drawn a few tubes of blood, she complained of chest pain. I thought, 'What is this with me and chest pain in white patients in my care?' I jumped into action, got an EKG, and suggested to the CCU that it would be better to transfer her to them immediately where she could be monitored. They agreed and shortly after the transfer, her ST segments began to increase, so they began their intervention without delay.

I visited her every day until she was finally returned to my care on Osler 6 after she had been stabilized post a small myocardial infarction. Two weeks after discharge from the floor she came to my clinic for a follow-up assessment. When it was her turn to see me, she brought her male companion with her into the office. I gave him my chair.

She said, "This is my boyfriend, Greg. I would like you to be his doctor." I smiled and said, "Of course. I would be pleased to see him."

I looked at him and stretched out my hand to shake his. "I am Dr. Douglas.

Do you need a Doctor?"

He nodded affirmatively.

Then she said to me, "I guess they told you."

I said, "Yes. The nurses did tell me that you were not sure you wanted a Black Doctor to be examining you."

She apologized and I smiled and said, "I understand. I am sure that you had never encountered a Black doctor before. I am honored to take care of you and Greg."

She became one of my most compliant clinic patients.

The third month I was assigned to the CCU and the first thing our Resident told the team was that we were lucky because we were going to have Dr. Bernadine Bulkley as the Attending Physician. He told us that she had already become famous for having identified fibrous bands below the root of the aorta and extending to the mitral valve in patients with ankylosing spondylitis and aortic regurgitation. These were called 'Bulkley's Bumps'.

"She's a very attractive woman – and if you get out of hand with any off-color comments, believe me, she will rip your b.... out," our Resident warned us. Dr. Bulkley was one of the youngest physicians on staff and became the youngest woman to receive a full professorship at the Johns Hopkins Hospital. As I recall, at that time, there was probably only one other female professor at The Johns Hopkins Hospital, and that was Dr. Mary Betty Stevens, the world famous Rheumatologist.

Dr. Bulkley introduced herself to the team and started to lead the rounds on the patients. She listened to the presentation on each patient, asked a few questions and then commented on the pathophysiology of the condition and treatment. She was business-like, but pleasant. A couple of weeks later, I knew that I had made a good impression on her because she actually made a joke to the nurses, somewhat at my expense, when she told them that she was a few months younger than I. This was true. Thereafter, whenever I ran into her in the hospital, she would stop briefly and enquire about my family. She also introduced me to her husband, Greg, who at that time was a Chief Resident in Surgery at Hopkins.

The fourth month I was back on a private ward, this time Nelson 5. The month was relatively uneventful. I had gotten much more efficient and could actually spend more time at the bedside listening to the patients. Often, I would surprise them by commenting on the soap operas, the characters of many of which had not changed since I first came to America and had started watching Soap operas instead of attending my classes at Lehigh University.

There was one not so pleasant event while on Nelson 5. I had a patient who was admitted with pleural effusion and was suspected of having a lung tumor. Her attending physician had asked me to tap her chest and send off the fluid for diagnostic evaluation. I did the chest tap and sent the samples to the lab. Early, the following morning, I checked to see whether any results had returned. There were no reports. Shortly thereafter as we were rounding her attending physician joined us and asked, "How is my patient doing?"

"I did the chest tap yesterday and as yet no results are available. I will check again after rounds," I explained.

He raised his voice and said, "There are no results because you did not do the Chest tap!"

The Resident, the two other interns and the two students took a slight step back so that the Attending and I were directly facing each other.

"I called the lab and they said that they had received no samples from this floor." He said with angry emphasis.

I was puzzled and told him that I would check.

My resident was also puzzled. She said, "Frank, I know that you would never say that you had done the tap if it were not true."

I said, "Thank you, Martha. Would you mind observing me when I repeat the tap?"

"Of course, Frank."

We sent the samples off to the lab. Later that night I called the lab and again they claimed that they had not received the samples. My resident called the attending physician and told him what had happened and thus spared me another barrage of insults. I did a third tap two days later and the Resident took the samples herself to the lab. This time we got the results.

As the months went by, it occurred to me that I seemed to have been luckier than some of my fellow interns because I had almost no major crises during the night when I was on **long** call. On one of those on call nights as I was sitting at the

Nursing station, I said to the two nurses who were also in the station "You know, I have been really lucky in that I have had almost no crises during the night."

One of the nurses said, "Frank it is not luck. We have your back." I said, "Really. How so?"

She said, "It is simple. Whenever we call you, you listen. You ask our advice. You come immediately when we suggest you need to look at a patient and you don't treat us like we are just nurses."

The other nurse said, "And we can actually read your hand writing." "Thank you for that feedback. It is probably because, Lynnet, my wife is a nurse and I had heard her complain about the way some doctors treated nurses. As a result, I promised myself to learn as much as I could from nurses, and to print my notes."

My two most exhausting months in my first year were my month in the ER and my month on the Bone Marrow Transplant (BMT) service. It was March when I was assigned to the BMT service and I thought to myself, 'This will be a breeze. I am almost at the end of my first year. I should be able to do this even more efficiently and get home more nights when I am on short Call.' Well, Bone Marrow Transplant was an order of magnitude of medicine greater than I had experienced thus far. Fluid balance was a major challenge, not only from a view point of input versus output, but also ensuring appropriate electrolyte balances and understanding the differences in the body compartments during fluid and electrolyte shifts. Managing infections in neutropenic patients (patients with extremely low white blood cell counts. White blood cells are needed to fight bacteria and other infectious agents) was also another challenge. These were the early days of Bone Marrow Transplantation (1978) before cyclosporine and neupogen. It was the time when the parents waited hopefully to get our 9 am report on white cell counts and body temperature, each hoping that their child would not have another 'shake and bake' session from the amphotericin B, which was used to treat fungal infections.

Bone Marrow Transplant Service was physically and emotionally draining. I slept in my own bed at home only two nights that month. It also had other human aspects to it as families waited to discover whether potential family members would match and be bone marrow donors for the transplant. One particularly difficult case was a family from South America. There were four children and neither the father nor the other three children were compatible enough for a donor match. The Attending Physician discussed the difficulty with the team and decided to speak with the wife alone to determine whether this child was adopted. It turned out that the boy had a different father, which fact was not known to her husband. The Attending concluded that it was the wife's responsibility to discuss this with her husband and that we would only give the relevant information, which was there was no match among the family. I imagined how painful that conversation between this woman and her husband must have been and hoped that it did not ultimately lead to the dissolution of the family.

My most difficult shift in the Emergency Room was 8 pm to 8 am. The ER was always busy from 8 pm to midnight. Once patients were stabilized and either sent home; admitted to the floors or CCU; or were being held in the ER for observation; the last four hours, 4 am to 8 am were most difficult. Often, there was little activity in the ER during those hours. I struggled to stay awake when there was no activity and I was also too tired to read medical articles.

One morning I got into my car after my shift, headed up North Broadway to North Ave and awoke sometime later when the car bumped into a ditch on the other side of the intersection. Evidently, I had fallen asleep at the traffic light and the car had drifted through the intersection and into the ditch. I was incredibly lucky as I had absolutely no memory of anything after stopping at the traffic light and before being jolted to consciousness when I hit the ditch. Thereafter, I would sleep 3-4 hours in one of the On-Call rooms before driving home.

I also learned quite a lot in the ER. The first was that many of the Black patients were afraid to be admitted to the hospital. They were concerned that the Doctors would 'experiment' on them. As a result, as soon as they felt better in the ER they would refuse admission and leave. A second learning was that many patients were distrustful of the social worker, hence the accompanying problems associated with the illness were often not addressed. A final learning was that poor black patients with sickle cell anemia, who came to the ER in crisis, were often suspected of trying to get pain medication when it was not needed. I must admit that I found myself at times having this prejudice and waiting for Hgb values and neutrophil count before starting pain medication in these patients. It was always difficult to discern whether any particular patient was truly in pain or merely exhibiting narcotic drug-seeking behavior.

The Second year was less strenuous, with more time to read medical literature and learn more about the diseases with which patients presented. It was also a different role in which I learned how to quickly assess whether the intern had made an accurate decision with respect to which patients needed immediate and urgent intervention.

I also enjoyed teaching the medical students on rotation and because I had had excellent residents who had given me many opportunities to perform procedures, such as placing catheters in the subclavian veins and also inserting swan catheters, doing lumber punctures and tapping chests to extract pleural fluid, I could be equally helpful to interns and students by allowing them to learn these procedures.

In one case I was supervising a sub-intern on Osler 6 floor. He was doing his first lumbar puncture. His patient was positioned on her right side and he had prepared the area of her back well for the procedure. Then I noticed that he was sitting there motionless and sweating profusely. I tapped him on the shoulder motioned for him to step out of the room.

"What is the problem?" I asked.

He said, "I don't know. I am afraid I might do something wrong."

I told him to change his gloves, wash his face and get a fresh Lumbar Puncture kit. While he went off to do this I went to the patient and said, "Madam, please relax but remain on your side with your knees drawn up to your chest. You doctor will return momentarily."

When he returned I told him, "I want you to know that I would never let you do anything that would harm the patient."

He returned to the bedside, donned his fresh set of gloves, swabbed the L3-L4 area a second time, palpated the area to feel for the break between the two vertebrae, and with a careful but purposeful motion he placed the needle into the lumbar space and a drop of clear spinal fluid appeared at the end of the needle. He attached the syringe and withdrew a cc of spinal fluid.

I placed my hand on his shoulder and could sense his smile of pride.

At the end of the second-year I received a call from Dr. Victor McKussick, chief of medicine at the Johns Hopkins Hospital. He informed me he had gotten a phone call from the National Institutes of Health and they wanted me to join them as a Clinical Research Associate one year earlier than planned. I would spend the first year on the clinical services in hematology, pulmonary, cardiology and endocrinology after which I would join one of the labs.

I was so engaged in my residency at Hopkins that I had quite forgotten that I had received an NIH Pratt fellowship to do research in the lab of Dr. Juli Axelrod, a Nobel Laureate. The original plan was for me to go directly to Dr. Axelrod's lab after completing my M.D. at Cornell. However, on my visit to the NIH to discuss starting date and other details, Dr. Jack Orloff, the Director of the National Heart Lung and Blood Institute, advised me to do at least one year of residency before starting my fellowship at the NIH. Because of my experiences during my two rotations at Hopkins, I was quite open to this recommendation. Dr. McKussick assured me that he supported this course of action and that I would get full credit for my third year of Residency at Hopkins.

In June of 1979, I Joined five other Clinical Research Associates in NHLBI. My five other colleagues had completed their three years of residency in medicine and were very able and collaborative young physicians. Cardiology was the busiest service so usually two of us were responsible for managing the cardiology and pre-cardiac surgery patients. Patients were referred from all over the world to be evaluated or treated for various difficult cardiac problems, particularly valvular and septal defects. A major area of leadership in cardiac surgery at the NIH was the treatment of Idiopathic Hypertrophic Subaortic Stenosis (IHSS) in which condition asymmetric septal hypertrophy was a characteristic feature. Dr. A. G. Morrow, the cardiac surgeon and Dr. S. Epstein, the cardiologist were world leaders in this area. Thus, I had the opportunity to take care of patients with rare or very difficult cardiac pathologies.

In the midst of loads of hard work and dealing with patients with challenging disorders, two episodes occurred during my time on the cardiology service that still cause me to smile. One of my patients was a seven-year old girl from Greece who had a significant atrial septal defect. On my return to the floor after a day off one of the nurses told me that my little patient was quite upset that I was not there the day before and kept asking for the 'Chocolate Doctor'. Thereafter, I became Dr. Chocolate to some of the nurses.

The second chocolate episode occurred one night when I was on call.

One of the nurses asked me to go to the utility room, where there was a slight problem. Without asking the nature of the problem I accompanied her to the room, which was a few feet from where we were. There was a cake sitting on one of the trolleys. Cecile, the Head Nurse of this Cardiology floor and two other nurses were present. Cecile was the stereotypical British Charge Nurse and had been a former nun. She had a stern visage, was always serious and task oriented. It was my birthday and Cecile, on learning that I loved cheesecake, had made a cheesecake as a surprise birthday gift. As I stood there looking at the cheesecake, somewhat overcome by this gesture, one of them said, "Is there a problem, Frank? We thought you loved cheesecake."

I replied, "It looks wonderful. The problem is that it has two layers and the bottom is chocolate. I do not like chocolate."

Cecile burst into hilarious laughter and said in her strong English accent, "We must let everyone know that Dr. Douglas does not eat Chocolate bottoms."

We all enjoyed the play on words but were somewhat surprised by this mildly risqué comment and the laughter that came from Cecile.

Working on the other services was equally rewarding in getting the opportunity to take care of patients with unusual conditions. For example, on the endocrinology service, taking care of young patients with Familial Alphalipoprotein Deficiency, a rare inherited disorder that is characterized by severe HDL reduction was sometimes heart wrenching. One patient was a 14year old boy from Tangier Island, Virginia, where the condition was first discovered by Donald Fredrickson of the NIH, in 1961. At age 14, he had advanced atherosclerosis, and had already had a myocardial infarction. The only medicine that could reduce his serum cholesterol levels was niacin. However, this could only be taken at low doses because of severe flushing. As a result, he often refused to take the niacin. Unfortunately, at that time, the prognosis for these patients was poor as many organs in the body, notably the tonsils, spleen, nerves, liver, and heart could be affected by these yellow fatty deposits.

Another common condition seen on the Endocrine service was in anorexic young girls with hypokalemia, and severe secondary hyperaldosteronism that had been brought on by their self-induced purging or vomiting. Both conditions presented not only medical but also psychological challenges.

The medical effects of low potassium from the self-induced hyperaldosteronism could be life threatening.

At the end of this clinical year I went to Dr. Orloff to ask how to effect my transfer to Dr. Axelrod's lab to start the research portion of my fellowship. Dr. Orloff informed me that since I had done my clinical year in NHLBI I would need to find a lab in NHLBI for Research. I was assigned to Dr. Walt Lovenberg's Lab.

Walt was really more interested in my Chemistry background, while I had developed an interest in neuropeptides such as Substance P. I spent 3-4 months in in a lab in Walt's area, somewhat isolated from the rest of his group, and with an old HPLC instrument that I was trying to bring to life as I was sure that I could develop an HPLC assay to measure Substance

P. One day, Ms. Pat Hall from the Waters Corporation, who occasionally would stop by to entice me to purchase their HPLC system, asked a critical question.

"Do you think that you could develop an HPLC Assay to measure biogenic amines?"

At that time the assay required use of radioactive isotopes that only a few labs could perform. I said that I thought I could. She then said that she would loan me their system, complete with an automatic sampler and tray to do this.

This changed my life immediately. In short order, I was able to develop the assay, which I gave to her in return for the Waters HPLC system!

Shortly thereafter, I was in the glass shop in the basement of building 10 when I ran into Dr. Axelrod.

"Where have you been?" he asked, looking grumpily at me. "I've been waiting for you for more than a year."

I explained to Juli what had happened and he said that he would take care of it. One week later I was released to join Dr. Axelrod's group. Juli's group was in the National Institute of Mental Health, NIMH. Since I was interested in the role of neuropeptides in cardiovascular function this turned out to be a good solution for my fellowship in Neuroendocrinology. This spanned both NHLBI and NIMH. I arrived at Juli's Lab and he explained that he was semi-retired and had turned over running the group to three of his directors. Juli had two labs, in one of them he had his desk and the other was across the hall where a female technician had her desk. Juli then cleared off one of the benches in the lab where he had his desk and said, "This is your area. I want you to work with me."

I was thrilled and one of my 'Foggy feelings' descended on me. I could never explain these, but they seemed to occur whenever I had experienced something overwhelming, as for example, in my early days at Lehigh University, or my wine-induced Fog at my Ph.D. Candidacy oral examination.

As I left Juli's Lab, Mike Brownstein one of Juli's most prominent mentees, invited me to come into his lab for a chat. He told me that he had heard that I was interested in neuropeptides and that this was one of his areas of interest. In addition, Dr. Palkovits, the world's expert in mapping the brain histologically was also a member of his group, spending his time between his lab in Hungary and in Mike's Lab.

I am not sure why I made what was undoubtedly a life-changing decision, but all I could think of, was that I did not feel welcome by Walt Lovenberg's group and I did not want to end up in an uncomfortable position with Mike. So, I went back to Juli and asked his advice. Juli told me it was my decision. I was given lab bench space with two other of Mike's post docs, on the second floor, two floors away from Juli. Nonetheless, periodically, Juli would call me into his office to discuss my research. And every time, as I tried to give what I thought were scientifically thoughtful answers, Juli would say, "Frank, ask the simple questions: the answers are always very complex. So, if you start with complex questions, you will never see the trees."

One day, after one of these sessions, as I was leaving Juli's lab, his technician, who was a Black woman motioned to me. I entered her lab and she came directly to the point.

She said, "I have never met an idiot like you."

I was stunned. I took a step back, away from her and said, "What is that about?"

She continued with an angry tone, "People would give an arm and a leg to work with Juli. The man clears off his desk for you to work directly under his guidance and you decide to go and work for his mentee. I have never seen such stupidity."

I tried to explain. I said weakly, "Mike is working on Substance P, which is one of my interests and I do not want to get into an uncomfortable situation." I knew that she was correct. I had made a major error in judgment.

"What situation could you get into? Juli IS the Leader of this entire group." She shook her head slowly with obvious disgust and disbelief.

I have been asked, on occasion, whether there is anything that I had ever done that I regretted. And I have always answered, 'No, with one possible exception, and that was giving up the opportunity to work directly for Juli Axelrod.' The collaboration with Niki Palkovits was quite rewarding as Niki would supply dissected areas of the brain, such as the Substantia Nigra and I would assay them for neuropeptides, such as Substance P and Somatostatin. I also began to look for ProSubstance P peptide and had achieved its isolation. All that was left was to characterize its structure. Unfortunately, Mike was reviewing a paper which would have been published before my paper. Mike shared this information with me and said that it was my decision. I could submit a paper or consider that I had been 'scooped'. (In retrospect, I should have submitted a paper anyhow, because I did not know any of the details of the paper that Mike was reviewing.) The rest of the time in Mike's Lab was actually quite productive, but what I had not figured out was that in the biological sciences, one published as one was building the 'case', as compared to the physical sciences, where one published after the 'case' had substantially been made.

At the end of the second year in the Lab, Mike was considering moving to Harvard and invited me to join him in this move. Juli asked to see me and without explanation, said, "I want you to do me a favor. My Friend, Alfred Heller is the Chair of the Department of Pharmacology at the University of Chicago and I would like you to go there and give a seminar on your work." A one-day visit turned into a three-day visit in which I was recruited to join the department of Medicine and the Division of Clinical Pharmacology at the University of Chicago's Pritzker School of Medicine.

At about the same time, The Johns Hopkins Hospital offered me a similar position including being a member of the Hypertension Clinic. University of Chicago countered by adding the Directorship of their Hypertension Clinic. Hopkins had the additional benefit that it was close to the NIH and therefore I could continue my research in Mike's group until I was ready to transition it to labs at Hopkins. I discussed this with Juli, who said simply, "Al is a friend of mine and I would like you to go there."

I decided to go to the University of Chicago, not only because I felt that I could not disappoint Juli a second time, but because I also felt that I was ready to be a Director of an effort.

The time at the NIH was also significant for one other reason. Shortly after arriving at the NIH, Dr. Keiser discussed my joining the military. He explained that since I had chosen to be in research, I would have a better chance of getting government grants if I were a citizen. If I were to join the military, during my time at the NIH, I would be in the US Health Services branch, which is administered by the Navy. I would have the rank of Lieutenant Commander and it would be my choice whether I wanted to wear the naval uniform every day or work in civilian clothes. Were I to do this they would be able to facilitate my citizenship.

I joined the Public Health Branch of the US Health Services and received my military clearance with full privileges to use the Commissary and Health care coverage. Shortly thereafter I received the application for citizenship which I promptly completed and returned. As part of the anticipated interview to qualify for naturalization, I read the constitution and reviewed some of the key aspects of the history of the US. Of particular note was the oath to which I would have to swear in a Naturalization ceremony, to become a citizen. Parts of it said:

'I hereby declare, on oath, that I absolutely and entirely renounce and abjure all allegiance and fidelity to any foreign prince, potentate, state, or sovereignty, of whom or which I have heretofore been a subject or citizen; that I will support and defend the Constitution and laws of the United States of America against all enemies, foreign and domestic.'

Although I had for quite some time accepted the reality that the US was my home, and that Guyana was no longer 'home', finality of those sentences above, produced more of a nostalgia than a homesickness.

About a month later I had an appointment for an interview with a judge at the Immigration and Naturalization office in Baltimore. If I passed the interview I would be sworn in as a citizen in a ceremony that was occurring that day. I arrived at the Judge's office. She invited me to sit.

She was business like. I guess judges have to always project seriousness and detachment. She began immediately. "I must remind you that the requirement that you not meddle in Guyana's politics remains a condition for the success of your application to become a citizen of the US."

"I understand, Judge." I replied.

She looked at my completed application that she had before her. And then just as I thought that she was going to skip the Civics test, she asked, "What is the purpose of the Constitution?"

I responded, "To frame how the government works and to protect the basic rights of Americans."

She nodded affirmatively. "what are the first three words of the Constitution?"

I answered, "We the people."

"How many senators are there in the US Congress?"

"There are 100 senators, Judge." With that answer she turned back to my completed application that lay on the desk before her. Then she got to the killer questions, the incorrect answer to any of which would disqualify me.

"Are you a member of the Communist Party?" I replied "No."

"Do you use or have you ever used or dealt in drugs? "

"No." I replied hoping that she did not know of my experimentation with such agents when I was in graduate school. She looked at me directly, as though she was trying to make a decision. I had planned for the possibility that this answer about drugs would be challenged. If that occurred, I would say, 'Judge, I have never dealt in drugs. Yes, it is true that I did have a small experimentation when I was in graduate school, but my fear of being visited by 'the men in suits' brought a rapid end to my experimentation.' I would explain if she asked about the 'men in suits.'

However, she reached for a form, stamped her signature on it, gave it to me and directed me to a room where the Naturalization Ceremony would be held.

There were about 50 of us in the room. It was only the second time in my life that I was in a room with people from at least half as many countries as the number of people present. The other occasion was at the Fulbright Fellowship Orientation Program at Yale University.

Everyone seemed both excited and nervous. Finally, the ceremony began.

We stood, raised our right hand and took the pledge.

One could see the pride and joy among all who had just gone through this simple but life changing ceremony. On my way out, I passed the office of the judge. I tapped on the door and went in. She was still sitting behind her large desk with papers in front of her.

She asked, "Did something go wrong?" "No." I said. "I just have a Question." She asked, "What is it?"

I asked, "Now that I am a citizen, can I do everything that citizens do, like voting etc.?"

She said, "Yes. Of course."

I said, "Thank you. Now I will go and join the Communist Party, do Drugs and all the things that non-citizens cannot do."

She looked at me quite shocked and I rushed out of her office before she rescinded my citizenship.

While at the NIH a small group of us took call at night for the Physicians working at the Bethesda Hospital. One night I had a patient who was dying and the distraught family remained at his bedside all night. At about 2 am, the nurse taking care of him paged me to come to his room. She thought that he had passed on.

I went to the room where the tearful family was huddled around his bed. I asked the nurse to bring an EKG machine. I observed him. Checked his pulse, listened to his chest and heart. Then I attached the EKG leads and ran a rhythm strip which was flat. The family could see the flat EKG. I turned to the family and expressed my condolences. I went to the nurses' station and recorded my examination and time of death in the chart.

About one hour later, I was awakened by a phone call and not a page. It was the Charge Nurse.

She said, "Dr. Douglas, we have a problem. One of the nurses on the floor where you pronounced the patient told the family that the patient is still alive."

I said, "REALLY!? Where is the patient?"

The Charge Nurse said, "He is already in the morgue."

I continued, "Please bring the nurse who said he was alive and an EKG machine to the morgue. I will meet you there."

I met them in the morgue. We removed the sheet that covered the deceased patient. I deliberately repeated the examination that I had done in front of his family, before pronouncing him dead.

I then turned to the nurse in question and said, "There is something that I want you to do. The nipple of the breast is one of the more sensitive areas of the body. I would like you to squeeze his nipple as hard as you can. If he flinches he is alive."

Now clearly quite embarrassed she declined. I then made a show of squeezing his nipple. The charge nurse apologized to me and said that she would immediately talk to the family members who were still in the hospital. The next day I received a call from the Head Nurse to tell me that they had fired that nurse as they had had other problems with her.

In 1982 I joined the Department of Medicine and the Committee of Clinical Pharmacology at the University of Chicago's Pritzker Medical School. I was also appointed Director of the Hypertension Clinic. I immediately set about implementing several things that I had learned as a medical student, resident and Research Fellow to increase my chances of success in this my first independent position in a research-based medical school and hospital.

For example, I was responsible for hypertension consultation within the University of Chicago Hospital. I had done a fourth-year elective in Clinical Pharmacology with Dr. Marcus Reidenberg. Dr. Reidenberg had recently joined Cornell University Medical Faculty and as a result was unknown to most of the clinical staff. Every morning, at the time when the teams would be making rounds, he would walk by with his small team, introduce himself and ask whether there were any problems where we could be of help. For the first week everyone politely said, "No. Thank you."

Then in the second week, one team asked him to look at a patient who was having a reaction to her antibiotic. After that consult, we had more work than we could handle.

I did the same at University of Chicago and suddenly the hypertension clinic that had been struggling for patients began to become busy as university of Chicago Physicians referred their hypertension patients to me.

I joined the Chicago Heart Association and suggested we implement a Church-Based Hypertension Screening Effort. I had assisted Dr. Elijah Saunders in Baltimore who had introduced this effort to improve blood pressure control in Black communities. The Chicago Heart Association agreed to develop a similar program and assigned Ms. Diana Schmidt to work with me on this. Diana was really quite committed to this effort and we developed an approach that was adopted by the National American Heart Association for implementation in other areas of the country. I received the Chicago Heart Association's Heart of the Year Award (1984) and later, the American Heart Association's Louis B. Russell Award (1986). The Chicago Heart Association's support for this effort contributed significantly to its success. I was elated that this contribution was considered worthy of note by the American Heart Association. I was also elected a Fellow of the American Heart Association's Hypertension Council.

I also visited some of the local physicians and explained my background and my interest in their referring to me any of their patients whose blood pressure was difficult to control. They told me they did not refer their patients to University of Chicago because their patients were never returned. I assured them I would return their patients. I developed the following practice for every patient referred to me. I would call the primary physician and let her/him know what was done, what else needed to be done, and that I had informed the patient to return to her/his primary physician for follow-up and ongoing care. These actions led to the Hypertension Clinic growing from about 300 patients to about 1000 patients over 2 years. In fact, this was so successful that Dr. Arnsdorf, Chairman of the Department of Cardiology invited me to join the Department of Cardiology and bring the Hypertension Clinic under Cardiology. I actually considered this move since cardiac problems is one of the sequelae of uncontrolled hypertension and an echocardiology expert with interest in hypertensive heart disease had joined the Department of Cardiology. However, other events intervened before I could join this team.

Dr. Leon Goldberg, the Director of the Division of Clinical Pharmacology, was an expert in dopamine and hypertension and was a very engaged researcher. I recall as I was stuck while trying to write my first grant application, he called me into his office, turned on a small recorder and said, "Start talking."

I asked, "About what?"

He said, "about the grant you are writing. Start with the introduction."

I started to talk and after a couple of hours, he stopped me. Got up and gave the recorder to his assistant and said, "please do a rough transcription of this and give it to Frank."

Then he looked at me and said, "That is your first rough draft."

I have used a semblance of that approach ever since, without the recording part. That is, I would simply get that first very rough draft done!

The grant application was for a five-year training grant from the NIH. One of my colleagues, Dr. Sol Rajfer, who had completed his Fellowship with Leon, had gotten one of these grants the previous year. Everyone, who reviewed my grant application, felt there was no way I would not get one of these grants. We were all stunned when I was denied with the only critical comment being that since I had a PhD, I should be applying for an RO1 grant.

This was absolute nonsense because my Ph.D. was in Spectroscopy and this was Neuroendocrinology in which I had just completed a Fellowship. I recall that Dr. Arthur Rubinstein, the Chairman of the Department of Medicine, was so angry when he saw the comments that he told me that if he heard that I was giving any more of my time to the NIH on their Hypertension Committees, he would fire me. I visited the Department at the NIH that managed these grants, to learn why my application was unsuccessful. The NIH specialist was quite apologetic and said simply that they had to follow the recommendations of the review committees.

In the meantime, I had two active ongoing collaborations; one was with Sol Rajfer and Leon on their work with novel therapeutic dopaminergic agents. I measured dopamine and various metabolites using the HPLC. Another was a study of orthostatic hypotension, particularly in young women, and the potential role of central nervous system agents such as clonidine, in ameliorating this effect.

One day, during a tilt test procedure and sample collection with one of these subjects, a nurse came to the room and said, "Dr. Douglas, there is a call for you. It is from the White House."

"Are you sure?" I asked, thinking that there must be a mistake. She said, "Yes. It sounds important." Although I wanted to be sure that the tilt test would proceed without incident, I was puzzled by, but eager to take the call. I asked the nurse to stay with the patient as I accepted the call. I straightened my tie and straightened my White Coat as I headed to the Nurses station to take the call. It was from Dr. Bernadine (Bulkley) Healy.

"Hi, Frank. How are you? As you know I am now at the White House as a White House Advisor and I would like you to join me."

"Wow." I said. "That would be an incredible honor, Bernadine."

I paused, I was conflicted. An opportunity to work for Bernadine was not to be taken lightly. 'This is not an easy decision,' I thought. Then I said very slowly, and pensively, also hoping that she could hear my inner struggle.

"I really wish I could. I have been at University of Chicago a short time. I feel that I need to stay at least a year before making another move. This is really difficult."

Bernadine then said, "Frank, it is good periodically to go out and interview for other positions. It helps you assess how you are perceived by others and the best time to look at other opportunities is when you do not need a job."

A couple of months later Bernadine came to the University of Chicago to deliver a lecture and I was one of the faculty members who were invited to have dinner with her. This was a small group. She greeted me warmly and said, "Morton (Arnsdorf, who was Chairman of the Department of Cardiology) says that you are doing an excellent job. Let me know if you change your mind about the White House opportunity." I felt quite special because I knew that my colleagues had observed that she had had a brief, private conversation with me.

About 18 months after joining the faculty of the University of Chicago's Pritzker Medical School. I began to receive calls from Pharmaceutical companies. Initially, I ignored them until one headhunter said that there is someone at Ciba Geigy who knows you and would like to talk to you. I had been visited by a team from Ciba Geigy, but had thought nothing of it. I was intrigued.

I went to Ciba Geigy and was greeted by Dr. Thomas Glenn, who was the leader of the team who had visited my lab. Tom came straight to the point. He told me that he had been promoted to Senior Vice President and Head of Research for the U.S. and he would like me to come to work for him. I also met with Dr. Max Wilhelm, who was the Global Head of Research and Development and Tom's boss. They told me that they were impressed with the fact that I was doing both bench research and clinical research, while running a very busy Hypertension Clinic and they needed someone on the research side who could do something similar in industry. I stayed an additional day and met with several leaders in Research and in Development Departments. At the end of the visit, they said that they would like me to set up a group that would do Phase 11a type studies to determine whether their new mechanism-based compounds were likely to become drugs. They also added that I would also run the Drug Metabolism and Pharmacokinetics (DMPK) Department.

I returned for a second visit. Ciba Geigy had peaked my interest because the possibility to continue my research while still contributing to improving the health of patients was attractive. In the interim I was also approached by Smith Kline French to consider joining them to lead their DMPK Department. On my second visit to Ciba Geigy, I told Tom that after considering their offer, I did not think that I had enough experience at that time to take over the DMPK Department AND also set up a new group, which we decided to call Clinical Biology. if I were to join Ciba Geigy, it would be to do one or the other task, not both. In addition, if I did join Ciba Geigy, I had some concerns about the political climate between Research and Development. The reason was that Dr. Joe Mollica, the SVP of Development, had made it clear during my interview with him, that he thought that Clinical Biology should be set up in Development and not in Research. Tom assured me that

Dr. Wilhelm was in agreement that it should be established in Research.

After this exchange, Tom asked, "which assignment would you prefer: leading DMPK or establishing Clinical Biology."

I said, "I would prefer to build the Clinical Biology effort."

Tom replied, "That is what we hoped you would say. There is, however, one problem. If you only did Clinical Biology, you would be hired at the Director Level, and not at the Executive Director Level."

I responded, "Tom the title is less important to me as is the opportunity to successfully build an innovative effort."

When I returned to Chicago I met with Dr. Arthur Rubinstein to discuss the visit to Ciba Geigy. Arthur was extremely magnanimous. He offered the following: he would keep my position open for a year at the end of which if I did not like the experience I could return to my position and all of my responsibilities. During that 'sabbatical' year I would need to give my lectures in Pathophysiology of Hypertension and Clinical Pharmacology of Hypertension Drugs. Dr. Michael Murphy, who had recently joined me on a two-year sabbatical from Ireland, would run the clinic with the able help of Delores, who was the very competent administrator of the clinic.

Leon was equally supportive but had a slightly different view on the situation. I had gotten a Pharma Career Award to do my research, but it was not enough to do my full program. I had gotten some very exciting results in 1983, by demonstrating that Substance P could cause smooth muscles of vessels to relax, but only when there was an intact endothelium. This was quite exciting as others were beginning to suspect that there was a vasoactive endothelium factor. Leon had even recommended that I take a year off and go and work with Dr. Robert Furchgott at Brooklyn Hospital, as he was working to isolate this factor.

Leon, reminded me. "Frank, do not overlook taking a year sabbatical with Furchgott to identify the endothelial vasoactive factor."

I said, "Actually, I briefly considered that but the stress on Lynnet and the girls will be too much."

He reflected for a moment, then said, "You are trying to do the impossible. In my day, the only MDs who went into research were those who could afford to do so. They had nannies to take care of their kids and money was not an issue. You are without financial resources and you are presently running a busy clinic, doing both bench and clinical research and have a family to support. That is a tall order."

Then, almost as though he had accepted the inevitability of the decision, he added, "I predict that you will do very well in industry."

I asked, "Why do you say that?"

"Because you have been able to navigate Academia successfully; a place where dogs fight over scraps."

Dr. Furchgott was awarded the Nobel Prize in Physiology and Medicine in 1998 for his discovery of the role of Nitric Oxide in the endothelium of mammalian systems.

Entering Industry-CIBA Geigy

On October 29, 1984, I arrived in Summit, NJ, the major Research and Development site at Ciba Geigy. I was introduced to Charlie O'Brien, the CEO of Ciba Geigy USA, and Dr. Roy Ellis, the SVP of Medical Affairs. I then spent time with the accountant Chuck Savarre and the head of Human Resources, Diana Farley, both of whom were incredibly helpful to me in those early days of navigating Ciba Geigy. The following day I spent several hours being oriented to the Research Department by my three colleagues; Drs. Heinz Schwend, the Head of Chemistry; Dieter Scholer, the Head of Biology; and Vince Traina, the Head of Toxicology and Pathology. My office was on the first floor of the Biology Building and I had a lab in that building.

Then came the first of many Tom Glenn unexpected maneuvers. A trailer suddenly appeared next to the Biology Building and Tom informed me that that was to be the Home of Clinical Biology. He explained there were some organizational changes and they needed my office. I learned later that when Tom was asked why Clinical Biology was in the Trailer, he replied that Clinical Biology was an experiment and if it did not work he would remove the trailer in the middle of the night and no one would remember Frank 'Who?' This was typical Tom Glenn humor.

I embarked on the task of building a team and was quite fortunate in attracting several excellent academic researchers. These included: Dr. Pierre Etienne, who was a psychiatrist and pathologist; Dr. John Turk, who was a Pharmacologist and Internist, with expertise in prostaglandins; and Dr. Al Kotake, an expert in the Breath Test and one of my former colleagues from the Division of Clinical Pharmacology, at the University of Chicago.

I also brought on board Mr. William Hirschorn as the Director of Operations. Bill was recruited from the Development Department and he was key in helping me with all things administrative. However, although my counterparts in Development, such as Drs. Margaret Hurley, Malcolm McNab, Irene Chow and Joyce Moscaritola were helpful and welcoming, the word had gone out not to assist Clinical Biology with infrastructure needs. This became critical immediately as we decided to demonstrate our capabilities on a project that had languished in Development. There was a compound that Ciba Geigy was considering licensing from a German Company. The drug was a magnesium aspartate compound called Magnesiocard. I took this on and immediately set about writing the IND and first protocol. Bill Hirschorn took on the task of designing and producing the CRF forms using the new Apple computer and Tom identified an expert in the cardiovascular effects of magnesium to do the study on the effects of Magnesiocard on blood Pressure.

Everything changed when the FDA accepted the IND with minimal changes and gave permission to move ahead with the first clinical study. Our small team was ecstatic at this early success. Dr. Roy Ellis, the SVP of Medical Affairs, called a group consisting of Vince Traina and me from Research and three of the VPs from Development to establish the 'rules of engagement' between Clinical Biology and Development. He told us that if this worked well, we will all put the document in our desk drawers and collaborate without ever needing to refer to it.

As we worked on these rules, it became clear to me that Development's concern was that Research would use Clinical Biology as a backdoor to develop research compounds that Development had refused. On recognizing this I made two recommendations. The first was that there be a joint committee between Research and Development, where Clinical Biology would present the objectives of its clinical studies and Development would clearly state and document what results these studies needed to achieve for Development to accept the further development of the compound of interest.

The second recommendation was the breakthrough and really surprised everyone. I said that evaluation of my performance should be based also on the Department of Development's assessment as to whether I had fulfilled the goals agreed to by the committee. Thereafter, we received full support from Development for interactions with the FDA and regulatory submissions, for generation of CRFs and use of the Phase 1 unit at Hahneman Medical School for Clinical Studies, when needed.

With this agreement and clarity, we could now embark on the full mission of Clinical Biology. In the mid-1980s, drug discovery had moved from depending primarily on animal models of disease, in which known compounds were screened in order to identify potential activity. Active compounds would then be chemically modified in the attempt to improve the effectiveness/toxicity ratio for the target disease. The new approach relied on selecting a target, for example, enzyme or receptor, that was critical in the mechanism of the disease, and synthesizing compounds to interact with that target. This became known as the mechanism-based approach.

Two developments fueled this advance. One was the development of high throughput invitro assays to test effectiveness on target enzymes or receptors. The second was the development of computer assisted modelling of sites of activity or areas in the target receptor or enzyme where the designed molecule would interact. The chemists were producing very potent and highly selective molecules for the identified enzyme, receptor, or ion channel, that was considered the critical factor or mechanism producing the disease.

Thus, the mission of Clinical Biology was to identify and assist in developing relevant animal models for the targeted disease and to perform small studies in selected patients to determine whether these mechanism-based compounds were likely to become drugs, that is, be effective in treating the humans with the disease. I decided to take a reasoned approach based on a modification of Koch's Postulates, namely:

1. Select a patient population that had identifiable and measurable characteristics of the disease.
2. Identify a measurable parameter that is associated with the disease
3. Demonstrate that the compound increased or decreased the amount of the parameter, and finally
4. Determine whether the decrease or increase of the parameter is associated with a clinical benefit by improving symptoms or signs of the disease.

In the 1980's, enzymes and receptors connected with the Cyclooxygenase and leukotriene biochemical pathways were popular targets. For example, the cyclooxygenase enzyme is responsible for producing several prostaglandins and Thromboxane A2. The prostaglandins have various actions including dilation of smooth muscles of blood vessels, inflammation, pain and fever; and Thromboxane A2 is a potent aggregation of platelets, thus causing clot formation. Aspirin blocks the function of cyclooxygenase and thus, for example, prevents clotting. Several companies had programs focused on the selective inhibition of the formation or activity of Thromboxane A2, either by inhibiting thromboxane synthase enzyme or by blocking the Thromboxane A2 receptor.

This would therefore be more selective than aspirin in that it would only block the aggregation of platelets and hence the formation of clots. It was also hoped that as a result, activity of the cyclooxygenase enzyme would be shunted to the formation of more useful prostaglandins such as PGI2, which causes vasodilation. We had several potent oral and parenteral thromboxane synthase inhibitors, one of which was already being studied in patients. There was great anxiety in Ciba Geigy, as to whether these compounds would have any clinical benefit. These compounds worked very well in the animal models of disease. What was needed were what I called 'human models of disease'. We selected two such models. These models were associated with high levels of Thromboxane B2 (TXB2), the stable metabolite of Thromboxane A2 (TXA2). Thus, TXB2 was our selected parameter to be measured. It was known that high levels of TXB2 were formed during kidney transplant rejection and I felt that TXB2 could be a potential marker of transplant rejection.

The second model was idiopathic pulmonary hypertension, which was also associated with high levels of TXB2. We first investigated the ability of our compounds to reduce the formation of TXB2 in the animal models of these two conditions. After demonstrating significant reduction of TXB2 formation on administering the Thromboxane Synthase Inhibitors in the two animal models of disease, we performed pilot clinical studies in the two conditions. We administered our intravenous compound CGS 13080 via approved protocols for the respective patients. CGS 13080 markedly reduced the formation of TXB2. However, we saw no clinical effect in either condition. My team recommended that the Thromboxane Synthase Inhibitors program should be terminated. It was a courageous recommendation but both Research and Development Departments accepted the recommendation. Shortly thereafter, Glaxo and Smith Kline French, who both had sizeable programs, also terminated their efforts.

Today, more than 30 years later, that decision has been proven to have been a wise one, as no Thromboxane synthase inhibitor nor Thromboxane Receptor Antagonist has been demonstrated to be an effective treatment for diseases such as angina, where formation of platelet clots plays an essential role. I have often joked that I was the first person in the Pharmaceutical Industry who was promoted because he killed a major Drug Development program.

Clinical Biology was the forerunner of Personalized Medicine, in which the **parameter** of interest is called a **Biomarker**.

Tom Glenn had done quite a lot to improve the rigor of the research programs. He had introduced flow charts and decision trees, so presentations became much more focused on the hypothesis and the flow diagram of tests that would be performed to support or reject the hypothesis. He supported the development of high throughput screening and use of computer assisted design methods. He also demanded scientific rigor during review of all programs, including those from headquarters in Basel, Switzerland. Unfortunately, Tom, who was a very strong deductive thinker, also seemed to like chaos.

Vince Traina once described Tom, as being in a boat traveling down the rapids of a river, and when everyone else in the team is ready to take a few breaths because they have finally arrived in calm water, Tom would be furiously paddling to stir up the calm water to simulate the rapids. This was often evident in the way he challenged the scientists to defend their projects. Every morning, Tom would peruse the Current Contents and read articles related to the projects being pursued by our teams. On the one hand this was quite exciting because it led to constant evaluation of hypotheses and a focus on the DATA.

On the other hand, however, although Tom wanted to use the most recent information to confirm or invalidate the rationale of each project, his style of challenging often developed fear instead of open scientific discussion. One meeting in which he challenged the projects was at the Research Assessment Group or RAG meeting, where project leaders would present their projects. Unfortunately, this became a forum in which some scientists felt more attacked than helped. I was able to get Tom to agree to discuss his concerns with me and let me act as a go between so that the scientists would be better prepared for their RAG presentations and feel less as though they were 'on the rack'.

Tom could also be somewhat devious. On one occasion he took a team of us to visit McMaster University, in Hamilton, Canada. At the end of a day of very interesting research presentations by various faculty, Tom asked his team to leave the room while he had a closed discussion with the McMaster Research Leaders. When we rejoined the meeting, Tom said, "We have agreed to a Research collaboration over 3 years, at $750, 000 per year and that would be paid from the Clinical Biology Budget."

The rest of the team looked at me because they knew that the Clinical Biology budget was only $3 million per year.

Tom looked directly at me and I said simply, "Tom, if you believe that this will help me meet my present goals, I am fine with it."

The collaboration never happened.

In the meantime, Vince and I had become very close friends and we often went to the New Providence Diner to debrief after one of Tom's invariably lengthy meetings. It was never clear to me why the meetings needed to be so long but Tom always found additional areas to explore. Often these meetings lasted all day.

On one occasion, a meeting ended rather early and Vince and I went to our favorite diner to debrief and unwind. Apparently, Vince's wife called Tom's office to find out when the meeting would be over and Tom's secretary told her that Vince and Frank were probably at the Diner where they usually go after meetings.

So, we got 'busted'. Our secret was out. Nonetheless, we continued our post Tom meeting debriefs at the diner because it helped us think of ways to translate Tom's challenges to the rest of the organization, or ways to alert Tom to a potential unwanted outcome. I rather enjoyed these post meeting discussions because Vince not only had a keen sense of humor, he was also a kind of company historian and could put many issues in a broader context.

Fourteen months after joining Ciba Geigy, Tom gave me the good news that I was being promoted to Executive Director and a portion of the Drug Metabolism group was being added to my responsibilities to ensure support of Clinical Biology projects. I was quite delighted as this signaled to me that Dr. Max Wilhelm, Tom's boss and Global Head of Research and Development, was pleased with my performance. Shortly after this promotion, Tom started to present other roles that I could assume in the company. I began to wonder if he was trying to get rid of me. The one that seemed to have gathered the most steam was for me to go to India and become the Head of Research for India. I explained to Tom that we had recently moved from Chicago to New Jersey and my family would not agree with such a move. I also doubted that I knew enough about the company to take on such an important assignment. I asked Diana Farley, the Head of HR for Research, for her advice and she told me that if I declined, I would probably never be asked again to make such a move. I decided it was better never to be asked again and so I declined.

In 1987 I was sent to Greensboro, North Carolina to participate in a weeklong Leadership program at the Center for Creative Leadership. I consider this week, the time I spent as a graduate student in the Department of Chemistry at Cornell University, and my time as an Intern and Resident at Johns Hopkins to be among the significant transformational periods in my life's journey. I did not know why I was selected to participate in this program, nor did I know whether I fell in the category of high potentials, or employees about to derail, but I am forever grateful that I had this experience. The mantra for this course was: Perception is Reality.

Twenty-four individuals from industry, academia and other walks of life were brought together, with great care having been taken to ensure that all were strangers to each other. There were combinations of presentations to the entire group as well as working sessions in six membered sub-groups. Each participant was being observed by three of her/his co-participants, and neither the person being observed nor the co-observers knew each other's identity. Each one was coached on how to accept and to give criticism.

Prior to attending the week-long program, each participant and individuals from that person's place of work, in a 360-degree manner, were requested to complete several detailed questionnaires. The questionnaires were completed anonymously. Psychologists from the Center observed the participants. At the end of the five days, the participant sat with her/his peer observers and received criticism of observed behaviors. The observed participant could only ask questions for clarification. No explanation nor defense for the observed behavior was permitted. The only acceptable response was, 'Thank You.'

Finally, the participant met with the psychologist who had analyzed the participant's responses to the questionnaire in comparison to the responses from her/his superior, subordinates and peers in her/his work setting. They also compared these with their own observations during the five days at the Center. At the conclusion, the psychologist would point out that if individuals at different levels of a participant's organization and new observers **perceived** the participant's behaviors similarly, then that was the participant's **reality.**

In my session with the psychologist he had two closing comments. The first was that the concordance between how I saw myself and how I was perceived by all was exceptionally close. This degree of concordance was not often seen. The second was a question. He asked, given this concordance between my self-perception and perception of others; my significant problem-solving ability and my IQ, why was I not in a higher position in my company. I explained that often when it came time for promotions my ethnicity would be an issue, so I would either consider leaving that environment or suppress my disappointment. He advised that I was NOT responsible for the misdeeds of others and the next time such a situation arose, I should confront my superiors and ask them why I was not being given the role.

About six months later, in March of 1988, Tom suddenly announced his resignation from Ciba Geigy to become Head of Research at Genentech. He asked me to join him, but again I told him that having moved twice in 5-6 years, a move to California would be out of the question, no matter how appealing. In fact, I was very interested in getting into the biotechnology space and helping solve some of the drug discovery challenges in this exciting new field. In spite of this interest, a move to California was not feasible for us. My colleague, Heinz Schwend, was appointed acting head of Research and was considered by many as the likely successor to Tom. Heinz was from Switzerland, had been with the US organization many years, and his school friend Dr. LePlatenier, who was on the Vorstand (Board) of Ciba Geigy, was responsible for R&D across the Ciba Geigy world. In fact, when Dr. LePlatenier visited the US, Heinz hosted a dinner and invited the team to meet him and discuss Research in the US.

Doug Watson, the successor to Charlie O'Brien as CEO of Ciba Geigy Pharma, USA, had started an external search and I was told confidentially, by Charlie Lay, the then head of Human Resources, that I was the internal candidate. I shared this with Vince, who began to share his analyses of the situation with me. Vince was like an archivist. He was famous for having stacks of 5x7 cards, on which he tracked the toxicology findings of every CGS and CGB (Ciba Geigy Summit and Ciba Geigy Basel) compound in development or that was on the market and could also tell you the toxicology findings of other marketed compounds in their class. Vince also tracked organizational changes within Ciba Geigy and knew the relationships and history of many of the leaders in the US and Basel. He therefore had his own predictions of who would succeed Tom and was convinced that it would be Heinz.

In the three years since I had joined Ciba Geigy, Heinz had become quite powerful. When Dieter Scholer had to return to Basel because of illness in his family, Tom had combined Biology and Chemistry together under Heinz. This meant that Heinz controlled more than half of the workforce in Research. Heinz, who disliked Tom's style and probably had never accepted that Tom was selected to head Research instead of him, began to undo research approaches that Tom had introduced. The major difference was that Tom had changed the Research paradigm from a chemistry driven approach to a mechanism-based approach, which was biology driven. Heinz began to reverse this and both Vince and I thought this was a step backwards, particularly since molecular biology was beginning to emerge as a potential discipline. I brought this to Doug Watson's attention as I wanted to avoid a direct confrontation with Heinz during a time of significant uncertainty. Doug listened but made no comment.

One day I was called by Doug to be interviewed for the position. The interview was somewhat brief and in my view was quite perfunctory. Shortly thereafter, Charlie Lay came to my office. He sat down, let out a sigh, and said, "We have made a verbal offer to a scientist at Smith Kline French. You need to know that I and others on the management committee were quite upset because, as we told Doug (the President of Ciba Geigy, USA), we compare every candidate to Frank Douglas. He is our Gold Standard. Why don't we give him the job?"

I thanked Charlie, who said as he rose to leave, "I do not know what to advise, but I thought that you should know."

It was after 5 pm and I reflected on my exit session at the Center for Creative Leadership and the advice I was given.

I called Doug's office. He answered. I said, "Doug, I know that you are close to a decision and I would like to know where I stand."

He said, "Well you are not number one and you are not number three." I said, "Could you tell me briefly why I am not number one?"

He paused for a moment, then said, "Come over to my office and let us discuss it."

I ran over to his office, not knowing what to expect. He invited me to take a seat and what then followed felt more like a serious interview.

At the end of it he asked, "Why did you not tell me these things before?" "Like what?" I asked.

"For example, you never mentioned that you had worked for Nobel Laureates, the last time we discussed your candidacy. For example, I learned recently that when the Nobel Laureate, Dr. Axelrod visited us, he specifically asked for you to join him at dinner and told everyone that you were one of his fellows at the NIH."

I said, "Well I should have been his fellow, but I decided to work directly with someone else in his group."

He said, "I also learned from one of our Chemists that one of the Professors on your Ph.D. Committee won the Nobel Prize."

I said, "Yes, that is Professor Hoffmann. He was my Theoretical Chemistry Advisor."

"I am still surprised that you never mentioned this." He said.

"I thought that the focus would be on my performance, and on an assessment of the leadership capabilities that I have demonstrated here at Ciba Geigy." I explained.

The discussion ended on that note.

About four days, later as Vince and I were having our usual visit to discuss compounds and then the politics of the day, I received a call from Doug's office. His assistant said that members of the DL (Pharma Division Leaders) from Basel were visiting and they wanted to learn about Clinical Biology. I told Vince and we started selecting transparencies from different files as I hurriedly put together a talk on the concept, the projects, the decisions, and the examples of how Clinical Biology was contributing to Drug Discovery. I did a quick runthrough with Vince and then headed for Doug's office. I was ushered into Doug's office and present were Mr. Orsinger, the Chairman of the DL and two other DL members, who were sitting in chairs next to each other. Dr. Max Wilhelm was sitting on a chair a small distance from and perpendicular to the chairs of the other DL members and there was a chair for Doug that faced the others. I looked around for the projector, but there was none.

Doug introduced the visiting members of the DL and said, "Frank, the members of the DL have a few questions for you."

I thought, 'This is strange, but as long as it has to do with drug discovery, I am on safe ground. If it has anything to do with Heinz and the mood in Research, I would be non-committal and simply say we are all trying to deal with the uncertainty.'

I answered the first question and Max immediately disagreed. I nodded acknowledgement of his comment but did not engage. A second question was asked and again Max disagreed with my answer. I thought it strange, but again did not engage Max.

On the third question, when Max disagreed, I said, "Max, I would like to disagree with you on this issue and here is why."

I gave my reasoning in a straight forward and succinct manner. I noticed Mr. Orsinger nod to Doug.

Doug then said, "Frank, Mr. Orsinger and the members of the DL are here to interview you for the job of Head of Research, so from here on address all answers to Mr. Orsinger and the other two members of the DL and not to Max or me."

What followed seemed like a serious but somewhat 'sympathetic', by which I mean that it was not confrontational, interview.

At the end of the meeting they thanked me for making myself available at short notice, and I thanked them for the opportunity. As I drove home to pack for my flight to Boston where Max and I had a meeting the following day, my mind was a whirr of thoughts.

'For DL members to fly from Basel, Switzerland, to meet with me must mean that they are really considering me for the position', I told myself.

'Did Doug request their presence to make the decision?' 'Why was Max opposing my answers?'

That evening I got a call from Max to meet him in the lobby of the Hotel in Boston, where we were staying for the meeting. I met Max in the lobby.

He greeted me in his usual understated manner and said; "let's go for a walk."

It was dark and dreary and we walked in silence for a while. My usual Fog had descended on me as I was uncertain about the purpose of the walk. 'Was it to deliver the bad news?' I wondered.

After we had walked a few blocks, Max asked, "Have you ever thought of doing Doug's job as CEO?"

I said, "No. I see myself like you Max. I am an R&D guy."

We turned back towards the hotel and nothing more was said. I went to bed in my fog state.

The following evening as I was waiting for my cab to Logan airport, Max came over to me and said, "After I asked you to take a walk with me last evening, I got a call to tell me that I could not congratulate you then on becoming Head of Research. Mr. Orsinger needed to get Mr. Krauer's approval. He received it today and you are now SVP and Head of Research for Ciba Geigy, US. You will be reporting to Doug and me. Congratulations."

He shook my hand. "As you know, Mr. Alex Krauer is the Chairman of the KL (Corporate Leaders) in Basel."

I told Max that I was absolutely delighted at this great news.

On my way to the airport, I called Vince to be sure that he had heard it directly from me. I was sure that Max would have told Heinz and Heinz would have informed his team. Vince told me that I had his full support. I told him that I was delighted that I could count on his support. The next morning, I went directly to Doug's office who congratulated me and took me around to meet some of his team and to introduce me to the assistant who had supported Tom, and my new office in the administration building. (Unfortunately, I could not bring my assistant, Ms. Sheila Gibb, who was excellent, with me. Tom's assistant was known for doing very little work and as a result, the assistant of the Head of Administration for Research did most of the actual secretarial support for Tom). Doug told me that we would discuss goals and expectations later. I spent the next two days working with Vince to understand the problems that I should expect from Heinz and the conversations I needed to have with both Doug and Max, since I would be reporting to both of them: to Max as the Global Head of Research and Development and Doug as the CEO of Pharma, USA.

On the question of Heinz, I did not have long to wait. Al Hutchinson, one of his lead and very gifted chemists came to see me. He said, "We have a simple message for you. Just as how Tom was head of Research but Heinz actually controlled everything, the same thing will happen to you."

I said, "Al, I want you to tell Heinz the following. I am not Tom. If he chooses to battle with me he will lose."

"Are you sure?" Al asked, looking at me incredulously.

I said, hoping he heard the irony in my response. "The reason is simple.

He wants this job badly and having this job is not that important to me."

He looked at me somewhat surprised and left without further comment. A few days later I was visited by another of the lead chemists.

He said, "People want to know how they will be evaluated by you."

I took a piece of paper and quite spontaneously drew a 2x2 matrix with four quadrants. I labelled the Y-axis Values or Goals. I labelled the X-axis Behaviors. I said, "Here is how I see the organization. In the bottom left quadrant are what I call Rebels. These are employees who neither share your goals nor behave productively to help you achieve your Goals. I say to such employees that they owe it to themselves to leave the organization and find a place where they at least could support the company goals. On the bottom right quadrant are employees to whom the goals are not particularly important, but they behave appropriately so that those goals can be accomplished. I call those Conformers. In the top left quadrant are what I call our Mavericks. They share our goals, but while everyone is marching left, right, left, they are sometimes out of step, going right, left, right. Finally, there are those in the upper right who both share our goals and model behaviors that move the organization forward. They are the Future Leaders. In any organization that I run there is a place for everyone except Rebels."

I gave him the sheet of paper and said, "Please share this with your colleagues." After he left I quickly scribbled, on a new sheet of paper, what I had told him in my moment of inspiration. I did not want to forget it.

Three weeks later Max called me from Basel to tell me that Heinz had requested a transfer back to Basel. He had been in the US about 20 years and this was a good time for him to repatriate. Max had found a leadership role for him in Central Research, Basel. I asked Max if there was anything that I could do to facilitate this. Max told me that it was all arranged. The reason for the visit from the second Chemist was now clear. Heinz had already shared with his team that he was returning to Basel.

From the day of the announcement of my promotion to Senior Vice President and Head of Research for USA to this day, I never saw nor heard from Heinz.

I asked Pat Murphy and her HR Team to help me rapidly organize an offsite meeting to develop the goals for the organization. I had discussed some of my plans with Doug and he was totally supportive and had helpful advice. His major concern was that we not lose many of our lead chemists whom Heinz had recruited. An off-site meeting, such as this, had been held once a year but only the 'Best and Brightest', as identified by Tom, were invited. In this workshop I not only invited the key leaders in each department but asked them to identify their young scientists AND technicians whom they considered to be innovative.

It was the first time that technicians were included in an off-site meeting. The first evening we listened to Zubin Mehta explaining how an orchestra creates exceptional music. Each musician needs to be expert on her/his own instrument while simultaneously listening to the other musicians to harmonize and create the sound and tone the conductor seeks to evoke from the entire orchestra. He illustrated this with the orchestra playing Bolero, the sound of which became a background theme throughout the next three days.

We then followed this by everyone telling the group something that was not known about him or her. We learned, for example, that we had a Rabbi in our midst. One female technician had walked up and down the Grand Canyon three times. One scientist had been flying planes since age 16. There were many stories of involvement and leadership in their communities. I shared with them my Evangelical Christian background and being Director of Youth for Christ, Guyana. The following days were focused on ways to improve innovation in our labs.

This workshop yielded many new approaches. For example, technicians could apply to spend up to 10% of their time to work on ways to improve an assay, process or procedure with the goal of improving productivity. Ph.D.s could use up to 20% of their time on an innovative project, and the remaining 80% on their assigned project. I also moved to a Therapeutic Area (TA) structure where each TA had Departments of Chemistry and Biology under the same leader.

Thus, I hired Dr. Manuel Worcel to lead the Cardiovascular and Atherosclerosis Therapeutic area, and Dr. Frans Stassen to run the Rheumatology Therapeutic Area. I combined Research Drug Metabolism with Toxicology and Pathology under Vince and recruited a Head of Clinical Biology. By so doing, I not only flattened the structure but reduced the friction between Chemistry and Biology because the Head of Chemistry often determined which projects would receive chemistry support, without which, a project could not succeed. Now both Biology and Chemistry had a common mission and had the appropriate resources to achieve that mission. I also began to recruit organic chemists who had also done a post-doctoral fellowship in enzymology, pharmacology or medicinal chemistry. Within 18 months, productivity had improved and we were producing twice as many Pre IND-compounds as the Basel Research group, although this group was twice as large as our US group.

The focus on innovation and involving the talents of the technicians led to a very important decision. We were developing an anti-cholesterol compound with a novel mechanism of action, which was in Clinical Phase 2. We were all excited about this compound until the technician who was doing additional profiling of the compound observed that at very high doses the animals were getting fatty livers. He brought it to the attention of the head of his department, who took it seriously and decided to engage Toxicology.

The initial toxicology studies were unremarkable. However, on review of the groups of animals, who had received a very high dose of the compound, incidences of fatty livers were seen. I told the team to work on understanding this as rapidly as possible. Very quickly they discovered that the compound was stimulating macrophages to ingest and store lipids. We terminated the clinical trial and project. I met with the team. Their disappointment was palpable. I looked at the technician and I could not help but feel his pain as he probably was second guessing whether he should have voiced his observation or simply have remained silent about his observation.

I stood silently and observed their concerned and, in some cases, sad faces. I spoke slowly, "I want to compliment everyone for discovering this issue early. You avoided further exposure of patients to an innovative compound that, unfortunately, could have also had an unwanted side effect. You adhered to the statement important to every Physician. It comes from the Hippocratic Oath: First Do No Harm."

I paused for a couple of seconds, then continued. "In my view there are three possible positive outcomes in Drug Discovery. The best is that we discover a drug that advances science and treats unmet medical needs. The next is that we find a drug that does not necessarily advance science but does treat an unmet medical need. And finally, we find a compound that advances science. This compound is in this last category. I would like you to complete your analyses and submit a paper on the mechanism of this compound." I left them looking relieved that I did not fault anyone, particularly since they knew that I was quite hopeful that this compound would make it to the market place. Because of this increase in productivity, Dr. Max Wilhelm suggested I rebuild the Central Nervous System Therapeutic Area group in the USA. (Tom in one of his more manic moves had recommended transferring the group to Basel. To his surprise Basel accepted and the group was terminated in the USA. At that time the CNS group was the most productive group in the USA and our scientists were among the most highly respected in the industry). I explained to Max that I would not be successful in doing this as we had lost credibility in the Neuroscientist community.

I also began to observe that during our global portfolio meetings, Max frequently sought my opinion before making final decisions on compounds and the portfolio. However, although he never dismissed my recommendations out of hand, he rarely adopted them.

One day I asked Max, "Why do I get the impression that you do not really want my opinion."

Max' response surprised me. He said, "I purposely do not accept your first recommendation, because whenever I turn down your first recommendation, you always come back with a better one. I wait for the better one."

As he said it I recalled the interview with the DL where Max contradicted my answers to the first three questions posed by the DL, and where the course of the interview changed when I challenged his third contradiction. I wondered whether what he wanted to demonstrate to the DL members present was that I had the courage to offer a different opinion when needed.

The increase in productivity was rewarded in another very significant and dramatic way. We were desperately in need of new labs in Summit. Tom had tried twice and was unsuccessful in getting the requisite agreement and funding from Basel. I told Max that I wanted to make a proposal for two new Lab buildings and I needed his advice on how best to approach this. He told me that I would first need to get the agreement of my counterparts in the other Ciba Geigy businesses in the USA, as they also had significant capital needs. He said after that, I would need to be sure that I had the support of Professor Nusech, my counterpart in Basel. If I had those, he would then organize my presentation to the members of the DL in Basel.

I immediately engaged Gus Pushparaj, who was responsible for all major capital projects for US Ciba Geigy, Pharma. Gus brought in Mitchell Giurgola, an excellent architectural firm, and personally took over full management and guidance of the proposal and project. I assembled a team of my senior leaders to discuss and give input to Gus on Laboratory needs, offices, special lab areas, hoods etc. I insisted on an open lab concept similar to that at the Salk Institute. It took a lot to convince the scientists, who counted their importance by the size of their offices and the lab areas under their control, to adopt this open lab concept. They finally agreed. I followed the steps outlined by Max and in the final pitch made by Gus and me to the DL, we asked for two buildings.

They approved one.

I then asked for permission to erect the external structures of the second building, which would not cost much and which building could be completed if we came in on time and under budget on completing the first building.

They agreed.

This was a major achievement and I was very pleased when Doug invited me to attend the dedication of the two buildings, (which some humorously named Fort Douglas), even though I was no longer working at Ciba Geigy at the time of this great event.

On aspects of running the overall Pharma business I was learning a lot from Doug and the rest of the team. Of particular help to me was Bill Sheldon, the SVP in charge of Commercial. In my first presentation to the Executive Committee to get approval to buy an NMR machine, I stood at the front of the room, facing my colleagues. I began the presentation somewhat hesitantly, but my confidence grew as I did not see any furrowed brows, pursed lips, or colleagues avoiding eye contact with me. At the end of the presentation and questions, I continued to defend the proposal.

Suddenly, Bill said, "Frank, I am going to have to teach you how to be a salesman. You have to know when you have made the sale and then you get the hell out of there."

Everyone laughed.

Bill and I shared an office suite and I would often get his advice whenever I had to make a presentation to the Executive Committee.

On another occasion, Bill was quite helpful. We had a large launch of Benazepril (Lotensin) in the US. This was the first time that I had attended a launch meeting for the sales force. I made a presentation at the opening session on the importance of Benazepril as an antihypertensive agent and a brief highlight of our Research pipeline. I was quite impressed with how masterfully Bill had stimulated and motivated the sales force during his presentation.

After dinner, I hung around for a while and then headed to my room. No sooner had I gotten to my room that Vince called me to tell me that I needed to return and mingle with members of the sales force, since I was but a name to them. On my way back, I encountered Bill walking in the direction of the rooms.

I asked, "Is everything alright with you?" I assumed he would be at the post dinner celebrations until the proverbial last light was out.

He responded, "Yes. I am fine. I am retiring for the night."
"So soon?"

He replied, "I always retire early because as it gets later, one of two things or both happen. Either you see your people doing things that they know they should not be doing, or worse, you witness your boss doing something you wished you had not seen."

I went back to the party and it did not take long for me to observe his concern.

Like Bill, I retired to my room shortly thereafter.

On the following day, I was assigned to one of the regional meetings to observe the Sales Force members preparing their 'elevator' pitches on the drug and reviewing the Pharmacology and Clinical data of the drug. The Director of this region was the only Black, female Regional Director (Ms. Saunders) in Ciba Geigy at that time. On the previous evening, as I stood in a corner nursing my glass of wine during the pre-dinner reception, I had observed this young Black woman, who, though unassuming in her appearance, seemed to be an authority figure because the four or five men and women around her were listening intently to her. A few minutes after the group broke apart, she came over to me and said, "It is clear that you are an introvert and events like this are difficult for you. Here is a tip. People want to TALK to you and get to know you. If you smile and look welcoming, you will be surprised how quickly the evening will pass. So, tell yourself: 'I am here for the next 45 minutes and I will enjoy it.'"

I thanked her.

She turned out to be correct. Little did I know that one day later I would again learn something important from her. She started her team meeting with a brief summary of the importance of ACE inhibitors, and Benazepril in particular, in the treatment of hypertension. Then she called on members of her team, individually, to deliver their 'elevator' pitch. After each presentation, Ms. Saunders asked for comments on what was very effective in the presentation. She would then select one of the offered comments to be noted as an example of what should be included in an effective presentation to the doctors.

I watched in amazement as each succeeding presenter incorporated what had been identified as excellent in the preceding presentations. By the time the last team member had presented, not only was it perfect, but all of the key aspects, that were previously identified as effective, had been incorporated in the presentation. It was one of the best examples of coaching by focusing on the positive that I had ever witnessed.

In 1991, about three years after I was appointed SVP and Head of Research I received a call from Max. He requested that I travel immediately to Basel and added that his assistant would take care of all arrangements. I flew to Basel the next day and was taken to the Drei Koenig Hotel.

The Drei Koenig Hotel was the most prestigious hotel in Basel and only the most senior members in the Ciba Geigy hierarchy were permitted to stay in this hotel. I could not sleep that night. I was sure that something of great moment was about to happen to me.

I arrived at Max's office at the appointed time of 9 am. His secretary Jose, who was always friendly and helpful to me greeted me and I sensed some discomfort on her part. She ushered me into Max' office. He was sitting behind his desk. The slight smile with which he often greeted me was not on his face. He looked preoccupied. His large, office, which was always bare, except for a few paintings on the wall, felt unusually empty that morning. Not even his large white note pad was on his desk. He motioned for me to sit on the opposite side of his desk, across from him. He came directly to the point.

"I will be retiring and although you should have been my successor, that will not happen. Some members of the KL believe that it would be inappropriate to have a Black person on the DL in Basel. They also fear that citizens of Basel would probably not like it."

I entered my Fog state. I was numb.

I was silent for a minute or two. Then I said, "Max, thanks for letting me know. Would you please ask Jose to arrange my return trip to the US? I think I have enough time to get a 1 pm flight from Zurich to Newark or JFK."

He rose, and it seemed almost with difficulty, and said, "I will have Jose take care of it."

I asked Jose to have the driver take me back to the hotel where I could check out and await the driver who would get me started on my trip home. I thought I saw a tear in her eye. I quickly averted my gaze because I could not really trust my own emotions. I was in my fog.

The next day I went to Doug and related my conversation with Max. Doug told me that he was aware of it and he was not sure what advice to give me. He further said that the only other option would be his job and since he and I were of the same age, and he did not want to work in Basel again, it was most unlikely that I would succeed him anytime. Doug was a Brit and had worked several years in Basel before becoming CFO for Ciba Geigy Pharma, US and finally CEO of Pharma, US.

I also recognized that the reason I was called to Basel for this conversation, Ciba Geigy could not tell me that I was being passed over because of my ethnicity in a meeting on US soil. My conversation with Doug lifted my Fog and Clarity reigned. I went back to my office and called a Headhunter and told him that I was interested in a position as Head of R&D, preferably for a US company. Shortly thereafter he called me stating that the recently merged company, Marion Merrell Dow and the US Division of Rhone Poulenc Rorer had both expressed interest. My interviews at Rhone Poulenc Rorer went very well and they expressed interest in making an offer.

My interviews at Marion Merrell Dow were quite interesting. In the semifinal round of interviews, I was interviewed by a team including the CEO, the SVP of Business Development, the CFO, the SVP responsible for Human Resources and their Head Hunter.

We sat around a relatively small round table and the questions came with an almost rehearsed tempo. After about an hour, Mr. Lyons, the CEO, leaned forward, looked straight at me and said, "If you were to get this job, you will have 3000 scientists worldwide reporting to you. How will being Black affect your ability to do this job?"

In a flash several thoughts flew through my mind. 'This is where they exclude me. No this could not be, this is my second visit to Marion Merrell Dow, so he knows that I am Black.' So, I tried to deflect and I turned to Mr. Barbour, who I thought had a British accent, and said., "Mr. Barbour, I assume that you are from Britain and have dealt with persons from the British Commonwealth, so I assume my being Black would not be a problem for you."

Mr. Barbour, who was the SVP of Business Development responded crisply, "I am not British. I am South African."

I immediately thought, 'What would Nelson Mandela do in this situation?'

I took a deep breath, then looked squarely at Mr. Lyons and said, "Mr. Lyons, the fact that I am sitting here should tell you that I have no problem with being Black. And the fact that I am sitting here tells me that you have no problem with my being Black. There might be people in the organization who have a problem, but as long as you and I have no problem with my being Black, I do not expect any problems."

Max' successor was named shortly after our conversation in Max' office in Basel. He had been the Head of Central Research in Basel. Over the ensuing 2-3 months there was general and growing disappointment with his performance. One day Doug called me into his office and told me that Mr. Pierre Douaze, the then Chairman of the Pharma DL was arriving that evening and had requested I have dinner with him. Doug did not offer more.

As I entered the Summit Hotel I could see Pierre walking slowly back and forth before the entrance of the restaurant. I waited a moment, then walked up to him and said, "Good evening, Mr. Douaze."

"Hi Frank, our table is ready." I followed him to our assigned table.

The waiter came over immediately and offered the wine list. Uncharacteristically, for a Frenchman, Pierre declined and I followed suit.

We declined the appetizer and only ordered the main dish.

Pierre said, thoughtfully, "We made a mistake in appointment of Max's successor. In fact, we hired a headhunter to look outside of the company for a replacement and after a search, the headhunter advised us that the best person to do this job is in our company. He said it is Frank Douglas. We have, therefore, decided to split R&D into two. Your colleague in Basel will be responsible for Global Discovery and you will be responsible for everything from Pre IND through Phase IV, including Toxicology and Drug Metabolism."

"Pierre, what about the issue of my ethnicity?" I asked. "And will I become a member of the DL and have to live in Basel?"

Pierre said, "I was personally very upset with the first decision. I have discussed this with Mr. Krauer and he has given his full approval. You will be a member of the DL and will have to move to Basel."

I said, "Pierre, when I learned that I would not be the successor of Max because of my ethnicity, I looked for other opportunities. In a couple of days, I have a final interview at Marion Merrell Dow (MMD), and I really would like to see this to the final conclusion." The advice from Dr. Bernadine Healy about when to interview for a job flashed across my mind: the best time to look for a job is when you do not need one.

Pierre said, "I understand. Please contact me or Max as soon as you have completed the interview."

Neither he nor I had interest in the meal. Pierre paid the waiter and I wished him a restful night.

Two days later, I went to the final round of interviews at MMD. I was told that there were two other final candidates.

We were each placed in a separate room, in separate parts of the building to minimize the likelihood that we would come in contact with each other. Three teams consisting of four company officials and board members of Marion Merrell Dow rotated every two hours as they interviewed each candidate.

In my preparation for this interview, my colleague, Eric Davidson had introduced me to the SOAR approach: S for Situation, O for Objective, A for Action, R for result. He recommended that I think of various questions that I could be asked and that I write out SOARs for actual examples that highlight the answer to the question. In my sessions, I had a blank yellow pad in front of me. Before answering each question, I would simply write down a single word, the name of the appropriate example, on my pad and then discuss it with the interview team using the SOAR approach. The following morning, which was actually a Saturday, I received a call from Mr. Lyons. He said that it was unanimous and that I will shortly receive a written offer to become their global Head of R&D. I asked him if I could have a few days because I needed to speak with Max Wilhelm, my boss in Basel. He agreed but stressed once more that they were quite eager to have me join the MMD team. After I joined the organization, Richard Bailey, the Head of HR, told me that he almost died when Mr. Lyons asked his ethnicity question. However, he assured me that although inartful, Mr. Lyons was seeking to see how I would react under significant stress.

The call from Mr. Lyons the following morning after the interview presented quite a dilemma. My youngest daughter (who was transitioning to high school) was quite interested in going to international school in Basel. I suggested that Lynnet and she should visit Kansas City as I flew to Basel to meet with Max that Thursday. I told them that I would wait until I heard from them as to which they would prefer, Kansas City or Basel, before talking to Max.

Because of the time difference, I had to wait until about 6 am Central Time the following day, which was 1 pm in Basel, to hear from Lynnet. I had arrived in Basel about 10 am. This meant hiding out in hotel Basel about 3 hours until I heard from Lynnet. Finally, the call came and Lynnet said Kansas City looked OK. Max, tired of waiting to hear from me, came over to the hotel to determine why I was not responding to phone calls. I knew that Max was expecting me to sign on for the new assignment in Basel, that day.

I ordered a cup of cappuccino and Max ordered an espresso.

Max, looking quite concerned, again no slight smile, asked, "Is something wrong at home?"

"No, Max, but Lynnet and Diah would prefer to stay in the US."

Max immediately called Pierre. Pierre was travelling but said that he would return to Basel immediately to discuss this. Max was clearly disappointed and I was wishing that I could head home without a meeting with Pierre. However, Pierre arrived for dinner.

In his usual direct manner, Pierre said, "Frank, everyone is expecting you to join us in Basel. Max says that you want to stay in the US. I don't understand it."

I said, "Pierre, when the decision to hire a head of Research for the US was being made, my ethnicity was an issue, but we got over that wall. This time, in the matter of my succeeding Max, my ethnicity was an even greater issue. This latter we have sort of addressed. My concern is that if I come to Basel, I would not like my family and me to have to face this issue again."

Pierre said, "Frank, it is truly unfortunate that this occurred. But I assure you that Mr. Krauer and the KL have approved your appointment and we will give all the support you and your family need."

I said, "I suspect that this assignment in Basel will probably not be my final assignment. I worry that my ethnicity will continue to be a recurring issue in Ciba Geigy."

Then Pierre said, "the present consideration is for you to return as successor to Doug Watson after a number of years in Basel."

I said, "what I need is assurance that my ethnicity will not play a role in decisions about my assignments in Ciba Geigy."

Both Max and Pierre looked more hopeful as they assured me that this would not be a concern for me in the future.

I thanked them and told them that I would discuss it with my family and get back to them by the following Tuesday.

The next morning, which was Saturday, I got an angry call from Doug who asked why I would have told Pierre that I wanted his job. I needed to know that he was not planning to go anywhere. I told Doug what had happened and that I had not yet made a decision. On Monday I came in to work and Lee, my assistant, asked me if I knew Doug was meeting with Vince, Frans and Manuel. I told her that I was not aware. Later that day Doug called me into his office and told me that it was decided that since MMD had some similar programs, such as the smoking cessation patch, I should clear out my desk and leave the company immediately. I reminded him that I had told Pierre that I would call him with a final decision the following day, Tuesday, as well as I had not yet accepted the offer from MMD. He told me that he had discussed it with Pierre and Pierre was in agreement with my immediate departure.

I called Mr. Lyons and accepted the job offer and suggested that I could start immediately. In January, 1992, I entered Marion Merrell Dow as EVP responsible for R&D and member of the Board of Directors. The reason given in Basel as to why I elected not to go to Basel was that I did not want to learn German. A month after being at MMD, a former colleague at Ciba Geigy, Dr. Irene Chow, who was SVP and head of Development, called me to tell me that Pierre wanted to talk to me. I called Pierre.

"How are you doing, Frank?" he asked and I could hear the warmth in his voice.

He continued. "Thank you for calling. I still do not understand why you did not come to Basel. However, there is still an opportunity to change things." "Pierre, this was a very difficult decision for me. I assure you, however, that if MMD was not meeting my expectations, I would have immediately accepted your kind offer."

I could sense his disappointment as he said, "Ok. Let's keep in touch.

Goodbye."

Aventis and Its Predecessor Companies – Child, You are Blessed!

In July 1995, I boarded Delta Airlines in Cincinnati to fly to Frankfurt, Germany, to assume my new assignment as Head of Research for the newly formed company, Hoechst Marion Roussel. As I settled into my seat in first class I reflected briefly on what Max and others would think now that I was actually going to be working and living in a German speaking country. Would I learn German? I was inclined to do so and had started taking lessons. My thoughts then went to the prior four years. It was during this time I realized that I had two choices: I could enjoy the Mystery of the Journey of my life, or I could enjoy the Journey of the Mystery of my life. In my case, I seemed to have a tendency to select the 'road less travelled' and hence was frequently faced with having to enjoy the Mystery of the Journey of my Life. This flight to Frankfurt was a continuation of a Journey that began in January, 1992, at Marion Merrell Dow, and one whose course could not have been predicted. I had assumed that I would have been able to rapidly increase the productivity of Research and Development and that Marion Merrell Dow would have increased in size and capitalization through organic growth. That was not to be.

My first week at Marion Merrell Dow was most welcoming. My office was literally about 15 feet from that of Mr. K's office. In 1950, Mr. Ewing Marion Kauffman (Mr. K) formed Marion Laboratories with a $5000 investment, initially working out of the basement of his home and selling ground oyster shells as calcium supplements from the trunk of his car. In 1988, the year before he merged the company with Merrell Dow, Marion Laboratories had revenues in excess of $900 million. During that first week, Mr. K. invited me to meet him in his office. He welcomed me and told me a little of the history of his company. He then asked with obvious pride in his voice, "Do you know of what I am most proud?"

"Please tell me," I said.

He said, "There are two things that give me great pride. A few years ago, when Marion company was doing very poorly, I did not downsize. People came to work and did whatever they could to get products out the door. Some even went and swept the manufacturing floors. Now that the company has been sold many of these associates have become millionaires."

Mr. K. called all employees associates and ensured that they had ownership in the company by giving ALL employees stocks and stock options.

"The second thing of which I am proud," he continued, "Is that there are now 12 associates who have started Foundations to help others. This is the one that gives me the most pride."

"I have a simple motto and it is: **Treat others as you would like to be treated.**"

I listened intently without interruption.

Finally, he said, "You have a very important mission, because I think you are probably one of the few people who can do it. Your Job is to say 'No' to Fred Lyons when you think something should absolutely not be done."

I would later come to understand how salient this comment was.

In my first meeting with Fred I was quite pleased when he told me that he wanted me to take some time to get to know the organization. He told me which meetings I should attend, including the CEO staff meeting and the Development Projects Meeting, which at that time he chaired and would later turn over to me. He also told me that he had mentored Dr. Judy Hemburger, who was the Head of Regulatory and would be reporting to me. He wanted me to know that he planned to continue working closely with Judy on Regulatory issues.

As an example, as a member of the Pharma Board, he was involved in development and ultimate passing of the

Prescription Drug User Fee Act (PDUFA) by the United States Congress in 1992. I thanked Fred for letting me know and told him that although I did not expect any issues with the administration of Regulatory, I did hope that I would be permitted to discuss any problems openly with him, should they arise. I also asked him if we could set up some criteria or milestones to be achieved to determine when it was time for me to assume the leadership of R&D. He said that that was not necessary and although the lack of specificity bothered me a bit, I was intrigued by the approach.

During my month of learning, a number of things became apparent. For reasons that were not clear to me, Fred did not like the Merrell Dow R&D organization. He spoke frequently and openly of how much better the Marion Development organization was compared to that at Merrell Dow. It was also clear that the presence of Joe Temple, who was a Dow leader, as Chairman of the Board was absolutely critical to ensure a successful merger. Joe was a Mensch in every sense of that word and had a practical wisdom that made it easy to address difficult problems with him.

In retrospect, perhaps I should have taken the opportunities offered by both Joe and Mr. K to be seen as having their support, but, as I had always done, I focused on navigating the waters myself and only reached out for advice and help after I had exhausted my own efforts in addressing any issue. I had done the same at Ciba Geigy, at Hopkins and at the NIH, where I had not availed myself of mentors, such as Max Wilhelm, Bernadettte Healy and Juli Axelrod. I had this need to demonstrate that I had worked hard and had earned my positions, and they were not given to me because of my relationships with eminent leaders.

After about a month, I told Fred that I was ready to take over and he agreed. One of my first tasks was to complete the merger of Research and Development departments of the two companies. It was generally felt that the Marion Labs had a strong Development Department. Its research was quite small compared to that at Merrell Dow. The former Marion Labs was better described as a Search and Development organization. Its largest selling drug, Cardizem, was in-licensed, and cleverly developed. Merrell Dow's largest selling drug, Seldane, had come out of its own research group.

I told Fred that I wanted to start off with a 2-day off-site meeting for the new team to learn about the two predecessor organization; to develop our operating principles; and to identify the major goals for the year. These things were critical as it was already February, 1992. I asked Fred whether there was a Facilitator that he could recommend, and he did. Fred also said that he wanted to participate in this off-site meeting. I told him that I would prefer him not to participate because I feared that, as CEO, his very presence might inhibit open and candid discussions. He insisted on attending and I said, "OK.", but could we agree on the following. If you have a major concern about anything I would like you to signal to me to take a break and you and I could discuss it off line." He agreed. I worked with Jerry Bartlett, the Head of Human Resources for R&D, a Marion background associate, and the external facilitator, to structure the meeting.

The meeting started quite well as the facilitator was quite capable. Introductions and descriptions of each department went well as did exploration of common themes that had been mentioned. I did notice, however, that as team members expressed their views they always looked towards Fred, as if seeking approval. Suddenly, Fred signaled me for a break. We went into a huddle and he told me that I was doing it all wrong and as a result the team was not participating fully. I thanked him for the input and told him that I would address it. In my usual open style, I shared with the team Fred's observation and asked their advice on what we could do to make the rest of the meeting more relaxed and open.

Fred shot up his arm and started to speak.

And I said, "Sir, you are out of order. We have an agreement that this is my meeting and if you have a comment you and I will take it off line." I could see the mixture of fear and astonishment on the face of the team members.

Fred continued to express his view that I was doing this meeting all wrong.

When he was finished, I said, "Thank you, sir. This off-site meeting is now officially adjourned."

Fred stormed out of the room and the others, with the exception of Jerry Bartlett and the Facilitator, followed him. We collected the flip chart sheets on which the Facilitator had captured key comments, in silence. After we had completed collecting everything Jerry looked at me. "You know that Fred will fire you," he said.

"I would prefer him to fire me now than after several months of fundamental disagreements," I replied.

"Well, you need to know no one has ever spoken to Fred like that." Jerry added.

We returned to our offices.

Fred and I did not discuss this incident.

We continued as if this event had not occurred. I started to meet with the team on 1 on 1 sessions. I had taken over the chairmanship of the Product Development Committee which Fred continued to attend. I would question data and also call on members attending the meeting to comment on some aspect that was within their level of expertise. The Marion background associates were clearly not accustomed to this open challenge of data, but the Merrell Dow background associates seemed eager to engage and defend their projects scientifically. It was abundantly clear I needed to develop a strategy to guide the organizational and pipeline alignment in a manner that could not be attacked by Fred. I reached out to my friend Eric Davidson, who is an expert in Organizational Development, for assistance. In typical fashion, Eric suggested something very simple. He suggested sending the following ONE PAGE questionnaire to the top managers and scientists and using the output from this questionnaire to develop a plan.

THE QUESTIONNAIRE:

What are the key strengths of your organization? What are the weaknesses of your organization?

What would you start doing to make your organization better? What would you stop doing to make your organization better? What are the barriers to achieving greatness in your organization?

What would you advise the Head of R&D to focus on to move the organization forward?

The answers to each question had to be brief and all answers were to be written in the space provided below the question.

Forty-seven associates received this questionnaire and all responded. I had Jerry Bartlett and his team summarize the responses and identify the major themes. I shared this with Fred and recommended we organize a 5-day workshop, to address these issues and develop a strategy to be presented to him and the CEO staff. I recommended that we hold the meeting at our CNS Research Center in Strasbourg, France.

Fred approved the plan.

Now that I reflect on it, I am surprised that Fred did agree to the venue for this meeting as I clearly wanted to minimize any attempts on his part to participate in the meeting. However, had he decided to attend, I intended to recommend that he attend on the final day at which time the associates would present the recommendations and he could challenge them. We could then make the appropriate modifications before presenting to the CEO staff.

All 47 associates who had completed the questionnaire were invited to Strasbourg and they worked diligently during the five days. We completed the key elements of the strategy and recommendations for organizational alignment. This included making Cincinnati the Research Headquarters and Kansas City the Development Headquarters. We confirmed the focus of our Anti-infectives Center in Gerenzano, Italy, and the Development activities in Winnersh, UK. In addition, the Strasbourg Center continued its focus as the site for Research and early Development in Central Nervous System disorders.

On return to the US, I presented the recommendations to Fred and the CEO staff and they were approved.

There was also lots of fun at this offsite workshop. As is very common in Europe, the French associates selected a restaurant in an old castle which offered dinners for groups. After dinner,

Steve Rubeg, one of the US associates started to play the piano and lead a 'sing along'. Then the associates began calling on me to sing a solo! Steve played a few bars of a few familiar songs but each time I declined.

On noticing that some of the French associates were dressed in costumes, like knights, I told them that I would sing a classical song that had won me second place in the Adult Baritone contest in British Guiana. I was 18 years of age at the time of this contest. So, I sang the stanza from the Secular Masque by John Dryden:

> Thy sword within its scabbard keep,
> And let mankind agree;
> Better the world were fast asleep,
> Than kept awake by thee.
> The fools are only thinner,
> With all our cost and care;
> But neither side a winner,
> For things are as they were.

The European contingent was quite impressed that I was a fan of classical literature. Little did they know that not only had I sung the role of The Major General in the Gilbert and Sullivan's Operetta, the Pirates of Penzance, but that at the same music festival I had placed second in the adult verse recital. I had recited William Shakespeare's Sonnet 116:

> Let me not to the marriage of true minds
> Admit impediments. Love is not love Which
> alters when it alteration finds,
> Or bends with the remover to remove. Oh no!
> it is an ever fixed mark
> That looks on tempests and is never shaken; It
> is a star to every wand'ring bark,
> Whose worth's unknown, although his height
> be taken. Love's not Time's fool, though rosy
> lips and cheeks Within its bending sickle's
> compass come;

Love alters not with his brief hours and weeks,
But bears it out even to the edge of doom.
If this be error and upon me prov'd I never
writ and no man ever lov'd.

The words of these two classical pieces have stayed with me and have often given me strength to know when to keep my sword within its scabbard and when to look on tempests and be not shaken, as I replaced the word 'Love' in the sonnet with the word, 'Grit'.

I remain amazed at how few people have True Grit and how many have values and principles that are like the grit that compose sands that shift with the prevailing winds.

We articulated the goals and every quarter I published our performance against goals, with full transparency and without excuses for shortfalls or terminations of projects. We also trimmed the pipeline but gave every project a sunset time by which the critical hurdle had to be solved or the project was terminated. There were far too many projects in the pipeline, some of which were more 'wishes' than there were potential winners. This process was well accepted and I got the impression that associates appreciated the transparency. The termination of projects created some anxiety about how associates would be evaluated. When asked the question, I responded, "I want our scientists to use quality, cutting edge science to solve problems in the fastest possible time, whether the answer is Yea or Nay! That is what we reward."

Since Regulatory Affairs was also officially my responsibility, I began to review the minutes of FDA meetings. I became concerned because it seemed I had a different interpretation of the minutes concerning Seldane (Terfenadine).

Seldane, a Merrell Dow innovation, was the first non-sedating antihistamine approved by the FDA. It was one of two Blockbusters, the other being Cardizem, in the MMD portfolio. MMD was working on taking Seldane over the counter and my interpretation of the minutes was that the FDA had concerns about the safety of Seldane and was unlikely to approve it as an over the counter medication. In fact, the more I studied the FDA minutes, the more I thought the FDA was considering taking Seldane off the market because of Safety concerns.

I discussed my concerns with Fred. However, he had a different interpretation of the FDA contact minutes.

I told Fred that I had looked at the structure of Terfenadine. There were three places on the molecule where metabolites could be formed. In addition, there was a mismatch between the pharmacokinetic half-life and the pharmacodynamic halflife of the drug: the pharmacokinetic half-life of Terfenadine was extremely short because it is rapidly metabolized by the liver, whereas its biological activity lasts for hours. This often suggests presence of an active stable metabolite.

Fred became quite frustrated with me and ended the conversation. Following my meeting with Fred, I went to Cincinnati to talk with Dr. Bert Carr, the chemist who had invented Terfenadine. He confirmed that there were three metabolites and more than one of them was active. He and the pharmacologist who had helped develop Terfenadine told me that they knew that Terfenadine was metabolized by the Cytochrome P450 3A (4) enzyme and it was also found by others to be a Potassium Channel Blocker, encoded for by the Herg gene. We looked at the data that he had on the three metabolites and I suggested that the metabolite responsible for its long duration of action was most likely Fexofenadine.

Armed with this information, I went back to Fred and told him that if our scientists could show that Fexofenadine was not metabolized by the CYP450 3A(4) enzyme and that it does not block the Herg channel, I could promise him that I could develop and get it to submission in three years. I implored him to let me start a small effort as we could, in any case, position it as a second-generation non-sedating antihistamine. He finally agreed.

The safety concern with Terfenadine (Seldane) had to do with a small number of individuals who at the same time had been exposed to the antifungal ketoconazole or the antibiotic, erythromycin. These individuals had suffered significant cardiac arrhythmias, such as Torsade de Pointe. Antifungals such as ketoconazole block the action of CYP450 3A(4) so that Terfenadine builds up in the body. Because Terfenadine blocks the Herg channel, heart arrhythmias, such as ventricular arrhythmias and Torsade de Pointe can occur. Ketoconazole is used in several shampoos, so restricting its use was impractical.

Seldane was not the only issue between Fred and me in 1992.

I found that he was calling members of my team and sometimes giving them orders to act contrary to decisions that I had made. Judy Hemberger also became an issue as it was generally felt that if one had a serious disagreement with Judy one ran the risk of being fired by Fred. On one occasion as I was having a meeting with Jerry Bartlett in my office, Donna, my assistant interrupted and said, "Mr. Lyons wants to speak with Jerry immediately."

Jerry looked at me a little uncertainly, and then said, "I do not like these meetings with Fred because Fred uses them to get information on Frank Douglas."

I told Jerry, "Believe me, there is nothing that I would say to you that I would not tell Fred directly. So, you can feel free to answer any of Fred's questions."

Jerry looked at me as he rose to leave for his meeting with Fred, and said, "Frank, the problem is that you are in charge but Fred is in control."

During all of 1992, Fred and I did battle.

I had reached out to Rich Bailey, the Head of Human Resources, who had a good relationship with Fred, for advice. Rich had little to offer. The situation was so tense that I was told that people referred to it as the 'Fred and Frank Fights'. Finally, after about 18 months at MMD, I decided I could not continue in this dysfunctional relationship with Fred. I asked Rich Bailey to facilitate a meeting between Fred and me, so I could discuss the best way to work with Fred.

Rich discussed it with Fred, and Fred agreed.

On the morning of the meeting, as I left the house, I told Lynnet and Diah, who was in high school, that that was probably my last day at MMD. I told them that I had written a resignation letter, which I was prepared to give to Mr. Lyons if we could not break through this impasse. I also had generated a list of things that I needed to be able to function successfully as the Head of R&D.

I came to the meeting and Rich and Fred were already seated and waiting. Rich started by stating that I had requested this meeting and Fred had agreed to participate. Then he asked me if I would like to address my concerns. I thanked Rich for arranging the meeting and Fred for agreeing to it. I said I would like to know, with examples wherever possible, what is it that I am doing that Fred finds inappropriate or simply wrong.

Fred responded angrily that he did not have to answer any questions from me.

To Rich Bailey's credit, he said, "Fred, I do think you owe Frank an explanation."

Fred again refused.

I could not hold my peace. I said: "Fred, you hired me to be Head of R&D, but it is clear to me that you want to run R&D. Well, that means that one of us is redundant and it is not you. This morning, I told my wife and my daughter that today is probably my last day at MMD." I rose from my chair and said: "Here is my letter of resignation." I handed him the letter and headed for the door.

As I reached the door, I heard Fred say, come back and sit down. I complied.

He asked, "Do you have another job?"

I said, "No, nor have I been looking. But over the last 18 months, I have tried everything to make this work and I have decided that it is time to accept the reality, which is, I have not succeeded."

Then Fred asked, "What do you want?"

"I have a list to which I would like to refer." I had previewed this list with Rich Bailey, who had advised me to remove any reference to Judy from the list. I had done so. I retrieved the list from my yellow note pad and I read them one by one.

> "I need the authority to develop the R&D strategy and to fully implement that strategy, once it has been approved by you
>
> I need the right, with observance of the appropriate HR requirements and your approval,

to hire and remove when necessary, individuals who will be reporting to me

I need to be assured that once decisions have been made in R&D that associates in R&D cannot bypass me and go to you to get those decisions reversed

As Head of R&D it is my responsibility to ensure rigorous scientific evaluation of projects. This means that associates should not be permitted to circumvent our processes by appealing to you to maintain projects that should be terminated."

After each point Fred said, "You got it."

Then he said, "There is something that you do not know. Your team is gathered in a room and is waiting to see the color of the smoke from the chimney of this building. Here is what we are going to do. You and I will walk over to them and I will tell them that you are the Head of R&D and from this day forward I will not meddle in R&D."

And Fred kept his word.

From that day forward, he never interfered. Before we left our meeting, I told him that there were two people whom I needed to reassign or terminate. We discussed them and he agreed to my recommendation. He also told me to go ahead and work quietly on the Seldane metabolite.

This was none too soon, because about two months later Dr. Kessler, the FDA Commissioner, during an interview on a morning news program, announced that the FDA was considering restricting the use of Seldane for the treatment of allergic rhinitis. The price of the MMD shares plummeted immediately because this meant that the yearly revenues would decrease significantly with potential loss of one of our two block busters.

At the CEO staff meeting we discussed how to manage this potential loss of value and investor confidence. I was asked to return with a proposal.

I recommended that we focus on the most promising projects in the pipeline and we develop Fast Cycle Teams to bring these projects rapidly to specified decision points. I further recommended that we take very senior R&D associates out of their present roles and have them lead these teams, with the written commitment that at the conclusion of their project, they will return to their previous or equivalent position in the company. The core team members would be assigned 100% to the team. Support functions, such as Drug Metabolism and Pharmacokinetics would support these teams as high priorities. Detailed Project plans would be developed and tracked and every opportunity would be used to do things in parallel. Finally, I recommended creating a medical writing group and NDA submission group to support these four teams.

We selected four projects for the Fast Cycle Teams. Two were MMD innovations and two were in-licensed compounds. Dolasetron (Anzemet), a 5HT3 receptor antagonist, which had been moving very slowly was given a tight timeline to complete analysis of the Phase 3 clinical trials and submission. Fexofenadine was given a three-year timeline for submission. The critical clinical trials to demonstrate clinical Proof of concept were identified and tight timelines were established to get go/no go decisions for all four projects. Anzemet and Fexofenadine (Allegra) met their timelines. The two in -licensed compounds, unfortunately, failed to show clinical Proof of Concept and were terminated.

The Fexofenadine project team was a great example of a Fast Cycle Team at work. This team was led by Dr. Dennis Giesing. Questions were raised as to whether he was the best choice. I insisted on him being the leader and he did an outstanding job. Animal models were rapidly setup and these demonstrated that Fexofenadine was not metabolized by the CYP450 3A(4) enzyme. Equally important, Fexofenadine did not have activity on the Herg channel, and administration to the animals showed no prolongation of QT on the EKG, which was one of the hallmarks of potential for Torsade de Pointe arrhythmia. Dr. Vijay Bhargava designed and performed excellent preclinical and clinical Pharmacokinetic studies and supported the clinical pharmacodynamics studies.

A Phase 1 study was performed and this also demonstrated no QT prolongation at high doses. My major reason for promising that we could go from not having a commercial synthesis to submission in three years was that since Terfenadine was rapidly converted to its metabolites, it meant that all the toxicology that was done on Terfenadine was essentially the toxicology of the metabolites. Thus, all we had to show was dose response presence of fexofenadine when Terfenadine was administered to the animals in brief toxicology studies. FDA accepted this reasoning. I was elated because this meant that I could make good on my statement to Fred that I could develop Fexofenadine in three years.

Another challenge was the commercial synthesis. I instructed the team to try several approaches in parallel, including a biotechnology approach. (In fact, the plant in Brindisi, Italy, that was built to work on biotechnology production of Fexofenadine was dedicated in my honor. The last time I visited Brindisi, the plaque with the dedication was still on the corner stone).

Dr. Philippe Bey, Head of Research, did a yeoman's job in using several approaches to rapidly develop a commercial synthesis for Fexofenadine. Clinical studies were less of a challenge. The Merrell Dow organization had learned a lot over the years about the best design to show clinical activity in a Phase 2a trial. We could also extrapolate from the serum levels of fexofenadine achieved with different active doses of administered Terfenadine, to find the best fexofenadine doses to use in the Phase 2a study. This allowed us to do the equivalent of a Phase2b/3 study for submission. With approaches such as these we were able to reach our target for submission in three years. The FDA placed a Black Box warning on Seldane and we were able, ultimately, to bring Fexofenadine (trade name, Allegra) onto the market, and remove Seldane from the market. Allegra D followed closely thereafter. Anzemet was submitted and approved for the prevention of chemotherapy induced nausea and vomiting.

In late 1993, Dr. Richard Markham the former COO of Merck joined MMD as President and COO and member of the Board of Directors. My life improved significantly with the addition of Dick Markham.

Dick had spent almost all of his professional career at Merck and thus had been impregnated with the culture of a strong research-based Pharmaceutical company. During the years that Dr. Roy Vagelos was CEO, Merck was voted 'the most Admired Company'. In my view it was also the most innovative company, even though it seemed to use a 'fast follower strategy'.

One of the first things that happened following Dick's arrival was that I received a significant increase in compensation including an award of shares and options. (This was one of the issues between Fred and me when I discovered that two of the individuals reporting to me were actually being compensated at a higher rate than I).

In any case, when I asked Rich Bailey, to what I owed this windfall, he said, "you owe it to Dick Markham." Apparently, when Dick saw my compensation, he told Fred that he (Fred) did not quite appreciate how highly regarded Frank Douglas was in the pharmaceutical R&D community.

I could also discuss exploratory projects with Dick, who, once given the scientific basis of the project, would suggest indications for development that we had sometimes not considered. Dick's leadership was also critical at this time as we considered strategic moves for the company. We pursued a small number of potential merger candidates and a company that expressed interest was Hoechst. In fact, Hoechst made an offer to acquire the company but Dow, the parent company of MMD, found the offer not satisfactory. Dick was tasked with keeping open lines of communication with Hoechst. Finally, in May, 1995, Hoechst purchased Marion Merrell Dow for $7.1 Billion.

When Juergen Dormann, the CEO of the Hoechst conglomerate, was asked why he had paid $7.1 Billion for MMD, he reportedly responded, 'for MMD's development and marketing expertise, MMD's good working relationship with the FDA, Dick Markham and Frank Douglas.'

This was evidently the case as with the formation of Hoechst Marion Roussel, Dick was identified to succeed Jean Pierre Godard as CEO of the merged company on Jean Pierre's retirement within one year.

My role was a little less clear initially. I had been approached by Bristol Myers Squibb and after a couple of interviews had received an offer letter to become their global Head of Development and succeed Dr. Leon Rosenberg, the EVP responsible for R&D, on his retirement which was targeted to occur one year later. I decided to stay with the newly merged company, HMR (Hoechst Marion Roussel), for two reasons. The first was to ensure that there was no delay in getting all Fexofenadine studies completed for the targeted submission date of the NDA. The second was my concern for the associates in Kansas City. Hoechst explained that for political reasons they had to split the responsibilities of R&D. Dr. Rothraut Lapps, a German Hoechst Associate would be responsible for Development, worldwide, and I for Research worldwide. They committed, verbally, that in 18 months, they would recombine R&D under me. My concern for Fexofenadine and the Kansas City Associates was enough for me to accept, with little concern about the final outcome with respect to the organizational structure of R&D.

With this commitment, I had already made a couple of brief trips to Frankfurt to secure housing and company ID, etc. On the return to Kansas City from my second trip, as I was walking by Fred's office, his assistant mentioned that Fred was in his office.

I went in to see him.

He was sitting behind his desk looking a little forlorn. In the past, his very presence seemed to fill the office, but now it felt eerily empty. He got up from behind his desk and invited me to sit at his large conference table.

We sat together at one end of the table with our chairs facing each other.

He asked about the status of the research integration plans. He then told me that he had decided to retire and his major concern was for the Kansas City associates and any impact on Kansas City. He had hoped that Kansas City would play a leading role in the new company, but that now seemed unlikely.

We sat there in silence for a while and then Fred, who always showed little emotion during meetings, leaned slightly forward towards me and said, "There is something I need to tell you because it is important for you to hear it. When you came to us I did not like anything you did. But you were always transparent. You reported progress on projects and did not hide problems. We could depend on anything you said. You pushed Fexofenadine forward, and because of you this company was saved. You need to know that."

"Fred, it takes an unusual person to do what you just did," I replied: "Thank you."

Then a smile came over his face. "You think that I am stubborn, but you are just like me!" he said.

We both laughed heartily. I rose to leave.

He stood up and gave me a firm handshake.

The flight had once again become smooth. The shaking from the momentary turbulence that the plane had encountered was over, so I motioned to the Flight attendant that I was ready to have my dinner, which I had delayed a couple of hours. I mused how much I liked sitting in the upper deck of a 747 and marveling that a 350-ton mixture of metal, wood, plastic, paper and humans can fly 5-6,000 miles non-stop, and on that night having encountered only 12 minutes of turbulences. And what if it were to crash? (Well the good news was that one would die on impact and not linger in some hospital hooked up to heart monitors and to a ventilator).

A ventilator…this transported me to the last memories of my mother.

Finally, in 1980, the Burnham government permitted my mother to migrate to America. I guess all those whom it concerned in Guyana were finally convinced that I had no political aspirations. Now that my mother was in Baltimore with us, she was able to sponsor my younger brother and two sisters, who were still in Guyana, to migrate to the USA. They joined her during 1982 and occupied the lower apartment in

Wyanoke Avenue, after our tenant, Sharon had vacated the apartment.

My other brother, Cheddie, had come to US a few years earlier as a visitor and had disappeared into the denizens of New York City. He suddenly reappeared to us in Rochester and appeared quite ill. I sent him to the hospital at the University of Rochester for evaluation and treatment. He went to the hospital and did not return to our home. We did not know what his problem was until we were visited by the Public Health nurse to tell us that they needed to evaluate his contacts as he had an STD.

Cheddie reappeared in 1982 after my mother arrived and he elected to stay in Baltimore with her in the house at Wyanoke. In 1991 he became very ill.

I knew for some time that he was on drugs and had discussed it with him.

I was also aware he was gay, although we had never discussed it.

I was also convinced that my mother was keenly aware that he was gay and suffered silently as she became aware that he was engaging in unhealthy behaviors. My mother had called me because he had had a seizure and she had noted that he was having difficulty walking. He was admitted to the hospital. I took the train from New Jersey to Baltimore to see him. I asked the doctor taking care of him what was his diagnosis.

"Do you not know?" the doctor responded. "He has not given us permission to discuss his diagnosis with anyone. However, since you are a doctor and his brother, I will tell you that his CSF was positive for Cryptococcus."

"It is clear he has AIDS. How bad is it?" I asked. "Very bad."

"We would like him to die at home." I said.

Several months ago, I had come to terms with the fact that my brother's life style choices would lead to his early death. My concern was the impact this final outcome would have on my mother.

A few days later he was discharged to home. I discussed with my mother and sisters how they should handle him, how to manage his secretions, and how to avoid contacting HIV from him. I left for a meeting in San Joachim, California.

Shortly after arriving at the hotel, my mother called and said that Cheddie did not look 'good' and was asking for me. I took the next flight back. When I arrived home, I went to his room and pulled up a chair beside his bed.

He requested to be cremated.

I sat there holding his hand and occasionally giving it a firm squeeze. I reflected on him as a young boy, whom all the women relatives loved, as they cuddled him and encouraged him to dress in our mother's clothes. I also thought of how beloved he was by many of his girlfriends during his teenage years and I recalled two of them who were frustrated that he did not respond to their romantic advances. I thought of my own initial anger and then resignation as I observed his dangerous life style with drugs and sexual activity after he came to live with my mother and siblings in the house on Wyanoke Ave., in Baltimore.

Thirty minutes later he passed.

A couple of days later, as we sat together mourning his loss, suddenly my mother said, "Well, now my work is done. I can go now." It surprised us because she had sat there silently, in deep grief for several minutes, when she made this statement, then descended again into deep silence.

We all told her that she would live for a long time, so she should not think of death.

Four months later, I received a call at my office at MMD that informed me that mom had been taken to the hospital, complaining of abdominal pain.

When I arrived at the hospital, she had already been discharged. They had tapped her abdomen and had sent her home with a clamped tube protruding from her abdomen.

I immediately called the doctor and asked him what type of medicine was being practiced and if they had done cytology on the fluid. They had not evaluated the fluid for cancer!

Of course, this was not The Johns Hopkins Hospital. That would never have occurred there.

I immediately took her back to the hospital and had her readmitted. After examination, they said that they suspected that she had a mass and would schedule her for a laparotomy the following day.

The next day she was back to the unit on a ventilator. They had found tumor at the head of the pancreas and involving the gall bladder. There was nothing they could do.

The days following, the fluid in her lungs increased and it was clear that she would remain dependent on the ventilator. One day, she asked for a pencil and paper and wrote that she wanted the tube out. I explained to her that if we did that she would probably die.

She wrote on the pad, "I know."

I talked to the attending physician on the floor. He also agreed that she would not survive long if she were disconnected from the ventilator.

I went back to the house at Wyanoke Avenue, shared mom's wishes with my aunt and sisters, and brought them to the hospital. I asked the attending to come to the bedside and to bring one of the nurses with him. When we were all gathered, I told mom that the doctor was the only person who could make that decision, so I have asked him to explain to her what would happen if she were disconnected from the ventilator.

"Do you want him to explain it to you?" I asked her. She nodded affirmatively.

The doctor explained and asked her if she understood. She nodded affirmation.

"OK. Mom, I will ask the doctor to give the order to disconnect the ventilator."

She reached for my hand. Held it in her two hands and brought it to her lips and kissed it.

"I'm going to leave now, so that the medical staff can disconnect the ventilator," I told her.

Four hours later she was gone.

I turned the light out at my seat to signal to the flight attendant that she could remove the untouched meal and to hide the tears that were rolling down my cheeks. Years later, that would still occur whenever I thought of the life of my mother.

She was a meek woman. As a young boy, I often thought that she was a weak woman, because she never defended me against the lies that were being perpetrated against me. She had a proverb for every misdeed, which we would have to recite as punishment. For example: what a tangled web we weave, when once we practice to deceive; and pride goeth before destruction and a haughty spirit before a fall; were two of her favorites.

I thought of the many years when, at Christmas-time, she would have me repaint the walls of the one room in which we lived. The smell of fresh paint, pepper pot, and the black-eyed peas and rice that she cooked, made it feel like Christmas and we did not notice that once more we had received no toys or new clothes for Christmas.

But most, I recalled how at times, as I sat on the little stoop studying, I would sense that she was looking at me. One day, when I was about 12 years old, I asked her, "Mom, why do you look at me like that?"

She sighed, then her face turned serious and tender at the same time. **"Child, you are blessed,"** she replied **"You just don't know how blessed you are."**

Hoechst Marion Roussel

A driver was waiting for me when I exited the Gepaeckausgabe (Baggage Claim area). He took me to the furnished apartment we had rented in Kohlberg, a suburb of Frankfurt. There Frau Kaehler was waiting for me. Frau Kaehler was assigned to help me with the daily needs of living. She took me to the Lebensmittelladen (grocery store) and assisted me in buying groceries and kitchen items, such as cleaners, soap and other essentials including toilet paper. I did have an uncomfortable moment as she replaced the toilet paper that I had selected with another and explained to me why it was better. She started to go into greater detail with the comparison when, I said, "I agree. Thank you." Frau Kaehler also showed me how to get to the Hoechst site and actually took me to the office and back to my apartment for a few days.

I was given the option to have my office in the building where Jean Pierre Goddard and Dick Markham had their offices, but I elected to have an office in one of the Research buildings. I knew that I was not welcome in that Research building when I saw the office that I was assigned.

It was clearly a large storage closet, barely wide enough to house a desk and a waste basket up against the window, and a cupboard against the wall between the door and window.

For secretarial help, I was supported by one of the young women in the secretarial pool reporting to Dr. Juergen Reden, who was the former Head of Research for Hoechst Pharma. She was a junior secretary, but one of the things I immediately came to appreciate was the competence of these very young people. At about age 16, they enter an apprenticeship program while simultaneously attending secretarial school. By the time

194

they had completed their secretarial program they were quite efficient and could manage complex tasks.

Frau Mazchak was the executive assistant of Jean Pierre Godard and I went to see her about appointment of my executive assistant. She told me that she had someone in mind, who, if she accepted, would be very good for the job. I told her that I would like to interview one candidate from each of the three companies: Hoechst Pharma, Roussel Uclaf and MMD. She actually found three candidates whom I carefully interviewed.

I called Frau Mazchak and asked if I could have a few minutes of her time. She said, "Of course, Dr. Douglas."

I said, "Frau Mazchak, I would like to discuss the results of my interviews with the three candidates."

Frau Mazchak responded, "Thank you. What is the start date for Frau Stoeber?"

I tried again, "I agree that Frau Stoeber is the strongest of the three candidates. I would like to discuss each of them to be sure that I have not missed anything."

Frau Mazchak replied, "When do you want Frau Stoeber to start?" "When is Frau Stoeber available?" I asked, finally understanding that the decision had been made, and my only role was to agree with Frau Mazchak's choice.

"Dr. Douglas, I will send Frau Stoeber immediately to discuss her start date with you."

Within minutes of my conversation with Frau Mazchak, Frau Stoeber called and asked for an appointment to see me. I told her that I was available.

Fifteen minutes later, Frau Stoeber appeared at my office. "Please have a seat." I said

"Dr. Douglas, I am very pleased for the opportunity to work for you, but I have a very good boss now and I feel badly about leaving him."

"Is Dr. Zerban your boss?" She nodded affirmatively.

"Alright, I shall call Dr. Zerban and discuss a transition with him. I will assure him that you will be available to complete any urgent projects over the next 2-4 weeks."

"Thank you, but I do have one other problem." "Yes?" I said "And that is?"

"My husband and I have planned a vacation, leaving the end of this week, and I would like to start after our vacation."

"That will be fine." I assured her. "Have an enjoyable vacation."

After she left my office, I called her boss, Dr. Zerban, to discuss the dilemma. He was quite gracious, praised her work and said that he had told her that this was a good opportunity for her. He said that he was sure that he could manage the transition.

One week went by and I had not heard from Frau Stoeber. Two weeks elapsed and no Frau Stoeber. Many of the memos that I received were in German and I needed her to translate and to advise which ones needed an immediate response. At the beginning of the third week I called Frau Mazchak and asked her if Frau Stoeber had decided against supporting me. She asked why.

"She hasn't shown up for work," I said.

"Oh, she will. She is still on vacation. She has one month of vacation." "One Month!" I exclaimed in disbelief.

"Yes," Frau Mazchak replied. "One month."

While waiting for Frau Stoeber, I had started to walk around to get a sense of the Labs. No one greeted me. They observed me silently. I asked to have a meeting with all of the senior scientists in the Research Department. The meeting was led by Dr. Juergen Reden, who introduced me. I went to the microphone and had hardly spoken 4-5 sentences when scientists sitting in the first two rows stood up. One said something in German, which of course I did not understand and he and those standing walked out of the meeting.

When I learned what was said, I responded spontaneously. "I have been told that your colleagues said that they are sick and tired of people who cannot speak their language coming to tell them how to do science. Well here is what I will do. I know that you believe that Americans are lazy and will not learn a foreign language. I will start learning German. I might not succeed, but you will see me trying. I will expect you to try to do science differently, because you have evidently not been successful in bringing drugs to the market."

I adjourned the meeting.

In the interim I had also discovered that there were members of the Hoechst Board who did not agree with having an American in this role. At least two of them were encouraging some of the senior scientists to resist anything that I tried to do. Two weeks later I assembled the group again. This time I decided to make it a question and answer session.

As I was about to start I noticed two late comers, a man and a woman, who came and sat in the front row. The first question came from the middle of the room. He stood and in perfect English said, "We don't understand it. We bought you and now you are the boss."

Immediately, I thought, 'I wonder if he knows the images the comment of 'being bought' conjures in the mind of a Black man?'

"Obviously, I did not give myself this job," I responded in measured tones "You have to pose that question to Mr. Dormann." Then I noticed someone give a piece of paper to the man in the front row. He and the woman left immediately. There were perhaps one or two more questions and the room went silent. We adjourned.

I learned later that the meeting was a setup. The man was the onsite Union leader who represented the non-Ph.D. associates. The Ph.D.s would never invite him to one of their meetings. On noticing that he was in the meeting room, one of the chauffeurs went to his boss, a board member, and told him that the plan was to catch Dr. Douglas in a trap and then the man, Herr Arnold Weber, the leader of the Betriebsrat (the Workers' Council) would go on television and exploit the error. The Board member had called him out of the meeting and, I am told, worked hard to persuade him to cancel the television appearance, which he did.

Shortly thereafter, Jean Pierre Godard called me and told me that he had received several complaints against me. He further stated that he was inviting my direct reports in Frankfurt and me to discuss this matter over lunch. He asked if I had any problems with his plan. I said, "none whatsoever. I do have one request and that is, I would like Dick Markham to attend the luncheon."

As we finished the main meal, Jean Pierre stated the reason for the luncheon meeting and asked me if I had anything to say at the outset.

I responded, "Jean Pierre, I have only one request and it is that I be given at least one concrete example for each complaint." The discussion started and the complaints were clearly not significant.

I practiced what I had learned at the Center for Creative Leadership. I offered neither excuse nor explanation. "Could you please give me an example, so that I can better understand?" was my only response.

Suddenly, Dr. Dieter Brocks, who was Head of Metabolism and one of the leaders of the resistance against me, blurted out, "The problem is that you are charismatic and in our history we do not like charismatic leaders."

"That is enough," Jean Pierre said as he stood up and terminated the meeting.

The next day, Prof. Feltch, who was the member of the Board responsible for Research & Development across the Hoechst businesses, came to see me. He was appalled when he saw my office. He left and ordered that I be moved immediately to an office compatible with my level and status. I was relocated to an office previously occupied by Dr. Rudi Kuntsman on the same floor with Dr. Juergen Reden, the former Global Head of Research for Hoechst Pharma. Dr. Reden was now reporting to me as Head of Research for Hoechst Marion Roussel (HMR), Germany.

The internal mail for all members of that floor, which was a kind of Research Executives' floor, was delivered to one area and collected by Frau Heil, the executive assistant to Juergen Reden. Before my arrival she was the Head Assistant in Research. My hiring of Frau Stoeber, in effect, meant that she replaced Frau Heil as the Head Assistant in Research. It did not take long for us to recognize that mail that should have been delivered to me was still going to Juergen Reden. In addition, there was a quiet hostility directed at Frau Stoeber, who was clearly ostracized and being treated like the enemy. One morning I received a call from Frau Mazchak. She said, "Dr. Douglas, we know what is going on over there. We want you and Frau Stoeber to move your office to our building, immediately."

"Frau Mazchak, although I wanted to be close to the Research Labs, we will take your advice and move our office immediately." I replied.

We began the process of rationalizing the Research Portfolio. I brought the Research Leaders together, Dr. Philippe Bey of the US, Dr. Jacques Raynaud from Roussel, and Dr. Reden from Hoechst, and gave them the task of agreeing on key criteria by which each project would be evaluated. They came up with about ten criteria, such as in vitro Proof of Concept, Selectivity, BackUp compounds, Pharmacological Proof of Concept, Clinical Proof of Concept, Toxicology, Patent Status, and Competitive Profile. Once this was agreed amongst them, I told them to select three external scientists and drug discovery experts who would evaluate the projects in an offsite meeting. I reserved the right to approve or disapprove the recommended individuals.

Frankly, I had no intention of disapproving any scientist that was presented. Then I selected a two-day period for evaluation of the portfolios by therapeutic area from each of the HMR predecessor companies. Presentations had to be focused on the established criteria. Frau Liane Stoeber, with the help of the trainee assistant, who was initially assigned to me, organized the entire meeting, including selection of the site for the meeting, invitations, and travel of invited senior scientists from the predecessor companies. The scientists, who were invited from each company, were encouraged to pose questions to the presenter and to score the projects on the evaluation sheets. The crucial evaluation results were those from the three external Evaluators. The evaluation from the participating associates was used as another and secondary confirmation of the external evaluation or to create further discussion if there was a marked disagreement between the two sets of evaluations.

At the beginning of the event Liane came to me and discreetly showed me a note she had written on her yellow pad. It said simply that one of the Frankfurt presenters, Dr. Kramer planned to disrupt the meeting during his presentation.

I nodded and said: "Thank you."

Although the stakes were high for me, I was betting on one thing: Pride: Personal pride, Scientific pride and Pride of country.

Without expressly saying it, I knew the scientists in the audience from Frankfurt, Paris, and the US would each be evaluating their colleagues, their own scientific projects, and the productivity of their site against that of their counterparts in the other countries. That is precisely what happened, so that when Dr. Kramer made his inappropriate remarks about the meeting, the silence with which his comments were greeted, underscored their incongruity. We came out of that meeting with recommendations for the Therapeutic Areas of focus at each site: US, Frankfurt and Paris.

Based on the strength and number of projects at a site, that site became the HMR site responsible for Research in that Therapeutic Area. This resulted in termination and transfer of projects, and in a small number of cases, transfer of people from one site to another. The recommendation was approved by the Hoechst Board.

Next, I had to address closure of sites, particularly in the US. I recommended that we close the large MMD Research site in Cincinnati and concentrate Research in Bridgewater at the Hoechst Celanese site. There would be a delay of about 18 months as we built additional Research Laboratory buildings in Bridgewater, New Jersey. I made the following offer to every Ph.D. in Cincinnati: if they were to find a Post-Doctoral position in an area that would enhance their present capabilities, we would support them at their present salaries and pay all additional costs. On their return to HMR, at the end of their Post Doc experience, we would expect them to operate at the level of a newly graduated Ph.D. in that field. (I did not have to address Kansas City at that time as this was a development site and was primarily the responsibility of Dr. Rothraut Lapps).

On the people side, after it was established that Juergen Reden was involved in the meeting to which the Betriebsrat Leader was invited, he was assigned to be the Hoechst representative in Brussels. Not a bad exile!

Dieter Brocks left the company shortly after he implied at the luncheon, that I was like Hitler. He went to work for Bayer AG.

In order to ensure that those remaining German leaders could not claim that I was acting in an autocratic manner, I introduced the following process. For every item on the Agenda that required a decision, I would go around the room and have every one state his understanding of the problem. Once we had agreement on the Problem Statement, I would then get to the Flip Chart and ask them to list the criteria by which each offered solution would be evaluated for best fit for the Problem Statement. I insisted that I wanted the best solution for the problem and I was agnostic as to whether it came from a Japanese, French, US or German originated approach.

This seemed to work well except that the German colleagues always seemed to want more discussion on every issue. I decided I needed help.

I went to see Mr. Dormann. I explained the problem and asked his advice.

It was simple.

"You are the Boss and they know it," he said. "So, you don't need to remind them of that. Simply set a time by which the decision must be made and tell them that if the decision is not reached by that time point, you will make it."

It worked like a charm.

Mr. Itoh from Japan was always first with his recommendation, followed by the US, Germany and France in that order. A final discussion and agreement on a course of action occurred before the deadline, each time.

I had started learning German in earnest to fulfil my part of the challenge that I had made. (I was commuting between Frankfurt and New Jersey). On Saturdays, when I was in Frankfurt I would take a 2-hour German lesson and during the two weeks when I was in the US, I would arrange similarly for 2-3 hours of lessons during those two weeks. One thing that I did tell my teachers was that I would learn faster if I tried to translate a paragraph from the Frankfurt Allgemeine Zeitung (FAZ) and discuss the grammar contained therein. I had a little notebook in which I would write down each word and, routinely, I would also record the words immediately above and below the one of interest. And thus, for every new word I encountered I ended up memorizing three words and their English meanings.

In December, an 'End of Year' meeting was held in the Jahr Hunderthalle for the entire HMR associates on site at Hoechst. This was about 3000 associates. Liane thought it a good idea for me to deliver my presentation in German. I took my planned presentation to my German teacher, asked her to translate it into German, and to assist me as I practiced presenting it.

At our next session, she asked me to read the first page of the German version aloud. After I had stuttered through a few sentences, she said, "Frank, let me be honest. It will take you an entire day to read this aloud. Why don't you do a 2 to 3-minute summary in German and have one of your colleagues present the full report."

I agreed.

I was also not making much progress on the summary. I just could not pronounce the German words correctly. Then I recalled my experience with a Japanese Post Doc when I was at the University of Chicago. One day, he asked me to record his presentation slowly and distinctly so that he could practice from my recording.

I asked my German teacher to do the same. I used it to identify when a vowel was expressed short, or long, and wrote 'ts' over every 'z' to remind myself how it is pronounced. Similarly, for 'w' I wrote 'v' above it. I began to make progress with my 'scored' sheet.

"Frank, when you begin your presentation, you have to pronounce the first few words accurately," my German teacher said. "If you do not achieve this, everyone will sigh and wonder how much longer they would have to endure this."

On the day of the 'End of Year' meeting, Liane came into my office, pulled a chair away from my desk, sat in it, and said in a somewhat serious tone, "Let us practice your speech."

I stepped away from my desk and stood about 6 feet in front of her and began, "Guten morgen, meine Damen und Herren. Ich freue mich Ihnen den Forschungsfortschritt zu praesentieren." I continued to the end of the three minute speech.

She listened in silence. She offered no criticism. At the end she said, "You are ready."

It was not easy to refrain from asking, "How did I do? or was it OK?" In the typical understated manner of the Germans, she had given her positive evaluation.

When it became my turn to speak, an eerie stillness descended on this enormous hall that on occasion would hold a couple thousand screaming concert fans. I looked at Liane who was sitting in the front row in my direct view. I could not read her expression. There was no smile, no frown.

I reminded myself, 'Frank, you have to nail this opening.'

I started, "Guten morgen, meine Damen und Herren." Thunderous Applause! I could not believe it. I said to myself, 'OK. You can do this.' I made it through the summary. Again, Applause. I looked at Liane and she had a small smile. She was clearly pleased.

(It made me wonder how many of her friends she had told that I would be the only American who would deliver a presentation in German). After the meeting I headed directly to the airport for Christmas vacation at home in Leawood, Kansas.

In January I returned to Frankfurt and everyone who encountered me said something in German and I had absolutely no clue about what was said to me. I discussed it with my German teacher who recommended my taking an intensive 3-week immersion course in German and she recommended S&W School in Meersburg. She said I had to be someplace where people could not bring work to me and the distance of Meersburg from Hoechst would achieve that. I could only afford two weeks in February so Liane signed me up for the course. In the meantime, it was recognized that I had only learned how to read a text but could not converse in German. So, I no longer had to go through the embarrassment of not being able to respond in German. Everyone reverted to English when speaking to me.

Niehls, one of the owners of the S&W (Sprachen und Wirtschaft) School, met me at the train station at Fredricksburg and took me to the home of Frau Baerbel Trautwein. Frau Trautwein had a large house with a great rose garden on the side of the hill that sloped down towards the main road below. Beyond this road, the center of the city stretched towards the east bank of the Bodensee Lake. There was a wonderful view of the calm waters of this lake as one enjoyed 'Breakfast at Trautwein'. Frau Trautwein would have 2-3 students in residence and Breakfast consisted of freshly baked dark and light-colored rolls, at least three types of cheese, marmalade, slices of ham, tea and coffee. There was always a small bouquet of flowers in the middle of the table. Frau Trautwein provided breakfast each morning from Monday to Friday. The first floor of her house consisted of the kitchen, breakfast area, and living room, which also had a wonderful view of the lake.

The entrance hall held a guest bathroom and, to the left opened onto the living room, and on the right were the stairs to the second and third floors, as well as entrance to the breakfast area through the kitchen. On the left of this living room were Frau Trautwein's private quarters. The students had large rooms on the second floor. These very large rooms each contained a bed, desk and chair, two easy chairs, and an incredible view of the Bodensee Lake. The early morning view of this lake from my bedroom window produced the calm I needed to face the day's barrage of German words that never coalesced into comprehensible sentences. The view of the gentle sunsets over the Lake slowly drained my head of the feeling that the day's jumbled vocabulary had not yet found the right networks for storage in my fevered brain, before I had to embark on my evening class. A kitchen and a common full bathroom were across the hallway and a public coin-operated phone was on the wall in the hallway, on the second floor. A full apartment was on the third floor.

After Fruehstueck with Frau Trautwein, we would walk down the hill, cross the main street and traverse the cobbled-stoned streets of the small, town center. The school occupied the second floor of a small building in the middle of this town center.

My program began at 8 am with a 1-hour break for lunch and a similar 1-hour break at 5 pm for dinner. The day ended at 7:30 pm after my session with Niehls. The rest of the day was shared by 4-5 other teachers. I dreaded my first session because Angelika had an accent that I could not understand and so I neither recognized nor appreciated anything she said. The other sessions were fine but at the end of each day my head felt like a solid heavy wooden block supported by my neck. I was supposed to have sessions on the week end, but by Friday afternoon I was in such a deep fog with a heavy wooden block for a head, that I cancelled out of it and used the time to relax. I was really ready for a motivational speech from Professor Henry Higgins. 'Eliza Doolittle, believe me: I understand what you went through', I would think to myself, at the end of each day.

That Friday afternoon, I was like an addict craving to hear and speak English. When I returned to Frau Trautwein's house, I broke the rules and spoke to her in English. Frau Trautwein had lived in America for 10-12 years when her late husband was an engineer at NASA so I suspected that she spoke English fluently. She looked at me with a blank, but yet kind stare, and never responded. I went up to the phone on my floor, made an overseas call to my assistant in the US and assuaged my throbbing head with the sound of fluently spoken English sentences. The content of the call was not important. I simply needed to hear the flow of understandable, connected thoughts spoken in sentences without being aware that those sentences had WORDS!

The following Monday, I stayed a little longer at breakfast and arrived for my session with Angelika, purposely a little late, in order to shorten my misery. I made it through the day and evidently the weekend break had been good for me as I came into my evening session without the feeling that I had a great wooden block for a head.

Niehls' session consisted of explaining the structure of business, unions and the economy in Germany. He covered the role of the Vorstand (Board of Management), Aufsichtsrat (Board of Directors or Supervisory Board) and the important Mitbestimmungsrecht des Betriebsrats (co-determination right of the Work Councils). (This last, where the unions have a seat on the Board of Directors and give input to major strategic changes in the company, is a major difference compared to the USA).

As I sat listening to Niehls everything was so clear that I finally raised my hand and asked, "Niehls, are you speaking to me in English or German."

A smile came over his face and he said, "Sie haben begonnen auf Deutsch zu Denken." (You have begun to think in German). Of course, everything he had said was in German.

The following morning, I could understand Angelika and to everybody's relief I began to respond in German. The previous week I had sat impassively, listening to everything but without ever uttering a word in response. I had had the breakthrough and I was not late for any of my remaining sessions with Angelika.

I could also see that my sessions with Doris and Iris were more enjoyable for them because I was conversing. Sprechen und Hoeren (Speaking and Listening) is how one learns a language, they would remind me.

On the morning that I returned to my office, I greeted Liane in German. She responded in German. I then asked her in German why she had responded to me in German because before that morning she had always spoken to me in English. She said that it was clear from my diction that I could speak and understand German. Prior to that morning, I had a little ritual with Liane. I would write out a sentence in German, practice pronouncing it, then go out to her desk and ask her my question in German. She would always respond in English.

Liane suggested that I should conduct my daily staff meeting auf Deutsch whenever only German speaking staff members were in attendance. I suggested that I would initially try it one to two days a week.

Shortly thereafter, I was conducting all of my staff meetings auf Deutsch. I requested my staff and others to correct my inaccurate translations from English to German, and not to refrain from laughing when they found a misstatement hilarious. I needed them to instruct me on the correct usage of the words or phrase. This was very important to me because I wanted to avoid repetition of an incident that had occurred in one of the Hoechst Board meetings. My colleague, Frau

Dr. Lapps, and I were invited to give a progress report on the merger activities of our departments, Development and Research, respectively. The meeting was conducted in English as I was the only one who could not speak German. My colleague had a very bad cold and after a fit of coughing, I turned to her and said, "Gute Aufbesserung." I quickly corrected it to, "Gute Besserung", when I observed the smiles on the faces of several of the Board members. To my relief, my self-correction, was greeted with much broader smiles from the Board members and Frau Dr. Lapps. Gute Besserung, refers to improvement in one's health. One would never say Gute Aufbesserung, Aufbesserung would be used, for example, to improve one's income. And to make it even more complicated, for improvement in one's capabilities, for example, one would use Verbesserung. (I love the specificity in the use of German words).

The Union or Workers' Council remained in opposition to my presence and lacked understanding of what I was planning to do. The BILD Zeitung, a popular newspaper in Germany had carried a front-page article complete with large photos of Mr. Dormann and me. The Title was DIE JOB KILLERS. Fortunately, I knew enough German to recognize that 'Die' there meant 'the' and not "die" as in "kill".

The Workers' Council asked for a Debate, to be attended by the non-Ph.D. technical staff and other members of the Workers' Council. I selected Guenther Wess to join me in the Debate. On the other side were a famous retired Professor of Pharmacology, the Minister of Finance for Hessen, a national union representative and a local union representative. The moderator was a famous radio personality.

Before the Debate I told Guenther that we should remember that this is really not a traditional debate, but rather an opportunity for us to explain what we were trying to accomplish. Therefore, we should not engage any of the speakers. If something was represented incorrectly by them, we should wait several minutes before making the correction. Finally, I told him that if I did not understand any question directed to me, I would ask him to explain it to me and then decide whether to ask him to handle it or to answer it myself.

We arrived at the venue which was off site in a small theatre style auditorium that probably held about 300 people. I immediately became alarmed because it sloped down to the front and the only mode of exit was to walk back up to the entrance of the auditorium.

(It was really a fire hazard, but I was more worried for my safety because I would have been trapped with no other means of escape if anyone desired to harm me physically. Guenther assured me that such an occurrence is most unlikely to happen in Germany).

The Debate started with the Pharmacology professor attacking me for destroying research in Frankfurt.

I listened carefully, but there was little substance.

The Finance Minister and the National Union Representative talked about loss of Jobs. After the three had spoken, the moderator said that it was time to hear from Professors Douglas and Wess.

I focused on two points.

The first was that in the early 1980s Hoechst Pharma was in the top three pharmaceutical companies worldwide. However, prior to the formation of Hoechst Marion Roussel, it had dropped to about 19th position. Now Hoechst Marion Roussel was in the top three pharma companies, worldwide, but that was the result of the merger and not because our productivity had improved. So now we had to earn the right to be among the top three Pharma companies. My second point was that we needed to hire scientists with new skills. For example, we were proud of the fact that we had one Molecular Biologist in Frankfurt. Our competitors had several times that number.

Guenther and I held to our plan of not engaging the other side and focusing on explaining what we were trying to achieve.

After about 90 minutes, Herr Weber, the leader of the Workers Council in Frankfurt, rose. "Professor Douglas, we understand that you need to bring new skills on board. My question is: Can you do that without reducing the workforce?" he asked.

I told him what I had done with the scientists in Cincinnati, where we were closing the site. I told him that we would offer the same to every Ph.D. in Frankfurt who would take 18-24 months to learn a new area and return to help improve our innovation capabilities.

The Debate ended without incident. Guenther said that he thought that we had performed credibly. The following day I also learned that the attendees were surprised that I could debate auf Deutsch and without need of a translator.

Later that day Herr Weber came to see me.

"Professor Dr. Douglas, die falsche Information wurde mir gegeben (I was given incorrect information)," he stated as he addressed me with German formality. "Es wurde mir gesagt, dass Sie die Techniker entlassen wollten. (I was told that you wanted to fire the technicians). Jetzt es ist mir sehr klar, dass Sie Wissenschaftler mit neuen Expertise in die Firma bringen moechten. (It is now clear to me that you want to bring scientists with new expertise into the company)." I said. "Herr Weber, das ist richtig. Zum Beispeil, wir brauchen Wissenschftler, die Expertise in Der Molekularbiologie haben. Im Moment, gibt es nur EINEN solchen Wissenschaftler in Frankfurt. (Mr. Weber, that is correct. For example, we need scientists who have expertise in Molecular Biology. Presently, we only have ONE such scientist in Frankfurt)."

"Professor Dr. Douglas, ich moechte Ihnen gerne helfen. Ich koennte das tun, wenn wir die wichtigsten Sachen zusammen diskutieren, bevor Sie Aenderungen machen. (I would like to help. I could do this if together we discuss important matters before you make changes)."

He continued, "Bitte, vergessen Sie nicht, dass ich Politiker bin. Das bedeutet, dass wenn ich zu den Mitarbeitern etwas sage, bedeutet es nicht, dass ich gegen Sie spreche. (Please do not forget that I am a politician. This means that when I say anything to the workers, it is not a signal that I am speaking against you)."

"Herr Weber, dass waere willkommen. Vielleicht koennten wir ein Meeting zweimal im Monat, oder wenn immer es noetig ist, haben. (I would welcome that. Perhaps we could have a meeting twice each month, or whenever it is necessary)."

"Vielen Dank, Herr Professor Dr. Douglas." We shook hands and that was the beginning of a productive collaboration.

A couple of weeks after this debate, as I was driving into work, Liane called and told me not to come onto the campus.

I was unsure what to do so I called Beate Lupprian in Bad Soden, a neighboring town, and asked if I could come by and stay at her place for a few hours. After about two hours of wondering what was happening on campus, I got the Entwarnung (all-clear) from Dr. Hildegard Nimmesgern and I went into the office. Once there I learned that a demonstration had been planned to block my access to my office. Since I did not show the demonstration fizzled.

Beate was an interior designer who had helped me with renovations in the apartment when I had moved from Kohlberg to Frankfurt City. She had given me a detailed Rechnung (Bill) for materials and the workmen's time, but I noted nothing for her time and expertise was recorded. I asked her about it and she waved it off. I asked Liane how to handle this and Liane advised that I should give her a gift that would have meaning for her.

During the time that Beate and her team were renovating the apartment, she and I would meet Friday's after work and practice languages (German, on my side and English, on her side). She had mentioned that she had never visited the US and that gave me an idea. I discussed it with Liane who was certain that Beate would be very excited by such an invitation. I invited Beate to spend Christmas with us in the US. She was delighted and spent 10 days with us in New Jersey during Christmas, in 1997.

A few months following the failed demonstration in front of my office, however, a more serious event occurred.

A Union demonstration organized by the Union of Hoechst City and supported by the national union was planned to occur outside the gates of the Hoechst campus.

I came onto the Campus that morning and saw white crosses covering the lawns outside the Research Laboratory buildings. The crosses were placed neatly in rows, several deep, and reminded me of the Luxembourg American Cemetery and Memorial that I had visited a few years earlier. White coats hung from the windows of the laboratories, simulating ghosts.

I could feel the hairs standing erect at the back my neck. And to experience this in a foreign land!

It was more eerie than the burning cross at Lehigh University.

It was also clear that this organized and planned event involved many individuals, and that it was no midnight prank.

I wondered whether the use of crosses was also an attack on my ethnicity. Since many individuals were involved, it could not have escaped everyone's consciousness of the implication of placing crosses on the lawn where a Black person worked.

I came to my office and before I could greet her, Liane in a very serious tone, said, "Mr. Waesche wants you to go to his office immediately." And she stressed immediately.

I walked over to Horst Waesche's office and, in his office, there were two other colleagues. I was already in my Fog state with thoughts flying with lightning speed through my brain, but none stopping long enough to be processed. He came directly to the point. "The National Union has planned a demonstration against Mr. Dormann and you. We expect about 8,000 demonstrators outside the gates of the Hoechst Plant. We are concerned about the actions inside the Plant, such as the crosses on the lawn, and although we doubt that any bodily harm would come your way, we want to take every possible precaution."

As he paused, my Fog was clearing. I began to listen intently. I noted that Charles Langston, our Head of Human Resources wore a look of deep concern. I said nothing. I listened for the planned action.

"We have selected a place some distance away from Hoechst and you will stay there with a guard."

I finally spoke. I said, simply, "Ok. I will go back to my apartment and pack a suitcase."

Horst Waesche responded quickly, "We do not want you to return to your office or apartment. The driver is ready to take you to the selected destination right now. Your driver will also be your bodyguard. We will get your personal items to you."

My Fog returned as I followed the driver/bodyguard to his car.

I spent the week wondering whether this was worth it. I considered resigning and returning to America, However, I reminded myself that the National Union Demonstration was primarily against Mr. Dormann and I was seen as his most visible Agent of Change.

I called S&W and reached Anka, the co-owner of the school. I asked her advice.

She expressed disbelief about the Crosses on the lawns but felt that there would be no attack on my person.

I also called Frau Trautwein since she had lived in Alabama and would be more aware of racial issues in the USA.

She expressed disbelief and horror but also felt that it would be unlikely that anyone would harm my person.

I refrained from calling any of my colleagues, including Dick Markham. I decided that the decision about whether to leave or stay was one that I alone could make. It also was for me a test as to how Mr. Dormann and the Board would respond.

Two of my mother's frequent sayings kept rolling through my mind. "Son," she would say. "Virtue is its own reward. And, Son, people can do to you what they want to do, when they want to do, how they want to do, but NEVER for as long as they would want to do."

The following week I returned to my office. Everything had returned to normal.

No one talked about the crosses which were all removed. There were still a few white coats in windows.

Mr. Waesche asked for a tour of the Research Labs. I used this tour to 'show off' a daring hire that I had made in order to illustrate the new skills that we needed. (I had hired Dr. Andreas Bush, who was very young, to replace Prof. Bernard Schoelkens as leader of the Cardiovascular Group). It was clear to me that Mr. Waesche had asked for the tour to demonstrate visibly that I had Mr. Dormann's and his support.

Apart from the few white coats still in display in the windows, no one, including Liane, ever mentioned the event. The major change was that I was given a driver/body guard and advised not to drive anywhere by myself. I was advised to have Mr. Ralf Weber, my driver, accompany me at all times.

Was Nicht Ist, Ja Kann Das Noch Werden

During this initial difficult 18-month period, I had found two sources of support. One was Liane and her husband Dieter and the other was the group at S&W. I would periodically call up Anka or Niehls and schedule a weekend for private German lessons. I would stay at Frau Trautwein's 'Bed and Breakfast' and enjoy an evening at one of the restaurants with one of the S&W teachers and Frau Trautwein. By now we were using the German familial form 'Du', in addressing each other.

(This was one of the things that I really liked about Germany. They make a clear distinction between an acquaintance and a friend. Once they consider you a friend and have offered the 'DU' form form of address, you are like a member of the family).

In my first weekend back to S&W, they expressed great surprise at my German capabilities. They told me that usually when executives came to them, they had been sent by their companies and were really not interested in learning German. So, these executives would spend three weeks at S&W and one year later they would return and have to start learning German, all over again. Anka continued, "Then one day, Frank Douglas came to us. We had great concern because the first week he worked very hard but was just not getting it. Suddenly, in the second week he was fluent. Now, several weeks later he is speaking and writing German at the level of a German first year University Student!"

Meersburg, teachers at S&W, such as Niehls, Anka and Iris, and Frau Trautwein (Baerbel) became my friendly places and faces away from Frankfurt.

Liane and Dieter and Manuela Blume at TExT (my German Teacher in Frankfurt) were my friendly faces in Frankfurt and Hoechst.

My unexpected rapid success in learning German was also captured in the Frankfurt newspaper. In a profile written about me in the Frankfurter Allgemeine Zeitung, the following comment was made (Seite 56/Samstag, 18 Juli 1998. Nr.164):

'Um das besser zu koennen, hat Douglas Deutsch gelernt. Kein Wort habe er gesprochen oder verstanden, als er Ende 1995 aus den Vereinigten Staaten zuerst nach Frankreich, dann bald nach Deutschland gekommen sei. Nun spricht er die Sprache des Ursprungslandes perfekt.'

Translation: In order to be able to do this better (the persuading of others), Douglas learned German. He neither spoke nor understood a word (of German), when, at the end of 1995 he left the USA, first to France and shortly thereafter to Germany. Now he speaks the language of the Country of origin, (i.e. Germany), perfectly.

Of course, this was slight exaggeration. By end of 1995, I had learned many German words, but understood absolutely nothing when they were used in conversation. However, at the end of my two weeks at S&W in February, 1996, they considered me to be fluent.

September, 1996, I called a large meeting to present the organizational changes I planned to implement in the Research Department. I asked to have a Dolmetscher (translator) to translate the questions after my presentation because I wanted to be sure that I understood each question before responding auf Deutsch. At the beginning of the Question and Answer period, as I stepped away from the podium the ear piece fell and I was disconnected from the Dolmetscher. I ignored the ear piece, stepped to the center of the stage and conducted the Q&A auf Deutsch.

A few years later Hildegard Nimmesgern told me that that was the turning point. The Associates knew that I could read a prepared text, but the debate performance had been somewhat overlooked. However, answering questions in that setting convinced the associates that I was fluent in German and that signaled to them, that I had had enough respect for them and their culture that I had exerted myself to learn their language. I was not the arrogant American who had come to tell them to do things the American Way.

I held periodic sessions with the Betriebsrat Representative, Herrn Arnold Weber and explained how I was approaching bringing in new talent. I extended to the German Ph.D.s the same opportunity as I had offered our associates in Cincinnati. We also offered early retirement which, initially, almost no one accepted.

I was puzzled by this until Liane explained that many of these associates and their parents lived in the same neighborhood all of their lives. They are identified with their profession and the firm or University where they work. It is therefore very embarrassing for them to have their neighbors know that they no longer work for Hoechst and that they no longer have a job.

On discovering this, I identified one of the buildings to which we could move individuals and provide them offices for up to one year, after which we would have to let them go, if no internal position was found. It was interesting to observe individuals come to work with their brief cases and sit all day in closed offices reading newspapers and magazines. Ultimately, most found other jobs and we were able to decrease the Ph.D. workforce by 30 % and to bring in talent with the needed areas of expertise.

About one year later, Mr. Waesche came to see me to tell me that they were planning to combine Research and Development under me, and it would help if I became a member of the Frankfurt Rotary club. This was important because one of the senior and prominent members of the Vorstand of the parent company, Hoechst, was a member of this Rotary Club and a strong supporter of Frau Dr. Lapps. I was introduced to the Rotary and became a member of the Frankfurt Rotary, a relationship I went on to thoroughly enjoy. A couple of months prior to this meeting with Mr. Waesche, I had noticed a lot of activity on the Development side as the senior leaders seemed to be flexing their muscles. I learned that a large meeting of senior Development Associates had been held in New York City, and the buzz was that Dr. Lapps would be taking over R&D, and this would be the end of Frank Douglas. Former MMD Development leaders, who apparently had been slow to integrate were now rushing to support Dr. Lapps. I heard these rumors but continued to do that which I told often to my good friend Vince Traina at Ciba Geigy, namely, "When the big guys are firing their guns, you get under the table and do your work."

In October 1997, Mr. Waesche came to me and told me it would soon be announced that R&D would be consolidated under my leadership and that Dr. Lapps would be coming to see me to discuss her role. It was up to the two of us to determine her role. Shortly, thereafter, Dr. Lapps came to see me. I arose from behind my desk and invited her to join me at my small round table. She was, as usual, fashionably dressed, with one of her trademark scarfs around her neck. Later I learned that these scarfs were not only a fashion statement but covered the surgical scar that was secondary to a thyroidectomy. We sat at my small round conference table in silence.

Unable to hold back the tears she said slowly, "The gentlemen lied to me.

The gentlemen lied to me." She repeated this 3-4 times.

Finally, I asked, "Which gentlemen?"

She only replied, "They lied to me and they will have to pay. I will resign." As we sat together in silence for another 2-3 minutes, the previous anger that I had felt towards her, as she had encouraged others to undermine my efforts, was replaced by a sympathy-a sympathy, borne out of the realization that she was misled and had evidently been assured that SHE would become the Head of Research and Development.

Somewhat cautiously, I asked, "Is there anything that I can do to help with this transition?"

She did not respond. After another minute she rose, now more resolutely, and without uttering another word, left my office.

The announcement came and Dick Markham, who was now CEO of HMR asked me how I would organize the combined

R&D. I told Dick I had a plan for which I needed his input and support. It was based on the answer to two questions that Mr. Dormann had posed to me in one of my very first presentations to the Hoechst Board in 1995.

The two questions were:

1. What are the differences between German scientists and American Scientists in Pharma? And,
2. Did Hoechst have good scientists in Pharma?

I had told Mr. Dormann that I would answer those questions after I had gotten to know the projects in Frankfurt and had made an assessment of the Frankfurt R&D organization.

The answers were the following:

1. American Scientists not only ask whether they are **doing things right**, but periodically ask whether they are **doing the right things**. Once German Scientists decide on a path, they focus mainly on whether they are doing things right, and seem to feel threatened by the question: Are they doing the right things?
2. For the second question, I told Mr. Dormann that I had looked at 3-4 of the most innovative drugs that had been marketed in recent years, for example: ACE inhibitors and HMG CoA Reductase Inhibitors. Hoechst scientists were among the first to be working in these areas but had either brought them to the market well after the the competitors, with little patent life left, as in the case of (HOE 498) Ramipril or had never made it to the market as in the case of HMG CoA Reductase. This latter was quite stark because their lead Cholesterol and liver expert, Dr. Kramer, was the only person in Industry to have received a prestigious Liver Research Prize. So, Hoechst had excellent scientists who were working on cutting edge mechanisms. The problem was that they were more focused on publishing papers than

on doing the experiments that help decide whether a compound would become a drug.

My solution was to do two things. One was to develop a Biotech Pharma type atmosphere at the sites, where there would be a focused portfolio and the sites would have to compete for global resources. Each site would be assigned enough resources for its projects, but global resources could be assigned to support projects at any site. The second thing was to have a Drug Innovation and Approval organization whose portfolio was determined by the company and not solely by R&D. Dick agreed and the Drug Innovation and Approval Organization (DI&A) was born.

The components of this organization were as follows:

- Each site had its own Therapeutic Areas of Focus and its task was to innovate for the entire company in Those Therapeutic Areas.
- For example, Frankfurt was responsible for Cardiovascular, Metabolism and Rheumatoid Arthritis, US was responsible for Oncology, aspects of rheumatoid Arthritis and Central Nervous System and France was responsible for AntiInfective agents and some aspects of Central Nervous System.
- Capabilities were clustered to accelerate the drug discovery process.

The Drug Innovation Process was divided into four parts: Target Identification and Validation, Lead Generation, Lead Optimization, and Product Realization. Target Identification and Validation was the responsibility of the Disease Groups (Molecular Biologists and Biologists).

Global functions included: Lead Generation(LG) consisting of High Throughput Screening, Chemistry and Combinatorial Chemistry, and Biotechnology; Lead Optimization (LO) consisting of animal and human Pharmacology through to clinical Phase 2a, Toxicology and Pathology, and Drug Metabolism and Pharmacokinetics; Product Realization (PR) consisted of Phase 2b and Phase 3 studies, Pharmaceutics,

Biometrics, Data Management and Analytics. Regulatory was a separate Global Function. The Site Head was responsible for the Disease Groups, that is Target Identification and Validation, at his/her site; for managing project teams through to Phase 2a; and, in addition, for managing the administrative functions at the site. All other functions, such as LG, LO and PR were global with groups resident at each site. However, global resources were given to priority projects, thus, for example, chemists, at one site could be assigned to support higher priority projects at another site.

Product Realization and Regulatory were headquartered in Bridgewater, New Jersey and supported the Global organization.

Why Drug Innovation and Approval?

It was important, particularly for the German scientists, to be aware that it was not enough to do great science; one must do great science with a purpose and our purpose was to innovate drugs that can be approved for the treatment of unmet medical conditions.

Two other concepts introduced included: Common Mechanisms of Action and the Network-centric Organization. The Common Mechanisms of Action concept was implemented to encourage the sharing of compounds for profiling in other Therapeutic Areas, in addition to the one for which the compounds were first synthesized, as long as the mechanism of action was relevant to the involved Therapeutic Areas. The second was the concept of a Network-centric Organization, through which, by developing networks within and external to HMR, especially in Lead Generation and Lead Optimization, opportunities to find innovative solutions to problems could increase.

Fortunately, I was blessed with superb Leaders.

Dr. Philippe Bey was Site Head for the US, Dr. Jacques Raynaud was Site Head for France and Dr. Guenther Wess was Site Head for Germany, and Jerome D'enfert was Site Head for Japan, without whom, this experiment would absolutely not have worked. Dr. Tim Gau was the first Head of PR, while Dr. Vince Traina (recruited from Novartis) was the first Head of LO.

An unexpected comment on my management style occurred during a press conference that was held to announce the DI&A organization and the appointment of Dr. Guenther Wess as Head of DI&A Germany.

After my brief presentation we invited questions from the audience.

After a few questions about the pipeline and our competitive position in the Pharmaceutical Industry, one reporter posed a question to Guenther. He asked, "Since Dr. Douglas is also headquartered in Frankfurt is your job merely that of a figure head?"

Guenther responded, "Let me explain something about Dr. Douglas. One day I was in his office. He received a phone call. He apologized and said he needed to take it but I could remain seated in the office. He listened to the caller. Finally, he said, "Here is my view of this situation. If I have to tell you how to do your job one of us is redundant and it is not I. That ended the call."

That response also punctuated the end of the Press Conference.

I wasted no time in identifying who on the former Development Team would be retained as leaders in the combined organization and invited the designated leaders in the new R&D organization to a Workshop in Ruesselsheim, Germany. Mr. Waesche joined us for dinner one night and spoke of the importance of moving forward rapidly.

One of the leaders came to me and expressed his confusion about how he should conduct himself. I asked, "Why the concern?"

He replied, "In Development, we spent a lot of time discussing how to keep Frank Douglas outside the tent. And now, here you are in the middle of the tent."

I advised, "Just do your job well and everything will be fine."

He resigned shortly thereafter thus giving me the opportunity to recruit someone from outside the company to replace him.

My next task was a solution for Kansas City, since we had established Bridgewater as Headquarters for Phase 2b,

Phase 3, and Regulatory. In a visit to Quintiles in Edinburgh, Scotland, as they expressed interest in having a larger presence in the US, I made a proposal to them. They expressed interest immediately. I assigned Dr. Ulrich Grau to work with Quintiles to bring this proposal to fruition and to manage the agreement. The agreement was that they would take over the operations in Kansas City and ensure support and completion of ongoing HMR development projects. They would be initially guaranteed 80% of the work load form HMR. This would decline by a specified percentage each year until year 5. Thereafter they would be a preferred provider to HMR.

This was a win-win-win solution.

A win for the associates in Kansas City, who were able to retain their jobs. A win for HMR in that there was no loss in time for completion of important ongoing development projects.

And a win for Quintiles who got facilities, an experienced work force and the opportunity to further build their business in the US.

The DI&A organization was implemented rapidly. This was probably because of a principle I had used since Ciba Geigy, and that was to focus reorganizations on realignment to achieve well defined objectives and to avoid unnecessary movement and transfer of associates. The newly constructed Research buildings in Bridgewater were completed and occupied. Product Realization and Regulatory Affairs Departments moved into a newly constructed leased building in Bridgewater, New Jersey, which was located not far from the Research buildings on the Hoechst Celanese site. This building was also a short distance from the buildings that housed our Commercial Departments. I persuaded Dr. Nahed Ahmed to relocate from Kansas City to Bridgewater and assume the position of Global Head of Portfolio and Project Management. I also hired Dr. Errol De Souza as the first Head of Lead Generation.

Review of the portfolio presented two opportunities to introduce changes, immediately, in the way we approached conduct of clinical studies and NDA submissions to the FDA. The first occurred with the drug Leflunomide (Arava), which had an imminent FDA meeting. I put it into a Fast Cycle team mode, held a week of intense preparations with participation of external experts to prepare for the FDA meeting. Arava was approved in September of 1998.

The next opportunity was the conclusion of the Phase 3 study of Insulin Glargine (Lantus), a long acting insulin.

It did not achieve its end point.

As I listened to the debrief with the lead investigator, I sensed that the Hoechst team had not followed the advice of the expert when they designed the Phase 3 studies. I told Dick that I was confident that I could recommend a design that would show the efficacy of this drug and get it approved for marketing. Dick was skeptical about whether we should be in the insulin business because short acting insulin was becoming a commodity. I told him that NPH was the only basal insulin and it was not clearly a once a day drug. We would be able to show that Lantus is truly a once daily basal insulin.

Dick agreed.

We rapidly redesigned and repeated the Phase 111 study and submitted the NDA, April 9, 1999. Approval was received one year later. Other Approvals followed, including: Risedronate (Actonel), a joint development with Proctor Gamble Pharmaceuticals, the innovator of the drug, for the treatment of Osteoporosis; Rifapentine for the treatment of Tuberculosis; and Refludan for the treatment of Heparin-induced Thrombocytopenia and prevention of thrombotic events.

Nahed Ahmed developed a more rigorous portfolio evaluation process which was co-chaired by Dick and me and in which cross-disciplinary teams (Drug Innovation and Approval, Business Development, Commercial and Manufacturing) evaluated the presented data on the compounds and voted on the portfolio. The entire process was Data-driven.

Apparently, sometime in 1998 Juergen Dormann and Jean Renee Fortou, the CEO of Rhone Poulenc Rorer began to discuss ways to protect their companies from hostile takeovers. They decided that being in a position to immediately announce a merger between Hoechst and Rhone Poulenc Rorer, if either were attacked, would be a good approach. Teams were assigned to evaluate the strengths of the key departments, pipelines, marketed products and patent life, etc., in the two companies. It seems that these analyses convinced the two CEOs that it actually made sense to merge and eventually focus primarily on Life Sciences. Merger plans started in earnest in 1999.

This decision to merge immediately presented a number of challenges. The first was intended to be a major game changer for the new company. Jean Rene Fortou had met Dr. William Haseltine on a plane and Dr. Haseltine had convinced him that he could transform Drug Discovery for the new company. (Bill Haseltine was the CEO of Human Genome Sciences which was actively identifying genes and submitting patents for such genes). Dr. Haseltine had convinced Mr. Fortou that were he to buy Human Genome Sciences he would have a 'lock' on a large number of genes which could be used both for gene therapy and production of proteins for treatment, as well as diagnosis.

I was asked my opinion. I said I strongly doubted that the courts would ultimately allow the patenting of genes that are in nature and that there was a real underestimation of the challenges involved in developing gene therapy. One example was delivering the gene to the target site to create the desired therapeutic effect. I suggested a better investment would be to collaborate with Millenium as that would give us access to their integrated functional genomics platform. This would improve drug discovery capabilities across all research sites of the merged company, which was to be called Aventis.

Since we could not come to an agreement I recommended to have our research teams put together a list of capabilities that were needed to modernize our target identification and validation platform and employ a company such as A D Little to evaluate the capability of Human Genome Sciences versus Millenium to satisfy these requirements. I further said that all I would like is to sign off on that list of requirements and once done, Dr. Francois Meyer, my counterpart at Rhone Poulenc Rorer could be responsible for interacting with the company doing the assessment.

This was agreed and implemented.

The result was that we decided to do a deal with Millenium. The collaboration with Millenium was quite unique. I wanted to ensure effective transfer of technology and codependence in the venture. So, in addition to Millenium transferring key elements of its integrated functional genomics platform, I recommended we create a joint venture in discovering, developing and marketing drugs in Inflammatory diseases, one area where functional genomics could play an important role in identifying and validating targets. The second was that we set up an Aventis group close to Millenium's site in Boston, where the platform would first be transferred, and which group would be responsible for establishing the platform in Aventis' major research sites. Aventis, as part of the deal, also purchased an equity interest in Millenium. This collaboration did much to rapidly improve the Lead Validation capabilities in Aventis.

The second challenge was the appointment of the Global Head of Research and Development: Francois Meyer or Frank Douglas. Mr. Igor Landau and Mr. Fortou both tried to convince me to take the position of CSO for the entire Aventis Life Sciences Group, which included Pharmaceuticals, Agriculture, Pasteur Vaccines and a Blood Factors Group.

I declined as I saw this as a purely administrative role with little impact on the discovery and development of products.

In order to make the final decision, Igor suggested a comparison of the productivity of the Rhone Poulenc Rorer R&D group versus that of the HMR DI&A group.

I responded that I would welcome such a comparison. I told him that it would be a good comparison because Francois Meyer had reorganized his R&D group about the same time that the DI&A organization was introduced. I told him that each year, we had summarized the performance of the DI&A organization and had just completed the summary of the 2-years performance since introduction in October 1997. I told him that I would give him two copies of that report and that I would live by the decision that was based on that comparison. I did not need to be part of the discussion.

A week later, Igor came back to me and told me that the decision was made to go ahead with the DI&A organization with me as the Head. This means that I would have led R&D for the Marion Merrell Dow merger, for the Hoechst Marion

Roussel merger and now for Aventis Pharma AG, in the Hoechst and Rhone Poulenc Rorer merger!

It became clear that the Rhone Poulenc Rorer was a very political group compared to the group at Roussel Uclaf. At every turn they sought an advantage. The battle for where the headquarters would be ended with the selection of Strassbourg, France. (This was probably chosen because it was close to the German border and had changed hands during the years between France and Germany). The reality, which was not lost on Rhone Poulenc Rorer associates and leaders was that the new company was Aventis **SA** and not Aventis **AG.** I was told that Mr. Dormann did reach out to the German government for more favorable tax treatment to ensure that the new company would be headquartered in Germany but was unsuccessful.

If this is correct, then the German government was responsible for transferring an historical and world renowned German industrial giant to its neighbor France.

The battle for ultimate supremacy of Aventis was joined between the French leaders and the German leaders, reporting into the CEOs of the former companies. The Board of the new company, Aventis Life Sciences, consisted of Mr. Dormann as chairman and Mr. Fortou as Vice-Chairman, with Mr. Waesche responsible for Agriculture and Mr. Landau responsible for Pharma, and Mr. Patrick Langlois as CFO. Dr. Richard (Dick) Markham was appointed CEO of Aventis Pharma.

I used the methods that had worked in the early days of HMR in merging and determining sites as well as areas of focus for the sites in the new Aventis DI&A organization. I also used the advice that had been given to me by Mr. Dormann: 'They know that you are the boss. You don't need to remind them. Just set a time when a decision needs to be made and let them know that if the decision is not reached by that time point, you will make it.' I also told the new team that I would be clear about decision making. I would state when, it is: 'You decide as a group and I will do it; when it is: I decide and you do it. In such cases I will explain why it must be done that way; and finally, when it is: I am seeking your recommendation as input to the decision that I must make.'

These approaches were very useful because in the early meetings, some of the Rhone Poulenc background associates would abscond to corners of the room to make private phone calls, during breaks. It seemed as though these calls were to their leaders as often previously made comments and positions would change after a call.

Unfortunately, with this merger I lost some of my best people, particularly Jacques Raynaud and Philippe Bey. They were really indispensable to the success of HMR. Fortunately, I gained some other excellent talent during this transition. These included Sol Rajfer from Bristol Myers Squibb to lead PR, Larry Bell also from Bristol Myers Squibb to lead Regulatory, Bob Lewis to lead Rheumatology in the U.S., Claude Benedict to lead LO, and Pete Loupos from Rhone Poulenc Rorer to lead IT. Thus, Francois Meyer became Site Head of France, Guenther continued on as Site Head of Germany and Errol De Souza became Site Head of US.

There was a battle for the head of Portfolio and Project Management. Rhone Poulenc Rorer (RPR) insisted on appointing to this position, a rather junior associate, who would be coached by their recently retired head of Portfolio and Project management for an unspecified period of time.

I argued that Dr. Nahed Ahmed was already doing the job and did not need a coach. In a final decision-making meeting, I simply said, "You are free to have the junior candidate but you will do that without me as Head of DI&A." With that they agreed to appoint Nahed to that role. Initially, they had the Head position of Regulatory as well as Head of Lead Generation, but both individuals resigned after a few months in their positions.

Although Dick had held a meeting with the designated executive committee to discuss Lessons Learned from previous mergers and what we needed to do differently to make this a better experience for all, the constant positioning of inexperienced RPR associates for positions of leadership led to much confusion on the HMR side. We tried to address this by having frequent off-site meetings to get the RPR and HMR associates working together on their new objectives.

At one such meeting I arrived late for my presentation to the group of next level leaders.

The reason was interesting. There was a large tree outside the bedroom windows of my Frankfurt apartment. At that time of year, I was always awakened between 4 and 4:30 am by the loud singing of the birds who had made this tree their home. On that particular night I had been awake until about 3 am before I fell into a very deep sleep. When I finally awoke I lay in bed expecting to hear the birds singing. Instead, I heard the honking of cars going by, the braking of heavy trucks and also the voices of the citizens conversing as they walked by on the pavement one floor below my window. As I lay there in a semi-conscious state, suddenly, in addition to the noise of car horns, screeching truck brakes and human chatter, I began to hear the birds singing. As I listened their sounds seemed to have grown louder as the other sounds faded into the background. I remained a longer time in bed and enjoyed that sound of life from my feathered neighbors. Finally, I got out of bed, showered, dressed and drove to the hotel where the meeting was being held. I stood in the hallway outside the room where the meeting was being held, somewhat in my Fog state. Suddenly the door opened and I was discovered.

Someone said, "We were about to take a break while seeking to locate you."

I entered the room and decided not to deliver my prepared talk but to have a conversation with the participants. I ended by sharing my experience of that morning with the noises and the singing of the birds. "As leaders," I said, "during this integration process there will be many rumors and even dysfunctional behaviors. This is like the noise of the car horns and trucks and people on their way to other places. As leaders, **your job is to listen for and discern the song of the birds.** Everything else is noise and irrelevant chatter."

Another indicator of this intense political character of RPR came to me from a most unlikely source. Liz, a former colleague of mine from my days at Ciba Geigy, called me. She had left Ciba Geigy and had set up her own consulting business. In this capacity she had been working with leaders in RPR Pharma for a few years. Her call was brief. After a few pleasantries she said, "I was at a reception with the RPR folks and there was a lot of conversation about Frank Douglas."

"Really? That's interesting." I commented as I waited to learn more from her.

"The gist of the conversation was that they could not figure out Frank Douglas. So, my advice to you is to continue doing whatever it is you are doing, because once they figure you out they will find ways to influence you for their own purpose."

I said, "Thank you, indeed, Liz. I shall stay the course."

Integration of DI&A in the Aventis organization went smoothly in the US. There was little to be done in Germany. France, however, remained a challenge. On a few occasions, Dick suggested that I should move to Paris and duplicate the changes that I had made in Frankfurt. I explained to Dick that I was refraining purposely from involvement in the French organization. My opinion was that if I intervened I would be blamed for anything that went wrong. In addition, since Igor Landau and Fortou wanted to make Francois Meyer Head of DI&A, certainly he could integrate the HMR and RPR sites and programs without intervention from me.

As was my custom, at each monthly Executive Committee meeting, which was chaired by Dick and to which Igor attended, I would present, without comment, a table showing compounds and the progress of each DI&A site: Germany, France and the US. Each month, the performance of the French site was considerably less than that of the other two sites.

After about 8 months of this Igor approached me after a meeting. "Jean Rene wants to know when you will fire Francois," he said.

"Why does he ask?"

'Because Jean Rene and I do not think that Francois is getting the job done and you should fire him," he said.

I was quite surprised by this, particularly because at every DI&A Leadership (DIAL) Team meeting, almost without fail, Francois would mention that, by chance, he had met Igor or Jean Rene on the campus and they had told him how pleased they were with the job he was doing.

I called Francois for a meeting in my office.

I asked him, "Have you talked with Igor recently?" He responded, "Only in passing."

"Well, I have some not so good news. Igor has told me that he and Jean Rene are unhappy with your performance and would like me to replace you."

He looked stunned. I offered a face-saving solution, but one which was also beneficial to Aventis.

"You have invested a lot of time and energy in the gene therapy project. We could spin it out as a small company, which you could lead and help develop its product."

"How would it be funded?" he asked. "Aventis will provide the resources."

Francois again said that he was surprised to hear this decision, but he was in agreement with my offered solution.

All agreed to assign Guenther to run France for 18-24 months. As was my custom, I gave Guenther the assurance in writing that he would return to his role as Head of DI&A Germany at the end of this period. Guenther had three heads of Therapeutic areas in Frankfurt: Dr. Andreas Busch, Head of Cardiovascular; Dr. Bernd Kirschbaum, Head of Rheumatology; and Dr. Werner Kramer, Head of Metabolism. I appointed the triumvirate as Interim Head of DI&A, Germany, each being chair for 6 months on a rotation basis. Andreas Busch was the first chair. This actually worked superbly and was well received by the associates in Frankfurt. I was quite pleased by the positive reception of this approach. On the third rotation, when it came Dr. Kramer's turn, my colleagues, who recalled how vocal he was in his opposition to my being named Head of Research for HMR, were amazed that I let him have his turn.

"A commitment is a commitment," I said simply.

Chemical Biology

In 1999, I had agreed to be one of two speakers in the opening session of the 2000 Drug Discovery Conference in Boston. Frankly, I had not thought about it until one morning in February when I awoke in a panic. Suddenly I realized that Dr. Craig Venter, the other main speaker would be presenting the results of the historic event of deciphering the Human Genome. What would I have to say after that?

First, I thought of withdrawing by explaining that deciphering the Human Genome was such an historic event, Craig should have the full morning to present and answer questions. Then I thought that I needed to step up to the plate. I pulled in my key drug discoverers for a Friday afternoon brain storming session. I posed the question, "What do we need today to accelerate innovation in Drug Discovery?"

They concluded that there were two major areas that present barriers. We had made a lot of progress in chemistry. We can use combinatorial chemistry to cover the structure space of small molecules but we had made little progress on the biology side with respect to knowing the structure of receptors and that of many enzymes. There was a mismatch between the Chemistry and Biological spaces. The second area was that we did not have good predictive animal models to predict efficacy or toxicity in man.

And as I listened to the discussion the light bulb went off and I said, "I've got it! Presently we are limited to about 480 targets for drug discovery and about 60 of the top 100 selling drugs come primarily from the target classes: G Protein Coupled Receptors (GPCR), Proteases, Kinases, and Ion Channels. Craig Venter will tell us how many genes control Kinases, Proteases,

GPCRs and Ion Channels in the human body. He will tell us that we can express these genes and produce the actual proteins from these genes. This will, in principle markedly increase the number of potential targets for drug discovery. We will still have a barrier because elucidating the molecular structure of theses enzymes and receptors will still take time. But it will become a Knowledge Management game. Hence we should introduce the concept of Chemical Biology in Industry."

In the concept of Chemical Biology, Communities of Practice would be set up around each of these areas: Kinases, Proteases, G-Protein Coupled Receptors and Ion Channels. Each Community of Practice would be led by a cross functional core team consisting of a Molecular Biologist, Structural Biologist, Chemist, Drug Metabolism expert, IT expert, Clinical Pharmacologist, and Knowledge Management expert. Each Community of Practice would be called a Platform, for example: Chemical Biology Kinase Platform. The role of the core team would be to identify common problems in their platform, stimulate both discipline specific and multidiscipline solutions, and to disseminate this knowledge to all teams working in that area. The Platforms would also be responsible to establish collaborations with academic experts in aspects of their platform. These Platforms would be a further development of the DI&A Network Centric Organization.

At the Drug Discovery conference, as I expected, Dr. Craig Venter told us that there were, for example, about 500 Kinases, 548 Proteases, 800 genes for G-Protein Coupled receptors in the Human Genome. He ended his talk by saying, "Now the guy who has the difficult task to convert this knowledge to drugs is Frank." I was quite honored by this introduction from Craig. This was a watershed moment in the history of molecular biology with the vast implications for innovation in medicine and drug discovery.

It was an excellent lead in to my talk, which started with the Chemistry-Biology Space mismatch. I discussed how the establishment of Knowledge Management Based Communities of Practice could be used to exploit the new genomics information that was presented by Dr. Venter. This new genomics information will increase identification of targets and discovery of compounds that interact with those targets. The presentation was well received and the slides prepared by Drs. Blumbach and Nimmesgern were particularly helpful in illustrating the concepts of the talk. I returned to Frankfurt with the compelling need to implement a concept that I had now introduced to the world of Drug Discovery. I called my leadership team together, including Dr. Hildegard Nimmesgern, who had joined the DIAL Team as Head of Knowledge Management, to discuss a pilot of the first Chemical Biology Platform. We selected Kinase and Dr. Andreas Batzer to be Leader of the Core Team. I asked a team from the McKinsey company to assist the Chemical Biology Kinase (CBK) Platform by doing two things: 1) to serve as an external gad fly and raise questions but provide no solutions. 2) to create a Book of Knowledge in which key steps, observations and learnings would be captured. We also sent out an email to all associates announcing the establishment of the Chemical Biology Kinase Community of Practice. About 250 associates from several disciplines, who had worked with Kinases, joined the Community of Practice or Chemical Biology Kinase Platform.

The first action of the CBK was the convening of a workshop to which all team leaders for Kinase projects across the DI&A Research sites were invited. It was revealed that we had 54 Kinase projects and there was little communication among project teams. At the end of the workshop the number of Kinase projects was reduced to 39. A second immediate benefit was that a solution for a pharmacokinetic problem that had been identified by one team was leveraged by designing additional libraries of compounds based on this solution. This increased the possibility of finding solutions for a similar problem in other Kinase projects.

This was the first breakthrough.

However, during this time many associates expressed concerns that they were no longer sure what areas of DI&A they controlled and whether the traditional departments were still operational.

I kept reminding them of my favorite motto, which was: **Focus more on what we contribute and less on what we control.**

A third benefit was my being invited by Dr. Stuart Schreiber at Harvard University, who was leading the development of Chemical Biology in Academia, to join him as an editor of a series on Chemical Biology. This became an initial 3-volume set entitled: Chemical Biology: From Small Molecules to Systems Biology and Drug Design. I thanked Stuart and explained that because of the many issues demanding my attention in the newly formed Aventis, I would delegate this to Guenther Wess. Guenther joined Stuart and Dr. Tarun Kapoor as Editors for this Volume. I contributed an article, "Managerial Challenges in Implementing Chemical Biology Platforms," in Part VI of the Volume.

About nine months into this experiment, as I was attending a meeting in Berlin, I had a visit from Mr. Raul and Dr. Koenig from the Mc Kinsey company. They were concerned that I was trying to do a sophisticated experiment with an unprepared and resistant work force. They came with a proposal to introduce a change management program.

I listened to their proposal because they had both been very thoughtful advisors for the HMR and Aventis organizations. I thought about it for a short while, then told them that it is normal for the scientists to be anxious whenever there is a change. I can deal with the present unrest and will know when to stop the experiment. So, no further discussion was held about change management programs. Shortly thereafter, I received my biggest surprise and what I consider the greatest compliment that I have ever received in my years of leadership. It is one of those events for which I enjoy great pride and will never forget.

I was on vacation but had decided to remain in Frankfurt and work from my apartment. I received a call from Liane to tell me that Dr. Hans Peter Nestler, one of our senior scientists was holding a workshop, and would like me to attend the closing session that afternoon. I agreed.

I attended and sat silently in astonishment. Hans Peter had organized a global workshop among associates with expertise and interest in Proteases. It was done via video conferencing, which of course meant that some associates, for example those in Japan, had to stay up during the night and early morning to participate in this workshop. At the end of the summary of the workshop's conclusions I asked simply, "Hans Peter, how were you able to do this?"

Hans Peter responded, "I have been reading the CB Kinases Book of Knowledge and have been discussing it with Andreas Batzer, the CBK platform leader. Now our question for you is: Do you think that we are ready to start a Chemical Biology Protease Platform?"

I responded, "Congratulations to all of you. Start the Chemical Biology Protease Platform immediately."

I left with a sense that it was all worth it. There is no greater compliment than when colleagues not only accept an idea, but on their own adopt and build on that idea.

It was finally all worth the effort of taking the road that had not been travelled. Three months thereafter, all Chemical Biology Platforms had been established and were functioning. One year later, 60 % of all compounds in preclinical evaluation had originated from the Chemical Biology Platforms.

In 2002, there was another change in the leadership of Aventis Life Sciences that in my view set the stage for the ultimate demise of Aventis. That change was the appointment of Igor Landau as Chairman of Board of Management of Aventis SA, Horst Waesche as Vice Chairman of Aventis SA; and Messers Dormann and Fortou to Chairman and Vice-Chairman of the Supervisory Board of Aventis SA. Dick Markham was appointed COO of Aventis SA. In my view, Igor had distinguished himself in the first 2 years of Aventis Life Sciences by being loud and uninformed about either the science or the business of the pharmaceutical industry. It was clear that Juergen Dormann could not tolerate Igor's loud and perpetual utterances of uninformed opinions. Horst Waesche had announced that he was going to retire in 2002, having shepherded the merger to this point, but he agreed to postpone his retirement as it seemed that he was the only person able to contain Igor. I expressed my concern to Mr. Dormann that it was unfair and inappropriate to have Igor Landau instead of Dick Markham as leader of Aventis Pharma. I also told Mr. Dormann that he had put Dick in a weakened role and it might help if I could be in a position to help Dick push back against impulsive and potentially damaging moves by Igor.

That was not to be.

In March of 2002 Horst Waesche unfortunately died suddenly at the end of a visit with his cardiologist. This loss was a personal tragedy for Mr. Waesche's family as well as for the many colleagues and friends who admired and were influenced by the calm, sensible and somewhat 'eastern philosophical' manner in which he interacted with everyone and managed business challenges.

It was an incredible loss for the Aventis world!

This unexpected loss of Waesche led to Igor behaving in an even more unbridled manner. His obsession with Sanofi was immediately apparent as he insisted on a repeat analysis on Sanofi as a potential partner for Aventis. This analysis had been done several months previously as part of the usual course of business as we evaluated competitors. The focused repeat analysis on Sanofi returned the same result but Igor continued to argue for further analyses.

This not so secret preoccupation with Sanofi played out during one of our Portfolio Reviews which was chaired by Dick. Dr. Kramer, my Head of Metabolism and world-recognized Liver expert was presenting one of our more exciting projects—a Cannabinoid receptor modulator for the treatment of Hypercholesterolemia. Igor started by ridiculing the mechanism of action, stating it was nonsense. Dr. Thierry Soursac, the Head of Commercial, joined Igor in this rather heated and uncharacteristic assault on a presenter. Finally, I thought that this was getting out of hand, so I said in a very measured tone, "Ladies and gentlemen, there is only one person in this room who has the expertise to determine the scientific significance of Dr. Kramer's presentation. I am that person. I have reviewed this project and support it. If you do not think that we should be developing antiatherosclerosis drugs, then please say so and let us have that discussion." Sanofi had a major effort in this field of cannabinoid receptor modulation for treatment of obesity and hypercholesterolemia.

Dick called for a 15-minute break and when we returned we moved onto other topics.

In another interaction we were preparing for a presentation at one of the Investor's meetings. In the past these were led by Dick and I would support him by giving the pipeline update. Igor insisted on attending the meeting instead of Dick. Dr. Patricia Solaro, who was the associate in my group who analyzed and displayed the most recent pipeline data and supported me in 1 on 1 investor meetings, reported to me that Igor's office had altered a few slides and the projections could be misinterpreted.

I looked at the changes and called Igor to explain that the new timelines were a bit too optimistic.

He refused to make the changes.

I told him that I could not present the altered slides.

He replied that he would do the presentation himself, to which I responded, that that was his choice but I would not attend because ultimately, I would be associated with the presented timelines.

I did not attend the presentation and never enquired about what happened. In early 2003 I asked for a meeting with Mr. Dormann, who in 2002 had become CEO of ABB. I went to his office in Zurich and left quite disillusioned. I shared with him my concern that the French contingent of Aventis was focused on doing a merger with Sanofi. Were that to happen, the whole history of Hoechst and the importance of this company to Germany would be lost. I told him that I also was planning to retire by the end of 2003 because I had always planned to return to Academia at age 60 and in any case an R&D organization needed a leader who was him/herself an expert in the molecular biological and genomic sciences to continue to transform and improve the innovation process. He assured me that a Sanofi merger would not happen because he and Jean-Rene Fortou were agreed on the strategy for the company. In fact, he said that since all of our positions would be up for renewal in 2004, the plan was for him (Dormann) to return as CEO of Aventis, Fortou would become Chairman of the Supervisory Board, Igor would become a member of the Supervisory Board. I asked what would Dick Markham's role be and was quite stunned when he said that had not yet been decided between him and Fortou, because the deal he had made with Fortou was that he, Dormann, would groom Thierry Soursac to replace him as CEO.

I left his office feeling somewhat betrayed as I was always of the opinion that his intent was to ultimately return Dick to the CEO role of Aventis. I reflected on what Mr. Dormann's opponents once sarcastically wrote on the walls of buildings in Hoechst, namely, 'Dieser Mann hat Visionen', and wondered about its aptness. At that time, I felt that the graffiti were unfair and an insult. Was it true now?

Did he not realize that by assuming the role of CEO of ABB and moving to Zurich that he had psychologically ceded any influence he had to direct the future of Aventis?

We continued the strategic evaluations of potential partners for the next merger and started discussions with Novartis. These went extremely well. There was great enthusiasm on both sides because of the obvious synergies between Aventis and Novartis. Joerg Reinhardt, my counterpart at Novartis had quite similar views on strategies for R&D as well as the most promising compounds in each other's pipelines. The agreement was that Joerg would be Head of R&D in the merged company and I would stay on for up to a year, as needed, to help with the transition. As these negotiations were proceeding two things occurred. The first was personal and the second was a real game changer.

On the personal side, Igor came to me and told me that he knew that because I had joined the predecessor companies that led to Aventis through Marion, I did not have much of a pension. If I were to retire immediately he would give me a handsome package.

I asked, who would run DI&A. He said that Thierry Soursac could do that. I told him that I would think about it and give him my answer in a week. I went see Dr. Martin Fruehauf, former member of the Board of Hoechst. I shared with him my concerns about Sanofi and the fact that I was planning to retire by the end of the year. I told him of Igor's suggestion and my concern that it was another sign that Igor was planning something with Sanofi. Dr. Fruehauf said that he found this all strange. He continued, "When a man such as you, who has contributed so much to the company, is close to retirement, we usually give him a year to transition and a very good financial package. I do not understand why they are not doing this with you."

(This was quite poignant because on the occasion of a grand celebration of my 60th birthday, organized by the Frankfurt Rotary Club, Martin Fruehauf had given me a 1933 vintage bottle of Port wine. I still have it!).

The second person I consulted was my friend and sometime counselor Eric Davidson. I described Igor's offer to Eric and my suspicion that it had more to do with secret moves with Sanofi.

"Frank," Eric said simply, "You have never focused on money, so why start now?"

The day prior to my decision I got a call from Igor to let me know that since I was in the US he would come to the US to hear my decision. The following morning, I met Igor in an unoccupied office that he had selected. His feet were on the desk and he had just lit his cigar. We shook hands and I sat a bit removed from the front of the desk and a bit off center so that I was not looking at the soles of his boots.

"What have you decided?" he asked.

I told him that I had consulted two of my advisors and shared what they had said.

Finally, I said, "I have decided to stay and not retire. The money is less important than moving a couple of our projects over the finish line."

He sputtered on his cigar, then got up and promptly left the office.

I went to my office and started my day. Shortly thereafter, Dick came to my office and asked, "What did you tell Igor?"

"Why do you ask?"

He was pretty upset and said, "I don't understand that man." I asked Dick, "Did Igor share our conversation with you?" Dick smiled and said, "Yes."

"So, what did you tell him?" I asked Dick.

Dick responded, "I told him that's Frank. When he says something he means it."

We both laughed.

In January, 2004, we received a hostile bid from Sanofi. Igor expressed surprise stating that he had exchanged Christmas greetings with Jean-Francois Dehecq and Dehecq had given no hint that this was coming. (Dehecq was the CEO of Sanofi.) We rebuffed the offer as being insufficient and word began to circulate that Novartis might step in as a White Knight and purchase Aventis. The French government began to put pressure on both Sanofi and Igor to create a 'French champion' by making the Sanofi deal happen. Sanofi increased their offer by 14 % and a Supervisory Board meeting was summoned to consider the revised offer. This meeting was held in Paris and we were hoping to receive a firm offer with financial details from Novartis to present as an alternative to the Supervisory Board. We waited until midnight before we finally received a letter from Dr. Vasella, the CEO of Novartis.

It was quite disappointing.

It reaffirmed Novartis' interest but required us first to reject the revised Sanofi offer before they would make their offer. The dye was cast. The Supervisory Board had no choice but to accept the one firm offer that was on the table.

Thus 'the sardine swallowed the whale'.

I had the real impression that Jean-Rene Fortou was blindsided by this outcome and that Igor's only concern was that Sanofi had bought Aventis and not the other way around, namely, that Aventis had bought Sanofi. However, Igor was handsomely rewarded as he was appointed to the Supervisory Board of Sanofi-Aventis, where he remained for many years.

I also found it incredible that Igor, in his announcement to the associates about the acquisition, mentioned that one advantage that Sanofi had, was Rimonabant, an anti-cholesterol drug that was close to approval. I found this incredible for two reasons. Igor had attacked our own effort in this mechanism, based on cannabinoid receptor modulation; and secondly, we had evaluated the Sanofi Phase 3 results and had advised Igor that in our view it was not approvable. The FDA Advisory committee subsequently voted 11-0 against approval of Rimonabant. Although subsequently approved in Europe in 2006, it was withdrawn from the market, worldwide, in 2008.

In my meeting with Mr. Dehecq I made it clear that I was not staying on and could depart my office as soon as was necessary. I thought, however, that it was important to have a global meeting for the senior associates in DI&A to prepare them for the transition. Initially, Igor refused to give his permission but I insisted. The meeting was held in the Magic Kingdom, Disney, in Orlando. The theme was: Every Exit is an Entrance Somewhere Else (Tom Stoppard).

The objectives of the meeting were to:

- Recognize and celebrate the contributions that were made by the DI&A organization to the success of Aventis
- Identify the organizational and personal behaviors that contributed to DI&A success and identify ways to fuel the success of the new company: SanofiAventis
- Eliminate Fear of the Future.

The meeting was kicked off with a dramatic presentation, complete with lifelike sound effects of the fire aboard the MIR Space Station. Dr. Jerry Linenger, the American astronaut who was aboard the MIR Space Station, recounted the event and problem solving during a life-threatening emergency. Astronaut Linenger stressed the importance of team work and remaining calm during extreme pressure. As the astronaut recounted this horrifying experience, I thought this is even more powerful than the Samuel Johnson derived statement: Nothing Focuses the Mind like an Impending Hanging. The astronaut was facing not **impending,** but **imminent** death. That must have focused everything he possessed: mind, instinct, intellect, creativity; the only things that he could use in a gravity free environment, to escape to nowhere! The challenges of a merger pales in significance. I felt like saying to the gathered associates as Bob Marley sang in his song, Three Little Birds: 'Every little thing gonna be alright.' You are getting another opportunity to create new medicines in a different space.

In my opening presentation, I recommended use of the SOAR: Situation, Objective, Action, Result method to capture these contributions. I illustrated this by reviewing the transformation in Aventis over the four years of its formation (2000-2004).

Situation: Formation of Aventis and need to rapidly integrate the R&D organizations of the new company.

Objective: Increase productivity in the relevant areas of organizational and scientific performance, by reducing gaps in genomics and other technology platforms.

Actions: Implemented the Drug Innovation and Approval organization: transferred the Millenium Functional Genomics platform; introduced and implemented Chemical Biology Platforms and other Knowledge Management Network approaches, such as Lessons Learned sessions; Lead Optimization strategies, including, Fast in Man and Proof-of-Concept clinical trial approaches; Phamacogenomics, Toxicogenomics, and Drug Rescue strategies; and improved IT solutions with focus on making data easily available to enable informed decision making.

Results: more than 60% of new Early Decision Compounds originated from Chemical Biology Platforms; High Performance Units (HPUs) concept implemented in several areas such as Functional Genomics, Protein Production, Robotic Screening, Compound Library Design etc.; Increased productivity through tailored screening; and an increased and more robust product pipeline. Aventis had also become a desired partner for many academic and biopharma alliances. And Aventis was in the top 5 with respect to size of R&D pipelines (Phase 1 to Registration compounds).

Sybil Schalo wrote in Pharmaceutical Executive, Built for Speed, February 1, 2004, "Aventis' goals are no different from those of its Big Pharma competitors. That it has already delivered on many of them is what sets the company apart.........With that track record, it's no surprise that Aventis has emerged as a potential target of Acquisition."

Hence, in a perverse way, success also led to the demise of Aventis.

On the second day of the Meeting we had the various teams spend a day visiting the Magic Kingdom, and Epcot Center, with the express task of observing the various innovations and using them as metaphors to describe and improve drug innovation. We recommended that they do two things. The first was to use the SOAR paradigm to capture their ideas and add to it Enablers: Technology, Processes and Behaviors or Values. The second was to represent the before and after state in a creative drawing or painting.

Fifty-seven teams descended on the Magic Kingdom and Epcot center and three days later presented their creative ideas on areas across the Value Chain for Drug Discovery and Development. Ideas ranged from generating Lead compounds and Early Development Compounds, to improving Ph1/11a, Ph11b, Ph111 trial design, to Submission and Approval processes. Of interest, the teams identified Behaviors required to achieve the improvements. These included: creativity, thinking outside the box, transparent discussions, networking, knowledge sharing, crossfunctional validation, and passion for data and compounds. Nemo, giraffes and lions inspired the creativity of many of the teams. These recommendations and pictorial representations were recorded in the **DI&A Book of Success**.

Helping a Man Rise

It is said, "It takes a village to raise a child".

I have found, "it takes only a few good people to help a man rise."

I take this time to comment on some of the people who helped me rise above the many challenges I faced in Germany. The first was my sad visit to Max Wilhelm in his home in Basel. In 1996, I learned that Max had been diagnosed with a glioblastoma and was not doing well. I called his wife, Bea, in Basel and she invited me to visit as Max had enquired about me. Bea met me at the train station and I could see how strained and sad she was. She brought me to Max and I pulled up a chair beside his bed. He was not frail but appeared to have little energy. He opened his eyes and smiled broadly when he saw me.

Bea said, "Liebling (Darling), Frank is here."

I addressed him in German and he smiled and said, "You did not join us in Basel because you did not want to learn German and now a few months at Hoechst and you are fluent in German."

I smiled and said, "Max, I think that you choose to remember the 'Basel' excuse but not what had really happened. "

He smiled. Then after a while he said, "When you joined us we kept pushing you into management but you kept insisting that you wanted to stay close to the Lab." He paused. His breathing was labored. I chose to be silent and let him speak at his own pace.

He continued, "It was clear to us that you were going to achieve more success as a leader of scientists than being on the bench yourself." He took a slow breath. "And this is clearly the case. Do you know why?"

I looked at him questioningly but did not reply. I just wanted to listen. Then he said, "You have two talents. You think naturally in systems." Another pause.

"So, your approach to problems tend to be more insightful because you see what others do not immediately see."

I continued to listen.

"Your second talent is that you look at preclinical data and see the clinical implications. You design early clinical studies that inform how to further develop the compound. That is unusual for either Ph.D.s or M.D.s."

I nodded slowly as I reflected on the comments that were made to me in my exit interview at the Center for Creative Leadership. I also recognized that he was thinking of my contributions in Clinical Biology at Ciba Geigy which he had witnessed and supported.

Max passed two weeks after my visit.

At the top of the list of those people, in Germany, who helped me to rise are Liane, my executive assistant, and her husband Dieter. In Germany, one part of Liane's role was similar to that which Jim Stamoolis played when I was at Lehigh. She had a quiet manner of helping me avoid missteps.

For example, having had a successful first portfolio workshop, I suggested we organize a second Friday-Saturday workshop to review projects. Liane said simply and in a low-key manner, "It is unusual for the scientists to work on Saturdays. I do not think that the scientists would be happy if you organize another one, particularly so soon after their first such experience." I accepted her advice and refrained from having another Saturday event.

Liane and Dieter would occasionally invite me to dinner either with their close friends Harald and Marie or with Gudrun and Gerd, her sister and her husband. These were always enjoyable because we talked about everything but work and since it was always in German, it was an opportunity to practice social conversational German.

The importance of Liane, however, can probably be underscored by an anecdote that occurred a couple of months after I had retired. I had committed to give a presentation in Washington, DC. I was proud because I had arranged the logistics of the travel myself, or so I thought. I had ordered my ticket online. I got to the Acela on time. I exited Union Station in DC and started looking for the limo driver. Of course, there was none. I went to the curb and stepped into a cab.

"Where to?" the cabbie asked.

I was confused for a short while. Then I realized that I did not have a clue where I was going. So, I said that I had to give a talk but could not remember the name of the hotel.

"Are you a doctor?"

I replied affirmatively.

"I have been taking a lot of Doctors to one hotel. Perhaps it is there." "Let's go there," I told him. Fortunately, it was the right hotel.

At the end of my talk, I immediately sent an email to Liane and thanked her that in the 9 years that we had worked together, not once, did I have a problem with travel. Everything was always perfectly organized. I simply took the folder she gave me and followed the instructions, therein, without thinking. Equally, important, Liane and the team of assistants, each year managed the logistics of our annual global innovation workshop for about 160 of our scientists, which always went smoothly.

Finally, I got an answer to a question that would periodically occupy my thoughts, but which I had never asked.

Liane and Dieter were spending a three-week holiday at our condo in Cocoa Beach, Florida. They had done this twice before in my absence from the condo. This time I could spend a week together with them. The condo is directly on the Atlantic shore. As we sat on the balcony, enjoying the sound of the waves, the gentle breeze, and a glass of sauvignon blanc, I said, "I imagine that it was a very difficult decision for Liane to come to work for me."

Dieter responded, "Yes. Our parents thought that it probably was not the best decision since you are Black."

After a sip of wine and a slow swirling of his wine glass as if to take a breath himself, as he allowed the wine to breathe, he added. "Actually, Liane and I went away for a weekend and discussed it and decided, in spite of the concerns of our parents, we would do it."

Then I said with a laugh, "Now I understand why Liane needed 4 weeks of vacation before starting." We all laughed and raised our glasses in honor of our friendship.

I have commented on the importance of leaders like Jacques Raynaud, Philippe Bey, Jerome D'Enfert, Guenther Wess, Andreas Busch, and Bernd Kirschbaum at different points in building Research and later the DI&A organization. A somewhat unsung heroine, however, is Hildegard Nimmesgern. Often, I would be asked, "why are you so positive about Hilde?"

Well, she was different, was very opinionated, a sometime common German trait, but in it all there was a creativity that was expressed differently. Her personal challenge was knowing how to avoid getting between her idea and her audience. She also had a significant knowledge of Hoechst. Hilde helped launch our Knowledge Management effort in support of the Chemical Biology Platforms. She along with Drs. Hildegard Seifert and Patricia Solaro, formed a backroom of knowledge on the strategic positioning of our pipeline.

Although not in Frankfurt, special mention has to be made of Nahed Ahmed. On one occasion, Dr. Felicitas Feick, the Head of Communications, said, "We have often wondered how Frank is able to manage all of the challenges in the US, when he has to spend a lot of time in Europe. We have discovered that he has a secret weapon. She is called Nahed Ahmed."

Nahed was the only female SVP in Aventis and had won recognition based on the quality of her leadership and of our Portfolio and Project Management process. She became my de facto COO in the US and all of her colleagues reporting to me sought her advice on many issues before discussing them with me. Having someone whom I could trust to work with her peers to ensure the functioning of DI&A in the US was of tremendous help during the challenges in Frankfurt and Paris.

Nahed and I had also collaborated on another project for many years. This started in 1996 when she solicited my participation in a workshop that she was chairing for the BPBC (Beijung Pharmaceutical and Biotech Council). This led to our assisting BPBC in establishing and running their annual Health

Innovation Forum and assisting them in establishing their Bio Box, an Association for startup Biotech companies. Nahed continued to work with BPBC as I had to step away in 2011, when an assignment with one of our government agencies required a level of government security that did not permit my advising foreign governments. As of 2017, Nahed was still an advisor to BPBC.

Another individual, who was not a member of the Hoechst family, but a longtime collaborator with our scientists, was Professor Chandra of the Wolfgang von Goethe University of Frankfurt. Prof. Chandra was not only a collaborator and a fellow Rotarian, but also assisted me in the establishment of a CRO type organization to leverage many of the capabilities of the University. This organization is called ZAFES: Zentrum fuer Arzneimittel, Forschung, Entwicklung, und Sicherheit, which used the research, development, pharmacology and toxicology expertise in the University to help startup and other pharma companies. I had assigned Dr. Bernd Stowasser to organize and later manage ZAFES which he did for several years. Prof. Chandra also nominated me for an Honorary Professorship and recipient of the Wolfgang von Goethe Medal of Honor. I shall always remember the event and reception that was held for this prestigious award. It is one of the awards of which I am quite proud. I was told that 60 medals were minted and I was the 24th person to receive the medal. The medal is awarded every 2-3 years.

My German Language teachers, Niels, Anka, Iris, Frau Trautwein, Manuela Blume, and Tina, were not only teachers, but individuals away from the Hoechst Family, to whom I could reach out and escape from the challenges of HMR and Aventis. They became friends whom I could visit in Meersburg or Frankfurt and be simply 'Frank' and enjoy the best of the German country side, cuisine and conversation. In fact, I now have a circle of friends that include: Dieter and Liane, Hilde and Harald, Prof. Chandra and his wife, Frau Trautwein and Manuela Blume, in the true German sense of friendship; something that I do **not** have in the US!

However, two weeks every month, as I worked in my office in Bridgewater, New Jersey, the support that I received from Rosemary Bancroft, my executive assistant, and Nancy Thornton, Dick's executive assistant, recharged my batteries and made me ready for the next two weeks in Frankfurt, Germany. In fact, at the end of the second week in Bridgewater, as I prepared for my trip to the airport, Rosemary, who is German, would say to me: Jetzt freust Du Dich, dass Du wieder nach Frankfurt, Deinem zweiten ZuHause, fliegst. (Now you are happy that you are again flying to Frankfurt, your second home).

I cannot leave my German phase without making a final comment on two drugs that were not successful. The first is Cariporide. Cariporide inhibits Na+/H+ exchanger and in the EXPEDITION Trial showed a significant decrease in myocardial infarction and mortality in patients undergoing Coronary Artery Bypass Graft (CABG). However, there were more deaths from stroke in patients who received Cariporide compared to those who received placebo, although the incidence of death was lower than that seen in other studies. A sub-analysis showed that the majority of the fatalities came from patients in whom Cariporide was administered peripherally compared to those who had received Cariporide via a large central vein. We decided to terminate Cariporide and did not try to understand whether the difference in route of administration was responsible for this result. Nonetheless, Cariporide demonstrated that inhibition of Na+/H+ exchanger was associated with protection of the myocardium. This was a clinical/scientific first.

The second innovative drug was Telitromycin (Ketek). Ketek was the first ketolide to enter clinical use. At the first presentation for approval, the FDA Advisory Committee voted 11-2 in favor of approval, but the FDA refused to approve.

That was the first and only time that I had ever been angry at an FDA decision.

I have always defended the FDA as having a very difficult task: a task in which they are required to bring innovative drugs to patients as rapidly as possible, but at the same time they have to ensure the safety of patients. In an environment where they are attacked by both citizen groups and the congress, on both sides of the equation, I often wonder why their employees work there. In the case of Ketek, there was one case of liver failure in Europe. However, the etiology was unclear. This was debated intensely at the FDA Committee meeting, which I attended. (I had assumed that this might have been the reason for FDA's rejection of the recommendation for approval). However, in our follow up teleconference with the FDA, I learned that there was an investigator, Dr. Campbell, who had enrolled 400 patients, and whom the FDA had been investigating because of suspicions of Fraud in another study. She was found to have also committed Fraud in our study. There were also one to two other sites where the FDA had questions. When I investigated what our associates knew, I found that they had had serious concerns about Dr. Campbell but had not reported their concerns to the FDA. (At that time, it was not a requirement to report these concerns to the FDA, but it was clearly poor judgment not to have done so). I immediately replaced the Head of the unit who had with held the concerns from the DIAL Team and the FDA.

We agreed to do a larger Phase 3 study of 24,000 patients in a Usual Care setting. This meant that the participants would not necessarily be restricted from using concomitant medications for conditions not associated with those for which Ketek was being investigated. A large pharmacovigilance evaluation of side effects in Europe, where the drug was already marketed, was also required. That study again showed statistically significant improvement with Ketek and it was approved. There were incidences of severe liver problems after Ketek was marketed and these were associated with several FDA actions to restrict use of Ketek, as well as Congressional hearings. I do not know whether any studies were subsequently performed to understand which patients were at risk to suffer liver damage. (Such knowledge, when attained, helps doctors to determine which patients are at risk and should not be treated with this drug, while allowing others to benefit from it. The information also informs the scientists working in that field).

A final highlight of my Aventis days was the trip that Dick and I made to Johannesburg, South Africa, to present a grant to Mr. Mandela and the Nelson Mandela Foundation, in May, 2002. The Nelson Mandela Foundation was training villagers to help AIDS patients better comply with their drug regimens. AIDS patients also often acquire Tuberculosis and compliance is a real challenge. The therapy is usually 6 months long and patients often stop taking their medications after a couple of months because they begin to feel better.

This practice, however, often leads to development of hard to treat, resistant strains of the Mycobacterium Tuberculosis bacterium.

Our Aventis Regional Director had reached out to me, and I reached out to Dick to provide Rifapentine tablets to the Nelson Mandela Foundation, at no cost, to help the Foundation in its fight against Tuberculosis. The grant also included funds to train local villagers to be compliance workers. The Foundation organized an event to celebrate the award. The event was held in a covered area outside a main building of the Nelson Mandela Foundation, in Johannesburg, South Africa. About 200 invited guests were in attendance. There was a subdued almost reverent buzz as we awaited Mr. Mandela's entrance. Finally, he entered with a very small entourage of 3-4 people. The attendees called to him in hushed, reverent tones, by the familiar Thembu tribe appellation: Madiba. At 84, and in spite of the 27 years of imprisonment and hard labor on Robben Island and other prisons, he still walked with authority and unbowed. Dick and I each made brief comments announcing the award and then turned to Mr. Mandela for him to speak.

I no longer remember what he said.

In fact, I remember little of what was said that day, but I will never forget the dignity in his poise, the ring of sincerity in his words, the hushed silence of the audience and the venerable aura that embraced the place where we sat. One could feel 'his unconquerable soul' and sense what it meant to be 'master of my fate...captain of my soul'.

And but for a brief, oh so brief moment, I could also 'thank whatever gods may be for **my** unconquerable soul'.

Back to Academia

In April 2004, I received a call from Prof. Harold Sheraga at Cornell University. He stated that when he and Prof. Roald Hoffmann had learned that I was retiring they had discussed recommending that I be offered an appointment in the Department of Chemistry and Chemical Biology. I responded, immediately, that I would be delighted to accept such an appointment. About one month later he called and told me that it was agreed and that they would like me to spend about three days to meet with several faculty and the president of the University. I immediately arranged a visit and was excited by the opportunity.

However, it occurred to me that there was a great need for a Center that would explore methods to improve innovation in the Biopharmaceutical Industry and Cornell University and Cornell Medical School would be an ideal place to establish such a Center. At the dinner on the second night all wanted to know my decision. I told them how excited and honored I was to be invited to join the department and help in the Chemical Biology effort. However, I was thinking of something that few people could do, and I described my idea. I could feel the general disappointment and could sense it particularly in Roald Hoffmann. (I think that Roald was also hoping to involve me in a project that he was doing in one of the African countries).

Near the end of the dinner, Bruce Ganem said, "Well, Frank, you will be meeting with President Lehman tomorrow. You could mention it to him."

The following morning my meeting with the president and his Provost was quite cordial. They expressed their delight that I was considering joining the Department of Chemistry and Chemical Biology. As I stood to leave, I suddenly got the courage to say, "Actually, I have another idea."

They invited me to describe it. They both loved it.

The President immediately set up a meeting with the Dean of the Business School. My visit with him was also quite positive and he offered a joint appointment in the SC Johnson School of Business. I left with a promise to return in a couple of weeks with a fuller description of the planned program.

I returned home to New Jersey and found a call from my colleague and friend Api Rudich. I returned his call. Api was quite excited. He told me that the Dean at the MIT Sloan School of Business had asked about me. MIT had been interested for some time in looking at the Biopharmaceutical Industry but had not found the right person. My name had come up in discussion and the Dean had asked Api if he could encourage me to meet with him.

I met with Dean Schmalensee and we immediately engaged on the issues that a Center on BioInnovation could explore. I also met with Provost Brown. They decided to assemble interested faculty in MIT and Harvard for a oneday meeting to discuss establishing this effort. It was a very interesting meeting. I gave a 15 minute overview of what the program would be and then was asked to remain silent while the faculty discussed the proposal. It was fascinating to sit there and listen to an open discussion on the interest, need, and potential conflicts of such a program. At the end the Faculty voted for the establishment of the center.

There then followed a number of interviews, among them an interview each with Professors Richard Hauser, Ed Roberts, Martha Gray, Robert Levi, Robert Langer, Nobel laureate Phillip Sharp, and Vice President of Research Prof. Alice Gast.

My interview with Ed Roberts was significant. I arrived at his office and he offered me a seat in the lone chair other than the one behind his desk. My chair was at one end of a small sofa. As the conversation started he sat at the far end of the sofa away from my chair. He had been an MIT 'lifer': Undergraduate, graduate, faculty for a total of about 50 years. Few could know MIT, its incredible scholastic, research, technical and business leadership and culture better than he. He asked many probing questions in a manner that enabled a dialogue as opposed to a recitation of facts about my life on my part. As we spoke I suddenly became aware that he was sitting at the end of the sofa closer to me. I do not know when that movement occurred but it reinforced for me that his recommendation that I meet with him and Prof. Hauser regularly, so that they could help guide me, was quite genuine. It was one of my warmest welcomes to MIT.

This reception and obvious longstanding interest in the topic of Biomedical Innovation was quite compelling. In addition, all of the elements for such a collaborative effort: Biopharmaceutical companies, Academia, Medical Schools, and Hospitals were within easy distance of each other. I called President Lehman and explained that although I was really excited about the opportunity of being a part of the Cornell Community, establishing the Center in the Cambridge-Boston area would enable a more rapid initiation of the concept. We agreed that once the Center was established at MIT, we would consider starting one at Cornell. I communicated this to Dean Schmalansee and we agreed to have me join MIT and develop the Center.

I started early in 2005 and began to organize the MIT Center for Biomedical Innovation. I thought a good launch of the Center for Biomedical Innovation would be a forum on ways to improve the speed of Drug Innovation and its Approval Process. We limited attendance to 150 invitees and ended up with many more as several individuals appeared and were, of course, not denied entry to the event. The speakers consisted of leaders from the Pharmaceutical Industry and the FDA. It was an auspicious launch of CBI and introduced our concept of the CBI being a Safe Haven, where academics, industry and government scientists could meet and discuss major issues under the Chatham House Rules.

It led one MIT professor to give me a brief compliment. "You certainly have tremendous convening power," he said, shaking my hand firmly.

I was appointed Professor of the Practice in MIT Sloan School of Business, The Departments of Chemistry, Biomedical

Engineering and The Harvard -MIT Division of Health Sciences and Technology. These appointments signaled MIT's positive assessment of my previous and potential future contributions. This further energized the vision I had for the MIT Center for Biomedical Innovation.

One of the first CBI projects was to look at ways to improve the Drug development process. The first discussion with a team composed of representatives from Pharma, MIT and Harvard was innovation in Clinical studies. This team was co-chaired by Dr. John Orloff of Novartis and Dr. Howard Golub of Harvard-MIT Health Sciences and Technology Division. The recommendations were published in the article, "The Future of Drug Development: Advancing Clinical Trial Design": Orloff J., Douglas F. et al, Nat. Res. Drug Discov. 2009 Dec.8(12) 949-957. We proposed combining an Adaptive trial design with dose ranging in Phase 2a clinical trials.

Adaptive clinical trial designs are now commonly employed in Clinical Development of innovative compounds.

The second publication of interest came from a brain storming session among Prof. Ernie Berndt, Mark Trusheim and me, as we sat in a cafe in Washington, D.C. Mark was the instigator of this discussion. He was quite passionate that we needed to, as he described it, occupy the space, by publishing our thoughts on Stratified Medicine. We were convinced of two things. The first was that present and developing genomic tools would help us stratify and sub group patients due to their possession of markers that would predict their likelihood to have either efficacy or side effects to mechanism-based drugs.

The second was that the ability to stratify patients would lead to fewer patients being exposed to any treatment, but efficacy would be more predictable, compliance would improve and the approach would be profitable for the Biopharmaceutical Industry. This resulted in the publication: Trusheim MR, Berndt ER, Douglas FL; Stratified Medicine: Strategic and Economic Implications of Combining Drugs and Biomarkers; Nat. Rev. Drug Discov.2007 Apr6(4) 287-93. Mark and Ernie have continued this work.

The Center was strengthened by the participation and leadership of three colleagues: Professors Anthony Sinskey,

Steven Tannenbaum, and Enrst Bernd. Together we presented a course on Case Histories in Drug Discovery and Development. Teams of students from a science or engineering discipline, an MBA and a Medical student or resident-were given a drug such as Cariporide or Mevacor to research. They were to evaluate the chemistry, the pharmacology, Clinical trial strategy and marketing assumptions and develop a critical assessment of the Development of the drug. The final consisted of presentation of the case to a member of the company that had innovated the drug for his/her evaluation and reflection on what actually happened in the company. The overall plan was to use this course to develop a library of Case Histories in Drug Discovery and Development that could be used as teaching aids. The introduction of this course was quite successful.

Teaching and guiding senior undergraduate and graduate students is one of those experiences one never forgets. I had always advised young students, trying to decide to which undergraduate college or university they should apply, that the most important factor was the students. MIT proved this to be true. Anthony Sinskey often described students as vectors that bring faculty together. These students were industrious, curious, challenging, innovative and entrepreneurial. They not only devoured information but focused on the application of that information. During the time I was there I had the opportunity to advise four students on their thesis projects, and assisted Tony Sinskey in teaching a second course.

The most exciting student project, however, was that organized by Ernie Berndt, Mark Trusheim and me. We were interested in evaluating whether the FDA was really slow in approving Drugs. Was this Drug Class dependent? Or were there other factors? Dr. Janet Woodcock, the Deputy Commissioner of the FDA, arranged for us and the five students to spend the month of January at the FDA examining approval documents and the FDA Advisory Committee's evaluations and recommendations. This project went so well that the FDA arranged for the students to continue this work at the FDA regional office near Boston, where they could get secure and supervised access to the information.

About this time, I was approached by Bayer AG to join them as their Chief Scientific Advisor. This role, which reported to Arthur Higgins, the CEO of the Bayer Health Group, involved assisting in evaluation of Pharma Projects and collaborations, and stimulating innovation across Bayer's various businesses: Health Care, Diagnostics, Chemicals and Agriculture. This latter supported Dr. Wolfgang Plischke, Member of the Board of Management of Bayer AG, responsible for Technology. Initially, I was hesitant in assuming this role. However, it was pointed out to me that as a Professor I was expected to consult because this was one way to provide current practical problems for the education of the students. It was also important for me as it also kept me current and stimulated. It also provided an opportunity to support Arthur Higgins who was a very talented Pharmaceutical leader.

In another development, I was also approached by a group from Taiwan, who came to see me about a fusion protein construct and visions of treating many diseases. Since they had a veterinary business I suggested they select an animal viral disease because if it worked in that disease, they would have proof of concept to justify study of similar constructs to treat diseases in humans. They chose Porcine Pulmonary Respiratory Disease and succeeded in marketing a vaccine (PPRS Free) to treat this disease. They have continued this approach with potential therapeutic vaccines to treat HPV-induced cervical precancerous lesions and chronic Hepatitis B infections.

These efforts also led to others inviting CBI to join in applying for major grants. This internal and external embrace of MIT CBI in such a short time led me to visit Ed Roberts to ask why our efforts had met with such a positive reception.

As I entered Ed's office he offered me a chair and sat at the end of his sofa, close to me. I said, "Ed, thank you for your guidance. Today, I have a somewhat unusual question."

Ed looked at me and with a slight smile, asked, "What is it?"

"I have been quite gratified by the external, and more importantly, the internal embrace of MIT CBI. I am trying to understand to what I owe this successful response so that I can nurture and grow it." I explained.

Ed leaned forward towards me and said, "There are two things that you do. First you have big ideas. Big ideas attract the best people. Second you never take other people's ideas as your own. In fact, you openly share ideas and give credit where it is due. The result is that no one hesitates to share their ideas with you."

I thanked Ed. I was delighted for this was a significant compliment from a venerable MIT Professor and leader.

I thanked him and as I left I began to feel that CBI was ready to move to the next level. What we needed was a major grant. Just at this point Arthur Higgins raised the possibility of creating a Chair for me at MIT. I told him that I would prefer an unrestricted gift to support the work of the Center. That would give us freedom to initiate some programs and fund a number of post docs. I discussed this with Steve Tannenbaum as he and I had discussed a project that could be started in his labs. Steve agreed with that approach and Bayer awarded MIT CBI a $3 million grant to support my work. This was the catalyst we needed to move CBI to the next level.

Another colleague who was critical in helping me navigate MIT was Bob Langer. Bob is one of a small number of individuals who are members of all three Academies (of Science, of Engineering, and the Institute of Medicine), and one of only four living individuals who have received both the U.S. National Medal of Science and the National Medal of Technology and Innovation. It was Bob who advised me on how best to handle the Bayer AG gift in order to achieve my objectives. Bob also invited me to become a Partner in one of his many companies, Puretech Ventures, where I am Partner Emeritus and enjoyed several exciting years evaluating novel startup companies to bring into our portfolio, including being the Chairman of the board for Solace, one of our Development Startup companies. I was also involved in establishing Enlight Biosciences, one of the Puretech Ventures major companies.

About this time, I was also invited to become Chairman of the Board of Directors for Alantos. This was an interesting company because the German parent company was in transition, subsequent to failure of its major development project. The young CEO did a marvelous job because instead of blindly reducing the work force in the U.S., he led an effort to determine what was the major strength of the scientists around which, they could conduct a focused drug research effort and show progress to the investors in a short span of time. They decided on enzymology and selected the Dipeptidyl peptidase-4 (DPP-4) inhibitors area for the treatment of type 2 Diabetes. They hired a superb chemist to lead the Research effort. This was a sensible approach because Merck had already demonstrated Proof of Concept, having received final FDA approval for Januvia in 2006.

The Head of R&D rapidly found a series of active molecules and two of them were advanced into the clinic. They both showed significant activity. I facilitated discussions with Amgen which finally led to Amgen purchasing the company for $540 Million.

I then became somewhat incensed when I learned that the contracts that were in place awarded the CEO several times the amount received by the Head of R&D. When I discussed this with the major firm that had invested in and controlled Alantos, I was told that this was because the CEO had taken the greatest risk.

I still find it inequitable that the compensation for CEOs and Business Development Leaders, in small Biotech companies, outpaces that of the Heads of R&D without whom taking a risk (and some talk about taking 'prudent' risk) becomes a vacuous statement.

This next development step for MIT CBI was, in a way, overtaken by the Prof. James Sherley's tenure situation. Shortly after joining MIT I was requested to evaluate a $30,000 grant proposal, from Prof. James Sherley. He was a stem cell researcher unknown to me, so there could have been nothing other than my scientific evaluation to influence my recommendation.

I recommended that his proposal be funded.

In his brief list of other grants and grant applications in evaluation phase, he mentioned that he had applied for the prestigious NIH $1 million Innovation grant award.

I stated that in my opinion Prof. Sherley had an excellent chance of getting this very prestigious Award.

Prof. Sherley did receive the NIH $1 million award but his application for a $30,000 MIT award was unsuccessful.

I thought this rather strange, so when James visited me and related to me his struggles to obtain tenure, I had no choice but to engage. I began to attend the Minority Faculty dinners and was astounded to discover that there was significant concern among minority faculty about how they would be evaluated for tenure. Even worse, there was lack of conviction that there would be an equitable process should they want to appeal a negative decision.

Eventually, James Sherley announced and commenced a hunger strike. I went by each day to see him and near the end of the first week of his Fast I asked him, "James, what is your Exit Strategy?"

He simply looked at me without response.

I continued, "Here is what will happen. At some point you will become weak from your Fast and they will hospitalize you. That will be the physical end of your Fast."

"You need an Exit or Final Strategy." "You are right," he said.

A well respected Black Faculty member and longtime MITer came to me and suggested we discuss with President Susan Hockfield an approach that could result in James ending his hunger strike. Our approach had initial success as President Hockfield agreed to take another look at his tenure case. James had been turned down twice for tenure. I also went separately and talked to President Hockfield. I reminded her that when women faculty had complained about experiencing discrimination, her predecessor, Dr. Vest, had brought a panel together to evaluate the issue. This led to a number of improvements in the way women faculty were being treated.

To my surprise Susan Hockfield declined to do something similar to investigate the environment experienced by Black Faculty.

I told her that the James Sherley situation was a very visible tip of the iceberg, and this was the reason why a similar panel should be held. I even argued that she had nothing to lose because the panel would come to one of three conclusions. They could conclude:

1) This is the worst environment for minority faculty and in such an environment it would be difficult for a James Sherley to get tenure. They would offer their recommendations on how to improve the environment. Or,

2) This environment is very supportive of minority faculty and it is unlikely that it affected the James Sherley tenure decision. Their recommendations would probably be to make processes more transparent. Or,

3) This environment is indifferent to the presence of minority faculty and thus it is difficult to judge whether it affected the James Sherley tenure decision. They would offer recommendations that would probably be a mixture of those that would apply to scenarios 1) and 2).

Thus, I told her, at the end of this panel she would have a set of recommendations to deal with the larger issue and the James Sherley situation could then be revisited at that time. We were able to get James to end his hunger strike after eleven days and it was our understanding that the President would have a review of the tenure decision. However, a few days after James ended his hunger strike, President Hockfield not only changed her decision but denied him access to his lab which ended his tenure (pun intended) at MIT.

One of the things that puzzled me was that no attempt was made to relocate James Sherley to another and perhaps more suitable department. I was given the names of two white MIT faculty, who on failing to receive tenure in one department were transferred to a different department where they subsequently achieved tenure. I was surprised by President Hockfield's lack of interest in convening an external panel to review the environment at MIT with respect to Black Faculty. Susan Hockfield finally did finally agree to an internal panel and did invite me to chair it.

I declined because I told her not only did I have a conflict, but it was not my area of expertise. She did convene a panel of internal MITers, which was chaired by an MITer.

I decided that it would be unconscionable for me to sit at MIT CBI enjoying the growing success and collaboration while other minority faculty were living in an environment that is less welcoming of their presence and contributions. Further, I became surprised that a number of close colleagues, who were aware of my deep struggles and concerns, were totally uninterested in hearing my concerns. This signal gave me the impression that MIT did not value its Minority faculty.

I concluded that I, Frank Douglas, did not **Fit** in this environment and I resigned.

I left MIT and over the years only five of my former colleagues, regardless of what their views of my action might have been, showed respect for what was somewhat of a life changing decision on my part. These individuals are Ernie Berndt, Martha Gray, Alice Gast, Bob Langer and Api Rudich. And of note, only Dr. Claude Canizares, the Vice President of Research and Dean Tom Mgnanti invited me to meet with them to explain why I had chosen to resign. It reminded me of something that many immigrants to America immediately find puzzling. It is that Americans rapidly call you their friend and just as swiftly you discover this is but a superficial and meaningless claim. It also reminded me of how quickly unquestioned norms in America lead to tyrannical execution by institutions with the best intentions. How different this was from my experience in Frankfurt, where Liane and Dieter Stoeber went against their peers and family to support me. Or the leadership of Guenther Wess, Andreas Bush, Bernd Kirschbaum and Hildegard Nimmesgern, who early stepped forward as leaders to support my efforts.

Here is a somewhat amusing but nonetheless sinister example of the tyranny of unquestioningly accepting norms. It had to do with meetings in my office.

Shortly after arriving in Frankfurt, Frau Dr. Felicitas Feick, the Head of Communications came to introduce herself and her responsibilities to me. I welcomed her into my office, offered her a chair at my small conference table, and sat across from her at the table. As soon as she began to speak Liane got up from her desk and closed the door to my office. After a few minutes, I excused myself, went to Liane and asked her for a yellow pad. She gave me the pad. I reentered my office and intentionally left the door open. Felicitas started to speak and Liane rose from her desk and again closed my office door. After Frau Dr. Feick left my office, I asked Liane why she had persisted in closing the door. Liane explained that the door must always be closed when I am having a meeting so that my visitor could be assured that the discussion is private and that neither she nor anyone could overhear the conversation.

So, for the eight years I followed that advice. I closed my office door when visited by anyone, including females. Yet, almost instinctively, the first thing I told my assistant, Ms. Cheryl Mottley, at MIT, was that she was never to leave her desk when I was visited by a female student or colleague and that my door must always remain open, unless that is expressly requested by the visitor. If such a request were made I would audibly let her know that the visitor wanted to have a confidential discussion.

Sometime later I was amazed by this when I recalled an episode that occurred in Frankfurt. Our executive team and staff were housed in a building in the city of Frankfurt while our headquarters building was being constructed on the main campus of Hoechst, in the city of the same name.

There was a stairwell from the lobby to a walkway that connected two parts of the building. The steps of this stairwell were made of glass. Charles Langston, our Head of Human Resources was given the task to negotiate the replacement of this stairwell with non-transparent material. Unfortunately, the owner of the building absolutely refused.

Charles kept on trying. One day, Charles was late for the start of our executive committee meeting, a rather rare occurrence. Charles finally arrived and could not contain his laughter. He explained that he was having one of his heated arguments, if one could call it that, with the owner of the building over the stairwell. When he emerged from his office visibly annoyed, Manu, his assistant, asked what was wrong. When he explained that he was having another fight with the owner of the building over the stairwell, Manu shook her head slowly and said, "You Americans are crazy. You obsess over strange things. First, none of the guys would hang around the stairwell trying to look up our skirts, and if they did we would probably like it."

I decided to check this out.

At the first opportunity that I had, I stood on the hallway overlooking the lobby and observed the traffic. Germans would rarely take an elevator for 1-2 fights. They would use the stairs. The women and men came and went up and down that stairwell. At no time did I see a man lingering trying to be a voyeur. I returned to that building about 5 years later and the stairwell was still there, unchanged.

Thus, to watch MIT effectively create an environment, on the one hand, that sensitizes all to the important issue of sexual harassment, an evidence of abuse of power, and not respond to an equally egregious abuse of power in the treatment of minority faculty affected me deeply. What follows are two letters that I wrote at the time of my departure from MIT, one to Vice President Claude Canizares and the other to my colleagues at MIT. I also note that Dr. Pamela Newkirk, Professor of Journalism and Director of undergraduate studies at the Arthur Carter Journalism Institute, New York University, included these two letters in her book: Letters from Black America: Intimate Portraits of the Black America Experience

MIT's statement on my resignation was carried in the MIT News on June 3, 2007.

It said:

> "MIT deeply regrets Professor Douglas' intention to leave the Institute. He is a valued member of the MIT community, and has been a visionary leader of the CBI since he joined MIT as Professor of the Practice more than two years ago. We believe his decision is based on inaccurate information, and we sincerely hope that, once the facts are clarified, he will reconsider his decision."

Letter to Claude Canizares, MIT Vice President for Research

June 1, 2007
Dear Claude,

It is with a deep sense of disappointment and a heavy heart that I have come to the decision to withdraw from MIT.

I have observed with consternation the inability of the institution to manage the James Sherley situation. My dismay is even greater because the Institute, after having agreed to arbitration, which led to Prof. Sherley ending his hunger strike, now, has negated the agreement and insists upon his departure by June 30, 2007. Frankly, I am so astonished that the Institute did not resolve this issue that it leaves me to believe that the *desire* to do this is lacking. Clearly *where there is no will, there is no way*!

I would like to thank you, the Deans, Directors and Leaders of the Schools, Divisions and Departments of which I am a faculty member, for their support of my work in establishing the MIT Center for Biomedical Innovation. I would also like to thank CoDirectors, Tony Sinskey, Ernie Berndt, and Steve Tannenbaum, as well as Dave Weber, for their help in giving form to the vision of MIT CBI. Finally, I would like to thank Gigi Hirsh, Sherene Aram, and Cheryl Mottley without whose dedication MIT CBI would not have achieved its success and prominence.

I leave because I would neither be able to advise young Blacks about their prospects of flourishing in the current environment, nor about avenues available to affect change when agreements or promises are transgressed. I will leave on June 30th, 2007 and would recommend that I work with Tony Sinskey to ensure a smooth transition of leadership of the center. I am gratified that I leave behind a center that is well funded and that provides a safe haven where experts from academia, Industry and government can collaborate to improve innovation and accessibility of novel therapeutics.

Sincerely Frank

Letter to my MIT Colleagues and Friends
June 1, 2007
Dear Colleagues and Friends,

Since you paid me the superb compliment of celebrating the Black History Maker Award with me, I wanted to give you a more detailed explanation for my resigning from MIT. I recognize that you might nonetheless still find it unfathomable.

I arrived in the USA in 1963 and almost from the first day have had to deal with the effects of racism on a personal basis. In 2005 I came to MIT and felt that my retirement from industry was also a retirement from having to deal with racism. I was accepted and judged, 'not by the color of my skin, but by the content of my character' and by what I had contributed. You will never know how exhilarating this experience has been! Gradually, however, I found an inner sense of unease as I witnessed both a lack of genuine commitment to something greater than oneself and a lack of a real focus on benefit to humanity.

Two events awoke me from my personal reverie. These were the James Sherley saga and a conference on Race that was held on campus by Dr. David Jones, leader of the Center on Race Relations. I will not comment further on the James Shirley issue as I addressed it in my second letter to Claude. I enclose that letter.

"I was invited to present on BIDIL (from Nitromed) at the conference on Race Relations. I was amazed by the lack of interest in data, as well as the dogmatic and uninformed assertion that BIDIL was a Race Drug and therefore should never have been approved by the FDA. There was no interest in the fact that BIDIL demonstrated a 43% decrease in mortality in the Afro-American patients in which it was studied and the fact that this patient population dies at a rate 1.5 to 2 times greater than that of the white patients with similar degree of congestive heart failure. As I remarked to the conference participants, I cannot believe that had similar findings been discovered for a non-minority group that we would have called it a 'race drug'. One only needs to see the enormous sums of monies that are raised to find cures for some diseases that disproportionately affect some ethnic groups, to appreciate this. I found it remarkable that this conference was led by an MIT Center, whose leader (?) was clearly on a mission against this drug and had little interest in understanding the complexities of the regulatory process or drug development. These two events caused me to look at the MIT environment, where many 'flowers bloom' more critically.

I also became troubled by the absence of a sense of business ethics, among some of the students and faculty. Yes, I know it is a large institution of individuals. However, every institution has a character, a soul. That character defines its graduates and I sense that MIT is in danger of losing the humanity side of its character.

As you know, following the release of my resignation letter, I spent some 10 days reconsidering my decision to resign. I had many discussions and was genuinely touched by the personal support and, I would even say, affection that was expressed and the many emails and discussions. So, what was missing?

Why was I not persuaded to reverse my intention to leave? It is very simple. I recommended that the Deans and some of the department chairs should call for an external group to evaluate and make recommendations to improve the climate and conditions that appeared to be unsupportive of minority faculty at MIT. Only one person, namely (Dean) Tom Magnanti, discussed this with me. None of you, my colleagues, offered to support me in this. Instead, people focused on the sanctity of the tenure process, which was not the issue. I do not believe in the sanctity of anything that is created by men. Others of you tried to overwhelm me with guilt for the adverse effect that my decision would immediately have on a number of colleagues. This lack of support for my recommendation was ultimately the deciding factor. It signaled to me that the environment at MIT is so insensitive to this issue, that even friends and close colleagues could not comprehend nor recognize the essence of my 'dilemma'. I often tell young people: institutions survive. Individuals do not. (incidentally, I did share this with James Sherley). MIT will survive and I hope my Legacy of launching and implementing MIT CBI will also survive. But I have no illusions. I will soon fade in your active memories. Such is the rhythm of life.

As I say to friends: Enjoy the Journey of the Mystery of your Life, and if you already know the Mystery, Enjoy the Mystery of the Journey of your life. I tried to do that also for my own sanity.

Frank"

Article in Scientist Magazine on why I resigned from MIT

Discrimination in Academia

On June 3, I resigned from faculty and administrative positions at MIT, effective June 30. I did so because I perceived unconscious discrimination against minorities and because my colleagues and institute authorities did not act on my recommendations to address these issues. The timing was such that many of my colleagues thought I was resigning over the case of James Sherley, who was denied tenure in 2004 and went on a hunger strike earlier this year, in protest. But my decision was based on the complex, insidious nature of discrimination in a university context. I will go into more detail about my decision below, but several things have become clear to me throughout my decades of experience in industry and academic science. Academia is where the leaders and change agents of society and the world are educated, imprinted and nurtured. Selecting and preparing these future citizens and leaders has historically relied on various methods. Foremost is that done on the basis of excellence, whether it is in ability to recite, repeat or find new solutions to historical problems. This is the discrimination of excellence to the disciplines and is widely held to be a good thing. The other two methods are not considered as positive because of the role that personal preferences, that is, prejudices, play in them. One, the curious phenomenon of fraternities, sororities and social clubs, which discriminate along social lines, is the discrimination of social acceptance. The other, based on a behavioral or style component, supportive of the goals of the department or discipline, is the discrimination of the best fit. What makes these selection methods particularly troublesome for minorities is that discrimination of excellence to the discipline is impacted by the other two criteria. Recent events at MIT have been no exception to this pattern.

MIT: from women to BiDil. In 1994, Women faculty at MIT expressed their belief that "unequal treatment of women who came to MIT makes it more difficult for them to succeed, causes them to be accorded less recognition when they do…. and that (as a result) these women can actually become negative role models for younger women." The response of the then MIT president Charles Vest was most instructive: "I, like most of my male colleagues, believe that we are highly supportive of our junior Women faculty members. However, I sat bolt upright in my chair when a senior woman, who has felt unfairly treated for some time, said, "I also felt very positive when I was young."

That sarcastic comment indicated that when she was a young faculty member, she did not realize the extent of the discrimination to which she was being subjected. These women faculty were facing discrimination of social acceptance and best fit and recognized the impact it would eventually have on their evaluation with respect to discrimination of excellence to the discipline. Although some women faculty believe that the gains made by women faculty at MIT have been modest, the movement initially led by Nancy Hopkins has sensitized MIT to discrimination against women. When it seemed that Nobel laureate Susumu Tonegawa wanted to actively block the hiring of Alla Karpova, a young woman faculty member, there was an immediate reaction from eleven senior women faculty, who engaged the administration in this issue.

They wrote that MIT had "damaged (its) reputation as an institution that supports academic fairness." Ultimately, Karpova declined the offer of a faculty position at MIT, saying, "I could not develop my scientific career at MIT in the kind of nurturing atmosphere that I and young people joining my lab would need to succeed." Given a potential discrimination against her with respect to best fit, her chances of meeting the criteria under discrimination of excellence to the discipline at MIT would be impaired. The fact that the administration and a large segment of MIT expressed dismay that this situation had occurred illustrates that fighting for the rights of women faculty has obtained social acceptance.

In March, 2007, I was invited to make a presentation at a symposium organized by David Jones in MIT department of Science, Technology, and Society. The attendees were primarily academics from MIT and other universities. I presented health statistics, focusing on BiDiL, a drug that is marketed for the treatment of congestive heart failure in self-identified African American patients.

Although I was forewarned that the group was hostile to this drug, which they labeled a "race drug" that should never have been approved by the FDA, I was astounded at the lack of appreciation of the realities of the situation. This drug had demonstrated a 43% decrease in mortality in a population that dies at a rate up to twice that of white patients. The group seemed uninterested in discussing the drug development and regulatory issues associated with BiDiL.

In short, it appeared that it was socially acceptable to ignore scientific facts and the impact on the lives of the affected patients in favor of pursuing a discussion about a "race drug".

As I told the audience, given the large sums that are raised each year for some orphan diseases, that happen to disproportionately affect other ethnic groups, I rather doubt that if we were fortunate to find a good treatment for those diseases, we would deny those patients access to the drug on the basis that it was a "race drug".

THE JAMES SHERLEY CASE

James Sherley was denied tenure by the department of Biological Engineering in 2004 and went through an appeals process which he claims was "tainted by racism and conflict of interest". In February 2007, he began a 12-day hunger strike in protest, which he ended because he thought that the administration at MIT had "committed to continue to work toward resolution of its differences with Prof. James Sherley," according to a letter to me from associate Provost Claude Canizares. Along the way, I had made the simple suggestion that MIT should assign an external panel to evaluate and make recommendations to improve the environment in which minority faculty at MIT work. I also recommended that depending on the findings of this external Commission a decision could be made as to whether the Sherley case should be further evaluated.

In April, MIT made it clear that it intended to enforce Sherley's departure by June 30.

What was astounding to me was that MIT said it had no intention of involving an outside mediator. They also withdrew from an agreement to discuss the "differences" as understood by Sherley. I began to wonder whether there was a lack of integrity at the highest levels of the Institute, or simply a lack of care in expressing the Institute's intention. I concluded that it was not an issue of lack of capability, but one of a lack of will to deal with a problem that had clearly polarized Minority faculty and the larger MIT Community. James Sherley's open and confrontational emails about his perception of racism and conflict of interest that led to his being denied tenure created both sympathizers and critics among the minority and majority faculty.

His unorthodox and somewhat "unacademic" approach made it difficult for some to openly support him. The administration failed to recognize that the case had become a complex mixture of the discrimination of excellence to the discipline, social acceptability, and best fit, and that they needed to deal with these separately and then reassess possible cross contamination.

While women faculty had used the metric paradigm, by, for example, highlighting differences in the size of the labs and access to resources, to make their case, Sherley focused on process. The approach by the women faculty met criteria for social acceptance. Sherley's unorthodox approach had little chance of success because it took many out of their best fit and social acceptance comfort zones. I decided to resign and did so on June 3.

Here is what I wrote Canizares in my resignation letter, which was released publicly. (This is the part that the press and MIT have chosen to ignore): "The Issue for me is not whether professor Sherley should be given immediate tenure or not. I cannot judge that and would not even presume to do so. The issue is: why has this great institution not been able to find a mutually, acceptable solution for a problem that affects, not only Prof. Sherley, but every present and future minority faculty member? I am convinced, and I have other reasons to believe this, that the will to do this is lacking."

Following my announcement of (planned) resignation on June 3, I engaged in three weeks of intense discussions with members of the administration and many colleagues. Several expressed dismay at my leaving and were convinced that my action was based on lack of adequate knowledge of the facts of the Sherley case.

It was striking that although I repeatedly stated that Sherley's tenure was not the reason for my resignation, my colleagues were so trapped by the sanctity of the tenure process that they could not see the larger problem. I decided that I do not "fit" in such an environment as I said in my resignation letter:

"I would neither be able to advise young Black faculty about their prospects of flourishing in the current environment, nor about avenues available to affect change when agreements or processes are transgressed".

What Next?

Institutions such as MIT will proudly parade successes of increasing the number of minority undergraduate and graduate students, and perhaps even the entry of young minority faculty. As promising as these statistics might be, they do not predict the success for minority faculty seeking tenure.

Indeed, they are irrelevant, because the issues are quite different at each stratum.

The absence of evidence of racial discrimination does not equate to evidence of absence of racial discrimination.

James Sherley's case may have been one of the interplay between the discrimination of excellence to the discipline and discrimination of fit. When there is insensitivity to the challenges of diversity, we get an institution trapped by its historical paradigms. Such an institution may not be relevant for tomorrow's world. I knew and worked closely with the many brilliant and humane professors and leaders at MIT, but there's a major problem that lies just below the surface.

MIT has not grasped the full and the global impact of diversity. It prides itself as a place where a 'thousand flowers bloom'.

These are independent blooms. It also needs to be a place where, through cross-pollination, hybrid and novel transformative solutions are involved and tested to address today's, as well as, tomorrow's problems.

MIT needs to re-examine its criteria for discrimination of social acceptability and best fit to ensure that it is relevant in the rapidly changing world.

Coming Full Circle

On leaving MIT, Dr. Carl Schramm, the CEO of the Ewing Kauffman Foundation, invited me to join the Foundation as a Senior Fellow and shortly thereafter, to join the Board of Directors of the Foundation. There was an excitement about entrepreneurship and innovation at the Foundation. The Foundation had recently introduced a program for post-doctoral candidates who had ideas with potential to become startup companies. I was assigned mentor for four of these young entrepreneurs and among my mentees one has succeeded in launching a company that uses polymers to enhance healing of wounds.

This period also gave me time to reflect on innovation and productivity in BioPharma. I joined forces with my former collaborator, Dr. Narayanan and interviewed 39 Biopharma leaders. We posed the question, "Is there Entrepreneurship in Large Pharma?" One of the amazing things we found was that although almost everyone started by expressing doubt that entrepreneurship exists in large Pharmaceutical companies, they quickly described actual examples where a dedicated individual found ways to generate excitement and solve problems in an innovative manner that ultimately resulted in the launch of a product. They also raised questions about a few of the strongly held beliefs, such as the need for 'Many Shots on Goal'.

Another observation had to do with the different expectations of scientists versus Manager-scientists. Early in their careers, scientists are advanced because of their scientific/ technical acumen. When they move into the middle manager level their evaluation is based on number of compounds advanced along the development path and reduction of cycle time. Less attention is paid to their contributions in anticipating and solving critical scientific/technical hurdles in the specific project.

Another idea resulting from our reflection of these interviews was that the structure of Research and Development will change over time. In early pharmaceutical organizations, the transition between Research and Development was at the end of the preclinical studies required to file an IND for first studies in humans. Thus, Development started from Clinical Phase 1. Later, as the importance of identifying patient subgroups and dose ranging became linked to having useful Biomarkers, several R&D organizations, including the DI&A organization, extended the research phase to the end of Phase 2a. It raised for us the question as to whether the typical Phase IV studies that were usually done by Medical Affairs departments, which were closely aligned with the Commercial Departments, would not actually benefit from a closer alliance with Research. We felt that with the genomic technologies, better biomarkers will be found to predict both efficacy and side effects, when one looks for them in patients taking various drug regimens. This field type study was reported in Nat. Rev. Drug Disc. Vol. 9, September 2010, 683-689.

As we were completing this study I was visited by a headhunter who told me that a group in Akron, Ohio, was interested in talking to me. He explained that the President of the University of Akron, the President of the Northeast Ohio Medical School (NEOMED), and the CEOs of the two adult hospitals and the Children's hospital wanted to create a collaboration to improve treatment paradigms by leveraging their joint capabilities. It immediately peaked my interest and I agreed to visit Akron and these leaders. The meetings were quite stimulating. It was immediately clear that the leaders most committed to this idea were Dr. Luis Proenza, President of The University of Akron, Dr. Lois Nora, the President of NEOMED and Mr. Considine, CEO of Akron Children's Hospital. I returned for a second visit which was what led to my decision to take on this challenge. In this second visit, I met 65 Ph.D.s, M.D.s, R.N.s, and administrators who had been working in cross functional teams for several months in order to develop a structure for the BioInnovation Institute. They had already identified five centers: Center for Biomaterials and Medicine (CBMM); Center for Simulation and Integrated Healthcare Education (CSIHE); Medical Device Development Center (MDCC); Center for Clinical Trials and Product Development (CTPD); and Center for Community Health Improvement (CCHI).

I invited these 65 leaders to a working session in which I presented my initial thoughts, and stimulated a discussion intended for me to sense where they saw the low hanging fruits. The discussion revealed a readiness to engage the Center for Biomaterials and Medicine as well as the Center for Simulation and Integrated Healthcare Education. I was quite surprised when I discovered that doing Clinical Trials was not a low hanging fruit. The issue had to do with control of the IRB process. This was an important signal which, in retrospect, could have been used to predict the failure of this experiment. Unfortunately, its significance only became apparent to me about two years into the experiment.

During this visit the support of a critical leader became apparent. That leader was Dr. Stephen Cheng, the Dean of the College of Polymer Science & Polymer Engineering. This was critical because the College of Polymer Science and Polymer Engineering was central to this multi-institutional collaboration. Fortunately, not only was Dr. Cheng a national leader in Polymer Science and Engineering, he was also a successful entrepreneur and, like Dr. Luis Proenza, an innovative and passionate supporter of the effort. Two additional committed and effective leaders of this nascent effort were Dr. Dennis Weiner, orthopaedic surgeon at Akron Children's Hospital and Dr. Walter Horton, Professor and Vice Pres. for Research at NEOMED.

During a dinner meeting with the leaders of the five institutions and Mr. Juan Martinez of the Knight Foundation, Mayor Don Plusquellic made an unexpected appearance and shared with me his commitment to the formation of the Institute and its importance to the city of Akron. This appearance was quite significant because it was on the eve of a recall election which the mayor did survive. I was quite impressed that on a night such as this, Mayor Plusquellic would demonstrate his commitment to this idea in such a dramatic way.

This surprise appearance by the Mayor, as well as the story of the trip made by the leaders of the five institutions to persuade the Knight Foundation to support creation of the BioInnovation Institute, resulted in my deciding that this was the right challenge for me. On that trip to the Knight Foundation Headquarters in Miami, the five leaders were accompanied by the Mayor, the County Executive, and several business leaders.

I gave my verbal commitment to Mr. Considine at the conclusion of the dinner. This decision was also made easier by encouragement from Prof. Bob Langer (former colleague at MIT), who confirmed that the University of Akron's College of Polymer Science and Polymer Engineering was among the top three in the U.S.

When I returned home I studied the grant that was awarded by the Knight Foundation. I was alarmed by two things in the award. The first was that the Foundation was giving $20 million over seven years to build the five centers and support the Program Office, with the expressed expectation that the participating institutions would raise an anticipated additional $50 to $70 million to build and run the centers over that five-year period. The second surprise was that it was estimated that it would only require $36.25 million, of which $11.80 million, would come from the Knight Foundation grant to establish and build the Center for Biomaterials and Medicine with an estimated **45 Principal Investigators** recruited over five years! I called Mr. Considine to understand the assumptions behind this projection and the likelihood that we could raise the additional $24.45 million. I concluded, that this would be a formidable challenge, but it would necessitate use of innovative approaches to meet it. I have often said that **if necessity is the mother of invention, then adversity must be the father of innovation.** This challenge required innovative approaches.

Having given a verbal commitment, I requested Mr. Aram Nerpouni, who had been the Project Manager of this effort and who had expressed interest in continuing with the organization, to find a fitting space to house the planned offices of the Institute. I also discussed further with Mr. Considine, the identified Chairman of the Board of Directors of the Institute, my initial assessment and potential initial steps. My initial steps were quite straight forward. First step: Exploit the present Momentum.

This could be done if one considered the following. A former student of mine, at MIT, had identified that four anchor pillars are needed in building a Biotechnology or Biopharmaceutical Hub. These anchor pillars are a large University with relevant faculty, a large Biopharmaceutical company, presence of entrepreneurial investors, and an incubator for startup companies. The College of Polymer Sciences & Polymer Engineering had the faculty with the relevant expertise to innovate Biomaterial solutions in Orthopedics and Wound Healing, as a beginning. NEOMED had additional faculty that could participate scientifically, and the Hospitals had the patients with the problems in need of innovative solutions. There was a group of Angel investors, which was a beginning and both the University of Akron and the City of Akron were providing space to incubate startup companies. The only thing missing was a large company as an Anchor Pillar. Given this situation and my assessment of readiness, I developed an action plan.

The initial step in 'Exploit the present Momentum', was to build a scientific collaborative environment among the five institutions. To initiate this we created the Collaborative Research Grant Program with the following characteristics: 1) Grant proposals would focus on Biomaterials in Orthopaedics or Wound Healing; 2) Grant applications would require co-leaders, one of whom had to be a clinical expert; 3) Proof of Concept must be achievable in 3 years, and 4) Grants should address how results would enable applicants to apply for national or other larger grants.

The second step was the creation of a **Place** where Simulation could be taught and developed in a multi-institutional manner, and where Device companies and other organizations could use the space to further test and develop their products. Both of these actions would immediately support specific expectations of the Knight Foundation Grant.

Mr. Considine agreed and arranged for the Research Development Grant Proposal to be presented at the upcoming Board Meeting which actually occurred on my first day 'on the job' as President and CEO of the BioInnovation Institute. Dr. Walt Horton presented the proposal to fund up to 40 collaborative grants and the Board approved it. The grant documents were structured; a review panel, including experts external to the Akron area was convened, and the key elements to create a multi-institutional collaborative environment were thus introduced. In the early days there were many humorous stories, such as a Polymer Scientist roaming through the hospital enquiring whether there were any physicians interested in working on his polymer.

In my first week, the John S. and James L. Knight Foundation held its Board meeting in Akron. Mr. William Considine introduced me to the members of the Board and Mr. Alberto Ibarguen, the President of the Foundation welcomed me with the following greeting:

"We are quite delighted that you have joined us in building the important effort in Akron. We hope that it will result in the creation of many jobs in Akron." He continued; "Could you tell us why you chose this assignment."

"Thank you for the welcome," I responded. "It is not often that I get an opportunity to help five Universities and Hospitals build an innovative collaboration to improve the health and the economic welfare of a city. It is a privilege to be part of creating a very important legacy for the city."

One of the members asked, "Do you have a personal mission statement?" I hesitated for a moment, then reached for my wallet and extracted a small somewhat aged piece of paper and said, "I have never shared this publicly, but given the importance of this effort, I think that it is a fair question and I should share it with you. It is what drives me."

I read it:

My Personal Statement
I want my life to be centered
On enabling others to discover and do
That which is noble and fair.

I want to employ the wisdom of knowing
When courageously to implement
New paradigms. And when, serenely,
To perceive and wait for the rhythm
And harmony; when the time has come
And I want never to lose the joy of striving
Always to do that which is noble and fair."

My impression was that the members were pleasantly surprised and pleased that I actually had a written Personal Statement and that the paper on which it was typed revealed signs of frequent use.

Over the next three months I continued my analysis of the capabilities in the five institutions comprising the BioInnovation Institute. NEOMED, founded in 1973, had the Vision of becoming the premier community-based inter professional health sciences university in the United States. Thus, it was a relatively young medical university, primarily admitting students from The University of Akron, Young State University, Cleveland State University and Kent State University. Its location in Rootstown, a rural area in Portage County, Ohio, probably made recruitment of faculty more challenging than is usual. (It ranked 130 out of 143 MD medical schools in the US (2015).

University of Akron, established in 1870 as Buchtel College, is a world leader in Polymer research. The first College in Polymer Science and Polymer Engineering was created at the University of Akron, which clearly benefited from the fact that at one time Akron was the headquarters of the major tire companies, such as Goodyear, Firestone, and Goodrich. The University has also been active in spinning out startup companies. Prominent among them are SNS Nanofiber Tech, which exploits the electrospinning technology developed by Dr. Darrell Reneker; and Akron Surface Technologies, Inc.

Among the three hospitals, Summa Health System, formed in 1989 through the merger of Akron City and St. Thomas hospitals, has more than 1300 inpatient beds. It has been ranked high performing in a number of areas such as pulmonary, urology, heart failure and lung cancer surgery. Summa has a modest effort in Clinical Trials Research.

Akron General hospital was organized in 1914 by F.A. Seiberling, the Founder of Goodyear Tire & Rubber Company and three doctors. It was initially funded by money raised by the community, having started as The Peoples Hospital to provide community medical care. After surviving many financial challenges during the Great Depression and two World Wars, The Peoples Hospital changed its name to Akron General hospital in 1954, and finally to Cleveland Clinic Akron General after being purchased by the Cleveland Clinic Foundation in August 2013. Akron General Hospital was an early leader in establishing Health & Wellness Centers.

Akron Children's hospital started in 1890 as the Mary Day Nursery and over 120 plus years has grown to become the largest pediatric healthcare system in Northeast Ohio and ranked among the best children's hospitals by U.S. News and World Report. It is also one of two pediatric hospitals in the nation that operate a burn center for both children and adults.

This constellation of Polymer Science and Engineering, other medical, nursing and engineering faculty, and patient needs, was in my view an unusual opportunity to create a community based, collaborative, open innovation and commercialization model. However, there were some critical weaknesses. These included:

- Subcritical mass of research physicians
- Very few experienced clinical trials investigators
- Lack of experience and history of attracting large center grants or large clinical trials
- No experience or history of large cross-institutional collaborations

As a result of the above, there was a lack of appreciation of the human and financial resources needed to achieve the vision for the BioInnovation Institute.

Building the Model:

Mission and Vision statements were developed for the Austen BioInnovation Institution in Akron (ABIA). These statements were:

- ABIA's mission is it to deliver value-added patient centered product innovation and commercialization.

The Vision:

Austen BioInnovation Institute in Akron aspires to be:

- A global leader in discovering, developing, and commercializing biomaterial solutions for patients with orthopedic and wound healing problems;
- Nationally distinct in use of simulation techniques in the education of the integrated healthcare team and early responders;
- Nationally distinct in improvement of health outcomes of the medically underserved

The Culture:

- Solution-Oriented
- Highest Expectations
- Entrepreneurial
- Resilient
- Patient-Oriented
- Adaptable-Embraces, and Acts on New Paradigms

Given the weaknesses cited above, I thought it was very important to build a culture that could be shared by all. I used a picture of base camp at the foot of Mount Everest to focus all on the enormity of the challenge ahead of us and the exhilaration that we will experience as we progress to the summit. I wrote then: "The ABIA partners have embarked on a tremendous journey to contribute to improving the economic well-being and health of our region-we are the Sherpas as we climb this Mountain to prosperity and personal vitality. It is a journey. And as I say to closest friends: enjoy the Mystery of the Journey of your life, and to others, enjoy the Journey of the Mystery of your life." The next order of business was building a leadership team.

Drs. Cheng and Horton of the University of Akron and NEOMED, respectively, assumed initial Leadership of the Center for Biomaterials and Medicine. They were subsequently replaced by Drs. Matt Becker from UA's College of Polymer Science and Engineering and William Landis, Professor and Head of Biochemistry at NEOMED.

There was a natural cross-institutional team for the Simulation Center. These were Martha Conrad, MS, RN from the Nursing college at the University of Akron; Michael Holder M.D. from the Department of Emergency Medicine at Akron children's Hospital; and Rami Ahmed, D.O., from the Department of Emergency Medicine at Summa Health Systems. I asked the three individuals to send me a one-page summary of the most important capabilities needed to build the Center for Simulation and Integrated Healthcare and to recommend which of them should lead the effort. Their responses were quite straightforward and honest. Based on their input I selected Mike Holder to lead this effort, and Mr. Considine, CEO of Akron Children's arranged for him to be assigned 80% time to support the BioInnovation Institute.

I appointed Aram Nerpouni Chief Administrative Officer.

The leadership for the Medical Device Development Center (MDDC) was rapidly filled when Dr. Brian Davis approached me at the end of a meeting and introduced himself and his interest in joining the Institute. Brian was a well-established researcher at the Cleveland Clinic. I asked him to send me his views on what should be done in MDDC. I also checked with Ken Preston of the University of Akron, who was the chair of the MDDC committee. Ken knew Brian by reputation and felt that he would be the right type of leader for MDDC. On receiving Brian's views on MDDC, I called him and offered him the position. (This was the fastest hire I had ever made-less than 48 hours).

Dr. Janine Janofsky was recommended by a professional recruiting firm and was an academic with experience working with community organizations at the University of Pittsburgh. She had also previously been Vice Provost for Research at the Central Michigan University.

Thus, within six months all leaders were in place to build the Institute. The Institute was officially named the Austen BioInnovation Institute in Akron (ABIA) in honor of Dr. W. Gerald Austen and his wife Patricia. Dr. Austen is a native of Akron who did his undergraduate degree at MIT and medical training at Harvard and the Massachusetts General Hospital. A pioneer in heart surgery and co-inventor of the open-heart bypass machine, he was Chief of Surgery for 29 years at Mass General Hospital. A member of the National Academy of Medicine and a Fellow of the American Academy of Arts and Sciences, he had been doctor to the Knight brothers and was chairman of the Board of Directors for The Knight Foundation for 24 years.

Sometime after the celebration in honor of Dr. Austen and his wife, I visited him at his offices at MGH to learn his expectations for ABIA. It was quite a warm visit in which Dr. Austen shared the tremendous successes he had had in raising millions of dollars to support MGH (Mass. General Hospital). He was very pleased that Dr. Martha Gray, who was the Director of the Harvard-MIT Division of Health Sciences and Technology, was a member of the Board of Directors of ABIA.

Of interest, as the visit was coming to an end, Dr. Austen said, "I have a question because I never understood what happened. Why did you resign from MIT?"

Although I did not expect the question, it was actually not surprising that Dr. Austen posed the question. Dr. Austen is a Life Member of the MIT Corporation and his question signaled to me that more than one year later there were still echoes of my departure.

I responded to Dr. Austen. "There were three reasons that were related to each other. The first was that the Sherley episode revealed to me that young minority faculty at MIT had questions about their treatment and felt that there was no way to address their problems. The second was that although Dr.

Vest, when faced with a similar concern from women faculty had assembled an external panel to evaluate and advise MIT on this issue, Dr. Hockfield refused to take a similar action for the minority faculty. Finally, Dr. Hockfield had promised to take another look at James Sherley's case. James agreed to end his hunger strike because of this commitment from Dr. Hockfield, who reversed her commitment immediately after he terminated his hunger strike.

It became difficult for me to enjoy my own successes at MIT when I could not assure young minority faculty that there would be an environment that would be committed to ensuring their success."

Dr. Austen said, "Your resignation always puzzled me."

With the key team members in place, I began to move rapidly to activate ABIA. A very visible metric, of which the three hospitals were quite conscious, was the number of inventions disclosed. A total of 11 inventions had been disclosed from the three hospitals over 9 years (2001-2009).

To address this challenge, we did two things. The first was to assign an engineer to each hospital whose task was to meet with surgeons, and when possible, observe procedures in the operating room, ask questions and stimulate ideas from the surgeons for solutions that could become inventions. The second was to introduce what we called our I Six process: Invention Disclosure, IP & Market Assessment, Technology Funded Projects, Active Projects/Prototypes, and Out License or Spin out of Companies. The differentiating step in this was **printing a 3D prototype of the Device** so that the inventor could have an actual model of the invention and work further to modify it.

These two interventions were extremely successful. In 2010, one year later, there were 27 Invention Disclosures and in 2011 and 2012 there were 129 and 102 Invention Disclosures!

Potential inventions were presented to the MDDC Evaluation Committee which included an entrepreneur, to determine suitability to move on to the prototype phase. Presentations for suitability consisted of Medical Need, Early IP and Market Assessment, and review of projects presently approved to be funded for the prototype phase. This information was used to determine suitability and priority for prototype phase. By middle of 2013, 36 projects were in the Technology Funded phase, six were in out licensed discussions and seven companies had been spun out.

Another activity that contributed to the productivity above was the introduction of the **Bioinnovation Design course**. This course was co-led by Dr. Ali Dhinojwala of the College of Polymer Science and Dr. Ashoke Dey of the Business School and me. In this course we formed teams of students comprised of a graduate student in Polymer Science & Engineering, a student in the MBA program, and a medical or nursing school student. The class received lectures in principles of Ethnographic Research, such as Observation and Problem Identification, Brain Storming Techniques, Needs Assessment, Prioritization, as well as Pathophysiology. Students selected a Physician whom they shadowed and observed. They identified potential problems and worked on root cause analysis on a selected problem. Completion of the course required design of a prototype to address the problem. A number of these designs were approved for prototype development. Our team of professors leading the course was subsequently joined by Dr. Matt Becker of the College of Polymer Science and Dr. Shiv Sastry of the Department of Computer Science. My appointment as University Professor in the College of Polymer Science and Engineering, as well as Professor of Integrated Medicine at NEOMED enabled rapid establishment and implementation of this course.

One modification of this BioDesign course led to a very rewarding result and demonstrated the importance of a patient-centric approach in finding novel medical solutions. A couple was referred to me by one of the pediatricians from the Akron Children's Hospital. The couple came to our offices with their 12-year son in his wheel chair. I invited a couple members of my team to join the meeting. The father was an engineer and the mother was a school teacher, who was now spending 100 % of her time caring for their son and trying to find solutions to help him manage his muscular skeletal disease. Their son Dan, was wheel chair bound and was outfitted with a computer connected to his wheel chair. A lever on his wheel chair allowed him to move the pointer on the computer. He operated this lever with his knee. His arms were strapped to the wheel chair to control the frequent involuntary arm movements which was an integral part of his muscular skeletal disorder.

The mother explained, "Dan is functioning at the same academic level as his age peers in school. However, it takes him several hours to complete his assignments. Now he has arthritis of his right hip from having to use his right knee to operate the lever to his computer.

We have approached several companies for help, but none is interested in working on problems encountered by a very small number of patients."

I thought for a moment and then said, "I have an idea. We have a BioDesign course in which a team of students shadows physicians to identify problems and work with the physicians to find solutions for selected problems. What if a team of students shadows Dan at home and at school to observe problems and to determine which ones we could address?"

The parents agreed and we formed **"Team Dan."**

Within one month of observing Dan, the team noticed that when Dan's arm was lightly secured to the arm of his wheel chair, he could move his thumb in a controlled fashion. With this discovery, the team designed a sleeve that lightly held his arm to that of his wheel chair. They also designed a switch to operate his computer with his thumb. This temporary solution provides Dan the opportunity to alternate between use of his knee and thumb to manipulate his computer, thus reducing the rate of deterioration of his hip.

This productivity was aided by two other programs I introduced. One was the **Women's Entrepreneurship Program**. This program was presented by ABIA and the University of Akron's College of Business Administration. Teams were comprised of a student specializing in technology and an MBA candidate. Teams were expected to develop a business plan for an existing project that could be commercialized within 18 to 24 months and an Industry Advisory Committee was assembled to provide mentorship to the Teams. We were lucky to have Mr. Thomas Ruhe, Vice President of the Kauffman

Foundation, lead the launch of this course. The course used the Kauffman Foundation Fast Trac Syllabus.

The second program was a concept that I called **Synergy Seminars**. Synergy Seminars were held once a month and had a special format. The presenter would present the technical background to the topic, then show a list of problems associated with the topic. The audience would suggest solutions to a selected problem. In order to reduce the tendency of the presenter becoming defensive, we used a specific format, as follows: the questioner would ask, "What would happen if you tried 'X'?"

This freed up the presenter to state what 'had happened' if that approach had been tried, or to engage in a dialogue with the questioner and others in the audience with interest or experience in the suggested approach. The format was intended to foster an Open Innovation approach. This became a very popular seminar and it was interesting to witness how often presenters struggled to transition from the typical 'expert' presentation style to that needed to lead an open innovation dialogue.

In 2010 an unusual opportunity arose for ABIA when the NSF and the Department of Commerce announced their i6 Grant program. Our I Six program seemed a potential fit. I approached Dr. Newkome, who was vice president of Research and responsible for the University of Akron's Research Foundation (UARF), with the suggestion that we collaborate on a submission. I assigned the writing and coordination of the effort to Drs. Brian Davis and Shauna Brummett. Initial problems arose as Dr. Newkome insisted that UARF should take the lead. I agreed, provided that my team wrote the grant. A few weeks later Brian and Shauna told me that they were of the opinion that UARF was interested in working with Michigan University on the grant. I requested a teleconference with Dr. Newkome and his Michigan partners to understand their submission plan and the role that ABIA would play. It was clear that there was no role for ABIA.

I told them that that was not a problem for me as I planned, notwithstanding this news, to submit a grant. I also offered Dr. Newkome that UARF could also be a collaborator with ABIA since they were not the principal party in the collaboration with Michigan. The ABIA grant was based on our I Six process and the achievements to date. ABIA won one of the six $1.5 million awards. The Michigan/UARF submission was unsuccessful. Our ABIA submission was entitled: Commercialization of Innovative & Marketable Ideas. The Award was presented by Mr. John Hernandez, U.S. Assistant Secretary of Commerce for Economic Development, in a ceremony on the campus of the University of Akron.

Winning this award had two additional significant sequelae. One led to the **Value-Driven Engineering** initiative and the other to the **Accountable Care Community** initiative. A few months after receipt of the i6 award I received a call from Mr. Aneesh Chopra, U.S. Chief Technology Officer and Associate Director of Technology at the White House. He asked whether I would be willing to look at the challenge of Medical Device Innovation and the problem of the BRIC (Brazil, Russia, India, China) countries copying and making less expensive versions of American innovations, which they would subsequently market in the US. I accepted the invitation to look at this problem. I invited Dr. Steve Fening, our Senior Engineer and Ms. Rita Filer, our Events Manager, to work with me on this effort. I also reached out to Faegre B. Daniels in Washington D.C., who assigned Ms. Debra Lappin, one of their senior Life Sciences experts, to assist us.

Rita Filer had joined ABIA in an interesting manner. She had applied for the job as my executive assistant, but during the interview, I sensed that she could work independently. I told her that I would never hire her as an executive assistant, but if she were interested, I would assign her special projects for about one year, and if she performed well I would give her a manager level job. She achieved her assigned objectives and in the process was often thought of as the prototypical ABIA associate.

Dr. Steve Fening had been hired from the Cleveland Clinic by Brian Davis. Steve was our senior engineer and Director of Orthopaedic Devices. He had observed several operation room procedures, in the manner of our I Six process, looking for potential inventive solutions. One of his observations led to the first company that we spun out: Aphto Orthopaedics. Presently this Device, invented for the treatment of children with scoliosis, is under out-licensing discussions.

We invited experts from Johns Hopkins University, Case Western Reserve University, Harvard, MIT, Stanford University, University of Akron, the National Institute of Biomedical Imaging and Bioengineering, Medtronic, Inc., and Orthopedic Research Laboratories to form a steering committee. Members of the Office of Science and Technology, Executive Office of the President, participated as observers to our committee teleconferences. After several discussions the steering committee concluded that we would not be able to prevent foreign countries from introducing copies of our technology for FDA approval and marketing at lower cost in the USA.

The real challenge was how to maintain U.S. Global competitiveness while adding value. In March, 2011, we organized a Safe Haven Summit of about 50 experts on the topic: Value-Driven Engineering and U.S. Global Competitiveness. Mr. Aneesh Chopra, U.S. Chief Technology Officer and Associate Director at the White House Office of Science and Technology Policy delivered the keynote address. He applauded the initiative and stressed the importance of the U.S. remaining a global leader in innovation of Medical Devices.

Mr. Dick Gephardt, the former House majority leader and President and CEO of Gephardt Government Affairs focused on the need for public-private collaborations to ensure the continued leadership of the U.S. in medical innovation. Mr. Gephardt said that the "Time is now to frame a new national imperative that joins the forces of the public and private sectors to sustain our country's vibrant medical innovation ecosystem and ensure our return on this shared investment through improvement of health for generations to come." Additional speakers were Dr. Charles Vest, President of the National Academy of Engineering and former President of MIT; Gus Jammy, President of SEMATECH, a public-private enterprise; and Dr. Seth Greenwald, the Director of Orthopaedic Research

Laboratories. We decided to focus on the concept of Value-Driven Engineering (VdE).

The Summit attendees, representing academy, industry, and government broke into four workgroups and discussed:

- Creating a framework for identifying areas of opportunity for VdE
- Developing current and new strategies that support VdE
- Creating a new public-private partnership model to advance U.S. VdE in a global marketplace.
- Training the next generation of Value-Driven Engineers

The Summit defined a number of Value-Driven Engineering Principles (VdE), which were: Quality being the sina qua non:

- Clinical Utility,
- Reduced Complexity,
- Cost Savings and Cost Efficiency

These became components of a VdE equation. Added to these was Patient Centricity which, when included from design phase, through prototype and final manufacturing, could be instrumental in driving competitive innovation. The Summit also recommended the creation of PAVE: Platform for Advancing Value-Driven Engineering. PAVE would foster Patient Centricity, public-private engagement and investment, and education programs in use of the VdE equation.

The VdE Equation was conceived as the following:
$$Value = f\{Clinical\ Utility/(Complexity \times Cost)\}$$

- Where Clinical Utility is a measure of the benefit/risk ratio of a new product or process;
- Design Complexity is a measure of the 'user-friendliness' of the design of the device to patients, physicians and manufacturers;
- Cost Savings represents healthcare expenditures over the course of the disease state currently (without the new innovation) minus healthcare expenditures over

the course of a disease state due to implementation of a new innovation

An excellent example of Value-Driven Engineering was contained in the quote of Dr. Matthew Callaghan, the Founder of One Breath (March 11, 2011) who said, "You can't suggest to make a cheaper ventilator, you have to make a new way of ventilating…. When we think now about things that are cost-effective, the platform he developed is cheaper, it's only got 12 parts, it's a wonderfully accurate, it's as accurate as a $30,000 ventilator. Just because something is cheaper doesn't necessarily mean that it's not as good."

Another example of a VdE innovation is that of the Zio Patch, of which, Dr. Uday Kumar is the co-inventor. The Zio Patch is worn by patients to detect irregular heart rhythms. The predecessor of this innovation is the Holter monitor, which consisted of a monitoring box with several leads attached to the chest. The system could only be worn for 2-3 days and was a major inconvenience for the wearer. The Zio patch can be worn for up to a month and records and transmits the heart rhythms wirelessly. Dr. Kumar was a member of the Value Driven Engineering Steering Committee that organized the Safe Haven Summit and developed the Value-Driven Engineering Principles and Equation.

The recommendations of the Summit were published in June, 2011 in a whitepaper titled, "Value-Driven Engineering for US Global Competitiveness". I must express my appreciation to Debra Lappin Esq. of Faegre Baker Daniels company and her team, who worked tirelessly with us to complete this whitepaper in a very short time after the Safe Haven Summit. Within a few months after publication there were about 11,000 downloads of our whitepaper.

One year later the first National Conference on Value-Driven Engineering and US Global Competitiveness, sponsored by The Ewing Marion Kauffman Foundation, was held in Akron and Speakers included:

Bob Litan, the Vice president for Research and Policy, Kauffman Foundation;

William Heetderks, Director Extramural Science Program, National Institute of Biomedical Imaging and Bioengineering, NIH;

DeVon Griffin, Project Manager, NASA Glenn Research Center; Thomas Fogarty, Founder, Fogarty Institute for Innovation;

Ernst Berndt, Louis E Seely Professor in Applied Economics Sloan School of Business MIT;

Megan Moynahan, Associate Director of Technology and Innovation, FDA;

Steven Welby, Deputy Assistant Secretary of the Defense for Systems Engineering, US department of Defense.

A special feature of this conference was also a competition for examples of VdE solutions for needed Devices in Developing Countries. Examples included monitors of pregnancy and simple stethoscopes. There were 300 attendees representing 18 countries, 45 companies, 11 government agencies and officials and 5 hospitals.

This was remarkable because few believed that anyone could attract people to travel to Akron, Ohio for a National conference. It did surprise me at this defeatist attitude about Akron given that it **is** the home of the prestigious College of Polymer Science and Polymer Engineering. They had forgotten that Topic and participating Experts convene scientists. Unlike Real Estate, it is less about Location.

As we were building national leadership in developing this important principle in medical device innovation, we also turned our attention to creating collaborations with industry in the Polymer Engineering space. ABIA, in collaboration with University of Akron's College of Polymer Science and Engineering, created the Akron Functional Materials Center to provide combinatorial and high throughput methods to address industry problems and processes. This Center, led by Dr. Mathew Becker, was housed in the National Polymer

Innovation Center and brought Polymer Scientists and Engineers together with industry scientists around industry relevant problems. This collaboration and the broad expertise within the ABIA partners was instrumental in the establishment of a partnership between the FDA and ABIA to improve the quality, consistency, predictability and safety of biomaterials in medical devices. This was one of only three FDA partnerships in the nation in Biomaterials and Regulatory Science.

Four additional events recognizing the growing capabilities in the greater Akron area were: 1) the State of Ohio designating Akron as an Ohio Hub of Innovation and Opportunity for Biomaterials Commercialization; 2) ABIA being honored as an Ohio Center of Excellence for Biomedicine and Healthcare; 3) ABIA becoming leader of an $8 million project to develop biomedical sensor technology with a consortium of Ohio partners that included Bertec Corporation, Case Western Reserve University, the Cleveland Clinic Foundation, Cleveland Veterans Administration, Future Path Medical, Ohio Willow Wood, Parker Hannifin Corporation and the University of Akron; and, the collaboration with Centre of Excellence for Polymer Materials and Technologies, Slovenia, in April, 2013.

A second 'Place' for fostering collaboration among the five founding institutions and industry was facilitated through the creation of the ABIA Simulation Center and BioSkills Lab. The team of Drs. Michael Holder, Rami Ahmed and Ms. Martha Conrad visited Simulation Centers at a number of institutions. They presented a proposal to create a simulation center that would be differentiated from those that they had visited. Their proposal focused on creating key hospital departments: including Emergency Room, Intensive Care, medical holding area, operating room, obstetrics and Gynecology suite, as well as a control room with computing ability to conduct simulated emergency and team interventions. This allowed physicians and students to be trained in a mock hospital setting using robotic patients and other simulation tools.

As Mike Holder often said, "The first time you do a procedure should not be with a patient."

In addition, there were rooms for distant observed training in history taking and physical examinations of volunteer human subjects. An additional major feature of the center was the inclusion of a Bioskills lab. This nine-bay facility was also linked to the operating rooms in the three hospitals. Young physicians could observe operations in real-time while they simultaneously operated on fresh frozen cadavers under the additional guidance of a senior surgeon. The Bioskills lab was also used by industry to train physicians in the use of their new devices and also to get input from the physicians on ways to modify the devices to improve the ease of use of the devices. It was a good opportunity for Industry medical innovators to focus on human factors in the design and ultimate use of their devices.

The 25,000 sq. Ft. new ABIA Headquarters and Simulation Center was formally opened on September 28, 2012. The building had quite a history having been initially a railway terminal and for many years the Ohio Edison headquarters. The opening ceremony was quite memorable as leaders including congresswoman Betty Sutton, mayor Donald Plusquellic, County Executive Russ Pry, Mr. Robert Briggs, (a former chairman of the Knight Foundation Board of Directors), members of the ABA Board of Directors, and Dr. Gerald and Mrs. Patty Austen participated.

We also had a surprise attendee in the person of NBA All-Star basketball player Dominique Wilkins, who was the guest of Dr. Maseelall. I recall feeling that we had finally created a physical space where scientific collaboration and shared training, as well as innovation, could be fostered among physicians and scientists from the founding institutions and between the institutions and industry. Everything was now in place to market the capabilities of the Austen BioInnovation Institute in Akron. The Collaborative Spaces and Places were now available.

Mike Holder, who drove the design and building of the Simulation Center, was quite a visionary and entrepreneur. Prior to the completion of the Simulation Center he and Rami Ahmed outfitted an old ambulance and drove to various sites to deliver simulated training to physicians and nurses. Once the Center was completed the trio of Mike Holder, Rami Ahmed, and Martha Conrad, joined by Dr. Paul Lecat from

Akron General Hospital, developed and conducted simulation training for nursing students, NEOMED medical students and young physicians. Dr. Lecat used the Ventriloscope, his invention, to train students to recognize normal and abnormal body sounds while evaluating the patients. Ms. Michelle Chapman, who managed the BioSkills Lab, facilitated an active collaboration between animal studies at Summa Health and studies on fresh frozen cadavers in the BioSkills Lab, and this combination was a significant benefit to companies.

We also used the Simulation Center to develop the week long BioInnovation Academy Summer Program for High School students. This course was a condensed BioInnovation Design course in which students could observe simulated procedures, identify problems and then, working with the ABIA engineers, design, and in some cases, print a 3D prototype of their solutions.

The third area of focus for ABIA was that of Access to Healthcare for medically underserved patients in the Community. It seems that I sometimes get my best innovative ideas when I look at the coin from the other side. During a small workshop in Washington D.C., where the role of Accountable Care Organizations (ACO) was being discussed, I drifted into my occasional foglike state.

I was sitting at one of the six round tables that each had about eight participants. I could vaguely hear the colleagues at my table in discussion. I was deep in thought. Suddenly, I heard, as though from a distance, the moderator asy, "Frank, what are your thoughts?"

I jolted myself back into the present moment, stood, and said, "Presently, ACOs are given incentives to modify their practice approaches so that costs are reduced. A major problem, nonetheless, is that uninsured patients wait until they are very sick and use the Emergency Rooms as their private physicians. Reality is that there are other healthcare providers in the community. For example, there are Neighborhood Health Centers; Open M in Akron, Ohio, that was formed by several churches to provide healthcare and nutrition support to the medically uninsured; and the Network of Physicians who see patients referred to them by Open M; as well as the hospitals who absorb the costs of laboratory tests for those patients that are referred by this Network of Physicians. What if we created what I would call an Accountable Care Community (ACC), which would have the following components: a central triage center into which patients with non-emergency ailments could call and be directed to the nearest healthcare facility in their area; these healthcare facilities would form a network that provides care for such patients and accept responsibility, and accountability, as a group, for improvement of the health of their community."

This concept resonated with the colleagues in this workshop.

On returning to ABIA I discussed this with Dr. Janine Janosky, our Head for the Community Healthcare initiative and delegated the further development and implementation of this concept to her. I recommended we use an approach similar to the one we used with Value-Driven Engineering, namely, to organize a Summit in Akron, develop a White Paper and seek funding to launch the effort. This task was facilitated by the presence of Open M, the Network of volunteer Physicians, and most importantly, the Summit County Public Health Group, who were all very committed to providing care for the medically underserved. Thus, in June, 2011 we organized a Summit in which national and regional leaders discussed a framework for implementing such a concept. The output of the Summit was published in a whitepaper, "Healthier by Design: Creating Accountable Care Communities" in February, 2012. We benefited again from the support of the FaegreBD team. The Planning Committee of the Summit and presenters included representatives from the Center for Disease Control and Prevention, the UNC School of Public Health, Association of American Medical Colleges, Robert Wood Johnson Foundation, Summa Health System, Akron Children's Hospital, Akron General Health System, Northeast Ohio Medical University, University of Akron, Summit County Health District, and Austen BioInnovation Institute in Akron.

In our Accountable Care Community (ACC) effort, we created a Wellness Council and brought together 70 healthcare and other groups to improve the health of the community while providing cost-effective care. These included the major hospitals and healthcare providers, employers, Chamber of Commerce, universities, a range of faith-based organizations, transportation groups, economic developers, and planners. ACC began with a focus on control of Diabetes, through obesity reduction. This effort was recognized by a $2.5 million Community Transformation Grant from the Affordable Care Act's Prevention and Public Health Fund. Dr. Janosky was also honored by the White House as a Champion of Change for her leadership of this effort. Mr. Scott Rainone, our Director of Communications, and Dr. Janofsky attended the ceremony at the White House, where President Obama presented the awards.

My contract with ABIA was for four years, which means that at end of 2013 I had to decide whether to continue for another 3-4 years or to leave ABIA. I decided to reduce my time to 50 % in 2014 while looking for my successor. By end of 2013, it was becoming clear to me that the experiment of ABIA was doomed to failure. The reasons were multifactorial.

The first reason, which I had recognized at the very outset, was that there was an unrealistic estimate of costs to build this effort. I had engaged, nonetheless, because I was convinced that within one year there would be measurable signs of progress and this would be a basis for successful fund raising. (I believe that people invest when they see measurable signs of potential success). When I probed with Aram Nerpouni the assumptions behind these cost estimates, it became clear that several were quite unrealistic. For example, he told me that their estimation was that if they were able to recruit senior scientists to UA and NEOMED, those scientists would probably have their own funding and would probably bring 2-3 younger scientists with them. So, they would only have to recruit about 12-13 such scientists to get to the desired 45 for the Center for Biomaterials and Medicine. They had not estimated how much it would cost them, apart from relocation, to convince those scientists to move their labs and also what additional costs would be incurred for instruments, etc. to support their labs.

Even worse, although $80 million was always quoted as the amount that was available to build ABIA over 5 years, in reality there was only $47 million available. The Knight Foundation had committed $20 million over 7 years with the expectation that the five institutions would match this $20 million with cash and/ or in-kind. This was the first problem. At the very outset there was an agreement that NEOMED would contribute less than $4 MM over the 5-year time frame. The second issue had to do with 'in-kind' contributions. Once we started building programs, the needed technical and scientific capabilities or resources were often not available for 'in kind' contribution. Actually, the only institution that could really give in-kind was the University of Akron's College of Polymer Science and Engineering. Akron Children's Hospital gave 80% of Dr. Mike Holder's time.

$10 MM was given by First Energy but this was restricted for construction, for example, the building of the Akron Functional Materials Center in the National Polymer Innovation Center. The State had committed $20 MM. However, with change of the administration this was no longer viewed as a commitment, even though Dr. Proenza, the President of UA engaged in trying to convince the new administration to fulfill this commitment. The Knight Foundation stated clearly that it expected the five institutions to raise the remaining $10MM. Nothing was done by the institutions to raise this gap amount to get to the targeted $80 MM. ($20 M from Knight Foundation, $20 MM from the five institutions, $20 MM from the State, and $10 MM from First Energy Corp. accounted for $70 MM)

However, the lack of these projected funds was an important, but not the critical hurdle.

The real problem was that some of the institutions were really not committed to ABIA. They saw ABIA as a competitor, although, the reason for forming ABIA was a recognition that there were areas, where if they collaborated, they would 'raise all boats'.

Worse than that, whenever an ABIA program demonstrated success, a couple of them, particularly Summa Health System and NEOMED, would create a competing effort in house and stop collaborating in the ABIA effort.

Here are two examples:

- The Burton D. Morgan Foundation, on receiving a grant application from a department in Summa Health System, which they judged would be competing with the Accountable Care Community, refused to review the grant proposal and recommended that Summa work with ABIA and submit a joint grant proposal. This is how I learned that Summa was seeking to establish their own ACC effort.
- In a second effort, ABIA had applied to the state to build out some more space to extend the Simulation Center and provide space for startups that needed access to our 3D printing facilities and the Simulation Center. One day, I received a call from the office of one of the Ohio State Legislators to alert me to the fact that Summa had submitted a proposal to build a Simulation facility. It provided a political dilemma, so the decision was to fund 50% of each proposal. This then explained why Dr. Rami Ahmed, whose home base was Summa Health System, had suddenly resigned from ABIA. It was clearly to set up a competing simulation effort at Summa.

Perhaps, the most crippling effect on ABIA was that ABIA was restricted from engaging clients other than the five founding institutions. At the end of 2013, when the founding members stated that their annual support for ABIA would be $1.6 MM, instead of $4 MM over the next five-year period, it was abundantly clear to me that they were no longer committed to this open collaboration. The five institutions agreed to approve the new business plan that Joe Randazzo, the CFO, and I had created, which depended on bringing in new partners. Even so, there was still a reasonable outlook for ABIA as it now had a major asset. The combination of Simulation Center and BioSkills Lab was considered as among the best in the country. This however, required intense national marketing, for which we did not have the resources.

On the research side, there were a few successes, the most notable of which was the support ABIA had given for the work being done by Prof. Matt Becker. Matt had joined the faculty of the College of Polymer Science and Engineering in 2009, a few months before I arrived to lead ABIA. He was an instant supporter of ABIA, having been Co-Director of the Center for Biomaterials and Medicine, Co-Director with Prof. Dhinojwala, Prof. Dey and me of the Biodesign Course, Director of the Akron Functional Materials Center (an ABIA and UA collaboration), and Scientific Leader of the ABIA collaboration with the Slovenia's Centre of Excellence for Polymer Materials and Technologies. Matt was a recipient of one of the first ABIA Research collaborative grants.

The project supported by this grant led to a collaboration with scientists at Houston Methodist Research Institute. This collaboration recently received a $6 million grant from the U.S. Army Medical Research and Materials Command for their ground-breaking research in developing biodegradable polymers to stabilize and help rebuild bone in severe limb injuries.

Recently (Dec. 2017), Matt received a $2 Million grant from the State of Ohio for use of Biopolymers in treatment of pain and opioid addiction.

Presently, Matt is Associate Dean for Research and most fitting, holds the **W. Gerald Austen Endowed Chair** in the College of Polymer Science and Polymer Engineering!

Fortunately, Matt was not from Akron and was one of the few who truly recognized that it takes time and effort to move one's research to the stages of success.

I have often wondered why these five institutions had created ABIA and had wasted so many human and financial resources if they were really not serious about creating something special. It became abundantly clear that basically only two of the five institutions were committed to the collaboration.

I found a couple of events instructive. During one meeting, Dr. Steven Schmidt, who was in charge of Research at Summa, asked me a question. He asked, "What is the difference with respect to collaboration in Akron versus Boston."

I responded. "Good question, Steve. I have been thinking about this and I think I have an answer." I paused as I observed the other eight colleagues in the meeting look at me with evident interest. I continued. "In Akron people pride themselves on collaborating, but they collaborate on little things. In Boston, people don't spend a lot of time discussing collaborating on little things. When there is something big, someone takes the lead and invites their colleagues from MIT and Harvard to participate. The focus becomes on expertise and fielding the best team from the two institutions to win the Award."

There was silence. No further comments were made on this subject and we returned to the agenda of the meeting.

A second event that was instructive was a study that Mayor Plusquellic had commissioned to determine the best opportunities for Akron to build an industrial presence. To no one's surprise, the Technology Partnership Practice from Battelle recommended that Akron should focus on the area of Biomaterials. It identified "the need for an entity to push that effort forward". It was recognized that "the Austen BioInnovation Institute matches the description of a proposed Greater Akron Biomaterials Connector, a convener and facilitator, with flexibility and quickness, where the medical community, businesses and University researchers come together". (Commentary in Akron Beacon Journal, April 18, 2014). Nothing came of this effort because some leaders from the University of Akron felt that they should be the ones to coordinate such an effort. In the above-mentioned Commentary, ABIA was described as "the player who makes everyone else better".

Akron remains a rather strange culture. On the one hand there are leaders such as Luis Proenza, William Considine, Tim Stover, Joe Kanfer, Erwin Maseelall, Walter Horton, Ilene Shapiro, Anthony Alexander, Matthew Becker, Sam Gibara, Stephen Chang, Fran Buchholzer, Don Plusquellic, and Russ Pry (dec.) whose commitment to Akron is deep and is supported by their actions.

And on the other hand, there are many leaders in Akron who profess concern for Akron but whose personal ambitions and agendas cloud their mirrors. They remind me of the crabs in a barrel, although this barrel is quite gilded. For example, although many individuals praised the contributions that ABIA was making, few actually donated to ABIA. After we opened the Simulation and Integrated Healthcare Center, I held a small reception to celebrate the naming of the Maternity Simulation Suite in honor of our then two grandchildren (Abisayo and Ayodeji), both of whom were emergency, C-section deliveries. In fact, Abi was delivered at 24 weeks and spent 10 weeks in the Neonatal Intensive Care Unit at Columbia Presbyterian Hospital, in New York City.

Attendees at the reception could appreciate the flow of this simulated hospital, which is equipped to be functional during major emergencies. Attendees could walk from the Emergency Intake Area into a general treatment area through a door on the left. On the right, a door opens onto the section for conducting emergencies, such as bedside cardiac arrests in a hospital setting. In the center and overlooking these two rooms is a central 'command station' equipped with computers and communication systems to conduct simulated emergency and treatment protocols using programmable mannequins. Beyond the treatment area is a fully outfitted operation suite. From the cardiac emergencies simulation area one enters the maternity suite where programmed mannequins are used to conduct simulations of vaginal deliveries and resuscitation of infants. The attendees were given brief descriptions of each area as they interacted with my team and each other. Finally, I introduced Nataki, my daughter, Mayowa, my son-in-law and their two sons, Abisayo and Ayodeji, for whom the Maternity Suite was named.

Now that I reflect on that reception, I am surprised that it did not motivate others to support the Simulation Center. In fact, this led me at one time to say, "I scratch my head and stroke my non-existing beard and ponder and puzzle over, what is it about Akron that makes the nature of collaboration so different from what I have experienced on the East Coast of USA and in Europe?"

There are three people whom I often think of with great appreciation because they, by their own commitment to ABIA and Akron, always reminded me of the reason why I agreed to join the team in Akron; namely, 'that the patients are waiting!'

These individuals are Juan Martinez and Jennifer Thomas of the Knight Foundation, and Ms. Bonnie Griffith, my Executive Assistant, whose technical capabilities and more importantly, judgment, were of tremendous help during my last three years at ABIA.

In one of my first interviews, I was asked the question, "Why Akron?"

My answer was that I wanted to be part of the vision of these five leaders (Considine, Proenza, Nora, Strauss, and Stover) to leave a **Legacy** that improved the health and well-being of patients.

I end this section by displaying a copy of a few pages of a report that showed the key developments of the Austen BioInnovation Institute in Akron, from the inception of the idea in 2007, to 2012 when the Simulation and Healthcare Center was opened.

Austen BioInnovation Institute in Akron timeline

January 2007
A1 - 26 community leaders travel to Miami to meet with the John S. and James L. Knight Foundation seeking support to create a medical research partnership.

October 2008
B1 - BioInnovation Institute in Akron forms. Knight Foundation pledges $20 million toward the effort.

June 2009
C1 - ABIA wins Team NEO Economic Impact Award

September 2009
D1 - Institute changes name to the Austen BioInnovation Institute in Akron (ABIA), honoring Akron native and retiring Knight Foundation board chair Dr. W. Gerald Austen and his wife, Patricia.

D2 - Dr. Frank L. Douglas joins the BioInnovation Institute as president and chief executive officer.

December 2009
E1 - Federal lawmakers approve $1 million in funding to help ABIA purchase equipment for orthopedic devices.

January 2010
F1 - Partnership reached with Orthopedic Research Laboratories, a Cleveland company specializing in testing orthopedic devices.

February 2010
G1 - ABIA awards six grants for $100,000 each and two grants for $40,000 to local research teams.

G2 - Ohio Board of Regents names ABIA, The University of Akron and Northeast Ohio Medical University an Ohio Central of Excellence for Biomedicine and Healthcare.

July 2010
H1 - ABIA announces plans for new downtown Akron headquarters.

H2 - Ohio Gov. Ted Strickland designates Akron as an Ohio Hub of Innovation and Opportunity.

August 2010
I1 - ABIA's Medical Device Development Center begins offering grants up to $25,000 to support local inventors.

September 2010
J1 - State approves $2.5 million low-interest loan to help fund new headquarters.

J2 - BioInnovation design course launched with UA and NEOMED

J3 - ABIA receives $1 million from the i6 Challenge, a national innovation competition.

J4 - State awards ABIA and partners $2.6 million grant to develop medical sensors.

November 2010
K1 - *GQ Magazine* features Dr. Frank Douglas as a "2010 Rock Star of Science."

December 2010
L1 - GAR Foundation awards ABIA $150,000 for new diabetes patient education program.

January 2011
M1 - Akron Foundation Materials Center opens at UA National Polymer Innovation Center

M2 - Women's Entrepreneurship Program launched with UA

March 2011

N1 - Institute leads national conference in Washington D.C. on "Value-driven Engineering" effort to make U.S. medical service industry more competitive.

N2 - ABIA holds inaugural BEST (Bridging Engineering, Science and Technology) Medicine Fair, attracting more than 100 students.

June 2011
O1 - Partnership launches "Accountable Care Community" program to improve local health care.

O2 - Dr. Frank Douglas meets with the Obama administration to discuss Value-driven Engineering initiatives.

August 2011
P1 - With Summa Health System, ABIA unveils creation of first prototype, a simulator called PacerMan.

Sept. 2011
Q1 - Institute lands one-year, $550,000 CDC Community Transformation project grant for Accountable Care Community project.

Nov. 2011
R1 - Douglas leads educational briefing in Washington, D.C., on Value-driven Engineering.

R2 - ABIA's Center for Simulation and Integrated Healthcare Education holds first large-scale simulation for emergency staff.

Dec. 2011
S1 - FDA selects ABIA to provide assistance with new polymer biomaterials.

S2 - ABIA announces partnership with Lubrizol Corp. to share experience.

Jan. 2012

T1 - First spin-off company, Apto Orthopaedics, announced.

T2 - ABIA's Center for Clinical Trials and Product Development formed.

T3 - Medical simulation fellowship with Summa Health System launched.

April 2012

This performance of ABIA was underscored when Mr. Considine in a Beacon Journal interview (Nov. 25, 2014) said, "I really admire and applaud his (Dr. Douglas') value system and what he was able to do with a concept, because there was no substance in terms of the Austen Bioinnovation Institute, truly, when he came. He pulled people together and developed a startup company over his tenure here that truly did impact our community in a very positive way."

Awards and Recognitions

In this chapter I describe some of the awards and gifts that I have received in recognition of my contributions. I have selected those awards that have anecdotes associated with them.

In 2001, while on vacation in Africa, I received an email telling me that it was important for me to fly to London for the Global Pharmaceutical Awards meeting.

I told them that unfortunately, I could not because I was on a family vacation in Tanzania, on my way to Kenya.

They offered to fly me to London and back with minimum time away from my family.

I declined.

Two days later I learned that I had been awarded the Global Pharmaceutical Research and Development Director of the Year Award and that Dr. Nahed Ahmed, who was in attendance, had accepted it on my behalf. I did not share this with the family, so that they would not feel any sense of conflict or guilt.

During this vacation among the areas we visited was Thika, a village outside of Nairobi. This was an unforgettable experience and made missing the award ceremony much less important. This was my second visit to Thika. My first visit occurred a full decade earlier on the occasion of an International Hypertension Conference that was held in Nairobi.

The convention center was about a 15-minute walk from my hotel. At the beginning and end of each day I would walk by a young man with his shoe shine box. Business never appeared to be especially good as I rarely saw a customer in his chair that stood beside his box of rags and small cans of shoe polish. There were always two or three other young men conversing with him as he sat in the chair where the customer would sit. I observed as I walked towards them that the friends treated the shoe shiner with an indescribable respect.

One day, on my way back to the hotel, I stopped to get my shoes shined. As I sat in the chair, my impression that he was the leader was reinforced. I had brought a small suitcase of children's clothes that I intended to give away. I addressed him as he worked on my shoes, "I am Dr. Douglas. What is your name?"

He responded, "I am Peter Waweru. Waweru." He had a strong accent but was understandable.

"I have some clothes that I would like to give to some children. Do you know of anyone who might want these clothes?" I asked him.

He responded, "I have small children."

"If you would like to have them, you need to come over to the hotel to get them."

About 30 minutes later he came with two large brown paper bags into which the clothes did fit. He thanked me and said slowly, "I need a note from you to show the police that I did not steal these clothes."

I gave him a note written on the hotel stationary and included both my full name and signature, both of which he told me were needed. He thanked me profusely.

The following day, he stopped me as I walked by on my way to the conference and said, "Doctor, my family would like to meet you. Can you come?"

"I can only do that on Saturday, provided that it is not a long journey." "I live in Thika. It takes less than 1 hour on the Matatu."

"OK. I can do it on Saturday."

He arrived about 9 am on Saturday morning and we travelled the 50-60 minutes from Nairobi to Thika in a Matatu (mini bus). It had literally been decades since I had ridden in a vehicle that held two to three times as many people as was originally intended, and in which many people hung their heads out the windows as there was no place for them in the vehicle. The rough ride over the pot-hole filled road reminded me of similar bus rides in some parts of Guyana.

When we arrived in Thika, Peter (Waweru) took me to the neighborhood bar where he introduced me to his former school principal and a couple other older people in his village. I had the same indescribable sense that they treated him with respect. Then we went to his home. He and his wife, Mary, had two small children and lived in a one room mud thatched shack with an unattached similarly constructed small kitchen. His mother, who lived about a mile's distance from them, was also present. She had walked the mile or so to meet me. Both Peter and Mary spoke haltingly, but their English was understandable. They were proud of their little home and thanked me repeatedly for my kindness. I was the first Black American that they had met.

At the end of the visit, I asked, "How could I help you?"

He said, somewhat falteringly, "I know to drive a car. If I had a car I could do a taxi business and help my family more."

Mary said, "If we had a small place with 3-4 rooms, located between Nairobi and Thika, the men could sleep there and not have to find places in Nairobi."

We discussed the two alternatives. Peter expressed concern for Mary's safety. We decided to go for the car. We went to the bank and I opened an account into which I transferred money and arranged for him to have access to an agreed sum that was specifically identified for the purchase of a second-hand car. When I returned to the U.S., my family agreed also to help pay for school tuition for his kids as they entered high school.

About five years later, Peter told us that he had saved some money and now he would like to buy a matatu. His argument was that he could use it to take people along the way from Thika to the market place which was some five to 10 miles away. His further support for his request was that he could hire a couple of people to collect the fares as he drove the matatu. I agreed to send him money to help him purchase the mutatu. So, the morning of my second visit, he came to the hotel in Nairobi to take Lynnet, the girls and me to Thika. He arrived in a matatu that had New Jersey in large print on the rear window. Our home was in New Jersey.

We boarded the matatu. Peter explained that the original seats of minibuses are replaced with wooden benches so that there is room for more people. When we disembarked from the matatu at his home in Thika, I had one of the most moving experiences in my life. As we disembarked the matatu, a small group of villagers waving small branches, greeted us and sang; "Welcome to the Douglas family" as they escorted us up the small incline to the modest two-storied concrete house, that was now the home of Peter and his family. This small concrete house had two bedrooms on one side and a living room on the other side, on the first floor. We did not see the second level and suspected that it was probably unfinished. The unattached kitchen was larger and better built than the one I had seen on my first visit. Peter also proudly showed us that they had a vegetable garden and one milk cow. Peter's obvious pride at the success that he and his family had achieved served to suppress the tears that were welling up in me from the greeting.

I was overwhelmed by this greeting.

They had prepared some cakes and drinks. There were eight adults and several children in addition to the four of us in this crowded living room. The chairs were reserved for us and Peter's mother. The rest of the group remained standing. I looked directly at the woman who had led the little procession from the matatu to the house, and said, "We are very moved by your greeting. Could you tell us why you are happy to see us?"

The woman said, "Because you have been kind to Peter and Mary." Then a younger woman, who identified herself as a cousin of Mary's said,

"And whenever you send money to Peter, he always shares some of it with the rest of us."

Then the younger woman's husband said, "So lots of people in our village know about the Douglas family."

As on the first occasion, I asked what we could do to help.

Peter said, "If I had a second matatu I could hire 2-3 more people. We could also convert part of the living room to a small shop where Mary could sell various goods. Then people won't always have to travel lots of miles to the market."

We agreed to do both.

Their four children are doing well. Robert has a Bachelor's degree in Finance, Naomi is studying nursing in the U.S., and the other two children, Eunice and Eric, have graduated from high school.

The Black History Maker Award in 2007 was quite a surprise. It was a surprise because consistently, I had been ignored by Black media. For example, when I joined Marion Merrell Dow, Fred Lyons, the CEO, told me that he had arranged for Ebony to interview me. He further explained that he knew the Johnson Family well. Fred was surprised that I was never contacted by Ebony. Each year when Black magazines identified prominent Blacks, they would highlight Blacks in the Pharmaceutical industry who were two levels below me. So, when I received the first letter that I had been nominated for this honor, I actually discarded it immediately after reading, assuming that it was a hoax. My Executive Assistant, Cheryl Mottley, (I was at MIT at the time), brought the second letter directly to me and recommended that I call the Associated Black Charities organization as requested. I called and when it became clear that this was in earnest, I asked why I was selected. I was told that my name had come up on occasion, but no one seemed to know me. However, that year Dr. Shirley Ann Jackson, renowned Physicist, National Medal of Science awardee and President of Rensselaer Polytechnic Institute, told them that she knew of me and in fact, I was presently at MIT. (Dr. Shirley Ann Jackson was 2001 Black History Maker Awardee).

Dr. Richard Markham, my colleague and later boss at Hoechst Marion Roussel and Aventis paid me the significant honor of introducing me. In his introduction Dick (Markham) referred to the situation in Frankfurt where I went from being the "Job Killer' to member of the prestigious Frankfurt Rotary Club and honored with the Wolfgang von Goethe Medal of Honor. As I stood to make my acceptance speech, I looked out into the audience and saw my immediate family members, colleagues from the faculty of MIT, leaders from the Pharmaceutical Industry and a few of my former students. For a brief moment I reflected on my Journey in the USA where I evolved from young man to adult, from student to professor, from struggling disciple to leader. As I quickly reflected on this journey, I recognized that my Journey was a 'walk in the park' compared to that of Dr. Percy Julian for whom my award was named. Dr. Julian, the grandson of slaves, in spite of being denied many jobs and positions, nonetheless became the first person to synthesize physostigmine. He became a renowned world chemist at age 36. His research also made it possible to produce large quantities of progesterone and hydrocortisone at low cost. I left the event even more inspired and humbled by the life story and achievements of Dr. Julian. The event was a silent motivator for me to contribute even more.

The George Beene Foundation and GQ Magazine Rockstar of Science was an enjoyable moment, but only after I had called one of my daughters to find out what was GQ Magazine and whether it was credible. I asked how I was selected and was told that several organizations were asked to nominate one candidate. For example, Nobel Laureate Phillip Sharp was nominated by the National Cancer Institute. I was nominated by the National Organization of Rare Diseases.

I had the wonderful opportunity to meet with the member of the organization who had brought my name forward to his organization. He explained that many years previously, he had read one of my articles on Photoselection of Chlorophyll-a Microcrystals in a Russian scientific magazine. Since then he had followed my career. He had seen a number of my presentations on Clinical Biology and importance of using Biomarkers to select patient subpopulations. This approach is used in many orphan diseases. Finally, he was excited by my introduction of Chemical Biology in the industry to take advantage of the new and evolving information from genomics. He also shared with me that his son had Niemann Pick's Disease. He did not have to say anything else for me to recognize how vitally important it was to him that innovative approaches be used to find treatments for life threatening diseases. I thanked him for honoring me by recognizing my humble contributions.

The Life Time Achievement Award from the National Organization for the Professional Advancement of Black Chemists and Chemical Engineers (NOBCChe), in 2002, provided another interesting episode. As I sat on the dais looking out at the many young Black scientists and engineers, I thought that sharing with them those non-academic skills that are also important for future success would be different but important for them. I checked with the Master of Ceremonies whether it was OK to change my planned address. I thought of SOARS and scribbled the following at the back of the program:

- Believe in Yourself
- It is about Hard work
- To Thine Own Self be True
- Assume that others have the best intentions
- Lead by example
- Focus more on what you contribute and less on what you control

At the start of my presentation, I explained to the audience why I had made a sudden change in my presentation and I was going to share a few anecdotes as examples of successful characteristics that are not often discussed. In fact, this presentation to NOBCCHE in some ways motivated the writing of this autobiography.

I described the interaction with the psychologist at Lehigh to illustrate: **Believe in Yourself.**

I recounted the meeting with Prof. Roald Hoffmann to illustrate: **It is about hard work**.

My interviews at Ciba Geigy, in which I told them that I was not ready to take on both assignments were used to illustrate: **To thine own self be true**. My interview at Marion Merrell Dow where the CEO asked how my being Black would affect my ability to do the job was used to illustrate: **Assume others have the best intentions**.

Lead by example was illustrated by my commitment to learn the German language

And my general approach to management when dealing with reluctant employees was used to illustrate: **Focus more on what you contribute and less on what you control.**

I received many requests for a copy of that impromptu presentation.

Another award which was associated with one of those personal unforgettable moments was the Caribbean Heritage Award for Entrepreneurship in 2011. When we were informed of my being an awardee, Scott Rainone, my Director of Communications and Bonnie Griffith, my Executive Assistant, at ABIA, told me that they would handle it. The presentation of my Award was among the last that evening, so I sat and enjoyed the videos that other awardees had made to present themselves and their work. But I was also in a panic because I had not prepared anything, but a brief 'thank you' speech. Then they introduced me and as I proceeded to the stage there began a video of an interview with Mr. William Considine, ABIA's chairman, Hon. Don Plusquellic, Mayor of Akron and Dr. Luis Proenza, President of the University of Akron.

Mr. Considine, in a Beacon Journal interview, in 2014, as my transition to 50% time was announced, made a similar comment to the one that he made in the video. He said, in that interview, "Dr. Frank Douglas is one of those truly transformational leaders. He is a phenomenal visionary, extraordinarily proactive in his thinking. He's one-of-a-kind."

Dr. Proenza commented, "Most strikingly, Frank rapidly conceptualizes ideas in novel ways that add value. He has a way of creating value in every idea he touches and the new ways in which he looks at things create opportunities and innovation."

Hon. Plusquellic commented, "Dr. Douglas has brought great credibility to Akron. In spite of his reputation around the world and in America he came to Akron and started to build an effort from the ground up. We are proud to call him an Akronite."

These words are as precious to me as the Award itself.

The Weill Cornell Medical Alumni Achievement Award was special in several ways.

It was a moment of bitter sweet memories. There were two awardees. Dr. Henry Murray, my fellow awardee presented his work in search of the treatment of leishmanaiasis. This neglected tropical disease is caused by the parasite Leishmanaia that is found in parts of the tropics and southern Europe and that can be lethal when patients are untreated. His innovative approaches and commitment to find a treatment for this disease were quite impressive. The first few minutes of his presentation were noteworthy. He showed photos and talked of his many mentors along his career, starting from college, through medical school, residency, his first post graduate appointment, and initiating his infectious disease research to the present. This was in contrast to my presentation, in which I did not mention any mentors. (In this memoir I have identified individuals who actually tried to be mentors to me, but which opportunities I often did not recognize). I think the contrast between the two presentations at this prestigious award ceremony led Dr. Kudo, the president of the Alumni Association and MC of the event to ask, "Frank, given the many innovative contributions that you have made to improve the health of patients in both Pharmaceutical and the Device industries, who would you say was your mentor when you were a medical student at Cornell?"

I replied, "Unfortunately, at that time it was not easy for Black students to find mentors."

Dr. Kudo asked further, "Well what would you say you learned at Cornell that helped your career?"

I responded, "I learned how to persevere in less than nurturing environments, and that helped me succeed in the Pharmaceutical industry."

Then I said, "There is one person, who evidently was a silent mentor. That was the late Dr. Walter Riker, who was Chairman of the Pharmacology Department. I discovered this in a congratulatory email that I received from Dr. Curtis, the former Dean for Minority students."

"I would like to thank both Dr. Riker and Dr. Curtis for their support during those challenging times as a Weill Cornell Medical student."

Here is a portion of that email from Dr. Curtis:

"I wish to join the others in congratulating you on your achievements. I asked her (Dr. Liz Anstey) to send me a resume of your career highlights so that I could get a glimpse of the reasons you are singled out for this award. I was amazed, really bowled over, by the significant leadership positions you have and still hold in the pharmaceutical industry here and abroad.

Recruiting you to come to Cornell was as it turns out, one of my greatest achievements. I recall clearly that when doubts arose about how much talent you had, Wally Riker our head of Pharmacology assured me that you were the real article. How right he was...."

The anecdote associated with this final example is described in the Epilogue and the photo on following page. This tree contains the names of some of the drugs with which I was involved, primarily from the Marion Merrell Dow, Hoechst Marion Roussel and Aventis companies. There are 20 marketed drugs on the tree. These include: Nicodem CQ, Anzemet, Ramipril LE, Arava, Lantus, Amaryl LE, Sabril, Refludan, Ciclesonide, Allegra, Ketek, Lovenox LEs, Exubera, Priftin, Taxotere LEs, Dynepo, Apidra, Actonel, Targocid, Nicorette. They represent treatments for several conditions, including: Smoking Cessation, Chemotherapy induced Nausea, Hypertension, Tuberculosis, Rheumatoid Arthritis, Diabetes, Seizures, Allergies, Infectious Diseases, Cancer and Prevention of Deep Vein Thrombosis and Pulmonary Embolism. This was given to me by my leadership team at the occasion of my retirement from Aventis.

The plaque said, "In recognition of your invaluable contributions to a significant family tree of products that continue to enhance life for patients around the world."

I am quite pleased that the words **contributions, enhancing life and around the world** were included.

Epilogue

As I sat in my office working on this manuscript, eight-year-old Abisayo (Abi), my eldest grandchild, came to me and asked, "What are you doing, Papi?"

I replied, "I am writing my Autobiography." "Papi, what is an Autobiography?"

"An Autobiography is a book in which you describe the important or significant things that happened in your life, starting with your childhood."

"Thanks, Papi," he said as he wandered off to another part of the apartment. About 15 minutes later he returned and said, "Papi, you know what I think?" "Yes, Abi?"

"I think that you should put a picture of the plaque with the medicines that you made, in the book," he said with a thoughtful look.

"Abi, that is an excellent idea. I shall do that. Thank you."

"Abi, why do you believe that I should include the plaque?" I probed. "Papi," he said, emphatically, "The plaque has many medicines that you worked on. These medicines make people better."

Abi had provided an incredible insight into myself. The values that I embraced as a fifteen-year-old: Mercy, Wisdom, Justice, Authenticity, Emotional Strength, and Self-Control were the values I needed to make the lives of others better. The imprint of these values was formed in the crucible of learning from living consciously in a poor environment and from the reading of the Bible.

In the introduction to this memoir, I mentioned three questions that often puzzled me as a young boy:

Why does God relegate people of color to poverty and being the colonized? Why does God have favorites?

Why do I behave differently from my brothers and sisters and cousins?

Although I do not have the answer to the questions that involve God, I recently received insight from a childhood friend, Molly.

Molly, her siblings and I grew up in the Evangelical church. She has been a Canadian citizen for over 40 years. I was therefore quite surprised and flabbergasted when I received a three-page epistle from her, which epistle was a defense? explanation? of why God has chosen Donald Trump to 'drain the Swamp of Sin' in America. She likened God's choice of Trump for this role to God's choice of Saul, the Pharisee, to help convert the Gentiles.

In my response to Molly, I told her that I do not profess to know the Mind of God. I can only follow that which has been recorded, namely, "When a lawyer asked Jesus: Master, which is the great commandment in the law? Jesus said unto him. Thou shalt love the Lord thy God with all thy heart, and with all thy soul, and with all thy mind. This is the first and great commandment. And the second is like unto it, Thou shalt love thy neighbor as thyself. On these two commandments hang the law and the prophets." (Mathew 22:35-40).

I added, that God sent Saul into the world to convert the Gentiles, after he was converted, was baptized, and had received the gift of the Holy Spirit, and had been transformed to Paul.

'And Ananias …. said, Brother Saul, the Lord, even Jesus, that appeared unto thee in the way as thou camest, hath sent me, that thou mightest receive thy sight and be filled with the Holy Ghost.' (Acts 9:17)

After the death and resurrection of Christ, God seemed only to call those who had received the Holy Ghost to minister and bear witness on His behalf.

There seems to be only one reasonable conclusion, and that is: when Evangelical Christians do not adhere to what the Lord Jesus Christ identified as the two great commandments, and/or embrace and promote those who do not support these two great commandments, they have debased their religion to serve a diabolic hatred that has historically led to crusades and lynchings. As Samuel von Pufendorf said in 1673: "More inhumanity has been done by man himself than any other of nature's causes." This is particularly true when these heinous crimes are driven by the primeval sin: GREED. It is probably hopeless to wait for 'Road to Damascus Blinding Light' solutions, when the problems of the world are created by humans.

On the question as to why I behaved differently from my siblings, I do not have an answer as to where and when my tendency to take the road less travelled began. In retrospect, however, as I travelled that road, I found that having true grit in adhering to my values made me stronger in good times as well as bad.

This Journey made me truly **A Free Man from a Black Stream**.

CPSIA information can be obtained
at www.ICGtesting.com
Printed in the USA
FSHW020415180719
60117FS